# Author's Note

Like most fantasy writers, I have found it challenging to write material influenced by real (if bygone) cultures. In some ways I think it would have been easier to write pure historical fiction, because then I could have used all the artistic and factual information provided by scholarship and science. Since this is a fantasy novel, not a history text, I found myself in the odd position of having to *de-historify* these tales as much as possible—in effect stripping away the substance of reality while leaving behind only the thinnest broth for flavoring. My goal was to give homage; my goal was *not* to ape reality. Armchair Egyptologists, you have been forewarned.

In particular I struggled with character names, since many of these cultures' names were meaningful compounds of words in their languages—but this isn't Earth, so I couldn't use those languages. Instead I tried to capture a suitable structure and feel while avoiding compounds that would have meaning in those languages. Since I am by no means an expert, this makes it entirely possible that one or more of my characters has a name that means "beloved of cheese" or something similar. My apologies if so.

"All men dream, but not equally. Those who dream by night in the dusty recesses of their minds wake in the day to find that it was vanity; but the dreamers of the day are dangerous men, for they may act their dreams with open eyes, to make it possible."

—T. E. Lawrence,
*The Seven Pillars of Wisdom: A Triumph*

# Praise for the Inheritance Trilogy

"Many books are good, some are great, but few are truly important. Add to this last category *The Hundred Thousand Kingdoms*, N. K. Jemisin's debut novel... In this reviewer's opinion, this is the must-read fantasy of the year."

—*Bookpage*

"A complex, edge-of-your-seat story with plenty of funny, scary, and bittersweet twists."  —*Publishers Weekly* (Starred Review)

"An offbeat, engaging tale by a talented and original newcomer."  —*Kirkus*

"The very best kind of sequel: as lush and evocative and true as the first, with all the same sense of mystery, giving us the world and characters we already love, and yet with a new story and a wonderfully new perspective on the whole dazzling world and pantheon the author has built."  —Naomi Novik

"This is a book that readers won't be able to put down...A magnificent novel and one of the best books this reviewer has read this year."

—*RT Book Reviews* (Top Pick!)

"The key is just to tell a great, exciting, engaging story that keeps you turning pages long past your bedtime. And Jemisin has definitely done that here."  —io9.com

"N. K. Jemisin has written a fascinating epic fantasy where the stakes are not just the fate of kingdoms but of the world and the universe."  —sfrevu.com

"A similar blend of inventiveness, irreverence, and sophistication—along with sensuality—brings vivid life to the setting and other characters: human and otherwise....*The Hundred Thousand Kingdoms* definitely leaves me wanting more of this delightful new writer."  —*Locus*

"A compelling page-turner."  —The Onion A.V. Club

"Jemisin's talent as a storyteller should make her one of the fantasy authors to watch in the coming years."  —*Library Journal*

"*The Broken Kingdoms* had everything I loved about the first book in this trilogy—an absorbing story, an intriguing setting and world mythology, and a likable narrator with a compelling voice. The next book cannot come out soon enough."  —fantasybookcafe.com

"*The Broken Kingdoms* is an excellent sequel to *The Hundred Thousand Kingdoms* because it expands the universe of the series geographically, historically, magically and in the range of characters, while keeping the same superb prose and gripping narrative that made the first one such a memorable debut."  —fantasybookcritic.blogspot.com

"Wild and sharp...an engrossing, magic-filled thriller."  —*Newark Star-Ledger*

**By N. K. Jemisin**

The Inheritance Trilogy

*The Hundred Thousand Kingdoms*
*The Broken Kingdoms*
*The Kingdom of Gods*

Dreamblood

*The Killing Moon*
*The Shadowed Sun*

# THE
# KILLING
# MOON

BOOK ONE OF DREAMBLOOD

( ⊙ )

## N. K. JEMISIN

www.orbitbooks.net

Orbit
Hachette Book Group
1290 Avenue of the Americas, New York, NY 10104
www.HachetteBookGroup.com

First Edition: May 2012

Orbit is an imprint of Hachette Book Group, Inc. The Orbit name and
logo are trademarks of Little, Brown Book Group Limited.

The Hachette Speakers Bureau provides a wide range of authors for
speaking events. To find out more, go to www.hachettespeakersbureau.com
or call (866) 376-6591.

The publisher is not responsible for websites (or their content) that are
not owned by the publisher.

The characters and events in this book are fictitious. Any similarity
to real persons, living or dead, is coincidental and not intended
by the author.

Library of Congress Cataloging-in-Publication Data

Jemisin, N. K.
   The killing moon / N. K. Jemisin.—1st ed.
      p. cm.
   ISBN 978-0-316-18728-2
   I. Title.
PS3610.E46K55 2012
813'.6—dc22

                                        2011028110

                    10

                 LSC-C

Printed in the United States of America

# 1

*(⊙)*

*In the dark of dreams, a soul can die. The fears we confront
in shadows are as reflections in glass. It is natural to strike a
reflection that offends, but then the glass cuts; the soul
bleeds. The Gatherer's task is to save the soul, at any cost.*

(Wisdom)

In the dark of waking, a soul has died. Its flesh, however, is still
hungrily, savagely alive.

The Reaper's task is *not* to save.

\*       \*       \*

The barbarians of the north taught their children to fear the
Dreaming Moon, claiming that it brought madness. This was a
forgivable blasphemy. On some nights, the moon's strange light
bathed all Gujaareh in oily swirls of amethyst and aquamarine.
It could make lowcaste hovels seem sturdy and fine; pathways of
plain clay brick gleamed as if silvered. Within the moonlight's
strange shadows, a man might crouch on the shadowed ledge of
a building and be only a faint etching against the marbled gray.

In this land, such a man would be a priest, intent upon the
most sacred of his duties.

More than shadows aided this priest's stealth. Long training softened his footfalls against the stone; his feet were bare in any case. He wore little altogether, trusting the darkness of his skin for camouflage as he crept along, guided by the sounds of the city. An infant's cry from a tenement across the street; he took a step. Laughter from several floors below his ledge; he straightened as he reached the window that was his goal. A muffled cry and the sounds of a scuffle from an alley a block away; he paused, listening and frowning. But the disturbance ended as sandals pattered on the cobblestones, fading into the distance, and he relaxed. When the love-cries of the young couple next door floated past on a breeze, he slipped through the curtains into the room beyond.

The bedchamber: a study in worn elegance. The priest's eyes made out graceful chairs upholstered in fraying fabrics, and wood furnishings gone dull for lack of polish. Reaching the bed, he took care to avoid shadowing the face of the person who slept there—but the old man's eyes opened anyhow, blinking rheumily in the thin light.

"As I thought," said the old man, whose name was Yeyezu. His hoarse voice grated against the silence. "Which one are you?"

"Ehiru," said the priest. His voice was as soft and deep as the bedchamber's shadows. "Named Nsha, in dreams."

The old man's eyes widened in surprise and pleasure. "So that is the rose's soulname. To whom do I owe this honor?"

Ehiru let out a slow breath. It was always more difficult to bestow peace once a tithebearer had been awakened and frightened; that was why the law commanded Gatherers to enter dwellings in stealth. But Yeyezu was not afraid, Ehiru saw at

2

once, so he chose to answer the old man's question, though he preferred to do his work without conversation.

"Your eldest son submitted the commission on your behalf," he said. From the hipstrap of his loinskirt he plucked free the jungissa: a thumb-long polished stone like dark glass, which had been carved into the likeness of a cicada. Yeyezu's eyes tracked the jungissa as Ehiru raised it. The stones were legend for their rarity as well as their power, and few of Hananja's faithful ever saw one. "It was considered and accepted by the Council of Paths, then given to me to carry out."

The old man nodded, lifting a trembling hand toward the jungissa. Ehiru lowered the stone so that Yeyezu could run fingers over its slick, fine-carved wings, though he kept a good grip on its body. Jungissa were too sacred for carelessness. Yeyezu's wonder made him look much younger; Ehiru could not help smiling at this.

"She has tasted many of your dreams, Yeyezu-Elder," he said, very gently drawing the jungissa out of the old man's reach so he would hear Ehiru's words. Yeyezu sighed, but lowered his hand. "She has drunk deeply of your hopes and fears. Now She bids you join Her in Ina-Karekh. Will you grant Her this final offering?"

"Gladly," Yeyezu said, and closed his eyes.

So Ehiru bent and kissed the old man's forehead. Fevered skin, delicate as papyrus, smoothed under his lips. When he pulled away and set the jungissa in place of his kiss, the stone quivered at a flick of his fingernail and then settled into a barely-visible vibration. Yeyezu sagged into sleep, and Ehiru laid his fingertips on the old man's eyelids to begin.

In the relative quiet of the city's evening, the room sounded only of breath: first Ehiru's and Yeyezu's, then Ehiru's alone. Amid the new silence—for the jungissa had stopped vibrating with the dream's end—Ehiru stood for a few moments, letting the languor of the newly collected dreamblood spread within him. When he judged the moment right, he drew another ornament from his hip—this one a small hemisphere of obsidian whose flat face had been embossed with an oasis rose, the crevices tamped full of powdered ink. He pressed the carving carefully into the skin of Yeyezu's bony, still chest, setting his signature upon the artwork of flesh. The smile that lingered on the elder's cooling lips was even more beautiful.

"Dreams of joy always, my friend," he whispered, before pulling away the sheet and arranging Yeyezu's limbs into a peaceful, dignified position. Finally, as quietly as he'd entered, he left.

Now flight: along the rooftops of the city, swift and silent. A few blocks from Yeyezu's house Ehiru stopped, dropping to the ground in the lee of an old broken wall. There he knelt amid the weeds and trembled. Once, as a younger man, he would have returned to the Hetawa after such a night's work, overwhelmed with joy at the passing of a rich and full life. Only hours of prayer in the Hetawa's Hall of Blessings could've restored his ability to function. He was no longer a young man. He was stronger now; he had learned discipline. Most nights he could perform a second Gathering, and occasionally a third if circumstances required—though three would leave him giddy and half a-dream, unsure of which realm he walked. Even a single soul's dreamblood could still muddle his wits, for how could he not exult with Yeyezu's happiness so palpable within him?

Yet for the sake of other suffering citizens of Gujaareh, it was necessary to try. Twice he attempted to count by fours, a concentration exercise, but both times he failed at only four thousand and ninety-six. Pathetic. At last, however, his thoughts settled and the tremors ceased.

With some concern he saw that Dreaming Moon had reached zenith, her bright expanse glaring from the sky's center like a great striped eye; the night was half over. Faster to cross this part of the city on the ground than by rooftop. After a moment's pause to turn his loindrapes and don several gold ear-cuffs—for not even the poorest man in Gujaareh's capital went without some ornamentation—Ehiru left the old wall and walked the streets as a man of no particular caste, nondescript in manner, taking care to slouch in order to lessen his stature. At such a late hour he saw only caravanners, making the final preparations for a journey on the morrow, and a yawning guardsman, doubtless headed for a night shift at one of the city gates. None of them noticed him.

The houses became less dense once he reached the highcaste district. He turned down a side street lit poorly with half-burned-out lanterns, and emerged amid a gaggle of young shunha men who reeked of a timbalin house and a woman's stale perfume. They were laughing and staggering together, their wits slowed by the drug. He trailed in their wake for a block before they even marked his presence and then slipped aside, down another side street. This one led to the storage barn of the guesthouse he sought. The barn doors stood open, barrels of wine and twine-wrapped parcels in plain view along the walls—unmolested; Gujaareh's few thieves knew better.

Slipping into the shadows here, Ehiru removed his show-jewelry and turned his drapes once more, rolling and tying them so they would not flap. On one side, the drapes bore an unassuming pattern, but on the other—the side he wore now—they were completely black.

The day before, Ehiru had investigated the guesthouse. As shrewd as any merchant-casteman, the house's proprietor kept his tower open year-round to cater to wealthy foreigners, many of whom disliked relocating during the spring floods. This tithebearer—a northern trader—had a private room in the tower, which was separated from the rest of the building by a flight of steep stairs. Convenient. Hananja made way when She wanted a thing done.

Within the house, the kitchen was dim, as was the serving chamber beyond. Ehiru moved past the table with its low cushions and through the house's atrium garden, slowing as he turned aside fronds of palms and dangling ferns. Beyond the garden lay the sleeping chambers. Here he crept most stealthily of all, for even at such a late hour there could have been guests awake, but all of the rooms' lanterns remained shuttered and he heard only slow, steady breathing from each curtained entrance. Good.

As he climbed the tower steps, Ehiru heard the trader's unpeaceful snores even through the room's heavy wooden door. Getting the door open without causing its hinges to creak took some doing, but he managed it while privately damning the outland custom of putting doors on inner chambers. Inside the room, the trader's snores were so loud that the gauze curtains around his bed shivered in vibration. No wonder the proprietor had offered him the tower, and probably discounted the room. Still, Ehiru was cautious; he waited until a particularly harsh snort to part the curtains and gaze down at his next commission.

This close, the scent of the man mingled rancid sweat, stale grease, and other odors into a pungent mix that left Ehiru momentarily queasy. He had forgotten the infrequent bathing habits of people from the north. Though the night was cool and breezy, the northerner—a trader from the Bromarte people, the commission had specified, though in truth Ehiru had never been able to tell one northern tribe from another—sweated profusely, his pale skin flushed and rash-prickled as if he slept in high noon's swelter. Ehiru studied that face for a moment, wondering what peace might be coaxed from the dreams of such a man.

There would be something, he decided at last, for Hananja would not have chosen him otherwise. The man was lucky. She did not often bestow Her blessings upon foreigners.

The Bromarte's eyes already flickered beneath their lids; no jungissa was necessary to send him into the proper state of sleep. Laying fingers on the man's eyelids, Ehiru willed his own soul to part from flesh, leaving its connection—the umblikeh— tethered in place so that he could follow it back when the time came. The bedchamber had become a shadow-place, colorless and insubstantial, when Ehiru opened his soul's eyes. A reflection of the waking realm, unimportant. Only one thing had meaning in this halfway place between waking and dreaming: the delicate, shimmering red tether that emerged from somewhere near the Bromarte's collarbones and trailed away into nothingness. This was the path the man's soul had taken on its journey to Ina-Karekh, the land of dreams. It was a simple matter for Ehiru to follow the same path *out* and then *in* again.

When he opened his soul's eyes this time, color and vast strangeness surrounded him, for he was in Ina-Karekh, the land of dreams. And here the dream of the Bromarte revealed itself. Charleron of Wenkinsclan, came the name to Ehiru's consciousness, and he absorbed the name's foreignness and as much as he could of the person who bore it. Not a soulname, but that was to be expected. Bromarte parents named their children for the hopes and needs of the waking world, not protection in sleep. By the reckoning of this Charleron's people, his was a name of ambition. A name of *hunger*. And hunger was what filled the Bromarte's soul: hunger for wealth, for respect, for things he himself could not name. Reflected in the dreamscapes of Ina-Karekh, these hungers had coalesced into a great yawning pit in the earth, its walls lined with countless disembodied, groping hands. Assuming his usual dreamform, Ehiru floated down through the hands and ignored their silent, scrabbling, blind need as he searched.

And there, at the bottom of the well of hands, weeping with fear and helplessness, knelt the manifestation of the unfortunately named Bromarte man. Charleron cringed between sobs, trying and failing to twist away from his own creations as the hands plucked at him again and again. They did him no harm and would have been only moderately frightening to any properly trained dreamer—but this was nevertheless the bile of dreams, Ehiru judged: black and bitter, necessary for health but unpleasant to the senses. He absorbed as much of it as he could for the Sharers, for there was much of use in dreambile even if Charleron might not agree. But he reserved space within himself for the most important humor, which after all was why he had come.

And as they always did, as the Goddess had decreed they must, the bearer of Hananja's tithe looked up and saw Ehiru in his true, unadulterated shape.

"Who are you?" the Bromarte demanded, distracted momentarily from his terror. A hand grabbed his shoulder and he gasped and flinched away.

"Ehiru," he said. He considered giving the man his soulname and then decided against it. Soulnames meant nothing to heathens. But to his surprise, the Bromarte's eyes widened as if in recognition.

"*Gualoh*," the Bromarte said, and through the filter of their shared dream, a whiff of meaning came to Ehiru. Some kind of frightening creature from their nightfire tales? He dismissed it: barbarian superstition.

"A servant of the Goddess of Dreams," Ehiru corrected, crouching before the man. Hands plucked nervously at his skin and loincloth and the twin braids that dangled from his nape, responding to the Bromarte's fear of him. He paid them no heed. "You have been chosen for Her. Come, and I will shepherd you to a better place than this, where you may live out eternity in peace." He extended his hand.

The Bromarte leaped at him.

The movement caught Ehiru by such surprise that he almost failed to react in time—but no common man could best a Gatherer in dreaming. With a flick of his will, Ehiru banished the well of hands and replaced it with an innocuous desert of wind-waved dunes. This afforded him plenty of room to sidestep the Bromarte's headlong rush. The Bromarte ran at him again, roaring obscenities; Ehiru opened and then closed the ground beneath the Bromarte's feet, dropping him to the waist in sand.

Even thus pinned, the Bromarte cursed and flailed and wept, grabbing handfuls of the sand to fling at him—which Ehiru simply willed away. Then, frowning in puzzlement, he crouched to peer into the Bromarte's face.

"It's pointless to fight," he said, and the Bromarte flinched into stillness at the sound of his voice, though Ehiru had kept his tone gentle. "Relax, and the journey will go soft." Surely the Bromarte knew this? His people had been trading goods and seed with Gujaareh for centuries. In case that was the source of the Bromarte's panic, Ehiru added, "There will be no pain."

"Get away from me, *gualoh*! I'm not one of you mud-grubbers; I don't need you feeding on my dreams!"

"It is true that you aren't Gujaareen," Ehiru replied. Without taking his attention from the man, he began adjusting the dreamscape to elicit calm. The clouds overhead became wispy and gentle, and he made the sand around the Bromarte's dream-form finer, pleasant against the skin. "But foreigners have been Gathered before. The warning is given to all who choose to live and do business within our capital's walls: Hananja's city obeys Hananja's Law."

Something of Ehiru's words finally seemed to penetrate the Bromarte's panic. His bottom lip quivered. "I, I don't want to die." He was actually weeping, his shoulders heaving, so much that Ehiru could not help pitying him. It was terrible that the northerners had no narcomancy. They were helpless in dreaming, at the mercy of their nightmares, and none of them had any training in the sublimation of fear. How many had been lost to the shadowlands because of it? They had no Gatherers, either, to ease the way.

"Few people desire death," Ehiru agreed. He reached out to stroke the man's forehead, brushing thin hair aside, to reassure him. "Even my countrymen, who claim to love Hananja, sometimes fight their fate. But it's the nature of the world that some must die so that others may live. You will die—early and unpleasantly if the whore's disease you brought to Gujaareh runs its course. And in that time you might not only suffer, but spread your suffering to others. Why not die in peace and spread life instead?"

"Liar." Suddenly the Bromarte's face was piggish, his small eyes glittering with hate. The change came so abruptly that Ehiru faltered to silence, startled. "You call it a blessing of your Goddess, but I know what it really is." He leaned forward; his breath had gone foul. "*It gives you pleasure.*"

Ehiru drew back from that breath, and the fouler words. Above their heads, the wispy clouds stopped drifting. "No Gatherer kills for pleasure."

"'No Gatherer kills for pleasure.'" The Bromarte drawled the words, mocking. "And what of those who *do*, Gatherer?" The Bromarte grinned, his teeth gleaming momentarily sharp. "Are they Gatherers no longer? There's another name for those, yes? Is that how you tell your lie?"

Coldness passed through Ehiru; close on its heels came angry heat. "This is obscenity," he snapped, "and I will hear no more of it."

"Gatherers comfort the dying, yes?"

"Gatherers comfort those who believe in peace, and welcome Hananja's blessing," Ehiru snapped. "Gatherers can do little for unbelievers who mock Her comfort." He got to his feet and scowled to himself in annoyance. The man's nonsense had distracted him; the sand rippled and bubbled around them, heaving like the breath of a living thing. But before he could resume control of the dream and force the Bromarte's mind to settle, a hand grasped his ankle. Startled, he looked down.

"They're using you," said the Bromarte.

Alarm stilled Ehiru's mind. "What?"

The Bromarte nodded. His eyes were gentler now, his expression almost kind. As pitying as Ehiru himself had been, a moment before. "You will know. Soon. They'll use you to nothing, and there will be no one to comfort *you* in the end, Gatherer." He laughed and the landscape heaved around them, laughing with him. "Such a shame, Nsha Ehiru. Such a shame!"

Gooseflesh tightened Ehiru's skin, though the skin was not real. The mind did what was necessary to protect the soul at such times, and Ehiru suddenly felt great need of protection— for the Bromarte *knew his soulname*, though he had not given it.

He jerked away from the man's grip and pulled out of his dream in the same reflexive rush. But to Ehiru's horror, the clumsy exit tore free the tether that bound the Bromarte to his flesh. Too soon! He had not moved the Bromarte to a safer place within the realm of dreams. And now the soul fluttered along in his wake like flotsam, twisting and fragmenting no matter how he tried to push it back toward Ina-Karekh. He collected the spilled dreamblood out of desperation but shuddered as it came into him sluggishly, clotted with fear and malice. In the dark between worlds, the Bromarte's last laugh faded into silence.

Ehiru returned to himself with a gasp, and looked down. His gorge rose so powerfully that he stumbled away from the bed, leaning against the windowsill and sucking quick shallow breaths to keep from vomiting.

*"Holiest mistress of comfort and peace . . ."* He whispered the prayer in Sua out of habit, closing his eyes and still seeing the Bromarte's dead face: eyes wide and bulging, mouth open, teeth bared in a hideous rictus. What had he done? *O Hananja, forgive me for profaning Your rite.*

He would leave no rose-signature behind this time. The final dream was never supposed to go so wrong—certainly not under the supervision of a Gatherer of his experience. He shuddered as he recalled the reek of the Bromarte's breath, like that of something already rotted. Yet how much fouler had it been for the Bromarte, who had now been hurled through Ehiru's carelessness into the nightmare hollows of Ina-Karekh for all eternity? And that only if enough of his soul had been left intact to return.

Yet even as disgust gave way to grief, and even as Ehiru bowed beneath the weight of both, intuition sounded a faint warning in his mind.

He looked up. Beyond the window rose the rooftops of the city, and beyond those the glowing curve of the Dreamer sank steadily toward the horizon. Waking Moon peeked round its larger curve. The city had grown still in the last moments of Moonlight; even the thieves and lovers slept. All except himself—

—And a silhouette, hunched against the cistern on a nearby rooftop.

Ehiru frowned and pushed himself upright.

The figure straightened as he did, mirroring his movement. Ehiru could make out no details aside from shape: male, naked or nearly so, tall and yet oddly stooped in posture. Indeterminate features and caste, indeterminate intent.

No. That much, at least, was discernible. Ehiru could glean little else from the figure's stillness, but *malevolence* whispered clearly in the wind between them.

The tableau lasted only a moment. Then the figure turned, climbed the cistern's rope to its roof, and leaped onto an adjoining building and out of sight. The night became still once more. But not peaceful.

*Gualoh*, echoed the Bromarte's voice in Ehiru's memory. Not an insult, he realized, staring at where the figure had been. A warning.

*Demon.*

# FIRST INTERLUDE

( ☉ )

*Did you know that writing stories down kills them?*

*Of course it does. Words aren't meant to be stiff, unchanging things. My family were talekeepers once, though now they make funerary urns and jars. Many, many generations ago, before pictorals and numeratics and hieratics, words were kept where they belong, in mouths. The people who made sure those words passed on were my ancestors. Written words did not kill my lineage's purpose, though gone are the crowds—and the riches—we once commanded. We retell the stories regardless, because we know: stone is not eternal. Words can be.*

*So. At the beginning of time—*

*Yes, yes, I must begin with that greater story. I tell this in the Sua way, first the greater stories, then the lesser, because that is how it must be done. That was our bargain, yes? I will speak, and pass my tales on to you since I have no sons or daughters to keep them for me. When I finish speaking, you may summon my brethren, and I will go gladly to Hananja. So.*

*At the beginning of time the Sun was a swaggering oaf. He strutted about the heavens proclaiming his greatness day and night, heedless of the hardships he caused to the world below: rivers dying, deserts born, mountaintops burned ugly and bare. He shone himself brightly so that the two Moon Sisters would admire him and grant him their favor.*

*Waking Moon was a small and homely thing who rarely strayed far from her sister's shadow, fearful of being alone. She permitted the Sun her pleasures and he continued swaggering about, more certain than ever of his greatness.*

*But Dreaming Moon was full and beautiful. She loved the dark places and the cool nights, and sometimes she would gaze down into the ocean to paint her face with four bands of color: red for blood, white for seed, yellow for ichor, and black for bile. She felt no pressing need for a lover, and she found Sun's behavior offensive, so she scorned his attempts to court her.*

*Sun grew mad with longing for her, and even Waking Moon could not distract him from his lust. He sought solace in smaller, younger Stars, who would sometimes bend themselves to him, but at last his desire became too great even for that. He fell to the earth and masturbated, and when his climax came the earth tore and the heavens split and a great white spear of his seed flew forth and struck Dreaming Moon. Where the earth opened, plants and beasts emerged and began to spread across the land. Where the Dreamer was struck, gods came forth and began to spread across the heavens.*

*In a fury at this great insult, Dreaming Moon declared that if Sun could not control himself, she would control him. So she demanded that he bring her gifts to make amends and food to feed the children he had so carelessly spawned. She confined him to the day, where he could swagger as much as he wished and no longer annoy her with his foolish-*

*ness. She forbade him ever to lie upon the earth again, lest his lustful inclinations lead to more chaos. Meekly he submitted to these restrictions, for she was powerful with magic and he desired her still, and if this was the only way she would have him, then so it must be.*

*Now they live apart as husband and wife, she in the night and he in the day. Always he longs for her, and the days shorten and lengthen as he strains to rise earlier, set later, all for a chance to glimpse her. With time she has grown fond of him, for he has been humble and well-behaved since their marriage. Every so often, she rises early so he can gaze upon her. Once in a great while she lets him catch up to her, and he darkens his face to please her, and they join in careful lovemaking. And sometimes in the night when he cannot see her, she misses his foolish antics and pines for him, and darkens her own face. She is always bright again when he returns.*

# 2

(◦)

*Give Hananja peace and She shall dream peace and so*
*return peace upon the dreamer. Give Her fear or suffering*
*and She shall dream these, and return the same. Thus is peace*
*made law. That which threatens peace is corruption.*
*War is the greatest of evils.*
(Law)

There was magic in Gujaareh.

So the Protectors had warned all Kisua. Yet Sunandi's master Kinja Seh Kalabsha had required her to study Gujaareen magic as part of her apprenticeship, though it made the elders shake their heads and the sonha nobles sigh. Kinja had been adamant, however. Magic was mother's milk to the people of Gujaareh. They were steeped in its necessity, proud of its benefits, dismissive of its consequences. It was impossible to understand Gujaareh without understanding the source of its power.

And so Sunandi had learned. Gujaareen magic centered around the powers of healing, which the Hetawa—the governing temple of the Hananjan faith—controlled. But though the Hananjan priests served as gatekeepers for the magic, they were not its source. The people of Gujaareh made the magic, in the wild bursts of imagination and emotion called dreams; the Hananjans simply harvested that wildness and refined it into a purer, usable form. And so Gujaareen citizens brought their nightmares and nonsense dreams to the temples, where the priests called Sharers used them to shrink tumors or speed the healing of wounds. Sometimes a different kind of healing was needed, perhaps to regrow a severed limb or end a disease passed down through the lineage. Then Hananja's whores would go forth—no, Sunandi chided herself. Dangerous even to think with the usual Kisuati scorn while within Gujaareh's borders. Hananja's Sisters, they were called, though a handful were males in female garb; more Gujaareen strangeness. In solemn rites the Sisters would coax forth the most carnal dreams from Her supplicants, and those too would be given to the Sharers for the good of all.

And for those citizens of Gujaareh who were too old, or too sick, or too selfish to bring their offerings to the Hetawa...there were the priests called Gatherers.

Oh yes, there was magic in Gujaareh. Great, reeking heaps of it.

"You're afraid," observed the Prince.

Sunandi blinked out of her reverie to find him smiling at her, unapologetic. It was the Gujaareen way to speak of such things—desires that should remain private, concealed anxieties. He knew it was not the Kisuati way.

"You hide it well," he continued, "but it shows. Mostly in your silence. You've been so forceful up until now that the change is striking. Or is it that you find me a poor conversationalist?"

N. K. Jemisin

If only Kinja had not died, Sunandi thought behind the mask of her answering smile. He had understood the peculiarities and contradictions of Gujaareh better than anyone else in Kisua. In this land flowers bloomed at night and the river created lush farmlands in the heart of a desert. Here politics was half religion and half riddle, for under Hananja's Law even a hint of corruption was punishable by death. And here Sunandi had discovered that even Kinja could make mistakes, for though he had taught her the language and the magic and the customs, he had not been a woman. He had never been forced to contend with the most elegant, most dangerous charms of Gujaareh's Sunset Prince.

"I'm forceful when force is needed," Sunandi replied. She waved a hand: a touch of unconcern, a hint of coquetry. "Trade discussions with the zhinha most definitely require it. I was under the impression, however, that this meeting between us was..." She pretended to grope for the word in Gujaareen although she suspected that he, unlike most of his countrymen, would not be so easily lulled by her accent and feigned ignorance. "How do you say it? Less official. More...intimate."

"Oh, it is." His gaze followed her every movement; the smile had not left his face.

She inclined her head. "Then here I may be more myself. If you read fear in my silence, I assure you that it has nothing to do with you." She smiled to soften the snub. His eyes flared with a mingling of amusement and interest, as they always seemed to do when she parried his verbal feints. Small wonder he found her so alluring; to Sunandi's mind, Gujaareen women were painfully demure.

20

The Prince abruptly rose from his couch and sauntered over to the terrace railing. For a moment Sunandi set aside subtlety to drink her fill of the sight unobserved—though there was hardly any need to conceal her interest. The Prince's movements were studied, the epitome of grace; he knew full well she was watching. The black ropes of his hair had been threaded with cylinders of gold and strings of minute pearls, and this mane surrounded a face that was fine-planed and flawless, apart from the misfortune of his coloring. Ageless, like his lean warrior's body. Here in his private quarters he'd shunned the more elaborate collars and adornments of his office for a simple loinskirt and feathered waistcloak. The plumes of the cloak whispered as they swept the floor's tiles behind him.

He stopped beside a raised plinth bearing a platter, gazed at it for a moment as if to assure himself of the suitability of its contents, then brought the platter over to her. He knelt with careless ease before the bench she'd chosen and offered the platter to her with his head bowed, humble as any lowcaste servant.

On the platter lay a profusion of delicacies for the taking: crisp vegetables flecked with hekeh-seed and sea salt, balls of grain held together with honey and aromatic oil, medallions of fresh fish tied into bundles around wine-soaked raisins. And more, each arranged in neat rows of four—forty in all. An auspicious number by Gujaareen reckoning.

Sunandi smiled at that implicit hopeful message. After a moment's consideration she selected a wafer of sugar-stalk around which some sort of river crustacean had been baked. He waited while she took her time chewing, savoring the salt-sweet flavor; that was the proper way to show appreciation in both

Gujaareen and Kisuati custom. Then she inclined her head in acceptance of the offering. He set the platter on his knee and began feeding her more with his fingers, showing no sign of eagerness or haste.

"Kisuati speak often of Gujaareen courting-customs," Sunandi said while he selected another morsel. "My people find it amusing that men here use food to lure women into pleasure. In our land it is the opposite."

"The food is only a symbol," the Prince replied. His voice was low and smooth, and he spoke softly as if to soothe a wild animal. "It is the act of offering that—hopefully—tempts a woman. Some offer jewels; the shunha and zhinha favor such things as a mark of status. Lowcastes offer poetry or song." He shrugged. "I feared that jewels, given our relative positions, might be misconstrued as a bribe. And poetry is such a subjective thing. Offerings can offend, after all." He gave her something redolent of nutmeg, and wonderful. "Delicacies, however, tempt the appetites."

She licked her lips, amused. "Whose appetites, I wonder?"

"The woman's, of course. Men need little incentive to take pleasure." He smiled self-deprecatingly. Sunandi resisted the urge to roll her eyes at his foolishness. "And we Gujaareen revere our women."

"As much as you revere your goddess?" The statement edged along their notion of blasphemy, but the Prince only laughed.

"Women *are* goddesses," he replied. She opened her mouth and he placed the next item on her tongue, where it melted in an exquisite mix of flavors. She closed her eyes and caught her breath, inadvertently overwhelmed, and saw when she opened them again that his grin had widened. "They birth and shape the dreamers of the world. What better courtship can a man offer than worship?"

"Until you've had your pleasure. Then your goddesses return to making babies and keeping house."

"Just so. Honorable men continue to make offerings to them, though the offerings are nightly pleasure and helpful tools rather than frivolities." His eyes snapped with humor as if he sensed how much his words irritated her. "So you must forgive my courtiers and counselors if they are uneasy at having to deal with you as Kisua's Voice. In their eyes you should be secure in some man's kitchen, receiving the adulation that is your just due."

She laughed, not as gently as he. "Would they be displeased to find me here with you now?"

"Doubtful. A man and a woman associating for pleasure makes far more sense to them than a man and a woman associating for business."

When Sunandi politely turned away the next morsel, he set aside the platter and took her hands, pulling her to stand. She rose with him, curious to see how far he meant to go. "In fact," said the Prince, "they will actually be pleased that I have seduced the Voice of Kisua. No doubt they'll expect you to become more acquiescent after a day and a night spent offering dreams of ecstasy to Hananja." He shrugged one shoulder. "They do not understand outland women."

A day and a night. Mnedza's Hands, he had a high opinion of himself.

"I see," she said, keeping her face serene. The Prince made no move to pull her against him, did nothing more than hold her hands and gaze into her eyes. She met his eyes without wavering, wondering what a Gujaareen woman would do in such a situation. He had strange eyes: a clear, pale brown, like polished amber from the tall forests across the sea. His skin was of a nearly matching shade—not unattractive, but certainly improper for a nobleman. Amazing that these Gujaareen had allowed even their royal lineage to be diluted by northerners.

She decided to banter. "And you understand outland women?"

"I have two hundred and fifty-six wives," he replied, his voice rippling with amusement. "I can understand any woman."

She laughed again, and after a moment's further consideration stepped closer. His hands tightened immediately, pulling her nearer still until her breasts brushed against his chest through the folds of her gown. He leaned close, putting his face beside hers, cheek against cheek. He smelled of sandalwood and moontear blossoms.

"You find me amusing, Sunandi Jeh Kalawe?" His voice held only the barest hint of roughness; the lust was in him, but firmly controlled.

"I am a woman, my lord," she replied, in the same tone he'd used a moment before. "I find any man amusing."

He chuckled, breath warm against her ear, and began pulling her toward the couch, his grip coaxing her to stay close. "You'll find I'm unlike any man you know, Sunandi."

"Because of your great experience?" She posed the question carefully, knowing he would sense her true meaning but leaving him a safe outlet. He had two hundred and fifty-six wives, and was duty-bound to please them all. He was also far older than he looked. No one knew his age for certain, but he had ruled

Gujaareh for more than thirty floods, and he didn't look a day over that much. His lineage was famous for its longevity, said to be the gift of the Sun's scions.

But the Prince only sat down as they reached the couch, pulling her to sit beside him. Not until she was seated did he release her hands, shifting his grip to her hips instead.

"Because I am the Avatar of Hananja," he said, his golden eyes hungry as a lion's, "and I will give you beautiful dreams."

\*    \*    \*

Once their business was concluded and the Prince slept, Sunandi rose from the couch to attend herself in the wash-chamber. She took care to confine her exploration of the Prince's apartments only to what was in sight, for there was no telling when he might wake and come looking for her, and he would already be suspicious of her motives. Though she had expected to find nothing of note, her attention was caught in his study, where an iron case bristling with four elaborate eastern locks sat bolted to the desk.

There, she realized with a chill. The secret she had come to Gujaareh to find: it was *there*.

But she did not approach the case, not yet. Most likely it held dangerous traps; Gujaareen were fond of those. Instead she returned to the terrace, where with some unease she found the Prince awake, as alert as if he had never slept, and waiting for her.

"Find anything interesting?" His smile was a sphinx's.

She returned it. "Only you," she said, and lay down beside him again.

\*    \*    \*

She returned to her suite late that night, just as the Dreamer passed zenith. The Prince had not made good on his boast of a full day and night of pleasure, but he'd given a respectable accounting of himself nevertheless. The pleasurable aches she felt in the aftermath told her that it was probably just as well. She'd gotten out of practice; by morning she would doubtless be sore.

More important matters claimed her attention as soon as she crossed the threshold of her suite, however, where Lin waited for her.

Few of the Gujaareen had paid any heed to the skinny, wheat-haired child among the other pages in Sunandi's entourage. Northblooded youngsters were common in Gujaareh, and in any case it was the fashion for nobles of both lands to keep a few curiosities on hand as entertainers. It pleased her to let them think this was her only purpose.

"A long appointment, mistress," the girl said, speaking in Sua since they were alone. She lounged across a chair in the corner, her impish face not quite daring a smile.

"The Prince was kind enough to teach me a few Gujaareen customs that Master Kinja neglected."

"Ah, a valuable lesson, then. Did you learn much?"

Sunandi sighed, flopping onto a suede-covered bench that reminded her obliquely of the Prince's couch. Not as comfortable, sadly; her aches twinged. "Not as much as I'd hoped. Still, further tutorings might prove useful."

"That knowledgeable, is he? A hint, mistress: question him *before* the lesson begins."

She leveled a look at Lin. "Disrespectful infant. You must have found something if you're so insufferably smug."

In answer, Lin held up a hand. In it lay a tiny scroll barely as long as her forefinger. When Sunandi sat up in interest, she crossed the room to offer it to Sunandi—keeping to the shadows, Sunandi noted, and away from the open window. She filed this oddity away to ponder another time, however, snatching the scroll from Lin's hand. "You found it!"

"Yes, 'Nandi. It's in Master Kinja's hand, I'd swear, and..." She hesitated, glancing toward the window again. "It speaks of things no Gujaareen would commit to print."

Sunandi threw her a sharp glance. Her expression was unusually grim.

"If it's that serious, I'll send the scroll back to Kisua. But I'm not yet certain how far some of Kinja's old contacts can be trusted... especially the Gujaareen ones." She sighed in annoyance. "You might have to go, Lin."

Lin shrugged. "I was getting tired of this place anyway. It's too dry here, and the sun makes me red; I itch constantly."

"You complain like a highcaste matron," Sunandi replied. She opened the scroll and scanned the first scrawled numeratics, translating the code in her mind. "Next I'll find you demanding servants to oil your spoiled backside—*groveling Sun!*"

Lin jumped. "Keep your voice down! Have you forgotten there are no doors?"

"Where did you find this?"

"General Niyes's office, here in the palace.—Yes, I know. But I think it's all right. The general claimed some of Master Kinja's things because they'd been friends. One of the decorative masks. I don't think Niyes noticed the false backing."

Sunandi's hands shook as she read further. The scroll was not long; Kinja had been spare but eloquent in the limited space.

When she reached the end she sat back against the wall, her mind churning and her heart tightening with belated grief.

Kinja had been murdered. She had suspected, but the confirmation was a bitter tea. The Gujaareen had called it a heart-seizure, something too swift and severe for even their magic to cure. But Sunandi knew there were also poisons that could trigger heart-seizures, and other techniques to make death look natural. Here in Gujaareh, where only custom and curtains kept a bedroom secure, it would have been easy. And why not, given what Kinja had discovered? Monsters in the shadows. Magic so foul that even their murderous priests would cry abomination—if they ever learned of it. Clearly, someone meant to make certain they did not.

But now Sunandi knew those secrets. Not all of them by far, but enough to put her in danger of Kinja's fate.

Lin edged close, concern plain on her face. Sunandi smiled sadly at her, reaching up to smooth a hand over her thin, flat hair. Her sister of the heart, if not the lineage. Kinja had not adopted Lin outright as he had Sunandi—foreigners had no legal standing in Kisua—but Lin had proven her worth time and again over the years. Now it seemed Sunandi would have to force her to prove it once more. She was barely thirteen...

And she was the only one out of their whole delegation who could escape the palace and city without alerting the Gujaareen. It was why Sunandi had brought the girl, knowing they would never expect a Kisuati to entrust vital secrets to a northerner. And Lin was no untried innocent; she had survived alone on the streets of Kisua's capital for years. With aid from their contacts, she could handle the journey.

Unless Sunandi's enemies knew she had been sent to look for this. Unless the scroll had been left in place as a trap. Unless they knew of Kinja's penchant for finding and training talented youngsters.

Unless they sent their Reaper.

She shivered. Lin read her face and nodded to herself. She took the scroll from Sunandi's limp fingers, rerolled it, and tucked it out of sight in her linen skirt.

"Shall I go tonight, or wait until after the Hamyan celebration?" she asked. "It means two days' delay, but it should be easier to slip out of the city then."

Sunandi could have wept. Instead she pulled Lin close and held her tightly, and shaped her thoughts into a fervent prayer that she hoped the mad bitch Hananja could not hear.

# 3

⟨ ⊙ ⟩

*A child of a woman may have a four of siblings, or an eight.*
*A child of the Hetawa has a thousand.*
(Wisdom)

There were many things that one could feel when surrounded by a four of the Hetawa's finest guardians, Nijiri considered. Fear, first and foremost—and oh, he felt that in plenty, souring his mouth and slicking his palms. But along with the fear, and dread for the beating these men would almost certainly administer to him before they were done, he felt something new, and surprising: anticipation.

*Lack of emotion is not the ideal.* Nijiri licked his lips, practically hearing Gatherer Ehiru's night-soft voice in his mind. Ehiru always knew just the right thing to say when Nijiri came to him with a boy's frets. *Control of emotion is. Even we Gatherers feel—and we savor those feelings, when they come, as the rare blessings they are.*

Could the urge to grind his opponents' faces into the sand truly be a blessing? Nijiri grinned. He would meditate upon it later.

Sentinel Mekhi glanced at Sentinel Andat, his kohled eyes narrowing in amusement. "I think perhaps Acolyte Nijiri wants peace, pathbrother."

"Hmm," said Andat. He was grinning as well, turning his fighting stick in the fingers of one hand with careless expertise. "I think perhaps Acolyte Nijiri wants *pain*. I suppose there's a kind of peace in that."

"Share it with me, Brothers," Nijiri breathed, crouching low and ready. With that, they came at him.

He did not wait for their sticks. No one could deflect, or endure, blows from four armed Sentinels. Instead he dropped low, presenting a smaller target and slipping beneath the zone of their fastest response. They were fast enough with their feet, though, and he only just dodged Sentinel Harakha's sweeping kick by rolling over it. This, thankfully, put him outside the Sentinels' circle and forced them to turn. That gave him a precious half-breath in which to formulate a strategy.

Harakha. As the youngest of the four, he had yet to develop a Sentinel's proper serenity. He was dangerous; any Sentinel who survived his apprenticeship was dangerous. But Nijiri had observed Harakha in sparring matches several times, and noted that whenever his blows were deflected, he tended to flail for an instant before recovering, as if shocked by his failure.

So Nijiri swept at Harakha's ankles with first one leg and then the other, rolling on his forearms to execute the sweeps again and again, forcing Harakha to dance back. The other Sentinels quickly altered their formation to avoid Nijiri's whirling legs and to keep from tripping over each other—just as Nijiri had hoped. Then, when Harakha grew justifiably annoyed and angled a stabbing strike at Nijiri's head, Nijiri closed his legs and rolled—*toward* Harakha. This brought him under Harakha's stick; the tip struck the ground beyond Nijiri and lodged, just for an instant, in the sand. At this Nijiri kicked up, aiming for Harakha's hand. He did not score, for Harakha realized what he was doing at the last instant and jerked back, retaliating with a furious kick that Nijiri bore with a grunt as he rolled away. A small pain-price to pay, for he had achieved his goal: Harakha stumbled back a step more, overcompensating in typical fashion for the fact that he'd almost lost his weapon. This forced the other three Sentinels to move *more*, gracelessly, to avoid their clumsy younger brother.

Distraction was a Gatherer's beloved friend. Rolling to his hands and toes, Nijiri darted forward and slapped his hand against Mekhi's calf. It was hard to find the soul from a limb, and harder for Nijiri to cool his thoughts enough for narcomancy, but perhaps—

Mekhi stumbled and fell to the ground, groaning. He was only groggy, but from an awake, aware man whose blood was fired for battle, Nijiri could expect nothing better. When Mekhi went down, however, Harakha hissed and nearly tripped over Mekhi's stick. Nijiri rose behind him like a shadow, and too late Harakha realized the danger. By that point Nijiri had touched two fingers to the nape of his neck, sending dreambile coursing along his spine like cold water to numb everything it touched. Harakha was unconscious even as his body whipped around. He kept spinning until he hit the ground, hard enough that he would no doubt curse Nijiri for his bruises when he woke.

Delighted, Nijiri rounded on Mekhi, who was trying to

stumble away until his sleep-mazed mind could clear. Forking his fingers and humming the song of his jungissa, Nijiri lunged after him—

—Only to halt, statue-still, as the tip of a stick came to hover before his face. Another stick, light as the touch of a lover, came to rest on the small of his back.

It was only a sparring match, he reminded himself in an effort to summon calm. (It did not come.) Only a test...but he had seen Sentinels impale men using sheer strength and angles to make their blunt sticks sharp as glass-tipped spears. And Andat liked to leave flesh wounds whenever he felt Nijiri had not fought to his fullest effort, as an encouragement to greater diligence.

"Good," said Andat, who held the stick to his face. That meant the one behind him was Sentinel Inefer. He had bested two, but been caught by the two most experienced. Had that been enough to pass the test? *I should have left Mekhi; he was no threat. Should have gotten one of the others first, should have—*

"Very good," Andat amended, and with relief Nijiri realized the man was truly pleased. "Two of us, with you unarmed and all of us ready? I would have been satisfied if you'd gotten one."

"It would've been Harakha, regardless," said Inefer behind Nijiri, sounding disgusted. "Blundering, peaceless fool."

"We'll drill him until he learns better," Andat said easily, and in spite of himself Nijiri grimaced in sympathy.

Nijiri felt Inefer's stick leave his back. "Other matters take precedence for now," Andat said, looking up at the balcony that overhung the sparring circle. Nijiri followed Andat's gaze and tensed in fresh dread, for there, gazing down at them with a wry expression, stood the Superior of the Hetawa. Beside the Superior stood two men in sleeveless, hooded robes of loose off-white linen. He could see nothing of their faces, and the angle was wrong to glimpse their shoulder tattoos, but he knew their builds well enough to guess which was which—and which, since a third man should have been among them, was missing.

Suppressing a frown, Nijiri got to his feet so that he could raise his hands in proper salute toward his brethren.

"That should do, I think," said the Superior. "Sentinel Andat, are you satisfied?"

"I am," said Andat, "and I speak for my pathbrethren in this. Anyone who can beat two Sentinels out of four has more than sufficient skill to carry out the Goddess's will beyond the Hetawa's walls." He glanced at Nijiri and smiled. "Even if he chooses to follow the wrong path in the process. Alas."

"I see. Thank you, Andat." The Superior's dark eyes settled on Nijiri then, and privately Nijiri fought the urge to cover himself or apologize for his unpeaceful appearance. He was still out of breath, drenched in sweat and dressed only in a loincloth, and it felt as though his heart had made a dancing-drum of his sternum. But he had done well; he had no reason for shame.

"Come then, Acolyte Nijiri," the Superior said—and paused, amusement narrowing his dark eyes. "Acolyte for now, at least."

Nijiri tried not to grin, and failed utterly.

"Go and wash," the Superior continued, emphasizing the latter word enough that some of Nijiri's joy turned to embarrassment. "At the sunset hour, come to the Hall of Blessings." To take your Gatherers' Oath, he did not say, but Nijiri heard it anyhow, and rejoiced anew. Then the Superior turned away, heading through the balcony hanging into his offices. Silently, the two hooded men flanking him followed.

"That was quick," muttered Mekhi, who grimaced and rubbed the back of his neck as he joined them. He still moved stiffly, shaking his free arm as if the hand had gone to sleep. Nijiri lifted his hand, flat with palm down, and bowed over it in contrition; Mekhi waved this off.

"A love match on both sides, I think," said Andat, though he also made an apologetic gesture when his brothers looked at him, so no one would think him resentful. "Go on, then, boy. Congratulations."

The word made it real. With a delighted grin, Nijiri bobbed a barely courteous nod to all three men, then turned and walked—with a speed just shy of running—into the Hetawa's dim silence.

\* \* \*

The bath restored his spirits, and the cool water was a balm after the sparring match in sweltering afternoon heat. No one else was in the bathing chamber when Nijiri used it, though once he returned to the small cell that he shared with three other acolytes he found that word had somehow spread: a four of pathing gifts had been left on his pallet. The first was a small, prettily enameled mirror, which had probably come from his roommates—yes, that was Talipa's work on the flowers, he would recognize it anywhere. Talipa had been claimed from a potter family. The second gift was a small set of finger-cuffs, engraved with formal prayer pictorals. Beautiful work, and probably that of Moramal, the acolyte-master. Nijiri set this aside. As a Gatherer he would need some jewelry, for a Gatherer went disguised among the faithful—but it was still not a gift that would see much use. Alas.

The third was a small jar of scented oil, which he sniffed and nearly dropped in amazement. Myrrh; could it be? But there was no mistaking the fragrance. Such an expensive gift could only have come from his soon-to-be pathbrothers. And that, no doubt, had been how the other acolytes guessed the news; one of them would've been dispatched to bring the gift to Nijiri's cell, and that one had apparently gossiped the whole way. Nijiri grinned to himself.

The fourth gift was a tiny statue of the Sun in his human form, carved in darkwood and polished to a fine gloss, right down to the prominent erect penis that any Sun statue bore. A popular gift between lovers.

Furious, Nijiri threw the thing across the room so hard that it broke in four pieces.

All his pleasure at passing the final test had soured, thanks to one tasteless, ill-considered gift. *What did the other acolytes think of that?* he wondered bitterly. But with the sunset hour coming, it was either go now or be late to his own oathtaking. So, fury banked if not fully extinguished, Nijiri hastily dressed in a plain loinskirt and sandals, though he also took the time to dab himself with the myrrh-oil and apply a bit of kohl to his eyes. It would not do to look ungroomed, or ungrateful for his new brothers' gift.

The Hall of Blessings—the massive, graceful pylon of sandstone and silver-veined granite that served as the entry to the Hetawa's complex of buildings—normally stood open to the public. As the main temple of Hananja in Gujaareh, and the only one within the walls of the capital city, the Hetawa was unique in housing only priests, acolytes, and those children who had been dedicated to the Goddess's care. Layfolk in Hananja's service were permitted to visit, but did not dwell within its walls. The lesser business of the Hetawa was conducted elsewhere in the city: schools for teaching children dreaming, law and wisdom, writing, and figuring; storehouses where tithes of money or goods were tallied; more. So during an allotted period by day, and again in the small hours of the morning for those who worked at night, the Hall was busy as the faithful came to do Hananja's greater work. They offered their prayers and dreams to Hananja, submitted commissions for healing or the Gathering of relatives, or obtained healing themselves for illnesses or physical complaints. Thus did all Gujaareh find peace. But at sunset, the Hall closed for all public purposes save dire need, so that each path of Hananja's servants could take its own communion with the Goddess of Dreams.

As Nijiri arrived, he found the Superior waiting on the tiered dais at the Hall's heart. Flanking him were the same two Gatherers—and behind them, above them, loomed the great nightstone statue of Hananja Herself. Nijiri fixed his gaze on the statue as he approached, trying to fill his heart with the sight: Her outstretched hands, Her white-flecked blackness, Her eyes perpetually shut as She dreamed the endless realm that was Ina-Karekh.

*His* realm, soon.

Such thoughts settled Nijiri's spirit at last, and by the time he reached the dais and bowed over his downturned palms, he felt sure of himself again, and calm.

(But where, he wondered again, was Gatherer Ehiru? Away on Hetawa business, perhaps. He fought disappointment.)

Silence fell, measured and still. When a proper span of time had passed, the Superior finally spoke. "Raise your head, Acolyte. We have something to discuss."

Surprised, Nijiri did so. Was this part of the oathtaking? As he looked up, the two men beside the Superior lifted their heads as well, each pulling back his hood.

"Your relationship with Teacher Omin," said the taller man. Sonta-i, he of the dead eyes and ashen-dark skin, eldest of the Gatherer path. "Explain it."

Everything in Nijiri went still. He stared at Sonta-i, too stunned even for alarm.

"Explain it *please*," said the other man, smiling as if that would soften the blow. He was stockier and younger and redder than Sonta-i. Curling copper ringlets trailed from his topknot, his eyes were a shade of brown that glinted red in the evening light, and even the tattoo on his upper arm—a four-lobed poppy—was the color of blood, where Sonta-i's nightshade had been done in deep indigo. Gatherer Rabbaneh, whom Nijiri had always considered kinder than Sonta-i. Until now.

*Omin, you useless, greedy fool.* Nijiri closed his eyes, thinking most unpeaceful thoughts. Anger had always been his weakness, the thing he strove most to control in himself. But now he could not help it, for if Omin's folly cost him the goal he had spent ten years striving toward...

"There *is* no relationship," he snapped, looking each man in the eye. Sonta-i's face remained impassive; Rabbaneh raised his eyebrows at Nijiri's tone. The Superior looked sorrowful—and by that, Nijiri guessed that he thought Nijiri was lying. This made Nijiri angrier still. "Though not for lack of trying on the Teacher's part."

"Oh?" asked the Superior, very quietly.

Nijiri made himself shrug, though he did not feel nonchalant at all. "The Teacher offered me favors in return for favors. I refused."

The Superior said, "Explain in fullness, Acolyte. When did this begin? What favors were offered, and what did he expect in return?"

"After I chose to leave the House of Children. The day I reported to him as an acolyte; he was to test me in numeratics. He found my knowledge acceptable, but he commented much on my face, my eyes, my walk. He said I was very pretty despite looking so lowcaste." He fought the urge to curl his lip, remembering that day and the way it had made him feel: low and weak and sick and afraid. The fear had changed, though, the longer Omin pressed him. He had grown angry, and that had always made him strong. So he took a deep breath. "Superior, now I must speak of that we do not discuss."

The Superior flinched. Rabbaneh's smile did not falter, but it grew harder, sharp-edged. Sonta-i did not react, but there was a palpable additional coldness in his voice as he spoke. "You imply that Omin made promises with respect to the pranje ceremony."

"I *imply* nothing, Gatherer." He watched that news settle in among them, and saw Omin's death harden on brows and tightened lips. At that, Nijiri did feel a moment's guilt. But Omin had brought this on himself—and Nijiri had his own future to consider.

"Continue," Sonta-i said.

"The Teacher offered me safety, Gatherer, from the annual selection of pranje attendants. In exchange, he made clear his desire that I attend *him*, in the small hours of the morning, at some location in a disused corridor of the Teachers' Hall. I do not know the place, since I refused him, but he said that he had used it with other acolytes, and there we would have privacy."

The Superior muttered something to himself in Sua; Nijiri, whose Sua was only passable, did not catch it. Rabbaneh let out a long sigh. For him, that was tantamount to a desert skyrer's shriek of fury. "And why did you not accept this offer?"

"I don't fear the pr—that we do not discuss." Silently Nijiri cursed the lapse. He had hoped to seem cool and controlled like a Servant of Hananja, and not a nervous child. "Why would I need protection from something I don't fear?"

The Gatherers looked at each other. There were no words exchanged between them—not that Nijiri could tell in any case. Rumor had it Gatherers could speak through waking dreams in some manner. But by that unvoiced agreement, Sonta-i abruptly moved away from his pathbrother and the Superior, coming down off the dais. Moving, his pace slow and steady and full of warning, to encircle Nijiri.

Now it took everything Nijiri had to stay angry, and not show his unease.

"You aren't afraid?" Sonta-i asked.

*I wasn't before now.* "No, Gatherer."

"An acolyte died last year. He served a Gatherer in the pranje and died. Did you know this?" Sonta-i did not look at Nijiri as he spoke; that was the worst of it. His eyes glanced over the moontear-vined pillars, the rugs, Hananja's starry knees. Nijiri did not rate even that much attention.

Nijiri did not turn to follow Sonta-i's movement, though the hairs on the back of his neck prickled whenever the Gatherer passed out of his sight. "I heard the rumors. I don't claim to be fearless, Gatherer; I fear many things. But *death* is not one of those things."

"Injury. Violation. Damnation. Despair. All these things can result when an acolyte attends a Gatherer sitting pranje." Abruptly Sonta-i paused, leaning in to examine a moontear flower with great intensity. Nijiri could not see what had so attracted the Gatherer's interest. Perhaps it was nothing at all.

"I am aware, Gatherer. I did sit pranje twice—" But those had been nothing, hours of boredom, while he sat with Sharers who'd been nearly as bored as he. Sharers faced the pranje's test only once every four of floodseasons, as a precaution, and no one could remember the last time a Sharer had failed. He had not trained to serve *Sharers*.

All at once Nijiri froze, as Sonta-i swung about and peered at him with the same taut scrutiny he'd given the flower. "You did not refuse the Teacher out of propriety. You refused him out of *pride*."

It was not a question, but Nijiri felt no need to deny it. They knew he had never been humble. "Yes. I wished to be a Gatherer."

"Acolyte," the Superior said, somewhere beyond Sonta-i. He sounded weary; Nijiri did not dare look away from Sonta-i's gray eyes to check. He didn't fear death, but somehow Sonta-i seemed worse than death in that moment. "You just said propriety was not your concern."

"Just so, Superior." He licked his lips—only so that he could speak clearly, of course, nothing more. "I felt that an acolyte who wished to become a Gatherer should do better, as illicit lovers go, than some greedy, undisciplined Teacher."

He was deeply relieved to hear a startled laugh from Rabbaneh, and the Superior's groan. Sonta-i, however, leaned closer to him, until Nijiri was breathing the man's exhalations. The tiny fibers of Sonta-i's iris, like spokes of a chariot wheel, contracted slowly as Sonta-i searched his face.

"You're hiding something," he said.

"Nothing I'm ashamed of, Gatherer."

It was a mistake; he knew it the instant he spoke. A lie. Sonta-i's eyes narrowed sharply. *He knew.*

"Your overly high estimation of yourself aside, Acolyte," drawled Rabbaneh, again somewhere behind Sonta-i, "why did you not report the Teacher to us? A man who would abuse his power over others should at the least be assessed for corruption. A Gatherer," and he said this with gentle emphasis, his voice growing serious, "would think this way."

Sonta-i was going to kill him. Nijiri knew that now. There was a stillness in the Gatherer that he had never seen before, though he found it somehow entirely unsurprising. Sonta-i was peculiar even by Gatherer standards—distracted by odd things, uninterested in emotional matters. Yet he was a Gatherer, and that honed all his peculiarity to an arrow-focus when he chose to do the Goddess's business.

So Nijiri spoke to Sonta-i. Not to excuse himself, because there was no excuse that any Gatherer would accept if he had already made his judgment. He spoke only to assuage his own pride. If he was to die, he would die like a Servant of Hananja.

"Because Omin did no harm," Nijiri said. "Not after that. He tried to harm me, but failed. And in his failure, he was tamed—for, after I informed him that I had only to speak a word to the Gatherers, he made no attempt to coerce other acolytes." Since then, in fact, Omin had been a model Teacher, save for his constant gifts and longing looks whenever Nijiri turned his back. And save for losing Nijiri his chance at the future he'd worked so hard to achieve.

Sonta-i shook his head slightly. By this, Nijiri knew his explanation had been insufficient to alter the Gatherer's assessment of him. Aloud, Sonta-i said, "And now that you're no longer an acolyte, this corrupt Teacher is free to press his attentions on other boys."

"I've dedicated myself to the Hetawa, Gatherer. I have friends among the acolytes, who would tell me—" But here he faltered for an instant, seized by sudden doubt. What would happen to him if the Gatherers did not accept him, and if Sonta-i did not kill him? He could go to the Sentinels, if they would still allow it, but he did not want to be a Sentinel, or a Teacher, or a layman, or anything but what he'd always, since the day he'd met Ehiru, *always* yearned to be—

"You've seen sixteen floods this year," said the Superior. "A man by law, and soon by duty as well. You cannot protect your fellows if you no longer dwell among them, never see their daily struggles. And you can't expect boys to bring their fears to you, either, for they'll have no cause to trust one grown man if another

has abused them." He sighed; from the corner of his eye, Nijiri
saw him shake his head. "Still too much the servant-caste."

At this, Nijiri flinched, stung enough at last to look away
from Sonta-i. "I am a child of the Hetawa, Superior!"

But it was Rabbaneh who nodded, to Nijiri's consternation.
"None of us are born to the Goddess's path, Acolyte. We come
from somewhere, and the past leaves its mark. Consider yours."

"I . . ." Nijiri frowned. "I don't understand."

"A good servant never complains, they say. A child of the
servant caste expects to be in others' power, and expects that
some of his masters will be corrupt. He seeks only to mitigate
the worst effects of that corruption so that he can survive. But
a Gatherer *destroys* corruption—and the power that allows
it, if he must. If that way lies peace. That is what I mean,
Acolyte Nijiri. You accommodated, where you should have
rebelled."

And belatedly, guiltily, Nijiri realized Rabbaneh and the
Superior were right. *A Gatherer does not seek help*, he had told
himself at the time—and so he had not, thinking himself stronger for handling the matter on his own. Thinking *of* himself,
when he should have held his fellow acolytes' peace foremost in
his mind. Of course Omin would do evil again; Omin was corrupt. There was no taming something like that.

Better to have brought the matter to the Superior and Gatherers, and damn his pride. Better even to kill Omin, with his
hands if not narcomancy, and then submit himself for the
Gatherers' judgment. Any action was better than complacency
while corruption festered and grew.

He knelt then, putting his hands and forehead on the floor to show the depth of his contrition. "Your pardon, Gatherer," he murmured against the stone, glad now that Ehiru was not present. Sonta-i still loomed over him, but that was right. How had he ever imagined himself ready to be a Gatherer? "I was wrong. I should never have...I should've done more. May Her peace ease my soul—I should have *thought*."

A moment of appropriate silence passed.

"Well," said Rabbaneh, with a sigh. "I suppose that will do. Sonta-i?"

Sonta-i took hold of Nijiri's arm, pulling him back to his feet. As Nijiri blinked in surprise, Sonta-i narrowed his eyes again. "He's still hiding something."

"Boys his age will have their secrets, pathbrother. Even we are permitted a few of those."

With a soft sigh that was not—*quite*, Nijiri thought—disappointed, Sonta-i released him. "Very well; I agree."

"And we know Ehiru's feeling on the matter." Rabbaneh clasped his hands behind his back and glanced at the Superior with a questioning lift of his eyebrows.

"He meant well, I suppose," the Superior said, nodding, though Nijiri heard a hint of reluctance in his voice. "And peace *was* achieved among the acolytes, if by unorthodox means, and if only temporarily."

"He's still young." Rabbaneh shrugged, his smile returning at last. "If we had nothing to teach him, what need would he have of us?"

"What, Gatherer?" Nijiri had begun to feel very stupid.

At this, even the Superior looked amused. "A necessary final test, Nijiri. There is peace in submission, but sometimes greater peace—*lasting* peace—in resistance. We needed to know that you understood this." He shrugged. "There are many paths to peace."

"We shall simply have to teach you to think farther ahead on that path, Apprentice," Rabbaneh added, smiling again.

Apprentice. Apprentice. Nijiri stood there, trembling; he barely noticed when Sonta-i shrugged as if losing interest and stalked away, returning to the Superior's side. *Apprentice!*

He wanted, very much, to leap into the air and shout, which would have been not only a mistake, but an offense to Hananja, here in Her hall. So instead he stammered, trembling for a moment with the effort to control his joy, "You honor me, Gatherers, to bring—to consider—" He couldn't think enough to form words.

"Yes, yes." The Superior glanced at the Hall's narrow, prism-glass windows, beyond which the sun's light still marked the western sky. The Dreamer had not yet risen. When it did, the Hall would fill with its silvered light, refracted further still by the windows into shifting, layered colors. That would help the moontear vines, which would not otherwise bloom indoors. "Please rise; we still have your oathtaking ceremony to complete, and then the Gatherers' dedication. And there's an additional matter we need to discuss."

Nijiri swallowed and nodded, feeling quite as though he could deal with *anything* now. He struggled not to grin like a fool. "Y-yes. What matter, Superior?"

"Ehiru," said the Superior. "You may have noticed his absence."

The Superior's grim air—and its sudden, sober echo on

Rabbaneh's face—abruptly made Nijiri realize that Ehiru was not just away on Gatherer business.

"He is indisposed," Sonta-i said, "because two nights previous to this, he mishandled a Gathering. The umblikeh was severed before the tithebearer could be pulled from the shadowlands; the soul was lost in the realms between waking and dreaming. What dreamblood could be Gathered was too tainted with fear and pain to be given to the Sharers for distribution."

Nijiri inhaled, stricken. No Gatherer had mishandled a soul in his lifetime. It happened, and everyone knew it; Gatherers were fallible mortal men, not gods. But for Ehiru, who had never failed to carry a soul to peace, to falter now—Nijiri licked his lips. "And the Gatherer?" *He cannot have chosen to end his service, not yet. The whole city would be in mourning if he had. They would not be talking to me of him if he had.*

Sonta-i shook his head, and Nijiri's belly tightened. But then he added, "Ehiru has chosen to seclude himself so that he may pray and seek peace. We believe he will choose to remain among us, for now, but..." He sighed, looking abruptly weary. "Well. What are your thoughts on the matter?"

Nijiri started. "My thoughts?"

"He was to have been your mentor," said Rabbaneh. "He is, after all, the most experienced of us now that Una-une has gone into dreaming. An apprentice should learn from the best. But given Ehiru's lapse..." He grimaced delicately, as if to apologize for his indelicate words. "So. Who is your choice, to replace him? Sonta-i, or me?"

Relief spread through Nijiri—and with it came a curious sort of eagerness, not dissimilar from what he had felt in the sparring circle, facing four Sentinels. Of this, if nothing else, he was certain. "If I was to be Ehiru's, Gatherer, then I will stay Ehiru's."

Rabbaneh raised his eyebrows. "A Gatherer can take months, or years, to recover from such a lapse, Apprentice. *If* he recovers. For Ehiru in particular this incident has been a blow. He's convinced that he is no longer worthy to be a Gatherer." Rabbaneh sighed faintly. "We're all prone to pride. But perhaps you should reconsider."

Rabbaneh and Sonta-i were trying to do right by him, Nijiri reminded himself; they meant well. They did not understand that Nijiri had made his choice ten years before, on a humid afternoon thick with the stench of suffering. Ehiru had shown him the way to true peace that day. He had taught Nijiri the beauty of pain, and that love meant doing what was best for others. Whether they wanted it or not.

How could he not repay Ehiru for that revelation, now that the chance had finally come?

"I will be Ehiru's," he repeated, softly this time. "I'll be whatever he needs, until the day he needs me no longer."

And he would fight Hananja Herself, if he had to, to keep that day at bay.

# 4

(•⊙•)

*It is the duty of the shunha to uphold tradition. It is the
duty of the zhinha to challenge tradition.*

(Law)

General Niyes's home was in the spice district, where the evening breezes smelled of cinnamon and inim-teh seed. The house
had been built Kisuati-style, with a roofed sitting area in the
side-yard, and elaborate patterns laid in colored tile about the
front door—though the ubiquitous Gujaareen river clay, sun-
baked to near-white, covered the outer walls. A necessity, in
this land of yearly floods; the clay kept the water from soaking
the house's support beams. Still, the design was familiar enough
in style and function that Sunandi felt right at home as she
stepped out of the carriage.

The additional sight of the general's family, all of whom stood
waiting on the steps, reinforced the illusion. The general himself was beaming in open welcome, a far cry from the usual
Gujaareen reserve. His two children wore brightly-colored Kisuati
wraps, though the boy had fastened his at the hip rather than in
front as was proper. By her elaborately coiffed and beaded hair,

Sunandi judged that the heavyset woman beside the general was his wife. Likely the only one, since the shunha nobility of Gujaareh prided themselves on maintaining the traditions of their Kisuati motherland.

"Speaker, we welcome you to our home." The woman spoke in flawless formal Sua; Sunandi was pleased by the use of her proper title. "I am Lumanthe. You will be my daughter for the evening, and my family your own."

"Thank you for the warm welcome, Lumanthe-mother. With this beautiful home and such perfect guest-custom, you might even tempt me to stay!" Sunandi grinned, too pleased to keep to tradition. Lumanthe raised eyebrows in surprise and then laughed, shedding her own formality just as easily.

"It must be difficult for you, Nandi-daughter, living here among the half-barbarian folk of this land." Lumanthe moved to stand beside Sunandi, taking her arm companionably. "It's hard enough for we who keep the old ways, but at least this is home for us."

"Not so difficult. After my apprenticeship with Master Seh Kalabsha I spent three years as the Protectors' Voice in Charad-dinh." She smiled. "Gujaareh at least has proper baths. In Charad-dinh I had to bathe in the local waterfall. It was very beautiful, but very cold!"

Lumanthe laughed heartily. "I spent a year in Kisua as a maiden. I remember being amazed at how different the two lands truly are. It seemed a wonder to me that your people and mine were ever joined."

"And will remain joined while the shunha endure." Niyes stepped forward, taking Sunandi's free hand for a moment in welcome. His Sua too was liquid and accentless, though more stilted than that of his wife. Shunha or no, Niyes was still Gujaareen, and no Gujaareen man was completely at ease with women. "Thank you for accepting my invitation, Speaker."

He sounded relieved, as if he'd half expected her to refuse. Sunandi filed that small bit of information away to ponder later and squeezed his hand. "I'll admit I'd hoped for an evening to myself, but having heard tales of your hospitality, I couldn't refuse." She gave him her most genuine smile and saw him relax just a bit.

"We'll work hard not to disappoint you. My children, Tisanti and Ohorome."

The children stepped forward to take her hand, murmuring greetings. Ohorome was the younger but already showed the beginnings of a muscular build: a warrior in the making. Tisanti was fifteen or so and just as muscular; perhaps she was skilled in dance. She had her mother's flawless skin—flawless, Sunandi saw, but lightly covered with some sort of powder, and she had marked her lips with a berry-colored stain. Sunandi suppressed a grimace. The girl was beautiful; she had no need of paints and powders. That was the way of barbarians—and the Gujaareen, who had adopted far too many barbarian customs.

Still, Sunandi smiled, and the girl smiled shyly back. The boy did not, but Sunandi took no offense.

"A fine family," she said to Niyes. "I'm honored to be welcomed into it, even if only for one evening."

Niyes beamed, but again Sunandi detected a hint of nervousness in his manner. More than the usual Gujaareen strangeness; something troubled the man.

"Come inside," he said, and she was forced to end her observations for the moment.

Inside, more familiarity greeted Sunandi. Sculptures of the Moon's children—Hananja of course, but also several of the gods worshipped in Kisua—stood on plinths set into the corners. Hanging brass lanterns filled the air with the fragrance of beeswax, though the more pungent scents of cooking spices and fresh fruit were dominant. Sunandi inhaled and sighed in pleasure.

Lumanthe chuckled. "Have you missed home so much, Speaker? You were only assigned to Gujaareh two months ago."

"The first few are the worst, Manthe-mother."

Niyes nodded to two servants, who pulled open a pair of handsome wooden doors. Beyond was the dining chamber, whose sole furnishing—a huge table, surrounded by sitting-pillows—was heavily laden with more dishes than Sunandi could count.

A servant crouched beside one of the pillows. Taking the hint, Sunandi sat at that place, inclining her head to the girl. To her surprise the girl visibly started, darting a look around with wide eyes as if she couldn't believe Sunandi had done such a thing.

Sunandi turned back to the table, concealing her distaste. Niyes had shown such careful adherence to Kisuati tradition; she had not expected this. The girl was almost certainly a free citizen of their servant caste, since in Gujaareh criminals were killed or imprisoned, not enslaved. Thus it was only proper to treat her with basic courtesy—but clearly the girl was not used to that.

*Kisuati on the surface, Gujaareen underneath.* An important distinction to keep in mind if she were ever so foolish as to consider trusting Niyes.

In the meantime the feast demanded her attention—for however diluted they might be in other ways, the family had clearly kept tradition intact in the kitchen. There was not a single fish or river-vegetable on the table, for which alone Sunandi thanked the fifty hearth gods. The servant girl presented her with slivers of spicy fowl roasted in cumin and jife nuts; fluffy barley cakes stuffed with yam, currants, and hekeh seeds; gingered lamb and tamban patties in rich gravy; and more. Over a dozen other dishes, all of them exquisite. She sampled as many as she could, aware that Lumanthe would be watching anxiously for her approval, but it took no great effort to display appreciation under the circumstances. The children grinned when she leaned back to belch.

Once everyone had eaten their fill, the servants took away the dishes and replaced them with decanters of mintmelon wine. Another pair of servants sat at the far end of the chamber and began to play soft music on a flute and twelve-note drum. Niyes lifted his cup and poured a small amount on the table as an offering to the gods; Sunandi and the rest of the family did the same, formally ending the meal.

She'd sensed Niyes's tension earlier and had guessed that he would wait to say whatever was on his mind, at least until guest-custom was satisfied. Sure enough, he nodded to Lumanthe a few moments after the wine was poured. Lumanthe stood, gesturing curtly to the children; Sunandi affected surprise.

"Is there some pressing matter? I'd hoped to spend the evening sharing gossip, Manthe-mother."

"Nothing important, Nandi-daughter, but we will have to gossip another time. Niyes wants to talk business—men's gossip." She rolled her eyes and smiled. "You may have been trained to endure it, but I've no taste for such matters. We shall leave you to it." Then she herded the children out, pausing to bow farewell from the doorway. "Not too much business, Niyes. She's had a good meal tonight; don't curdle it for her."

Niyes favored Lumanthe with a thin smile—and said nothing in reply, Sunandi noted while the family left. She watched Niyes over the rim of her winecup, noting that his tension seemed to increase as soon as the doors closed. He poured another cup for himself, spilling a few drops in the process.

"Will you walk with me, Speaker?" he asked at last. "I would give you a tour of my household."

She noted the darting glance of his eyes; the servants. She smiled and got to her feet. "A walk would settle my meal, thank you."

They left the dining chamber and strolled the halls of the sprawling house, exchanging small talk occasionally. She let Niyes control the conversation, knowing it would set him at ease and trusting him to know when it was safe to talk. To her surprise, he took a lantern and led her into the house's atrium, where a near-jungle of plants—most imported from Kisua, she gauged—helped to cool the night-breezes blowing through the house. Niyes fell silent here, though there was surely no one about; the crunching leaves underfoot would have alerted them to the presence of any listeners. Sunandi was growing impatient when Niyes abruptly veered off the atrium path and into the brush. She followed him to find a small door hidden behind the thickest of the vegetation.

Here she hesitated. Niyes was no fool. Half of Gujaareh knew he'd invited Sunandi to his home for the evening. If she disappeared, the Kisuati Protectorate would demand his execution at the very least.

"Please, Speaker." He kept his voice low; his tension was almost palpable now. "I would never violate guest-custom, and I must show you something important to both our lands."

Sunandi eyed him closely, noting the sheen of sweat on his brow and the tremor of his lantern. Whatever he was about, he was terrified, and not merely of offending a high-ranking guest. That decided her; she nodded.

Niyes exhaled in relief and opened the door. Beyond was a close, dark stairwell that slanted under the house. While he opened the lantern's shutters to full, she peered within, wrinkling her nose at the faint whiff of mildew wafting up from below. Mildew—and something else. Something fouler.

She went in anyhow, and Niyes shut the door behind them, leaving his small lantern as their only source of light. Most likely they were headed toward the family's private burial chamber. Despite tradition, few shunha families built such chambers in a city that flooded once a year, for only the wealthiest could afford the special shunts and gates that helped the chambers dry quickly once floodseason ended. The mildew she smelled was likely a remnant of the floods that had occurred a few months before. The other scent was newer. Stronger, as they drew closer to its source.

"I command legions only during war," the general said as they walked through the candlelit darkness. "In peacetime I manage the training camps for our soldiers. The prison included."

The last surprised Sunandi. There was almost no crime in Gujaareh. The realm had only one prison and it was small, housing the pettiest of criminals, food-thieves and the like. Gatherers killed the rest. Managing such a place did not strike Sunandi as the best use of a general's talents.

"The Protectorate considers conscripts more trouble than they're worth," she said carefully.

Niyes shook his head. "In Gujaareh, criminals may earn their freedom by proving themselves free of corruption. They may be tried by a Gatherer or in battle; most choose the latter, though it may take years. So we train them." He sobered. "A few four-days ago, however, prisoners began dying."

The smell had intensified, thickening the air, and now Sunandi recognized it: the early stages of decay, mingled with the spices and incense used in Kisuati embalmings. A tomb lay ahead, and it held a recent occupant.

Had some family member of Niyes's been in prison? No, any shunha foolish enough to land in prison would have been disowned, his corpse tossed into a dung ditch.

The stair led to a short tunnel, which ended at a heavy stone door whose thickness did little to diminish the reek. Sunandi put a hand over her nose and mouth, trying to breathe the faint scent of the lemon-water she'd used to wash her fingers after dinner.

Niyes glanced at her, concerned. "A woman of your station would not have seen death often."

"It is not unknown to me," she said curtly. An orphan girl-child on Kisua's streets witnessed all manner of ugliness and learned simply to thank the gods that it was no one she knew.

Niyes made no comment and pulled the thick rope that hung nearby. She heard the gritty roll of unseen pulleys and wheels, and the door slowly rose until the opening was of man-height. Foulness flooded out of the chamber to greet them; she gagged once but managed to keep her dinner down.

Setting the lever, Niyes released the rope and took up the lantern again. "I'm sorry to put you through this, Speaker, but you will understand once you have seen."

She nodded, not trusting herself to speak, and followed him within.

The chamber was beautiful, despite the smell. Niyes's line had clearly been wealthy enough to maintain it, despite the flooding, for many years. Elegant pillars, decorated austerely, circled the chamber's center; shelves along the walls held rows of gold- and lacquer-inlaid urns. At the center stood a massive stone sarcophagus, its sides lined with Sua prayer-glyphs. By tradition the next to last of the dead would be within it. But the newest of the family's ancestors held the honor of lying on the stone slab atop the sarcophagus, there to remain until someone else in the family died. Bodies were kept for as long as possible before cremation in case the soul had trouble finding its way to Ina-Karekh. Unless, here in Gujaareh, the corpse bore a Gatherer's mark.

Niyes stepped close to the sarcophagus, lifting the lantern high for Sunandi. Steeling herself, Sunandi stepped forward to examine the corpse.

It was not one of Niyes's relatives. Though the skin had darkened in death, Sunandi could still tell that the man, in life, had been much lighter-complected than any shunha of a respectable lineage. Perhaps even a northerner—although the hair was tight-curled and black, and the distorted features showed clear southern roots. A common Gujaareen, then.

But what truly shocked Sunandi was the expression on the corpse's face. The eyes had sunken, but lines of striation still showed around the lids and across the brow. He'd died with his eyes shut tight. The mouth was open, lips drawn back in a way that could have been caused by drying and shrinkage of the skin—but she doubted it. It took no embalmers' skill to recognize a mortal, agonized scream when she saw one.

"Twelve men have been found like this," Niyes said, his voice soft in the silence. "All were young men, healthy. All died in the night without warning, mark, or wound. This one had a cellmate, who said he was like this before he died—thrashing, trying to cry out but making no sound. Asleep."

"Asleep?"

Niyes nodded. "Asleep, and dreaming something so horrible that it killed him." He looked up at her, his face haggard in the lamplight. "I brought this one here to keep as proof. The others were burned. Do you understand what it means?"

She swallowed, her gorge rising anew. "The abomination. But if your Hetawa has failed in its vigilance, then you should be showing this corpse to the Prince of Gujaareh, not me. I am Kisuati; I can only say, 'We told you so.'"

"There's more to it, Speaker. Strange events have occurred lately, especially in the past few years. The Prince—" He grimaced. "The Prince has quietly poured money into the ship-docks along the Sea of Glory. They've slowed now, but until two years ago they were working night and day producing ships. Merchant-vessels, the orders say, but of a strange design, made with heavier wood than normal."

"The Sea of Glory has no connection to the Eastern Ocean," Sunandi said, confused. "Ships built there are no threat to Kisua."

"Those ships sailed away months ago and have never been seen or heard from again," Niyes said. "Where do you think they've gone, Speaker?"

"North? South? They're still no threat unless they sail west across the Endless and 'round the world to Kisua's front gate—a feat no vessel has ever managed, except in tales." Sunandi shook her head. "Leaving aside the fact that they might actually *be* merchant-vessels."

Niyes sighed and ran a hand over his balding pate. "The Prince has also recently sought alliance with several northern tribes. Not just our regular trading partners, either—ax-mad barbarians from the icelands, who make our Bromarte seem well-mannered and gentle-hearted."

"Perhaps he's found new trading partners. Which of course would require new merchant ships."

"But along with all the rest—including Kinja's death—you must admit it paints a disturbing picture."

It did indeed, but a picture that was far too indistinct to be of any use. Sunandi sighed. "I cannot bring this to the Protectors, General. Even if they believed me—which is no guarantee by far—they would ask the same questions I have, and you have no answers. I suspect you understand that. So I must ask: what did you really hope to gain from this meeting?"

"Your belief, if not the Protectors'. Kinja's message—have you deciphered it yet?"

Sunandi grew very still. "I don't know what you're talking about."

He grimaced. "There's no time for games, Speaker. We cannot stay here much longer or the servants—some of whom are surely spies—might miss us. Suffice it that Kinja gave me the message just before he died, though he told me nothing of its content. Said I knew too much already. He asked me to make sure his successor received it if anything should happen to him. Your girl's skills made that easy for me, thank the gods." He reached over and took her hand, gripping it firmly. "Believe the message, Speaker. Make the Protectors understand. The Reaper is only the beginning."

"I can't *make* the Protectors understand anything, General—"

"You can. You *must*. Go there to convince them—you'll have to leave anyway if you want to live; you know that, don't you? Do it soon. The Prince knew Kinja had discovered something, and Kinja died. He already suspects you. You're too obviously Kinja's heir."

"And you?"

Niyes smiled, bleakly and without a trace of humor. "I will doubtless take that place soon." He nodded toward the stone slab. "But before I do, I want to try and prevent a great evil. My men are loyal and more than willing to die for Gujaareh—but I won't let them die for *this*."

His face was grim, his eyes hard and resigned. He was either the greatest liar she'd ever seen, or he meant every word.

After a long and careful scrutiny, Sunandi finally sighed. "Then take me out of here, General, before I lose my dinner. I'll need all my strength intact if I'm to stop a war."

# 5

( • ⊙ • )

*Gujaareh's King is crowned as he ascends the throne*
*of dreams to sit at Hananja's right hand. In the waking*
*realm, it is the duty of the Prince to act in Her name.*

(Law)

In the sky above, the Dreamer had risen, her four-banded face
framed by thin wisps of summer clouds. In the streets below, the
same colors—red for blood, blue-white for seed, yellow for ichor,
and black for bile—glowed from banners on every torchpost
and windowsill, lintel and clothesline. The light reflected off
sweat-sheened faces and leaf fans, brightly dyed cloth and eager
smiles. Some while before the sun had set, its last sullen glow
fading reluctantly beyond the river. Already Hananja's city was
deep in the throes of worship, rejoicing on the night its Goddess
starved.

In the courtyard of the palace Yanya-iyan, the noblest of Her
followers had gathered to worship apart from the wilder street
celebrations of the common castes. Here the Hamyan proceeded in a more dignified fashion as the esteemed lords of the
shunha and zhinha mingled with their peers from artisan-hall

and warhall, the royal family and foreign lands. Every so often one of the guests would raise hands, proclaim some trinket or utensil a sacrifice, and exhort Hananja to accept it to supplement the sparse dreams She would receive on the shortest night of the year. Usually this ritual drew laughter from the other guests, though the Servants of Hananja in attendance maintained a pointed silence.

Had Nijiri known more of life beyond the Hetawa walls, he might have felt humbled by the presence of so many citizens of note. Instead he stood still as they ambled about him, his awe stolen by Yanya-iyan itself. The main structure of the great palace surrounded the courtyard in an open-ended oval. He and the other guests stood within a curving valley of marble tiers, each decorated with embossings and troughs of flowers that seemed to have been stacked to the sky. At the open end, bronze lattice-gates twice the height of a man allowed commoners to peer in, if they dared; the guards would allow it if they seemed no threat. Even as Nijiri watched, two women at the gate pointed in at something beyond him. He turned to follow their gaze and stopped in fresh wonder.

Far opposite the gates, at the other end of the courtyard, stood a pyramid-shaped elevated pavilion. Beneath the pavilion's glass roof, at the top of a mountain of steps, sat a deceptively simple oxbow seat carved whole from a block of pale, shiny nhefti-wood.

And there sat the Prince of Gujaareh, Lord of the Sunset, Avatar of Hananja, straight-backed and so still that Nijiri wondered for a moment whether the figure was flesh or painted stone. The answer came when a servant child crouched at the

Prince's left hand, offering a golden cup on a platter. The Prince moved an arm—no more than that—and took the cup without looking. Another child crouched nearly hidden behind the Prince, holding the staff that bore the Aureole of the Setting Sun: a wide semicircle of polished red- and gold-amber plates shaped like sunbeams, kept steady behind the Prince's head. Around the Prince's feet, twenty of his younger children sat arranged as living ornaments, reflecting their sire's glory.

"A rare sight," a voice said beside Nijiri, startling him badly. He jerked about to see a woman in a gown of palest green, translucent hekeh fiber. She smiled at his discomfiture, flexing the delicately patterned scars along her otherwise smooth brown cheekbones.

*Women are goddesses*, rang the old adage through Nijiri's mind before he swallowed and bowed over both hands, hazarding a guess. "Sister?"

"Gatherer." She inclined her head and spread her hands, her every movement grace. He stared, entranced by the way the black ropes of her hair caught the light. "Gatherer-Apprentice rather, given that I do not know you, and given that you gaze at me like a young man who hasn't seen a woman older than twelve for many years. That would make you Nijiri."

He quickly lowered his eyes. "Yes, Sister."

"Meliatua is my name." She nodded toward the Prince's pavilion again. "I meant the Prince's children, by the way. He rarely allows any but the oldest out in public."

"Ah, yes." Nijiri groped for some more polite way to address her. "Sister" alone seemed rude, like calling one of his brethren merely "Servant." But her order operated independently of the

Hetawa, and he knew nothing of their divisions of rank. Then it occurred to him that a conversation had begun between them and he was expected to respond, not stand there gawping like a fool.

"I, I was just thinking that it must be terribly dull for the children," he said, wincing inwardly at his stammer, "being forced to sit there for so long."

"The Prince will send them away presently. For the time being they're on display, both as a sign of his devotion to Hananja and as a rebuke to the rest of these fools." She looked around and sighed, either missing or ignoring Nijiri's shock at her casual contempt. "They offer Her trifles; the Prince presents his own flesh and blood. If the Hetawa laid claim to any of those children right now, the Prince would have no choice but to agree."

Nijiri blinked in surprise. That the Hetawa could adopt any child who showed promise—orphaned or not—he knew. During his own years in the House of Children he had met several adoptees with living parents. But they had all, like Nijiri, been children of the lower and middling castes. He could not imagine a shunha or zhinha heir, let alone a child of the Sunset, deigning to live as a mere Servant of Hananja when caste and family connections promised so much more.

She read his face and lifted an eyebrow. "Your own mentor is a brother of the Prince, Gatherer-Apprentice. No one knows the circumstances—Ehiru has always been private about such things—but he was the last child of the Sunset claimed by the Hetawa. Did you not know?"

Half-overheard whispers flitted through Nijiri's memory, but still the truth was a shock. He had guessed that Ehiru's origins were highcaste—who could notice that fine black skin, those angular features, those elegant manners and speech, and think otherwise?—but never so very high as that. He dared a look up at the seated Prince again and tried to visualize Ehiru in his place, beautiful and regal and perfect as a god. The image fit so well that a secret, shameful thrill flitted down Nijiri's spine before he banished it.

From the corner of his eye he spied Meliatua watching him. Realizing that half his thoughts must be obvious, he flushed and drew his hood closer about his face. "We all belong to Hananja now, Sister."

"Indeed we do." She took his arm then, startling him badly. He could do nothing but follow as she tugged him into a stroll.

"Where is your mentor, Gatherer-Apprentice? He should be at your side, protecting you from the likes of me." Her teeth gleamed in the firelight.

"He wished me to spend some time on my own, Sister." Nijiri felt the softness of her breast press against his elbow and fought the urge to nudge it back to see what would happen. He had a vague notion this would offend her. "Gatherers must blend in among people of many kinds; I am therefore to observe and learn." He glanced at her, hesitated, then dared humor. "Perhaps comfort is *my* sacrifice tonight."

To his relief she laughed, causing the scar-patterns on her cheeks to dance in the firelight. He admired the way the scars ornamented her beauty even as he realized with some surprise that he did not want her at all. She was a sculpture: to be observed and perhaps even touched, but not a thing one could take home.

"You should become a Sister if you'll miss such a small thing," she said. "Our business is comfort, after all. Although truthfully, there's little even we can do tonight."

Surprised, Nijiri followed her gaze and focused on his fellow revelers. It took him a moment to fathom the Sister's meaning, but now that she had pointed it out, the signs were obvious. A darting glance from a man who wore rich scholars' robes, at Nijiri—at his shoulder, which bore his new, just-healed Gatherer tattoo—and then away. A young zhinha woman, laughing at some joke by her companion, faltered silent for an instant as Nijiri and Meliatua passed. When she resumed laughing, it sounded forced. A tall soldier with a face like sandy foothills nodded gravely to Nijiri; there was a terrible sorrow in his eyes.

Meliatua shook her head. "And another measure of comfort is offered up to Hananja. They make proper sacrifices without meaning to."

"No one has ever looked at me with fear before," Nijiri said, troubled. "But then, I am a Gatherer now."

"Only the ignorant fear Gatherers on sight," the Sister said. "The rest know *when* to fear. There are no Gatherings on Hamyan Night."

This was true, and it was why Ehiru had been willing—after days of inactivity—to come out tonight. He was willing to train Nijiri, pray and spar with him, do everything an apprentice Gatherer needed him to...except Gather. That, however, was a different problem. "Then why do they fear me?" he asked.

"Observe, Apprentice, as your mentor commanded. Learn. *Listen.*"

So he did, falling silent as they wended their way through the crowded courtyard. At first he heard only snatches of words amid the babble. Gradually his ears sifted sentences from the mass, then finally snippets of conversation.

"—The shipping manifest didn't even show the extra cargo—"

"—Murdered in his cell. No marks, but his *eyes*—"

"—Bromarte. They usually hire the Feen to fight for them, but this time—"

"—Nothing natural, I tell you. He was gibbering when they pulled him out—"

"—Those military-castes. Tight-lipped bastards—"

"Rumors," Nijiri said at last. Above, the Dreamer's red band edged into Yanya-iyan's oval sky; they had circuited the courtyard for nearly an hour. "And gossip. But not of the mindless sort I expected. They speak of corruption, and madness, and war."

She nodded. "Just so. Not the stuff of comfort."

"That does not explain their fear of *me*, Sister."

"Doesn't it? Corruption and madness and war. Gatherers take the corrupt and those madmen who cannot be cured. War is anathema to Hananja, and thus to Her Servants." She turned to him, stopping abruptly and dropping her voice. "It may not be possible to find an explanation tonight. For now, it is enough that we have noticed. If She wishes us to understand further, She will let us find the means."

He frowned, remembering more rumors whispered among the Hetawa acolytes. "Can you not fathom it now, Sister? I know little about your path, but I have heard of your—er, powers—" He faltered when she smiled.

"Careful, Gatherer-Apprentice. Inunru the Founder had no

part in founding the Sisterhood. The Hetawa accepts us—grudgingly—because we supply the city with dreamseed, but never call us a 'path' in front of your Superior unless you want to annoy him." She nodded toward the left, and Nijiri glanced through the crowd to glimpse the Superior accepting a cup from a passing servant. Nijiri quickly looked away before their eyes could meet.

"For another, I possess only Outer Sight." She touched the scars on her face: two parallel lines of raised dots along her cheekbones and crossing the bridge of her nose. "Deciphering the realm of waking is my specialty, not dreaming omens. I can see the fear in these people and guess at its causes. I can investigate, to pierce the obfuscations and misdirections so common in the waking world. But to know for certain? That much will be beyond me until my fertile years end."

He groped for a suitable reply to this, then was surprised again as she disengaged her arm from his. "Sister?"

"Your mentor commanded you to observe and learn," she said, "not spend the evening consorting with a woman of dubious orthodoxy. And I have duties of my own on this night."

He flushed abruptly, realizing what those duties must be. She was a young Sister, perhaps only ten years older than himself, still nubile. The Sisters of Hananja served Her in many ways, but they never shirked their primary mission. There would be much dreamseed to collect on a night like Hamyan.

He inclined his head to her as he would to an equal, a silent acknowledgement of her rank in *his* eyes. "May She dream of your good fortune, Sister."

"And yours, Gatherer-Apprentice." She bowed to him—deeply, flattening both hands—and then turned away into the milling crowd. He gazed after her in wonder.

"If not for your vows she might have stayed with you tonight," said a voice behind Nijiri, and for the second time he turned to face a stranger. This one was a man of Nijiri's height, with eyes a startling shade of near-golden brown. It was impossible to guess this man's age. His skin was smooth and youthful, his thicket of long rope-braids—not a wig, Nijiri realized with some surprise—black and free of silver. But he felt older than he looked, as he watched Nijiri with all the patience and confidence of a waiting lion. And there was something fleetingly familiar about him . . .

"Young men your age are especially rich in dreamseed, I'm told," the stranger continued. "She might have drawn her quota for the night from you alone."

Nijiri bowed, carefully respectful while he tried to place the man's rank and that niggling familiarity. "Doubtless she will find others who have need of her skills."

"And you have no need? How old are you?"

"I have seen sixteen floods."

The man smiled. "Then you have need, young Gatherer! Does it trouble you that you could ease those needs right now, if not for your oath? Or are you hoping you still can, if you catch her in some discreet place along the way home?"

His words were offensive, and he knew it. Nijiri could see that in the man's smile. For a moment he was flustered. He should, as one sworn to Hananja, remind the man of his vows—but a highcaste might take that as an implication of ignorance

70

or stupidity. And yet to say nothing would make Nijiri faithless to Her...He wavered in indecision, his stomach knotting.

"We all have such needs, my lord. But directing them toward the service of Hananja is the sacrifice we of the Hetawa offer every day, with great joy."

The Gatherer Rabbaneh stepped out of the milling throng, his face carved into its usual smile, a cup in one hand. Before Nijiri could register relief, Rabbaneh handed his cup to Nijiri and dropped smoothly to one knee, crossing both arms before his face and turning his palms outward as if to shield himself from a blinding glare. A manuflection; Nijiri had heard of the custom from his Teachers, but never seen it performed outside of lessons. It was the highest gesture of respect, offered only to those specially marked by the gods—

*Dream of Inunru!*

The strange man—*the Prince of Gujaareh*—laughed good-naturedly at the look of horror on Nijiri's face, then waved a hand at Rabbaneh. "Stop that. I put aside the Aureole so I could walk among my people for a while without all that foolishness."

Rabbaneh rose and adopted the more traditional bow of respect instead. He was still smiling as he straightened. "You must forgive me, my lord. I meant only to model the proper behavior for Nijiri. His actions reflect upon the whole Hetawa now, and especially my path."

"Oh, he was perfectly polite, Rabbaneh. A credit to his Teachers."

"Thank you, my lord," Nijiri said. To his great relief he did not stammer, though he could not have vouched for the volume or pitch of his voice in that moment. He quickly bowed over his free hand, not trusting himself to manuflect without falling over. His hands shook so badly that Rabbaneh's drink sloshed and splashed in its cup. Rabbaneh reached over and deftly plucked the cup away before Nijiri could stain his robe.

"Nijiri." The Prince seemed to mull over the name. "Too pale to be shunha, too humble for zhinha. Were you common-born?"

"My lord." Rabbaneh smiled in a gentle reprimand even as Nijiri opened his mouth to say, "Yes." To Nijiri's surprise, the Prince chuckled.

"Oh fine, fine. You priests." He stepped closer, and Nijiri nearly started as the Prince reached up to take his chin between two fingers. "You're a fine-looking boy. It's a good thing your birth-caste no longer applies, whatever it was. You might have been sold in marriage to some wealthy, influential widow—or if you were lowcaste, someone would have made a pleasure-servant of you." He ran a thumb over Nijiri's lips and this time Nijiri did start in spite of himself, though he mastered the reflex to pull away in time. The Prince smiled, his eyes narrowing in amusement. Then—to Nijiri's intense relief—he let go.

"Sonta-i is your mentor?"

"Ehiru, my lord."

"Ehiru?" The Prince's eyebrows rose in impressive arches—though strangely, Nijiri had the sense that he was not surprised at all. "He's not the seniormost."

Rabbaneh coughed into one hand. "My lord, Hetawa matters..."

"Ah yes. Bad manners again. Do not take me as an example

of proper behavior, Nijiri. Old men take more liberties than young men can get away with." He tilted his head in a self-mocking bow. "Another time, Gatherer-Apprentice."

With that, the Prince turned away and wandered into the crowd, which parted before and closed behind him like water. In his wake, Nijiri exhaled a long breath and closed his eyes in a brief prayer of thanks. Rabbaneh waited politely for him to finish.

"Rabbaneh-brother, I have shamed the Hetawa. I did not recognize—"

"I know you didn't." For once, the older Gatherer was not smiling. That made the knots in Nijiri's stomach tighten still further. But Rabbaneh was gazing after the Prince. "He knew you, though."

Nijiri faltered to confused silence. After a moment Rabbaneh sighed and flashed a slightly strained smile at Nijiri. "You didn't shame the Hetawa, boy. Ehiru, Sonta-i, and I have taken turns shadowing you all evening. You handled the Prince well enough, and Meliatua before him." He assessed Nijiri then in a long glance. "You look tired."

"I—" Nijiri wavered, torn between the truth and pride. An apprentice should at least try to manage a full Gatherer's responsibilities, and Hamyan Night was only half over. But the combined stresses of the evening—the processional through Gujaareh's streets, the crowd, the Sister, the Prince—had drained him. He wanted nothing better than to go back to his quiet cell in the Hetawa and be lulled to sleep by the night-breezes.

Rabbaneh's hand settled on his shoulder and squeezed reassurance. "There's no shame in it, Nijiri. You were a sheltered acolyte only an eightday ago, after all. Go back to the Hetawa. You've satisfied protocol."

Nijiri could not deny his own relief, but guilt remained. "Ehiru-brother will expect—"

"I'll find him and tell him how well you've done." The older Gatherer's smile filled him with warm pride, and shyly Nijiri smiled back.

"Thank you, Rabbaneh-brother. I will have good dreams tonight." He turned to leave, pausing as he hunted for the shortest path through the crowd to the palace gate. It was only because he hesitated that he heard Rabbaneh's reply.

"Dream them while you can, little brother."

When he turned back, Rabbaneh had gone.

# 6

( ⊙ )

*In dreams did Hananja bestow knowledge upon Inunru, a*
*man of the sonha. "There is power in dreams," She told him.*
*"Harness it and therein lies magic. But only virtuous*
*men may wield it." Thus did Inunru bring forth*
*narcomancy, and for a time all people rejoiced.*

(Wisdom)

Ehiru had been watching the Prince's children for nearly an
hour when Rabbaneh found him. Most of the children had not
noticed him standing just beyond the overlapping circles of
torchlight around the throne pavilion. One of them, however—
a handsome lad of perhaps seven—occasionally peered into the
shadows that cloaked Ehiru, squinting and frowning as if
he sensed something he couldn't quite see.

"I sent Nijiri home," Rabbaneh said. He kept his voice low; it
was habit for both of them when in the dark. "He was beginning to get the look of a taffur that's been hunted too long."

"Mmm. He lasted longer than I did at my first public affair."

"*You* never learned to master tactful speech. That apprentice
of yours is at least circumspect. Too much so, really; still too

much the servant-caste, despite his pride." Rabbaneh sighed. "I hope he grows out of it soon."

"We *are* servants, Rabbaneh. Perhaps we should learn from Nijiri's example."

Rabbaneh glanced at him oddly; Ehiru noted this out of the corner of his eye. "Are you still troubled over that Bromarte, Brother? It's been an eightday."

"I destroyed a man's soul."

"I know that. But even the gods aren't perfect—"

Ehiru sighed. "That boy has the dreaming gift."

"—What?"

Ehiru nodded toward the child on the pavilion steps, who seemed to have given up the search for the moment. "That one. I noticed it as soon as I saw him."

Rabbaneh shifted impatiently. "Then notify the Superior so he can lay claim to the child. Ehiru—"

"The Superior knows. I saw him offer greetings to the Prince not long after the processional arrived. The child was watching a moth, oblivious to the world around him. Even the blindest layman could have seen that he was halfway to Ina-Karekh in that moment."

Rabbaneh sighed, rubbing the back of his neck with one hand. "The Superior must consider what is best for Gujaareh, not just the Hetawa. We cannot make the Prince appear subservient while Kisuati trade associations threaten embargo."

"I understand that very well, Rabbaneh. But it makes the situation no less offensive." He folded his arms and saw the boy on the pavilion steps peer sharply into the shadows again, perhaps catching some hint of the motion. "A child of true potential will be left undedicated and untrained. He'll grow up to become just another highcaste servant subject to the whims of the next Prince. *If* he grows up."

"Is that what might have happened to *you?*" Rabbaneh glanced at him sidelong, with an air of daring. They had all learned not to ask him many questions about his past. "If the Hetawa had not claimed you?"

Ehiru sighed, abruptly weary. "I would have died young, yes. And perhaps that would have been best."

Rabbaneh said nothing for a moment, though Ehiru felt the younger Gatherer's eyes on him. When he felt Rabbaneh's hand touch his shoulder, however, he brushed it off.

"Leave me this, Rabbaneh."

"The grief devours you—"

"Then let it." He turned away, unable to bear the look in his pathbrother's eyes. Was that what tithebearers saw when they found themselves facing a Gatherer? Sympathy for the loss too great, the pain too unbearable? How did they stand such meaningless pity?

"I'm going back to the Hetawa," he said. "In peace, Brother."

Ehiru walked away before Rabbaneh could mouth a response, opting to hike the long route around the courtyard's edges rather than a straight line through the lights and the crowd. A few revelers shared the shadows with him, some taking a break from socializing, some seeking a modicum of privacy for more intimate conversations. They did not speak and he gladly ignored them. If he had not recognized the Superior's voice when he heard his name called, he would have ignored that, too.

Instead Ehiru stopped and restrained the urge to sigh as the other man approached from the torchlight, stumbling once in the dimness. Ehiru stepped forward and caught his elbow.

"Darkness is the realm of Gatherers and dreams, Superior. Not the Hetawa's highest light."

The Superior chuckled, nodding gratefully as he righted himself. "The Hetawa's light would be you, Ehiru. I'm just a glorified clerk, and sometimes a gamesman." He sighed, smile fading as his eyes adjusted and searched Ehiru's face. "You're upset about something."

"Nothing important."

"Devout men lie poorly." Then the Superior's face softened. "But in your case the truth is painful enough that I suppose you can be forgiven. Which makes me even more sorry to have to do this."

"Do what?"

The Superior turned to gaze out at the crowd, which showed no signs of dissipating despite the lateness of the hour. It was thickest around the pavilion, where the Prince was visible on the steps, crouching to give a private good night to each of his children. A gaggle of strangers, black as shunha but dressed in foreign garments dyed shades of indigo, stood waiting nearby: Kisuati. The Prince's gestures of affection might have been a minstrel's show to judge by the avid way the strangers watched and commented to one another. Ehiru grimaced in bitter memory before the Superior's next words pulled him rudely back to the present.

"You have a commission. Forgive me, Ehiru."

For an instant Ehiru was too startled and angry to speak; he stared down at the Superior. "I desecrated a tithe only days ago."

"I'm aware of that. Yet as Superior I must also remind you of the practical implications of your self-imposed penance. Una-une gave his Final Tithe three months ago. Nijiri won't be ready 'til next season at least. I have asked Rabbaneh and Sonta-i to shoulder some of your duties given recent events and because you've taken on Nijiri, but it's simply unfair to ask them to continue much longer. Two Gatherers cannot do the work of four."

Ehiru flinched as guilt overlaid anger. Turning to gaze out at the crowd, he said, "I don't mean to burden my brothers unduly. But you must understand...I *doubt*, Superior. I no longer feel Hananja's mandate in my heart. I no longer know if..." He faltered, then forced himself to voice the fear that had been gnawing at his mind since the night of the Bromarte trader's death. "I no longer know if I am fit, if I am *worthy*, to perform my duties."

"Both Rabbaneh and Sonta-i have mishandled Gatherings, Ehiru—Sonta-i twice. Is your sin greater, or theirs lesser? Do you demand more of yourself than you expect of them?"

*Yes.* But he did not voice the thought lest he be accused of arrogance.

The Superior watched him expectantly. It was clear refusal would be unacceptable.

"As you wish, Superior," Ehiru said at last, with a sigh. "I can only pray that this is Hananja's wish as well. At least Nijiri will be pleased; he's been plaguing me to go out for a fourday now."

The Superior nodded and turned back to the crowd. His eyes roved for a moment before alighting on the steps around the pavilion. "The strangers there in grieving colors. They are Kisuati; they celebrate the Hamyan properly. Do you see them?"

Ehiru did. They stood higher on the steps now that the

children had been taken away by the Prince's wives and guardsmen. The Prince had resumed his place on the oxbow seat, his posture formal and the Aureole once again raised behind his head. Several of the strangers made a bow of supplication to him, but one woman amid the group remained tall and straight. The others bent around her like reeds to a bargepole.

"The woman."

Ehiru frowned. "Women need no Gatherer's assistance to reach Ina-Karekh—"

"In this case the commission is requested as a kindness, both to her and to the city. Her soul is corrupt, the supplicant says."

"Has an Assay of Truth been performed?"

"Unnecessary. The supplicant is beyond question."

Ehiru turned his head to stare at the Superior's profile.

The Superior smiled at Ehiru's skepticism, though Ehiru noted that the smile did not reach his eyes. "I did request proofs to support the charge of corruption. I was shown such proofs. But a formal assessment would take time and require a public record. In this case, that would cause greater harm."

Ehiru's frown deepened as suspicion flowered in his mind. "Who is she?"

"Her name is Sunandi. Jeh Kalawe in their nomenclature; a daughter out of the lineage of Kalawe, of sonha caste, in ours. She is the Voice of the Kisuati Protectorate, newly assigned to Gujaareh. The charge is that she has used her position to spy, to steal, and to corrupt Gujaareen officials. By her actions she foments unrest between Gujaareh and Kisua."

"Our focus is spiritual, not political." Ehiru folded his arms. "If the Sunset wants her killed, he has assassins for that."

"And if the Protectorate declares war? The assassination of an ambassador would be a violation of the treaty between our lands. The whole city would suffer if they sent an army seeking redress. Where is the peace in that, Servant of Hananja?"

*Long gone from my life,* Ehiru thought bitterly.

"Would they not also declare war if she is found dead with my mark on her?" he asked. "Gathering is not their way."

"They respect it as ours. Kisua honors Hananja too, even if they dilute their faith by worshipping other gods alongside Her. If this woman is Gathered, the Kisuati will be angry, no doubt—but not angry enough to declare war. That would enrage their own Hananjan sect and cause them no end of internal trouble." The Superior turned to him. "I won't pretend this isn't political, Ehiru. But there remains a spiritual component to the matter. The woman *has* committed acts of theft, deception, and malice. If she were anything but an ambassador, how would you judge her?"

"...Corrupt."

The Superior nodded as though he were still a Teacher, and Ehiru a particularly wise student. "As you said: our focus must be spiritual first and foremost."

Ehiru sighed. "Her location?"

"Here in Yanya-iyan, of course. The ambassadorial wing, largest suite. Will you require maps?"

"No. I remember the way."

"Will you be taking Nijiri? Palace guards draw swords first and ask questions later."

"The better for him to learn the hazards of our path." Ehiru turned to go, then paused. "I will carry out the commission tomorrow night."

"So soon?"

"If she is as corrupt as you say," Ehiru replied, "then for every day I delay, her soul grows more diseased. Shall I leave her to suffer longer?"

"No, of course not. In peace, then, Gatherer."

Instead, Ehiru left in silence.

# 7

## ( ☉ )

*In the dark of dreams, the soul cries for help. It summons
friends, loved ones, even enemies in the hope of relief
from its torment. But it is still in darkness. These
seeming allies will do no good.*

(Wisdom)

In the dark of waking, the Reaper's soul no longer cries. It has
no further need to summon others; others always come eventually, or it can fetch them if it so desires. It does not remember
the word *friend*.

*       *       *

Kite-iyan—Sun Above the Waters—was the Prince's springtime palace. Yanya-iyan—Sun Upon the Earth—was not flood-
proof, and during the rainy season most of the palace's denizens
suffered with the rest of the city. The Prince himself did not. He
retreated to Kite-iyan, where his four-of-four wives lived year-
round. There he spent the season of fertility in appropriately
symbolic labor, conceiving the children who would continue
his dynasty.

"I don't visit often during the dry months," the Prince said to

Niyes as they rode amid the caravan. "I find my wives are happier when I keep things orderly, and sudden unannounced visits create chaos. They scramble to adorn the palace for my arrival, make the children presentable, and so forth. The ones hoping for my favor rush to pretty themselves, while the ones who wish to punish me make themselves scarce. It's terribly detrimental to peace."

Niyes, keeping an eye on the soldiers around them, chuckled. "You sound as if you enjoy making unannounced visits a great deal, my Prince."

"Does it seem that way? How crude of me. Must be all this sun addling my brain."

The day was certainly hot enough for it. The Prince's caravan rode along the elevated roadway called the Moonpath, which led from the city right to Kite-iyan's front gates. Irrigation ditches feeding nearby farms flanked the path; there were no trees to provide shade. Niyes politely refrained from pointing out that the center of their caravan, where the Prince rode, was cooler than it could have been thanks to the canopy that four servants held above him.

"But yes, I do rather enjoy surprising them," the Prince continued. "I remember what it was like, growing up in Kite-iyan. My mother would alternately fuss over me and shoo me away, and the other mothers would be just as frantic, whenever the Prince visited. The guards and eunuchs, the tutors and chefs, my siblings—everyone was on edge. But at the same time we were all so *excited*. The Sun of our own little earthly kingdom was coming to shine on us. We were a family, after all, in spite of our numbers." The Prince's expression hardened. "My father—

may he dwell in Her peace forever—forgot that sometimes. I do not."

Kite-iyan had been built on one of the broad, squat hills that bordered the Goddess's Blood river valley. From there the palace stood sentinel over neatly sectioned tracts of farmland and orchards, and the maze of roads that connected each part of Gujaareh with every other. In the springtime, when the Prince usually made the journey, most of the farms were under floodwaters; now in high summer they were lush and green. As the party continued along the Moonpath, Niyes caught glimpses of workers in the fields below stopping to watch as the caravan rode by. Some knelt and manuflected; the rest shaded their eyes as if it were indeed the Sun himself who passed so near.

The gates of Kite-iyan opened as the palace came into view. When the troop drew to a halt, a dozen children poured out of the palace's entrance, the smallest of them running to meet the party. The Prince laughed and spurred his horse forward, waving the soldiers aside. He dismounted and then was mobbed by the youngsters, who showed no shyness in tugging on the Prince's shirt or skirt or even his braids to gain his attention. And he lavished it on them, Niyes saw, ruffling hair here or bestowing a rough hug there, picking up the youngest to carry on his hip, chatting with the rest as he walked.

Niyes signaled the soldiers to dismount and quietly flank the Moonpath and palace entrance. He expected little trouble; the Prince's decision to visit Kite-iyan had been spur-of-the-moment, and Gujaareh had no enemies—overtly—who could arrange unpleasantness on such short notice. It still never hurt to be certain.

Beyond the knot around the Prince, a handful of adults and older children waited more calmly near the gate. Among them Niyes spotted the Prince's firstwife Hendet, their son Wanahomen, and Charris, captain of the guard at Kite-iyan. The Prince patted several of the children to send them inside, handed the youngest off to an older sibling, and then paused to exchange affections with his wife and favorite son, kissing the former and playfully gripping the arm of the latter in a mock-combative gesture.

It would not be long before Wanahomen's combativeness became something more than playful, Niyes gauged, gazing at the young man's arms; they rippled with muscle beneath the finely tailored linen of his shirt. The Prince still outstripped his son in height and build... but it was cunning, and not physical prowess, that usually decided the contest for the Aureole. Wanahomen was more than old enough for that. Yet there was no cunning in Wanahomen's eyes, Niyes saw—nothing but adoration as he embraced his father.

"Did you really bring a full forty of men?" drawled a familiar voice.

Distracted, Niyes blinked away from the Prince to see that Charris had drawn near. The guard-captain was smiling, although his green eyes showed more than a little contempt. "Did you expect trouble, Niyes, or are you just becoming paranoid in your old age?"

Niyes set his teeth and smiled back. "When the safety of the Prince and his family are at stake, I take no chances."

"As you should not," the Prince said, turning away from Wanahomen to gaze at both men. There was a hint of censure in the Prince's face; Niyes knew he detested strife among his soldiers. He bowed over his hand in silent apology, Charris did the same, and the Prince inclined his head in acceptance. Then he added, "As no doubt Captain Charris takes no chances, even here within Kite-iyan's walls. We will trust his guardianship now, Niyes, and that of the men under his command. Tell your soldiers to relax and avail themselves of my wives' hospitality until we leave."

Niyes inclined his head obediently; Charris did too at the corner of his vision. So Niyes turned and gave quick orders to the men to stable their horses properly before taking their unexpected recreation, and then he followed the Prince and his family into the palace.

In the courtyard many more people waited—some of the Prince's other wives and children, the staff and servants. The Prince moved among them without hesitation, offering smiles and greetings as he walked. Niyes tensed, uncomfortable as always to see Gujaareh's ruler unguarded amid such a large crowd—but then he noted the scattering of soldiers' uniforms among the gowns and forced himself to relax.

"Come, Niyes," the Prince said, pausing at the archway that led into the palace's heart. "You've never been here before, have you? Though you knew Charris..."

"We trained together, my Prince," Niyes said, moving to join him.

"You're not friends, I gather."

The crowd was sparse here at the arch; Charris was still in the courtyard, giving orders to his men. Niyes cleared his throat. "No, my Prince. He is zhinha."

The Prince laughed, then led him forward into wide, airy halls of high ceilings and artfully arched windows. "Forgive me for laughing, old friend, but you must realize the rivalry between shunha and zhinha has always been amusing to those of my lineage. Look." He took Niyes' hand, lifting their hands together to show the contrast: river-earth black and desert-sand brown. "I have the same amount of gods' blood in my veins as shunha, zhinha, or even Kisuati sonha—leaving aside the fact that as Hananja's Avatar I hold godly status of my own. And yet because I am a few gradations paler in shade..."

"It is more than that, my Prince," Niyes said stiffly.

"Yes, yes." The Prince smiled and released Niyes' hand. "You're always so serious. We're here for leisure—although we must discuss one bit of business first. Come, let me show you around."

Kite-iyan was a women's palace; its walls were of rose marble threaded with occasional veins of gold. Troughs lined the hallways at intervals, abloom with flowering plants. Pictographs of Dreaming Moon and her children abounded in the decor, drawn from the more pleasant tales of the heavenly family's life. They also passed wide chambers devoted to women's interests—libraries and sculpture halls, practice rooms for stick-fighting and dance. A few of these were occupied, Niyes noticed, as not all of the Prince's wives had deigned to interrupt their routines for his visit.

"Things are very different here from my youth," the Prince mused, nodding to women or children as they walked. "In my father's day, this place was a flower-strewn prison. He took any woman to wife who caught his eye, regardless of her feelings on the matter. They were brought here, permitted no visitors or holidays, wholly cut off from the world beyond the gates. It was just as bad for us children, though we were at least permitted to visit the city from time to time. Beyond our lessons there was nothing to do but compete for status and our father's favor, and that we did with a will. Poisonous, all of it.

"Since I began my own marriages I have striven to do better. My children are permitted to know their maternal relatives. Their mothers may continue to manage their own separate households and businesses, and they can come and go as they please. And you see that I take no great care to keep men away. I saw a few of the younger wives considering that sloe-eyed archer of yours. I hope he's strong enough to endure them all." He shrugged and grinned as Niyes looked at him in astonishment. "It takes a great deal to keep two hundred and fifty-six women happy, man; your soldiers are doing me a great favor, believe me! Any children who result only add to my glory, after all."

Niyes nodded slowly, more unnerved than amused by this reminder that the Prince missed nothing. "The highcastes have been discussing your marital reforms, my Prince. Many find the changes... disturbing. But then we shunha have always revered our women in the old ways."

"Believe it or not, Niyes, I agree with the ideals of the shunha." They began to climb a staircase that wound in a gentle upward spiral; sunbeams from narrow windows slanted across it like wheel-spokes. "Gujaareh has been influenced far more than it should be by ill-mannered savages who bore holes through their skulls to cure headaches. It's disgraceful. I cannot marry fewer wives, but I can remember that they are human beings, not broodmares. I treat my children like the treasures they are. You were watching my son Wana. Were you surprised that he loves me?"

Niyes blinked in surprise. "Yes, my lord."

"You expected antagonism. The young lion, sizing up the leader of the pride. But we are not animals, Niyes. We are not meant to scrabble over scraps of power, pulling one another down like crabs in a barrel. My father followed that model. So did I, to succeed him. I killed most of my siblings and their mothers. I killed my father, for that matter—sent him to the Throne of Dreams with my own hands. He deserved no less honor."

Niyes flinched. Only habit, and the fact that the Prince did not slow, kept his feet moving up the steps. That the Prince had assassinated his way to the Aureole was no surprise; half the city suspected it. But for the Prince to admit his crime was another matter altogether.

*He speaks to me of treason. Why?*

"I mean to change all that, Niyes."

They passed a landing, heading toward the upper floors of what appeared to be one of Kite-iyan's towers. The walkways here were empty, Niyes noticed, the steps edged in a faint sheen of dust.

"I mean for my children never to have to murder their own flesh and blood. I mean for my wives to love me—if they wish—and not fear me. I mean for Gujaareh to have strong, wise leadership for as long as it stands. No more madness. No need to rely on the Hetawa for our peace and happiness."

Niyes frowned, distracted from his growing unease. "Admirable goals, my Prince—but while you are certainly a wise ruler, you cannot guarantee that all your heirs will be. As long as power is the prize, they will compete, and the ruthless will win."

"Yes. I know. It weakens us, all this infighting. Like you and Charris, shunha and zhinha, Gujaareh and Kisua. When we weaken ourselves so much, it becomes easy for others to dominate."

They stopped at another landing, this one fairly high in the tower. Afternoon sunlight cast an overlapping pattern of red-gold rectangles across the floor. At the end of the landing stood a heavy wooden door, braced and decorated with metalwork in the northern style. A large, ornate lock was set into the band across its middle.

*A door? In Kite-iyan?*

"My Prince..." Niyes swallowed and found his throat suddenly dry. "If I may ask, where are we? What are we to discuss, all the way up here?"

The Prince walked to the door and reached into his shirt, pulling out a long, heavy key on a slender gold chain. "One of my wives is here."

"One of your—" He stared at the Prince in confusion. The Prince gazed at the door, holding the key but making no move to open it.

"I grant my wives a great deal of freedom, but I expect loyalty in return. This one spied on me for the Hetawa." He glanced at Niyes, his eyes distant and hard. "Betrayal is the one thing I cannot forgive."

Coldness slithered along Niyes' spine. *I will die today*, he thought.

The Prince gave a slight, sad smile as if he'd heard those words, then turned to unlock the door. His voice, when he spoke again, was light, conversational, as it had been throughout their tour. Still, there was an edge to it now that Niyes did not miss.

"You must realize, Niyes: I understand why she did it. She was raised in the Hetawa's House of Children; they were family to her. She followed her conscience, and I don't blame her for that. Indeed, I admire her integrity... but betrayal is still betrayal, and it cannot go unpunished."

The Prince pushed open the door and stepped within, turning back to gaze at Niyes. After a moment, slower, Niyes followed.

Beyond the door was a narrow chamber lined along one side by windows—an extension of the hall that must have at some point been walled off to form a storage room. The windows here had been bricked shut, however, save a small one at the far end. Shadows shrouded the room, except where a single bloody rectangle of light spread across the floor. The air smelled of dust and wood resin, and things less wholesome. Stale sweat, unwashed flesh, an un-emptied toilet box. Niyes squinted into the gloom, waiting for his eyes to adjust. All he could make out at first was a woman's bare foot, lying motionless at the edge of the light. Her leg, and the rest of her, disappeared into the shadows beyond.

From somewhere in the direction of her body, Niyes heard harsh, uneven breathing.

The Prince closed the door behind them. The clack of its heavy foreign latch was very loud in the small space.

"The plain fact of the matter," the Prince continued, "is that the Hetawa is no threat. They can do nothing to me without harming themselves. But Kisua is another matter, Niyes. You've forced my hand by involving lovely, clever Sunandi. I must push my plans forward by several months because of this, even once I kill her. And that, too, is a true shame; I liked her very much."

"My Prince—" Niyes caught himself, even as his heart began to thud uncomfortably fast. It was too late. Had been too late the moment he'd decided to take the corpse from the prison as evidence; he had known that all along. Still, he was shunha, born of one of Gujaareh's oldest lineages. He would die with dignity. "…It was for Gujaareh that I did it, my lord."

The Prince's eyes softened. He gripped Niyes' arm for just a moment, then let him go. "I know, old friend. I don't blame you either, though I believe you judged me wrongly. I too do what I must, for Gujaareh."

From the far end of the room they both heard the harsh breaths quicken. A man's voice, thick as mud over stones, spoke. "I…can smell the Moons, Brother. Night comes." Then lower, hungry—"I am empty. I hurt."

The Prince glanced in that direction. With one hand, he plucked something from the hipstrap of his loinskirt and rapped it against a nearby wall. A faint, high-pitched whine sang in response, maddeningly familiar—and then Niyes remembered. The Hetawa. Every month when he went to offer his tithe of dreams. Jungissa, the stone that vibrated with a life of its own, essential for magic.

The Prince lifted the stone in front of himself as if to ward off whatever lurked in the shadows. "I've brought you something, Brother," the Prince said, keeping his voice soft. "This one is corrupt too. But you must finish him quickly, for tonight you have another task to complete. Do you understand?"

"Corrupt..." There was a shuffle from the dark, followed by a soft step. Niyes made out the figure of a man rising slowly from a crouch.

Escape was impossible. Even if he made it out of the room, Charris's soldiers would take him down at one word from the Prince. Heart pounding, Niyes drew his dagger.

"It's better if you don't fight," the Prince said. He kept his voice gentle, soothing, though his eyes marked Niyes's dagger. "He has enough control left to do it properly, if you don't agitate him."

Niyes smiled grimly. "I am also military-caste, my lord."

"So you are." The Prince sighed, then turned back to the door. "I'll tell your family that you died bravely, protecting me from an assassin. They'll not be harmed."

"Thank you, my lord."

"Farewell, Niyes. I'm sorry."

"So am I, my lord."

The Prince left. After a moment, the Reaper came.

# 8

(◦ ⦿ ◦)

*A Gatherer shall seek purity within the Hetawa, keep*
*hidden among the faithful, and reveal his whole self*
*only to the recipient of Hananja's blessing.*
(Wisdom)

A leaf had fallen into the fountain. The patter of water against
its surface sounded like rain. Ehiru closed his eyes as he sat on
the fountain's edge, listening.

Rain came only once a year in Gujaareh, during the spring.
When it came, the Goddess's Blood overflowed her banks and
flooded the entire river valley, from the Sea of Glory all the way
into the northeastern reaches of Kisua. Most Gujaareen hated
floodseason and the small discomforts that it brought—mud
everywhere, insects rampant, families forced to live on their
upper floors or rooftops until the waters receded. Ehiru had
always loved floodseason, himself. It cleansed, despite the initial mess; the city's sun-baked walls gleamed anew once the dust
of the dry seasons had been washed away. It renewed—for without the annual floods Gujaareh's narrow band of fertile land
would be swiftly devoured by the deserts beyond.

The boy would make a fine replacement once his training was complete, Ehiru decided.

But Nijiri was to replace Una-une; he grimaced, remembering this. There were one or two other promising youngsters among the acolytes who might replace Ehiru himself—none so clearly called to the task as Nijiri had been, but suitable nevertheless. Life would be difficult for Sonta-i and Rabbaneh until the new Gatherers gained seasoning, but soon their younger brethren would be ready to walk the Goddess's most difficult path. Then the Gatherers of Hananja would be renewed. Cleansed at last of weakness and taint.

"Ehiru-brother."

The patter of the fountain might have covered the boy's footsteps, but not the rustling of the palm fronds. These were so thick in the Water Garden as to be unavoidable. Yet Nijiri had approached undetected. Ehiru smiled to himself in approval.

"Hananja has given us to each other, Nijiri." He kept his voice only loud enough to be heard over the fountain. In the intermittent silence he heard the boy's soft intake of breath. "Me to you in your time of need; now you to me. I will be here until you need me no longer. Understand this."

More silence, just for a moment. "I may need you for many years yet, Ehiru-brother."

"Not so long. Only until your apprenticeship ends."

"And beyond!"

Ehiru turned away from the fountain and looked at him, surprised by the urgency in the boy's tone. Nijiri stood a few feet away, half-hidden amid the palm-tree shadows, looking every inch the handsome young highcaste in a tailored shirt and loinskirt of fine woven cloth. No one would guess him servant-caste given his manner, and his beauty. There was something perpetually deceptive about him: fine bones hid the strength that came from years of physical training, and his smooth-cheeked, pretty face drew attention away from his eyes—which Ehiru knew could turn very cold when circumstances merited. He had always had Gatherer's eyes, even as a child.

Not now, though. Now Nijiri's face seemed calm, but his body was rigid, betraying feelings that perhaps even he did not yet fully understand.

*I should never have allowed you to choose me as your mentor. Selfish of me, and confusing to you. Poor child.*

"A Gatherer must be strong enough to stand alone, Nijiri," Ehiru said. The boy's face twitched ever so subtly at this warning; Ehiru could not guess what was in his mind. "Your greatest lessons will come long after your apprenticeship, taught to you by the world. I cannot stand between you and those."

"I know that, Brother." There was an edge to Nijiri's voice, all of a sudden, that Ehiru had not expected. "I went with you, all those years ago, because I had already grown to understand it. *You* taught me my first lesson: that love means sacrifice. Making choices that are good for others, even at the cost of the self." He ducked his eyes suddenly, radiating unhappiness. "I *can* do that. But I see no reason to do it unnecessarily."

Suddenly Ehiru wanted to embrace him. It was the wrong thing to do—too familiar, too paternal. Nijiri was his path-brother, not his son; someday soon his opinions would hold as much weight as Ehiru's own. The relationship between mentor and apprentice required a careful balancing of affection with respect, on both sides. But in the wake of his mishandling of the Bromarte's soul, and the miserable self-loathing he had wrestled in the days since, it was both humbling and humiliating to realize that Nijiri still thought highly of him. Humiliating because he did not deserve the boy's admiration—but humbling to realize he could not abandon his duty so easily. The boy trusted him, needed him. He had to be worthy of that trust—*become* worthy of it, somehow, and stay worthy for long enough to get the boy trained.

A heavy burden, this unwanted reason to live. Yet in his innermost heart, he could not lie to himself: it was a relief, as well. The Superior had been right to require this of him.

"We have duties to complete," Ehiru said at last, and after a moment the boy took a deep breath to compose himself, then nodded. A fine replacement indeed, in spirit if not truth.

Ehiru turned and led the boy out of the Water Garden. They stopped in the silent, dim Hall of Blessings to kneel at Hananja's feet, where they asked Her to divert a fraction of Her attention from the Eternal Dream long enough to guide their endeavor. Then they left the Hetawa by the Gatherers' Gate, and went out into the night.

Ehiru had chosen not to travel the streets or rooftops this time. The hour was still early; too many of the city's folk were abroad seeking entertainments, or working now that the day's heat had faded. Ehiru and Nijiri had both disguised themselves as wealthy highcastes, so they traveled as highcastes would—hiring a small carriage drawn by a strong young man of the servant caste. With Hetawa-provided funds, Ehiru paid the servant to take them directly to the bronze gates of Yanya-iyan.

At the palace, other carriages had arrived to dispense passengers, and a number of waiting guests milled about the gates and courtyard. Most of them wore the rich colors and silks of foreigners—dignitaries in town for Hamyan Night—and all of them chattered loudly of the sights they'd seen and the pleasures they'd tasted and how marvelous was the Prince's hospitality. Ehiru had chosen to disguise himself as a wealthy shunha, which allowed him to glide through the crowd in haughty silence. Shunha scorn for foreigners was infamous; none of the guests even tried to speak to them. He drew Nijiri along in his wake as if the boy were a servant or favorite, and was pleased to see that Nijiri played along perfectly, keeping silent with his eyes downcast. The guises were so suitable that the gate-guards waved them through without a second glance until Ehiru paused to flash the Hetawa token concealed in the palm of his cupped hand. The guard who saw it stiffened and looked up at them for a moment, then jerked his head again to send them through.

Word would spread, Ehiru knew—first through the guards, then the servants and lowcastes. By dawn even the royals would know that a Gatherer had been in the palace on Hetawa business. Thus no one would suspect rivals or criminals when the body was found in the morning, and the guards would not be accused of laxity. Hananja's Law was paramount, but that did not prohibit Her Servants from showing professional courtesy.

Once within, Ehiru led the way up stairwells and through a labyrinth of curving corridors, seeking the halls designated for guests. He did not hurry, for shunha never hurried. The guards eyed but did not question them, and Ehiru did not bother to inform them of his true identity. He had satisfied practicality; now duty took precedence.

The guest halls were lined with thickly curtained entryways, each leading into an identical furnished apartment. The higher floors held even finer accommodations, and their target, but this floor was the means they would use to reach her. There were eight apartments here, two of which were dark and silent. Selecting the first of these, Ehiru pushed the curtain aside without jingling any of the tiny bells sewn along its bottom edge, and entered.

He held himself tense in case the chamber was occupied, but the rooms had a disused and impersonal air. Moonlight filtering through the sheer balcony curtain outlined brocaded cushions and plush couches, allowing them to navigate easily in the dark. Ehiru lit a single candle while Nijiri looked around, his face expressionless even though Ehiru knew the boy had rarely seen such opulence.

"The floors above us are for the lowest-ranked of the royal family and the highest-ranked of the guests," Ehiru said. "With the palace so full of strangers tonight, the guard will concentrate its efforts on protecting the Prince wherever he happens to be. That leaves all other areas—like this floor—vulnerable." He began to undress, laying aside the rich garments and jewelry of his costume. "The tithebearer should be in one of the suites on the next floor up."

Nijiri noted Ehiru's preparations and began to remove his own highcaste disguise. The boy had applied a cosmetic balm under his clothing, Ehiru saw with approval. The brown pigment would help to dim his conspicuously pale skin.

"Do we know which suite?" Nijiri asked, all business.

"The Kisuati ambassadorial suite is right above this room."

"I, I see, Ehiru-brother..." In the midst of donning his ornaments, Nijiri fumbled the jungissa—his own, newly issued, and carved in the likeness of a dragonfly. Ehiru winced, but the boy stooped and caught the precious stone before it could hit the floor. He straightened and attached it properly this time, shoulders hunching in shame.

Ehiru watched him. A degree of nervousness was understandable, but if Nijiri could not be calm, he would have to remain behind while Ehiru went up to perform the Gathering.

Either sensing Ehiru's scrutiny or realizing the problem himself, Nijiri drew himself upright and moved to sit on a nearby couch. His eyes closed; his lips moved in prayer; presently the wire-taut tension went out of his frame.

Pleased, Ehiru went to the balcony. Yanya-iyan's courtyard spread below, empty save for sand that had been swept into decorative patterns, and the Sun pavilion. No sign of the previous night's revelry lingered to spoil the image of perfect peace. It was a view so familiar that for a moment his mind wandered away from duty, remembering the other life of his childhood. He had visited Yanya-iyan only a handful of times, yet every visit was clear as water in his memory. In those days Gatherers had been nothing more than shadowy figures from his mother's tales, and the then-Prince had been more of a god to him than Hananja.

Movement across his field of vision caught his eye. He looked up to see a shadow fly across the bands of the Dreaming Moon. A skyrer, one of the night-hunting birds of the desert. They rarely hunted in the river valley itself, preferring the border-lands near the desert where there were scrubmice and lizards in plenty. Those of the farming caste considered it an ill omen to see skyrers over inhabited land outside of the rainy season—a sign that something, somewhere, was out of balance.

*A predator's silhouette etched upon a Moonlit rooftop* . . .

Behind him, Nijiri finished his prayer. "Brother? Forgive me for the delay."

Ehiru closed his eyes and listened. The Dreamer had risen fully, an immense four-hued eye filling the night sky. He could taste the subtle change in the air as people sought their beds and beasts settled in their stalls. Closer by, faint sounds from the other guest suites had ceased. For a moment he thought he heard whispers on the wind: a vision. Understandable, given the length of time since his last Gathering, and unimportant. He exerted his will and the illusion faded. All was still.

"Time," he said, and Nijiri drew close behind him.

It was a simple matter to stand on the railing and reach up to the ledge above, but he moved carefully anyhow. There were surely guards a few balconies up, protecting the Prince's quar-ters. Levering himself up, he settled in a crouch on his hands and toes, and peered at the balcony hanging while Nijiri swung up to join him. The chamber beyond was dark. The faintest hint of fragrance wafted out to him as a breeze stirred the silk: a woman's perfume.

Nijiri's bare feet padded against the stone as he landed on the balcony. Ehiru glanced at him and saw that the boy's face was calm, focused. Excellent.

Another breeze flickered past, causing the hanging to billow gently outward. Ehiru flicked it to widen the opening further and slipped within, pausing against a nearby wall to allow his eyes to adjust to the darkness. Nijiri did the same, both of them rising to a half-crouch. Moving away from the wall, they picked their way among the furnishings. Past the main chamber lay the bedroom. A set of wooden chimes swayed in the window, occasionally emitting random hollow notes. He heard a rustle and murmur from the bed; she slept restlessly. Only one breather: she slept alone.

He signaled Nijiri with a nod, and together they approached the bed.

Too late Ehiru heard the whisper of movement that the woman's stirrings had covered—shifting cloth, a careful step. In the same moment he heard the forceful release of a held breath and felt its warmth tickle the hairs on his right arm. He reacted without thinking, throwing himself forward just as something cold and sharp grazed his back, leaving a thin thread of fire along his skin.

Nijiri's blurt—"Brother!"—broke the silence. Ehiru abandoned stealth as he sensed his attacker closing in. Off balance, he caught himself against the edge of the bed and kicked out. His foot struck flesh and shoved something backward; he heard a muffled curse and garlic-tinged breath wafted past his face. In the bed the woman jerked upright, gasping.

Then Nijiri lunged past him, a blurred silhouette batting and shoving at another silhouette half his size. Something gleamed brighter against the shadows: a knife, poised to stab Nijiri's side. Ehiru struck first, his fist meeting bone; the knife clattered to the floor. In the same instant Nijiri made some sort of sharp movement and the smaller silhouette fell against the bedroom hanging, ripping it in a loud snarl of cloth. Nijiri closed in swiftly—

Lantern-light flared, painful in the dimness, and shocked them all to stillness.

"What in the names of the thousand Sun-spawn is going on here?" demanded the woman.

# 9

(•☉•)

*A Gatherer shall enter buildings in concealment, and*
*approach the bearer of the Goddess's tithe in stealth.*
*Thus is peace maintained into dreaming.*

(Law)

For several seconds after being jolted out of sleep, Sunandi
could not comprehend the tableau before her. Lin lay on the
floor, coughing and clutching at her throat. A slim, pale Gujaareen youth not far past the age of adulthood crouched over her
in a striking stance, staring at Sunandi in almost comical surprise. Another man—bigger, older, dark as a Kisuati and somehow familiar—stood in the foreground half-turned to her, his
eyes wide with shock and anger.

Then the fog of sleep lifted and details struck. Lin's knife on
the floor. The intruders' black-dyed clothing. A moontear-
embossed ornament on the man's nearer hip: the emblem of the
Hetawa.

Dearest Dreamer. Niyes had been right.

"'Nandi—"

Lin's croak startled her out of shock. She threw aside the

sheet, heedless of her own near-nudity—she wore only a light shift—and reached beneath the pillow to pull out the dagger she kept there. She snatched it from its sheath and leaped to her feet. "Get away from her!"

The man tensed as if to fight—and then some unidentifiable shadow crossed his face, replacing the anger with a strange, somehow detached calm. He straightened and then, shocking Sunandi nearly out of her skin, went down on one knee in formal manuflection.

"Forgive me. This should have gone peacefully." The man's voice was deep and so soft that she strained to hear him. He flicked some signal at the youth; the youth took Lin by the arm to help her up. Lin jerked her arm free and stumbled back to glare at both of the strangers. Her breath still wheezed alarmingly through her throat, though she seemed to be recovering. Sunandi edged over to her, knife still at the ready; with her free hand she pulled Lin's hand away from her throat. An angry red mark spread across the girl's larynx.

"I did not strike to kill," the youth said, almost apologetically. He too was soft-spoken, though his voice was higher-pitched. "I meant only to silence her."

"Nijiri," the man said, and the youth fell silent.

Reaction set in as Sunandi's fear eased, though anger replaced it. She shivered uncontrollably as she stepped around the bed, pulling Lin with her to put some distance between them and the strangers. The *killers.*

"Is this the piety of Gujaareh?" she demanded. Her voice sounded harsh and loud compared to theirs. "I was told the

Gatherers of Hananja had honor. I never dreamed you would allow yourselves to be used like this."

The man flinched suddenly as if her words had been a blow. "Used?"

"Yes, damn you, *used*. Why even bother pretending to serve Hananja's Law? Why delay? Kill me and be done with it—unless you mean to talk me to death?"

"'Nandi!" Lin's voice was a hoarse whisper.

It was not the wisest thing to say, true, but something in her words had jarred the older one; she had to keep talking. He was the greater danger, she saw at once. Not just physically; there was something else about him that set her nerves a-jangle every time their eyes met.

*Perhaps the fact that he wants to kill me.*

The Gatherer went still. His hand drifted away from his side, the fingers curling in an odd gesture—first and middle fingers forked, the rest folded neatly out of the way. For some reason that gesture sent a chill prickling along Sunandi's skin.

"I was trying to put you at ease," he said. "But I can calm you once you're asleep, if you prefer."

"Gods! No!" She took an involuntary step back. He did not lower his hand.

"Explain your statement, then," he said. The youth frowned at him in sudden surprise. "That we are being used."

"Are you mad? Get out before I shout for the guards. You're the worst assassins I have ever seen!"

"We are not assassins."

"You *are*. Doing it in the name of your bloodthirsty goddess changes nothing. Are you the one who's been killing the prisoners? Did you kill Kinja, too?"

The man's face changed subtly—still calm, but no longer detached. She thought she read anger in his eyes.

"I have never Gathered anyone named Kinja," he said. He began to pace around the bed, every step silent, his eyes never leaving hers. The youth followed him—less gracefully, but with the same soundless menace. "No one I have ever Gathered has been imprisoned, except within his own suffering flesh or blighted mind. I offer Her peace in exchange for pain . . . fear . . . hatred . . . loneliness. Death is a gift, to those who suffer in life."

He stopped, breaking the spell of voice and movement, and with sudden, chilling clarity Sunandi saw that the Gatherer had closed the distance between them until he stood only a few feet away. His hand was still poised in that odd gesture; this time he meant to strike. And when he did, no knife or half-grown bodyguard would stop him.

The fear spiked into terror—and then receded as Kinja's training reverberated through her mind.

"Two days ago I saw a corpse," she said. The Gatherer paused. "A man who had died in his sleep some while before. His face . . . I have never seen such anguish, Gatherer. In Kisua we tell tales of your kind, you priests who bring dreams of death. They say the dreams are not always pleasant. They say that sometimes, if one of your kind loses control, the victim dies *irusham*—wearing the mask of horror. Do you still want to tell me you know nothing of that?"

The Gatherer froze, the deadly intent in his eyes giving way to something unreadable.

"I know of it," he said, barely louder than a whisper.

"Then do you truly expect me to believe," she said, softening her own voice, "that you arrive here to kill me not even a four-day later, and it has nothing to do with the Prince's plans for war?"

The Gatherer frowned, and she realized she'd made an incorrect assumption somewhere. There was no mistaking the confusion on his face. Just then the youth stepped forward, apparently unable to keep silent. He did not quite step in front of the man, but his stance radiated protectiveness.

"The Prince has nothing to do with who is Gathered, or why," the youth said. "And my brother's mistake has nothing to do with any war."

*Brother?* Ah, yes. The boy was the man's physical opposite; it was unlikely they were related. He had to be the man's apprentice. Snippets of gossip overheard at the Hamyan merged with the niggling sense of familiarity, and abruptly she knew who the man was.

"You are Ehiru," she said. "The Prince's last surviving brother."

The Gatherer's eyes narrowed. Yes, that was it. Each man had clearly taken after his respective mother in most ways, but the stamp of the shared sire was in their eyes. Ehiru's were an onyx version of the Prince's, just as lovely—though far, far colder.

"My family is the Hetawa," the Gatherer snapped.

"But before that, you were of the Sunset. Your mother was Kisuati, a sonha noblewoman, probably some kin of mine. She gave you to the Hetawa to save your life."

The Gatherer scowled. "Irrelevant. Once the Hetawa accepted

me, I became wholly theirs. The Prince has no brothers; I have a thousand."

If this was his attitude, it was possible that he could be trusted. But trustworthy or not, it was clear only the truth would deter him from killing her.

Sunandi took a deep breath, straightened, then made a show of setting her knife on the bed. "Lin."

Lin looked at her incredulously, but the girl had learned long ago not to question her in front of others. With visible reluctance she set her knife down as well. At this the youth relaxed somewhat; the Gatherer did not. He lowered his hand, however, which Sunandi took for a positive sign.

"Explain," the Gatherer said again.

"This is not the best place for a discussion, you realize. The royal family's quarters are on the floor directly above."

"There are no listening-holes in this chamber. That would be foolish, since you might find and use them yourself."

And her enemies would be far more interested in what she did *outside* the guest suite, anyhow. "Very well. Perhaps you're not assassins—or at least, not knowingly. The end result is what matters in this case, rather than the intent."

"Not to us."

She resisted the urge to swallow at the menace in his tone. He still intended—no. He still *believed wholly* in the rightness of killing her.

"You say that someone named me corrupt. Who?"

"I do not know."

"Do you know why? What evidence they gave?"

"You were accused of spying, corrupting influential citizens of

Gujaareh, and attempting to foment war. I do not know the evidence given. That was evaluated—and accepted—by the Superior of the Hetawa."

"Hananja's Crusty Eyes." For a moment she was tempted to laugh, until she noted the affront on their faces and recalled her careless blasphemy. Silently she berated herself; now was not the time for amateurish mistakes. "—Apologies. I shouldn't be surprised. I *have* been spying, of course."

"Then you acknowledge your corruption?"

"Spying, as the Prince has spied on me, and as the ambassadors of Bromarte, Jijun, Khanditta, and every other land in spitting distance of the Narrow Sea have spied on one another for centuries. It is the job of an ambassador to spy. If there's corruption in that, then you'd better Gather a few other people in this palace tonight."

"Do you refute the other charges?" His expression was implacable.

"Corrupting highcastes and fomenting war? Let me see. I had a meeting with a highcaste who revealed to me one of Gujaareh's darkest secrets. He did it unbidden and uncoerced, and his intention was to *prevent* war. How would you judge that, priest of Hananja?"

"I do not judge."

"Then you had better start." She was growing angry herself in response to the tension of the moment and the Gatherer's obstinacy. "There is a Reaper in this land, priest, and I have seen the proof of it. I believe you and your brethren know of this abomination and conceal it."

The youth frowned in puzzlement. The Gatherer went rigid.

"There is no Reaper in Gujaareh," he said. "There has been none for centuries."

"I told you of the corpse I saw."

His jaw worked, and abruptly the affront in his face was eclipsed by something she hadn't expected to see: shame. "Sometimes Gatherers err," he said. Beside him the youth's scowl deepened, though the look he turned on his mentor was somber. The Gatherer fixed his eyes on the floor. "When that happens, we do penance. But I'm no rogue. Nor are any of my brothers."

"Twenty men have died like the corpse I saw, at the prison. Do Gatherers err so often?"

The man was already shaking his head, but in disbelief. "*Twenty?* No, that cannot be. Someone would've reported it. One or two mistakes the people can accept, but never so many, so quickly—"

"They don't know," Lin said suddenly. Sunandi looked down at her in surprise. Lin's pale eyes were narrowed at the Gatherer, though she spoke to Sunandi. "Someone in the Hetawa probably does, but not these two. Maybe none of the Gatherers know."

The Gatherer looked from one to the other of them, confusion plain on his face; his voice wavered with uncertainty and tension. "There's nothing to know. What you suggest is . . . is . . ." He faltered silent.

Sunandi snorted. "At least one of the Gatherers knows. Only Gatherers become Reapers."

"*There are no Reapers in Gujaareh!*" The Gatherer's composure shattered so suddenly that it startled them all. He glared at them, nostrils flared, fists clenched, body trembling with rage. Only his voice remained under control; he had not raised it, though he'd snarled the words with such vehemence that they might as well have been shouted. "That would be an abomination beyond imagination. We are tested regularly. When the signs begin to show, we give ourselves to Her. We all know our duty. To suggest otherwise is an attack upon the Hetawa itself!"

The youth looked genuinely alarmed now, and Sunandi felt the same. The sense of unease that she had felt from the beginning redoubled, joined now by an instinctive certainty. *Something is wrong with him.*

"I mean no insult," she said, carefully neutral. "It could be some new poison, whose effects mimic Reaping-death. Or a plague. There's no way to know for certain." She spread her hands, moving slowly and deliberately so he could see she meant no harm. "But if there's no rogue in the city, then someone certainly means to *suggest* that there is. Would that not also be an assault upon your brotherhood?"

The Gatherer's agitation cooled somewhat, though his stance remained stiff. "It would if it were true. But you have been judged corrupt. These could be lies."

Sunandi could think of no counter for that argument. Abruptly the whole situation wearied her; she sighed and rubbed her eyes. "They could be. For all I know, they are—lies fed to me, which I now feed to you. If I had all the answers, my job here would be done. As it is, I'm going to leave it unfinished; I must return to Kisua to tell my people what I've learned so far." She paused, looked at him, realizing that nothing had been settled. "If you allow."

That quick flex of his jaw muscles again, she saw, above neck-cords taut as ropes. After a long silence, however, the Gatherer jerked his head in a nod. "I declare your tithe in abeyance for now. Until I can confirm—or disprove—what you say." His eyes narrowed to slits. "If you have lied, do not think fleeing to Kisua will save you. Gatherers have tracked commissions across the world in the past. Hananja's Law outweighs the laws of any foreign land, to us."

"Of that I have no doubt, priest. But how do you intend to discover the truth?"

"I will return to the Hetawa and ask my brethren."

The man's naïveté astonished her. This was a brother of the Prince? "I would not advise going back to your Hetawa. In the morning when no one finds me dead, the conspirators will know I've told you secrets. The Hetawa—this whole city—may no longer be safe for you."

He threw her a look of withering contempt. "This is not some corruption-steeped barbarian land, woman." He turned to leave; the youth fell in behind him.

"Wait."

He paused, looking back at her warily. She went to her chest—still keeping her movements smooth and slow—and rummaged through it for a moment. "If you need to leave the city, give this to the guard at the south gate. Only before sunset, mind you; the shift changes at nightfall."

She stepped forward and held out a heavy silver Kisuati coin. One face of it had been scuffed and scored, as if by accident.

The Gatherer stared down at it in distaste. "Bribery."

She stifled irritation. "A *token*. The daytime guard at that gate is one of my associates. Show him that and he'll help you, even tell you where I can be found. I mean to be beyond the walls by morning."

He scowled, not touching the coin.

She rolled her eyes. "If later you decide I have lied, lay it on my breast after you kill me."

"Do not dare to mock—" Exasperation crossed the Gatherer's face and finally he sighed, plucking the coin from her hand. "So be it."

He turned and walked out of the bedchamber into the darkness of the main room. She saw him appear again as a silhouette against the balcony hangings, the youth a smaller shadow beside him. He vaulted the railing, his protégé followed, and both of them were gone.

Sunandi let out a long, shaky breath.

After an equally long silence, Lin inhaled. "I'll go now," she said in Sua. Rising, the girl went to the corner where an open pack sat, half-concealed by a large fern; she began rummaging through it, making certain she had everything she needed. "Arrange things with our contacts. Should've gone last night, but I wanted to wait until tomorrow when most of the foreigners began leaving after the Hamyan—" She paused, hands stilling their brisk movements for a moment. "Thank the gods I delayed. If I hadn't been here . . ."

Sunandi nodded, though absently. She hardly felt able to think, much less speak coherently. She'd faced many trials in her years as Kinja's heir, but never a direct threat to her life. The Gatherer's eyes glittered in her memory, so dark, so cold—but compassionate, too. That had been the truly terrifying thing. A killer with no malice in his heart: it was unnatural. With nothing in his heart, really, except the absolute conviction that murder could be right and true and holy.

Lin took her arm. Sunandi blinked down at her. "You need to leave now, 'Nandi."

"Yes...yes." Kinja had taken in Lin because of her quick wit and good sense; Sunandi thanked the gods for both in that moment. "I'll see you in Kisua."

Lin nodded, flashing one of her impish smiles. Then she was gone, slipping out of the apartment through the front door hanging, an oversized man's robe wrapped around her to conceal the pack. The hall guards would see her and assume she'd just finished some tryst with one of the high-ranking guests. They wouldn't question her as long as she headed toward the servants' quarters. From there Lin could leave the palace and be out of the city before dawn.

Kinja should have made Lin the ambassador, Sunandi decided in momentary envy. She was more ruthless than Sunandi, and eminently better suited to the whole process. But for now, Sunandi would simply be grateful for Kinja's good taste. She sighed, then turned to the chest to dig out her own pack.

Behind her, beyond the window, a man's silhouette flickered across the setting Moon.

# 10

(◦⊙◦)

*"This magic is abomination," said the Protectors to
Inunru, when the beast had been run to ground. "We
will not permit it within our borders." Thus Inunru
went north along the path of the river, and with him
went the most devout of his followers.*

(Wisdom)

The Reaper knows that it is an abomination. If it had a soul left,
it could mourn this.

*       *       *

Leaving Yanya-iyan had gone smoothly. The palace guards generally concerned themselves far more with unwanted intruders
than with departing guests—even those leaving in the small
hours of the night. Ehiru summoned another servant-drawn
carriage, ordering a drop-off along the quiet streets of the riverfront. Now Nijiri sat with his mentor on a rooftop near the river,
gazing out at the Goddess's Blood as it flowed in the near distance. Dreaming Moon had not quite completed her slow,
graceful journey across the sky, but already the horizon was

growing pale with the coming dawn. Nights were always short for a time after the solstice.

*Corruption and madness and war . . .*

Hamyan, and Nijiri's conversation with Sister Meliatua, had been only the night before.

At Nijiri's side Ehiru sat quietly, his eyes fixed on the river but seeing, Nijiri suspected, into some other plane. Though an hour had passed since the conversation with the Kisuati woman, Ehiru showed no inclination to return to the Hetawa. Nor was there any further sign of the temper that had seized him in the woman's bedchamber—though Nijiri knew the calm was only temporary. If Ehiru's control had slipped once, it would slip again. That was the way of the test.

He raised his hand, palm up. "Ehiru-brother?" Touch helped a Gatherer focus on reality when his other senses began to betray him; it was a trick taught to all who served as pranje attendants.

Ehiru's eyes flickered back from that other place, shifting to first Nijiri's face and then the proffered hand. Sorrow furrowed his brow, but he sighed and reluctantly took the hand. "Have I frightened you so much, my apprentice?"

"You have never frightened me, Ehiru-brother."

But Ehiru only looked down at their joined hands and sighed again. "She wasn't lying. In dreams I could be surer, but even in waking, there's a sense to such things."

Nijiri used his free hand to begin stroking the back of Ehiru's. This, too, was permitted in the pranje, but Nijiri suspected he was not supposed to pay such attention to the smoothness of Ehiru's skin, or the scents of incense and sweat that formed

Ehiru's distinctive musk... With an effort, he made himself lean back. "It's possible to lie without lying, Brother. She herself admitted that she didn't know the whole truth."

"She knows enough to be of concern." Ehiru gazed down at their hands. "But too much of what she said is... inconceivable. Unacceptable."

"This business of a Reaper?" Nijiri shook his head. "She must have been mistaken. She was, at first."

"No." Ehiru's expression grew solemn. "That mistake was mine. I assumed she spoke of... of my own error." He hesitated for a long moment. "The Superior told you?"

Nijiri looked out at the water. "Of course. I made the choice to have you as my mentor in full knowledge."

"*What* did he tell you?"

"That you failed to fulfill a commission, doing harm to the soul and perhaps even destroying it." Ehiru frowned as he spoke, however, and Nijiri stopped speaking, concerned. Was there more to the matter, then?

Ehiru took a deep breath, seeming to ready himself. "The tithe was to be taken from a foreigner—a man of the Bromarte. I found him already in Ina-Karekh and followed him in." Ehiru abruptly went silent; his fingers twitched a little against Nijiri's.

"Brother?"

"There was corruption in his soul." Ehiru still gazed out at the river, but Nijiri suspected he did not see the palm trees on the far shore, the reeds waving in the wind, or the flatboats bobbing gently at their moorings. His hand, in Nijiri's, felt cold. "Not enough to make him criminal, but enough to taint his dreamscape with ugliness and violence. I tried to take him to a more pleasant place, but then he had a true-seeing."

Nijiri frowned. "Foreigners don't see truly in their dreams, brother. They wander helpless in Ina-Karekh every night. A fourflood child has more control."

"Foreigners have the same innate abilities as we of Gujaareh, Nijiri. Anything a skilled narcomancer can do, they can— though only by accident."

Nijiri held back a snort; the notion of a barbarian managing the same feat as the most highly trained Sisters, Sharers, and Gatherers seemed ludicrous. Did children write treatises?

"In this Bromarte's case..." Ehiru sighed. "Up to that point he had been no different from any other stubborn, frightened dreamer. But then he said to me, 'They're using you.'"

Nijiri frowned. "What did that mean?"

"I don't know. But I *felt* the truth of his words. And tonight, when the Kisuati woman said the same thing..."

"So that was it." Nijiri squeezed his hand. "She is corrupt, Brother. A professional liar by her own admission."

"Then you dismiss her tales of dead prisoners, and a conspiracy to begin a war?"

"Dead prisoners would hardly begin a war. And anyhow, every account that I have read of war speaks of its terrible destruction and suffering. No one would start such a thing deliberately."

Ehiru glanced at him, and Nijiri was startled to see a smile on his mentor's face. "Ehiru-brother?"

"It's nothing. Just that I forget your youth at times." Ehiru drew up his knees and wrapped his arms about them, gazing up into the sky. Tiny pale Waking Moon peeked timidly out from behind her greater sister's curve; sunrise would come soon. "I envy you that youth."

Nijiri gazed at Ehiru in surprise and read faint lines of regret and worry in his mentor's profile. "You believe the woman's tale."

Ehiru sighed into a breeze. "When the Bromarte had his true-seeing, I mishandled the dream out of surprise. But after he was dead, I saw something else. A man, I think, on the rooftop across. He was *wrong*, Nijiri. I can't explain it. His movements, his shape, the feel of his presence; I have never been so frightened in my life."

Nijiri shifted uncomfortably. "A vision. A manifestation of your guilt." He had heard that strong narcomancers were sometimes plagued by such things. The dreaming gift was not always easy to control. "Flush with dreamblood—"

"No. The dreamblood was rotten; I was sick with it, not enraptured. What I saw was real."

"The Kisuati's Reaper?"

"I can think of nothing else that would have sent such dread through my heart."

"But to become a Reaper, a user of dream magic must fail the pranje, refuse the Final Tithe, go un-Gathered by our brethren for fourdays, somehow remain unnoticed by others while he goes slowly mad..." He shook his head, unwilling to believe. "It's impossible. Our brothers are too wise and faithful to let such a thing happen."

"I imagine those long-ago Reapers had faithful brothers too, once."

Nijiri sucked in his breath and stared at Ehiru. Ehiru smiled bleakly, his eyes lost in the distance. The words settled into Nijiri's heart like stones, and he fell silent beneath their weight. Perhaps out of respect for Nijiri's turmoil, Ehiru stopped talking as well, and they both brooded for a while.

Eventually, though, Ehiru sighed. "I saw what I saw, Nijiri. And if there are twenty dead men who saw the same thing..."

"Well, that's for the Superior to determine." Nijiri got to his feet and brushed off his loindrape decisively. Ehiru glanced up at him, a look of mild surprise on his face. "We must return to the Hetawa and report this. And you must go to the Sharers to request an infusion."

Ehiru raised an eyebrow. "One display of ill temper does not make me out of control."

"Not alone. But there have been other signs, haven't there?" It was unseemly to speak of such things, except when they had to be said. Ehiru squared his shoulders, radiating stubbornness; Nijiri pressed on. "I was trained, Brother, though I never got the chance to properly serve. Have you seen more visions than usual? Have there been times when your hands shook?"

Ehiru lifted a hand and gazed at it. "The morning of the Hamyan."

He'd let himself suffer for two whole days? Nijiri scowled. "Then it must be done. You Gathered no tithe tonight. By tomorrow night you might be hearing voices, seeing enemies under every leaf—"

Ehiru got to his feet and faced him. "I believe I know my own pattern, Nijiri, having experienced it every year for the past twenty."

It was a mild rebuke as such things went, but it silenced Nijiri anyhow. He bowed his head, fists clenched in shame and anger at being reminded of his place. But a moment later Ehiru sighed and put a hand on his shoulder.

"I'll go to the Sharers if that will ease your fears," he said. "And then we'll both go to the Superior—"

He paused then, cocking his head. Nijiri frowned and opened his mouth to ask what was the matter, but before he could speak, Ehiru held up a hand to shush him. He pivoted slowly toward the north, squinting along the flow of the river. The rooftops had become still as the Dreamer's fat curve at last sank out of sight, leaving only the deep monochrome darkness cast by Waking Moon's pallid light. No birds sang; not even a breeze stirred the laundry-heavy clotheslines. The city was silent.

No. Not silent. A few blocks away, echoing up from the street, Nijiri heard the slap of sandals on stone. Running.

"Light," Ehiru whispered. "A woman, perhaps. Or a child."

Nijiri swung about to orient on those running feet as well, tensing as a thousand possibilities—most of them dire—ran through his mind. "A messenger. A servant on an errand." A rapist. A murderer.

They fell silent again, listening. The rhythm of the runner changed, skidding now and again, faltering and then resuming. Nijiri frowned, for there was something indisputably urgent about the sound of those running feet. Something *frantic*.

Ehiru lifted a hand in a quick signal: *follow in silence*. Nijiri obeyed at once as Ehiru abruptly set off, leaping from the roof on which they stood to the next, and then running along another. Their course, Nijiri realized as he ran behind his mentor, would intersect that of the runner in a half-block or so.

Ehiru stopped at the edge of a squat storage house's roof, peering over its wall into the street below. No one was in sight. The patter of feet had stopped.

From an alley on the other side of the building—the direction in which they'd last heard the runner—they both heard a sharp, frightened cry.

Ehiru was moving before the cry's echo faded, running with no further attempt at stealth. Nijiri scrambled to keep up. Even after ten years of acrobatics training, it still shocked him when Ehiru reached the roof-edge and slowed not one whit before leaping off. He flipped in the air, his hands reaching back to catch the wall as he fell; his feet braced against the stone to cushion the impact. An instant later he let go, dropping another man-length to land on fingers and toes, his eyes fixed on the dark beyond the alley's entrance.

From that darkness came a soft hiss.

Nijiri skidded to a halt on the rooftop, his heart pounding. There was no easier way down. Swallowing, he took a deep breath to focus as the Sentinels had taught him, and concentrated on the opposite wall of the alley as he repeated Ehiru's flipping trick. He fouled the final leap, however, landing without injury but stumbling.

Before Nijiri could regain his balance, something flew out of the dark and struck Ehiru. It looked like a badly packed sack of clothes; it had yellow hair. The Kisuati woman's girl.

*Hananja have mercy!*

Ehiru grunted as he was borne down by the dead weight of the corpse. As he struggled to extricate himself from flopping limbs and a lolling head and horrible, horrible sightless eyes,

Nijiri moved to help—and gasped as something else came out of the dark and struck him so hard that his vision went white. He hit the cobblestones with painful force, too stunned to do more than flail weakly at the thing that had struck him. But this thing was no corpse.

"Pretty child," whispered a voice in Nijiri's ear. Fear froze him; the voice seemed barely human, low and rough. "I will enjoy your taste."

Hands as strong as iron caught Nijiri's arms. One of them pinned his wrists above his head. The other, smelling of dirt and bile and a four of other foul things, fumbled over his face. Nijiri shut his eyes in reflex as fingertips pressed against his eyelids. *Wait, this is*— But just as he understood—

—He woke screaming, somehow freed. Terror pounded through his blood so powerfully that he rolled to his side and vomited a thin sour trickle, then could not find the wit to move away from the mess. Instinctively he curled himself into a ball, praying for the fear to pass and for the sick throb of his head to either go away or kill him and be done with it.

Dimly he heard the sounds of flesh striking flesh, the scuffle of sandals on stone. A feral snarl, like that of a jackal.

"Abomination!" Ehiru's shout came to Nijiri through his misery and some of the fear faded. Ehiru would keep him safe. "You shall not have him!"

A rough laugh was the creature's reply, and Nijiri whimpered, for somehow he had heard that laugh in his nightmares—but he could not remember the nightmares.

The cobblestones vibrated as feet pounded over them, out of the alleyway, running away. Then hands lifted Nijiri, cradling him against warmth and muscle and a hard-beating heart. "Nijiri? Open your eyes."

It had not occurred to Nijiri that his eyes were closed.

Then fingers touched Nijiri's eyelids. He thrashed and opened his mouth to scream, terrified. But something sweet and warm and exquisite brushed against his mind, soft as flower petals, soothing away the terror.

When Nijiri opened his eyes, Ehiru's worried expression brought reality back to him, though in fragments.

"Thank the Dreamer. I thought your soul had come completely untethered." The world shifted dizzyingly as Ehiru lifted Nijiri in his arms. "The Sharers will be able to heal you fully."

Then the world began to bob and wheel in a mad dance as Ehiru ran with him. Nijiri's last sight before unconsciousness was the gem-layered glow of dawn.

# 11

(⦿)

It happened so rarely that Ehiru was summoned to perform his duty. Oh, the commissions were summonings in their way—submitted through intercessors, assessed by committee, and sanctified with prayer before a Gatherer ever saw them. So distant, that way. A direct summons was better. Then the Gathering could be performed by daylight, treasured, celebrated. The tithebearer could pass into eternal joy with family and friends near to witness the wonder, and bid farewell.

But so few truly believed in Hananja's blessing or welcomed it as they should. All the procedure, all the stealth had been designed for them—those of weak faith, or none at all. Even now Ehiru noted the ones who drew away as he walked through the streets in his formal Gatherer's robe, face hooded, the black oasis rose visible on his shoulder. It saddened Ehiru that so many of Hananja's citizens feared Her greatest gift . . . but perhaps that too was Her will. The greatest mysteries of life—or death—were always frightening, but no less marvelous for that.

In the merchant quarter: lovely, sprawling houses surrounded him. He reached the one he sought and found its inhabitants waiting, formally dressed and solemn, flanking the open door in twin rows to signal that the way was clear. A tall, pale-skinned elder was the master of the house. He bowed deeply as Ehiru passed, but not before Ehiru caught his eyes and read the faith there. Here was one at least who did not begrudge the Goddess Her due.

But for now his duty was to another. Ehiru said nothing as he passed the old man and entered the dwelling. She would be in the servant quarters. He stepped through a hanging and discovered a vast courtyard where a lesser house's atrium would be. Several tiny cottages clustered here. Some showed personal touches—a flower garden in front of this one, inexpert glyphs decorating the walls of that. He examined each house in turn, contemplating what he'd fathomed of the tithebearer from her note. It had been brief, using the blocky pictorals of a semiliterate rather than the more elegant hieratics taught to higher castes. Simple language, a simple request, written inexpertly but with care . . . His eyes settled on the nearest of the cottages. Conservatively decorated, comfortable in appearance, linked to the house by a neat path of river stones. Yes, this would be the one.

As Ehiru pushed open the front hanging, the smell hit him: old blood, feces, infection. Neither the herbalist's incense nor the sachets of dried flowers hanging from the ceiling could mask the stench. There were few diseases that magic could not heal, but those were always the worst. The cottage was little more than a single large room. A tiny altar stood in one corner; a firepit took up another. The far end of the room was dominated by a small pallet, on which lay a silent, shuddering form: the tithebearer.

But she was not alone. A boy-child who could have seen no more than six floods, seven at the most, knelt beside the pallet. Beside him were bowls, wadded cloths, a plate that held some sort of herbal *paste, and the incense-brazier. A child so young, nursing his mother as she lay dying?*

*Then the child turned and gazed at him with eyes like desert jasper gone dull with age, and Ehiru experienced a sudden flutter of intuition. The shaky, crude pictorals of the note. Not an adult's hand at all.*

*"Are you the Gatherer?" the boy asked. His voice was very soft.*

*"Yes."*

*The child nodded. "She stopped talking this morning." He turned back to the woman and laid his small hand on her trembling one. "She's been waiting for you."*

*After a moment's contemplation Ehiru stepped forward and knelt beside the boy. The woman was awake—but so far gone with pain that Ehiru marveled at her silence. The disease was a cruel one that he had seen before, infecting the bowels so that the victim's own body poisoned itself trying to fight the invader. Too late by the time the first symptoms appeared. She would have been passing blood for days, unable to draw nourishment from food, burning with fever even as she took chill from shock. Ehiru had heard the pain described as if some animal nested within the victim's gut and sought to chew its way out.*

*Her eyes were fixed on the ceiling. Ehiru passed a hand before her face but they flickered only a little. He sighed and reached up to lower his hood—then paused as he considered the boy's presence. The child had sent for him, but probably on his mother's request. Could a child so young comprehend the blessing that a Gatherer brought?*

*Yet as he looked again into the child's ancient, soul-weary eyes, he knew this one could.*

So he lowered his hood and put a hand on the child's shoulder, squeezing gently for a moment before returning his attention to the woman. "I am Ehiru, named Nsha in dreams. I come as summoned to deliver you from the pains of waking into the peace of dream. Will you accept Hananja's blessing?"

No response—save a faint racking shudder—from the woman. "She accepts," the boy whispered. After a moment, Ehiru nodded.

So he stroked her eyelids shut and sent her to sleep, and crafted a dream that brought her pleasure in place of torment. When he opened his eyes to observe her last breath, her cheeks glistened with tears and her face was rapt with joy. He lifted the sheet to arrange her and to set his mark on her breast. It was beautiful against her unblemished red-brown skin. He so rarely Gathered women, and this was a young one at that.

"Thank you," the boy whispered.

Ehiru focused on him, contemplating. "Where is your father?"

The boy only shook his head. He was servant-caste; any man who'd felt a passing fancy for his mother could've sired him. No relatives would be willing or able to support him. The master of the house might keep him, or release him to find a new master if he could. Then his life would continue in years of endless, mindless toil.

He held out a hand to the child. "Does it pain you?"

The boy's eyes lifted slowly. "Hn?"

"Your heart."

"Oh. Yes, Gatherer."

Ehiru nodded. "I'm no Sharer, but I have your mother's peace within me. If anyone has the right to it, you do. Give me your hand."

The child took his hand—with no hesitation or fear, Ehiru noted, pleased. So he pulled the boy into his arms and held him and shared with him an instant of the bliss that his mother would now know for eternity. A bit of cautery; no more than that. Dreamblood might soothe wounds of the heart, but it was never right to take the pain away completely.

The child went limp in his arms and began to weep, and Ehiru smiled.

A step behind him. He rose and turned with the child in his arms and saw the master standing at the threshold of the cottage. The rest of the family and servants hovered behind him, peering in. "Gatherer?"

"If you have no objection, Sijankes-elder, I'll take this child back to the Hetawa with me."

The elder's eyebrows rose. "I have no objection, Gatherer, but . . . are you certain? He's only a child, too young yet to be much use as a servant."

Only a child, and only a servant, but able to accept death and understand its blessing. Ehiru shifted the child to lean him against one shoulder and smiled as thin arms encircled his neck. As a Gatherer, he had never expected, nor wanted, sons. In spite of this, he stroked the boy's back, and for just a moment wondered if this was how it felt to have one.

"He will serve the Goddess now," he said.

And then he left with the boy safe in his arms, a mother's dreamblood warm inside him, and tears of love drying against his skin.

\* \* \*

Ehiru watched as Sharer Mni-inh, fingers on Nijiri's closed lids, sighed and opened his eyes.

"You were right to share peace with him immediately. His umblikeh was a hair from snapping." The Sharer took his hands from the boy. "He'll recover with no permanent harm—physically, at least."

Ehiru sent a prayer of thanks to the Goddess. "The creature was on him for only a breath. Gatherings are never so quick."

"You can't call this a Gathering." Mni-inh scowled so fiercely that his thin, fine brows almost met in the middle of his forehead. "It's too obscene for that. The humor was stripped with such speed and force that it left great rents in his mind. I've healed them, but there will be scars."

Ehiru ached in silent misery, lowering his eyes to the alcove floor. "My fault."

"Don't you dare blame yourself. Though if I hadn't seen the evidence with my own eyes, I would never have believed it. Gods; a *Reaper*." He shook his head as he got to his feet to stretch, eyeing Ehiru sidelong. "I would've said the madness had taken you."

"I would've said the same before tonight," Ehiru replied. He lifted a hand to one temple to massage the dull ache there. "But visions don't leave bruises, or bodies."

Mni-inh frowned, stepping closer and pushing Ehiru's hand away. Ehiru felt the Sharer's cooler fingers press against his temple, followed by the more subtle touch of another soul against his own. "You spent your last reserve giving peace to the boy. And took no tithe tonight?"

"No."

The Sharer's lips twitched, probably in disapproval. "You need an infusion, then. I'll wake Inesst. He has enough left to share with you, and it's almost time for his duty-shift anyhow."

Ehiru hesitated. "I think…I would prefer to face the pranje. Now, rather than at my usual time."

Mni-inh scowled. "You've been foolish about this long enough, Ehiru. You've served more than enough penance—"

"That is for Hananja to say, not you." Ehiru folded his arms and fixed his gaze on Nijiri, feeling more certain of his decision as he did so. "I tried to Gather last night, and circumstances demanded an abeyance. Then I tried to prevent a murder and failed. A child is dead, her soul banished to torment. Her body lies in an alley like trash, and now my apprentice has been harmed as well. Does that sound as though Hananja still wants me to work, Mni-inh?"

"It sounds like you're seeing omens around every corner!"

Ehiru pointed a finger at Nijiri's prone form. The boy still slept, but was beginning to breathe faster as he recovered. "*There* lies an omen. What do you think it means?" Mni-inh flinched at his sharpness, and with an effort Ehiru restrained his anger before it could alarm the Sharer further. More calmly he said, "Do you believe it was all a vision?"

Mni-inh rolled his eyes. "No, obviously something happened to Nijiri. But your reserves are low enough to be problematic, Ehiru, you cannot deny—"

"I don't want to deny it. I welcome it. I'll go into seclusion now if you think I should, but I won't ignore this coincidence, if that it is. I think She calls me to commune with Her, Mni-inh. I am Her Servant; I must obey."

"And your apprentice?" Mni-inh gestured toward Nijiri, his own anger bordering on the unpeaceful. "If you undergo the pranje now and She tells you to offer the Final Tithe, he'll be left alone."

"Sonta-i can—"

"Sonta-i has trouble mustering enough simple human compassion to comfort his tithebearers, much less anyone else!"

"Rabbaneh, then."

Mni-inh scowled in exasperation and poked Ehiru in the chest with a finger. "*You*, stubborn fool. You're the one the boy is in love with." Ehiru flinched at Mni-inh's bluntness—but then Mni-inh had always been too blunt, willing to say things no Gatherer would put to words. Most Sharers wouldn't have, either; that was just Mni-inh's way. "It's a good thing; only love can heal scars like his. And yours, if you ever decide to do more than just let them fester."

Ehiru took an involuntary step back, unbalanced by more than the jab. "I . . ."

Nijiri chose that moment, conveniently, to stir. Throwing a last glare at Ehiru, Mni-inh went to the boy's pallet and knelt, lifting one of his eyelids to peer within. Pursing his lips as he gauged something only a Sharer could fathom, Mni-inh then leaned down and whispered in the boy's ear.

Nijiri's eyelids flicked open, blank and disoriented—and then he bucked, throwing Mni-inh off and rolling away. He backed himself against the alcove wall in a crouch, eyes wild, before the Sharer could do more than gasp out a swift oath and reach after him.

Ehiru quickly caught Mni-inh's hand. Sentinel training functioned in concert with instinct; in this state, the boy might break the Sharer's arm. Pushing Mni-inh back, he crouched low so as to seem less threatening. "Peace, Nijiri. The danger has passed."

It took several breaths for sense to flow back into the boy's eyes. When it did he shut them again and sagged against the wall. "Brother."

Ehiru crept closer. "Here. The demon's gone. We've come home to the Hetawa, and you're safe in Hananja's own Hall. See?"

He got close enough to reach out and touch Nijiri's cheek with his fingertips. The boy's eyes opened and for a moment Ehiru was thrown ten years back in time. *Desert jasper.* Then the vision passed.

"Yes," Nijiri whispered. "I see you, Brother."

Beyond them, Mni-inh dared to take a step closer. "How do you feel, Gatherer-Apprentice?"

Nijiri sighed and shifted to sit on his knees. Ehiru took his hand as a pranje attendant would have, to help him focus. "Like a forty of children dance a prayer inside my skull, Sharer Mni-inh, with every one of them wearing thick, heavy sandals. Forgive my irreverence."

Mni-inh let out a chuckle breathy with relief. "Under the circumstances I'll gladly forgive you, Apprentice. Do you remember what happened?"

The boy's face grew momentarily still. "I remember...an alley. No. A darker place. There were creatures. I...I saw them breathing..." Abruptly he shook his head. "I remember nothing more."

The boy's furrowed brow and tight lips said otherwise, but Ehiru did not press and neither did Mni-inh. Instead the Sharer touched his other hand. "Your memory may return in time. For now, you need rest—"

"Sharers," Ehiru said. "Always putting body before soul." He got to his feet, pulling the boy up with him; Nijiri swayed a bit but then steadied. "The threat to the people is more important than our comfort, Mni-inh. We'll both rest after we've made our report."

The boy focused on him, nodded agreement. Mni-inh rolled his eyes.

"Gatherers, too stubborn for sanity!" He mimicked Ehiru's voice. "Very well. I'll send an acolyte to wake the Superior—"

"No need, Mni-inh."

They turned. The Superior stood in the doorway of the healing alcove, flanked by Dinyeru, a senior Sentinel. A hastily donned robe draped the Superior's shoulders, but his eyes were clear—and hard.

Two more warriors stood beyond him, Ehiru noticed abruptly. Strangers, wearing the red and gold of the Sunset Guard.

"Gatherer," the Superior said quietly, "present yourself for the judgment of the Hetawa."

Nijiri gasped. Ehiru stared back at the Superior, uncomprehending. Mni-inh recovered first. "Superior, you cannot believe that *Ehiru…*"

"I believe many things, Mni-inh." The Superior stepped aside; Dinyeru and the two strangers came into the alcove. In Dinyeru's hands was an odd contraption—two long, hinged cylinders sealed together down the length, each ending in a round bulb. Manacles, meant to enclose the forearms and force the hands into closed fists—a rogue's yoke. Ehiru had seen the device many times as a child, while cleaning items in the Heta-wa's archival vault. It had never been used in his lifetime.

"I believe in the beneficence of our Goddess," the Superior continued. "I believe in the honor and judgment of our Prince. Therefore I must believe it when his guardsmen come to tell me that a child was murdered in the city last night—a companion of the Kisuati ambassador Sunandi Jeh Kalawe. Your commission, Ehiru, was she not?"

Ehiru, shocked, made several attempts to speak before his voice worked. "Yes—that northblooded youngster. Yes, her body…"

"The child's body showed terrible desecration, Ehiru, of soul as well as flesh. It was found in an alleyway." The Superior's voice never rose, but his words grew sharp as blades. "What have you done with the Kisuati woman's body, Gatherer?"

Ehiru stared at him. "*Done?* There was no body. I declared an abeyance until I could discuss the matter with you—"

"No, there's no body. Her bedchamber is disordered by the signs of struggle; a weapon was found but *she* is gone." The Superior shook his head then, sorrow eclipsing anger in his face. "It's clear the madness hasn't taken you fully, Ehiru, or you would have been unable to stop yourself from killing your apprentice tonight. I thank the Goddess for that. Because of it I cannot cast you out; some part of you is still our black rose."

"All of him, Superior!" Mni-inh stepped forward. "I've examined this man. His reserves are gone, true. He may be afflicted by the early symptoms, but there's none of the spirit-wide corruption you're accusing him of. For the Dreamer's sake, he's *empty*, Superior—if he had taken a child and a woman and then attacked Nijiri, he wouldn't be!"

"The woman was alive when we left," Nijiri said, stepping closer to Ehiru. His tone bordered on disrespectful, Ehiru noted through a haze; he would have to take the boy to task for that. "She said she was leaving town, she and her girl. She feared an assassin would be sent, to kill her for her secrets."

"That may be," the Superior said, though he sounded less than convinced, to Ehiru's ears. "An Assay of Truth will determine the fullness of it. In the meantime, the Prince demands that the threat to his city be subdued."

Behind him Nijiri was compounding his disrespect, speaking with unseemly loudness. "The creature that killed the child was *not* Ehiru-brother. I saw it! It touched me and, and—" He faltered, took a shaky breath. "It was not my mentor. Ehiru-brother fought the creature off me, saved me. It was someone else. Some*thing* else."

"No other Gatherers went out last night, Nijiri." The Superior had regained control of himself; his voice was inflectionless. "Sonta-i and Rabbaneh had a much-deserved night off. The girl-child died in obvious agony, but no fatal wounds had been inflicted on her before death."

"That's because a Reaper—"

"That is a myth, *Apprentice*," said the Superior, and Nijiri flinched into resentful silence. "A myth told around campfires to make the desert nights pass. A rogue Gatherer has no special power or invincibility; he is nothing more than a pathetic creature consumed by his own weakness who may have to be put down for the safety of all."

"Then where are Ehiru's pathbrothers?" Mni-inh gestured sharply at the curtain and the Hetawa beyond. "Why these strangers, unsworn, untrained? We have always taken care of our own—"

"Because the Prince demands it!" Both Nijiri and Mni-inh flinched back from the Superior's flare of temper. Ehiru barely noticed; too much of him had gone numb. From the corner of his eye, he saw the Superior pause and visibly struggle for calm. "Some things are beyond even the Hetawa's discipline," the Superior said at last, and this time Ehiru heard an odd tightness in his voice. As if the words half-choked him coming out. "Ehiru will be held in Yanya-iyan. We must consider what is best for all Gujaareh, not just for the Hetawa." He gestured and Dinyeru came forward.

"Forgive me, Gatherer." Dinyeru raised the yoke, holding it so Ehiru could thrust his hands into the sleeves. The Sentinel's expression was sorrowful—but determined. Not even a Gatherer could best a Sentinel in combat.

Silence fell. Ehiru closed his eyes.

"I am still Her servant," he whispered, and thrust his arms forward into the yoke. Cold metal embraced them. He fisted his hands and grimaced as the straps along the sleeves were tightened, pulling his forearms together into an uncomfortably awkward position. A metal brace was snapped into place across his wrists, locking them together.

Then new hands took his upper arms—the hands of strangers, gripping him without love—and he was pulled along with them out of the Hetawa.

# 12

(• ◉ •)

*At the mouth of the river, which he named for the
blood of Hananja, Inunru built a city.*

(Wisdom)

"What do you mean, Lin hasn't arrived yet?" Sunandi demanded.

"*Seya*, Jeh Kalawe, I mean she hasn't come." Etissero eyed
Sunandi in mild surprise. "I haven't seen that straw-haired ras-
cal since your delegation passed through a season ago, when you
first came to the city. I would have remembered the girl: she
nicked my purse the last time she was here."

"And gave it back."

Etissero shrugged good-naturedly. "My people part fools from
their funds all the time. Our children play such games to learn
the trade. They don't usually put the mark on *me*, though, and
even more rarely do they manage to score." He smiled. "I could
make a fine tradewife of that girl, if you sold her to me."

"Alas, my father decided long ago that Lin and I should learn
to part fools from their secrets instead."

"A shame for both of you. There's no money in spying."

Sunandi shook her head in amusement, recognizing Etissero's effort to put her at ease. Dawn had broken nearly an hour ago, and she'd spent the two hours before that in harrowing flight through the corridors of Yanya-iyan and the streets of Gujaareh. But here in the Unbelievers' District, as the guest of a wealthy Bromarte, she could rest safely hidden in the sprawling community beyond Gujaareh's walls. The district had grown over the centuries to house foreign merchants and other opportunists who were eager to profit from Gujaareh's wealth, but unwilling or unable for reasons of their own faith to submit to Hananja's Law. Outside, the streets were thick with people eager to get their business done before the full heat of the day struck. Sunandi observed them for a few moments, momentarily surprised by how odd their bustling hurry seemed after the two months she'd spent in the city. Gujaareen rarely hurried.

Well, Kisuati-reared spy-girls were supposed to hurry, and it troubled Sunandi that Lin had not yet arrived at Etissero's. She'd had a good hour's start on Sunandi, and that was more than enough time for her to have talked her way past a gate or hired a ferryman.

Then again—

"I had trouble getting out of the city," Sunandi said, pulling the curtain shut. "None of my friends were on duty. That ordinarily wouldn't have been a problem—I had enough funds to pay the toll and a bribe, and they knew from my accent that I was a foreigner. But they were more wary than usual. They questioned me closely."

"Questioned you about what?"

"Who I was, where I was going, why I was leaving at the crack of dawn. I gave them my usual story for unusual circumstances—a timbalin-house mistress going to meet with a distributor to arrange an extra shipment." She brushed a hand against the gown she still wore, which was made of fine pleated linen rather than the more practical hekeh. The pleats emphasized the points of her breasts, which was something that had usually worked in her favor before. Men rarely remembered her face. "I looked the part, but they barely believed me. They checked my eyes to make sure I was a timbalin addict. They wanted to know which house could afford a mistress with such high coloring."

Etissero muttered something in his own language, then returned to Gujaareen so that she could understand him. "They're only that keen when they're on the watch for something. What did you say?"

"That I worked for the most expensive house in the high-caste district. That I was once an account-keeper in Kisua before I fell low, which explained the accent. And thankfully, my eyes were still bloodshot from being woken in the middle of the night by a *dekado* Gatherer and his little killer-in-training, so they let me through." She sighed and ran a hand over the brief, tight curls of her hair. "I think the gods must have granted me more than my share of luck in the last few hours."

The clan leader made no reply, and Sunandi was startled to realize he was staring at her, his face even paler than normal.

"You saw a Gatherer?"

"I told you someone tried to kill me. Though I talked him out of it."

"No one talks a Gatherer out of killing. At the most they stay their hand for a few days. Then they come after you again."

She sighed and went over to a bench between two carved plinths. It wasn't padded—a Bromarte custom intended to keep their traders' minds sharp even when they were at rest—and she winced as she sat down too hard. *Too many months living in luxury. I'm becoming as soft as the Prince.*

No. The Prince only seemed soft on the surface. Peacock and pleasure-hound he might be, but no one soft could play such dangerous, terrible games.

"Abeyance," she said at last. "That's what the Gatherer granted me while he investigates my story to see if it is true."

"Then, my sweet Sunandi, you are a dead woman." Etissero gazed at her solemnly.

She rubbed her face, still sleepy. "Perhaps. The fool planned to go back to his Hetawa and demand the truth from his masters. Hopefully they'll kill him and solve my problem."

"If they kill him, another Gatherer will be sent. The Hetawa always fulfills a commission once judgment has been rendered. They consider it a sacred duty." Etissero folded his hands and sighed. "Damn them. I never thought I'd lose anyone to their evil, let alone two in the span of a month."

"Don't put me in an urn already, man—" She paused, frowning as his words penetrated. "Two?"

"My cousin." Etissero leaned his elbows on the desk and sighed. "You met him. Negotiator in Gujaareh for his wife's clan; kept an ear to the ground among the merchants and common folk for me. He lived within the city's walls—*liked* it there, the fool. Said it was soothing. But several days ago they found him dead in his bed. The innkeeper said it looked as though he had been Gathered. To me it looked more like he'd had a heart-seizure or something else painful in his sleep, but those Gujaareen can always read a death."

Sunandi frowned at the dark flicker of memory brought on by Etissero's words. They'd called Kinja's death a heart-seizure, too. "I remember the man. Large fellow? He kept telling me how much he liked dark women."

"The very one. Charleron." Etissero shook his head. "Only the day before, I'd received a letter from him saying he was coming to visit. We never spoke about clan business, but he shared any interesting gossip that he heard with me. This time he'd heard something important that he wanted to tell me in person. Something about a rift between the Hetawa and the Sunset."

Sunandi inhaled and stared at him.

"Yes, I know. And then he turned up dead. Murdering *gualoh*." He rubbed his eyes with one hand, pausing for a moment to master himself; Bromarte men did not cry in front of women. "The Hetawa paid for his funeral. Hired mourners and a chantress, bought him a lapis-covered urn, put him in their own special vault above the floodline. Buried him like a king after they killed him. How I hate this city."

Silence had its own eloquence at times, so Sunandi kept hers.

It lasted only for a moment, however, until the house's heavy wooden door—a necessity in this district, and double-locked—banged downstairs. Light quick feet on the steps told them that Etissero's young son Saladronim had returned from his morning shift as a messenger. The boy came up the steps breathless, his cheeks flushed pink and eyes bright. He paused only long enough to offer a quick bow to Sunandi before blurting his news.

"Soldiers, Father. In the marketplace."

Etissero frowned. Sunandi rose and went to the window. Behind her she heard the trader quizzing Saladronim; the boy's careful recital of details and observations put a momentary smile on her lips. Kinja had not been the only one to see the merits of sharp-witted children, it seemed.

Below, in the streets, she saw what the boy meant. Amid the drab earth colors of common folk going about their business, flashes of brighter color stood out. A scattering of warriors in bronze half-torso armor moved through the crowd. Their skirts were a rusty red-orange, and their yellow headcloths swung from side to side. Searching. Cold prickled along her spine.

Etissero rose and came to the window beside Sunandi. "That isn't the city guard. I've never seen men wearing those colors before."

"I have," Sunandi said. She stepped back from the window, crossing her arms over her breasts to stop herself from shivering. "They are the Prince's own men, the Sunset Guard. They leave the palace only on his direct orders."

Etissero raised an eyebrow at her. "If you weren't Kisuati, you'd be pale now."

She took a deep breath, trying to calm her fluttering heart. "That Gatherer was sent to kill me. Perhaps the Prince has decided to make certain the job is done properly."

Etissero nodded slowly. Near the desk, Etissero's son sat cross-legged on the floor, watching both of them avidly.

"You'll have to remain here," the trader said. "No one knows you're in this house. Stay hidden for a few days and they'll decide that you must have reached the trade-roads. They'll move on, and then so can you."

She frowned at that. "No. Kinja's information—"

"Has waited since Kinja died, two seasons ago. Whatever recent discoveries you've made will survive another fourday's delay. Leaving now means the Protectors never get this information, because those men will catch you and kill you. Better late than never, hmm?"

He was right. Sunandi began to pace, in an effort to vent her restlessness. "Very well. But not a fourday."

"If—"

"If what I've learned is true, the Prince's plans could spell destruction for us all—northerner and southerner, Gujaareen and Kisuati and everyone who trades with either land. Better in time than too late, hmm?"

Etissero sighed. "I thank the gods of wind and fortune our women care more about money than politics in the north. I don't know what I'd do if I had to go home to one like you."

Sunandi permitted herself a small smile.

"Fine, then." Etissero flicked the hangings around the window closed. "How do you want to do it?"

"See if Gehanu's group is in town. I've traveled with them before, and they make the run from Gujaareh to Kisua often at this time of year." She took a deep breath. "That leaves me with only one worry."

Lin. Etissero saw her face and understood.

He went over to his son and put a hand on the boy's shoulder.

"Fetch refreshments for our guest—figs and almonds if we have them, kanpo-nut and cheese if we don't." The boy jumped up and went downstairs, and Etissero eyed Sunandi. "You should build your strength for the journey. The desert is hard on the weak."

His words chafed no less, she decided, for all that they were true. So she seated herself on the hard bench, and ate when Saladronim brought her food, and tried her best to invent new and scathing scolds to heap upon Lin when she finally arrived.

# 13

( ⊙ )

*A Gatherer shall neither marry nor acquire property.*
*He shall sully not his body with drug, sex, or other*
*impairment; nor his soul with personal attachments*
*beyond those of faith and brotherhood. He is the*
*right hand of Hananja, and to Her he belongs wholly.*

(Law)

The din of the late-morning market floated in through the narrow cell window in a babble of voices, clanging objects, and the clucks and bleats of animals. There was comfort in it despite the cacophony, for it was the sound of the city's daily routine. How could Hananja not be pleased by the order and prosperity of Her people? Ehiru smiled to himself as he knelt in the light and listened.

Then, from behind, the sound of his cell door's lock jarred the steady drone of the market. Ehiru glanced around, curious. The men in the guard-station had been solicitous toward him thus far, their ingrained respect for Gatherers still strong despite the ignominy of his circumstances. They had not disturbed him since he'd been brought to the station. But now three men stepped within, pausing until the door shut again behind them. Two were the Sunset Guardsmen who had brought him to the station. They took up positions on either side of the door, hands resting on knife-hilts. The third man was a bearded stranger in the garb of a midcasteman—an artisan, Ehiru guessed by the loose smock and headcloth the man wore. And yet...Ehiru narrowed his eyes, frowning at an odd sense of familiarity about the man's build and carriage.

"Don't you recognize me, Ehiru? I do this to fool the commoners when I walk among them, but I never imagined it would fool you as well." The artisan stepped into the patch of light, smiling with lazy—and familiar—amusement.

Ehiru caught his breath. "Eninket?"

The Prince raised both eyebrows, smile widening. "I haven't heard that name in years. Mind you—I'm supposed to have you killed for uttering it." He moved past Ehiru to the narrow shelf that served as the cell's bed, and seated himself with regal grace. "But I think we can ignore protocol under the circumstances."

As the shock faded, Ehiru composed himself and shifted to face the Prince. As best he could, for the rogue's yoke interfered with movement, he lifted his arms in manuflection and spoke in Sua. "Please forgive me, my Prince. I meant no disrespect."

"You need not retreat behind formality, either," the Prince replied in kind, then switched back to Gujaareen so they could speak casually. "I've yearned to speak with you in private for years, Ehiru. I'll admit this is unfair, doing this when you're effectively captive, but you refused all of my invitations."

"I am a mere Servant of Hananja. You are the Bringer of Night, Herald of Dreams, Her consort-to-be in Ina-Karekh. It is not the place of a servant to dine at the master's table."

"It isn't the place of a servant to avoid the master, either," the Prince retorted, then sighed. "No, this isn't how I wanted it. We're here now, Ehiru. Can't we be brothers again, at least for a few moments?"

Ehiru kept his eyes on the floor, though he finally lowered his arms and dispensed with Sua as well. "Can a bird return to its egg? You call me brother, but we have not been that for decades. And perhaps—"

He bit the words back, closing his eyes as memories assailed him with sudden, painful force. The scent of blood like metal on the tongue. His mother's mortal gasp. He could almost see the rose-marble walls of Kite-iyan around him…

*Vision*, he told himself, and grimly refocused his mind on the present.

"And perhaps we never were brothers?" the Prince asked. His voice was soft and sober in the dim chamber. "So I was right. You don't understand. Or forgive." Ehiru said nothing, and the Prince sighed. "There were those who would have used you and the rest of our siblings to sow chaos throughout Gujaareh, Ehiru. Think: your mother was Kisuati sonha, from an old and well-connected lineage. Would her son not have been more palatable to the nobles than the son of a commonborn dancer, as Prince? Even a daughter from a good lineage could have been used to foment unrest, for Gujaareh has had female Princes in its past. I did what was necessary for peace—though I'd never intended for our mothers to suffer. They were supposed to be set free, not killed." He sighed heavily. "That was an error, and the men who committed it were punished."

The vision was gone, but in its place Ehiru discovered a flicker of anger, swiftly growing. He fought to keep it banked and his eyes on the floor. "Death is always difficult to control," he said, very softly. "I live that truth every night."

"Then perhaps things would have gone better if I'd had a Gatherer's discipline." He paused, gazing steadily at Ehiru. "I kept expecting you to come for me, you realize. As soon as I heard you'd been chosen as the next Gatherer-Apprentice, I thought, 'Now I will face justice for my crimes.' But you never came."

Ehiru forced himself to shrug. "Heirs have assassinated their way to the Aureole since Gujaareh began. Even the Hetawa accepts the cruelty that is necessary to gain and keep power—so long as a Prince uses it to maintain peace from there on. Over time my brothers"—he put the faintest emphasis on the word—"have helped me to understand this."

The Prince made a sound of disgust, which startled Ehiru into looking up at him. "The Hetawa. You truly have become theirs, Ehiru. How they must love having another of our lineage in their thrall."

The anger grew by another measure, and Ehiru discarded protocol. "Explain."

"Ah, so I've offended you. But I won't ask your pardon, my Brother, for I am unrepentant in my hatred of your adoptive family. As should you be." The Prince gestured toward the rogue's yoke; Ehiru flinched. "It was they who unjustly put that on you, after all."

"The Superior said *you* commanded it."

"I commanded your removal, Ehiru, before the Superior could end your life. Not this humiliation." Abruptly the Prince gestured to one of the Guardsmen. "Find the key for that monstrosity he's wearing. I can't stand looking at it any longer." The Guard snapped a bow, banged a pattern on the door of the chamber, and exited when the door opened.

Ehiru's fists, already sweaty and cramped after hours in the yoke, tightened further. *"Explain."*

The Prince regarded him for a long moment. Then said, "There is indeed a Reaper in the city, Ehiru. It killed quietly until lately—men in the prison, elders whose deaths could be made to look natural, and the like. I've known of it for months."

"And you said nothing to the Hetawa?"

"They already knew."

Ehiru's jaw tightened. "I do not believe that."

"Of course you don't. And I have no way to prove my allegations to you. Nevertheless, they have kept the news of this Reaper quiet for reasons only the Superior and his highest subordinates comprehend. I've been trying to find some means of proving the Reaper's existence, to force them to act—but there have been other matters distracting me lately. This Kisuati spy, among many."

Ehiru nodded. "Then the commission came from you. You sent me to Gather her. For *political* reasons."

"I did indeed. She threatens this city. Why didn't you kill her?"

"Gathering is not assassination!"

The Prince rolled his eyes. "Have you never questioned your

commissions before, Ehiru? The Kisuati woman would not have been the first."

Ehiru caught his breath and stared at the Prince, too revolted to respond. In the intervening silence the Guardsman returned. He moved to kneel at Ehiru's side but the Prince abruptly rose from the cot, brushing him aside and taking the key. He knelt in front of Ehiru. The Guardsman gasped and immediately removed his front loindrape to lay on the ground for the Prince to kneel upon. The Prince waved it away, never taking his eyes from Ehiru's.

"Remember that I freed you, Brother," the Prince whispered, "while your Hetawa locked you away. Remember that much, if nothing else."

Ehiru blinked out of his shock and stared as the Prince deftly undid the locks and buckles of the rogue's yoke. He pulled it off Ehiru's arms and threw it into a corner, where it landed with a loud clatter. Ehiru jerked at the noise, then turned his eyes back to Eninket—the Prince—with an effort.

"Why?" he asked, meaning many whys.

The Prince smiled. "I can't tell you everything. You wouldn't understand anyhow, isolated as they've kept you. Suffice it to say that the Hetawa is corrupt; your brethren are dangerous to you now. I'll do what I can to clear your name and expose their crimes, but you must do something for me in return."

*The Hetawa was corrupt.* Ehiru shook his head, unable to absorb such a monstrous concept. "What?"

"The Kisuati woman. She cannot be permitted to reach Kisua, Ehiru, or there will be war. My men believe she is still in the outer city, the Unbelievers' District. Find her. Complete the

Gathering. Do this and I will see to it that you can return to the Hetawa in honor instead of shame. By our holy blood, I swear it."

To return to the Hetawa. To regain the order and peace that had been missing from his life for what seemed like ages… Ehiru closed his eyes, aching with silent longing.

The Prince smiled and lifted his hands to cup Ehiru's face. "I know you'll do what's right, my brother."

He kissed Ehiru then: once on each cheek, on the forehead, and on the lips. It was the way Ehiru's father had kissed him during his childhood before the Hetawa, and memories arose at once to buffet him like mountain winds.

Then the Prince released him, stood, and turned away to rap on the cell door. The Guardsmen fell in behind him as the door opened. When they were gone the door remained open, waiting for Ehiru.

Slowly Ehiru straightened, untied his waist-pouch, and poured the contents into one hand. His ornaments gleamed back at him, the Kisuati woman's scored coin among them.

Carefully—for his hands shook again and this time he could not still them—he put all except the coin back into the pouch. Then he got to his feet, moving slowly as an old man, and walked out of the cell.

# 14

*By the age of four floods, a Gujaareen child should be able to write the pictorals of the family name, count by fours to forty, and recite the details of every dream upon waking.*

(Wisdom)

Nijiri sat in the Stone Garden trying to keep his knuckles from turning white. They would be watching for that. He could give them no cause to doubt his self-control—not if he wanted to be left free and unchaperoned. Not if he meant to go and find Ehiru.

"Hiding something again," Sonta-i said. He stood across from Nijiri near a column of nightstone, just as unyielding. "You think we cannot guess your plans. You think we cannot smell the fury curling off you like smoke."

Damnation.

"Is my anger not understandable, Brother?" Nijiri kept his voice calm. "What surprises me is your lack of it. Does Hananja's peace silence all sense of propriety and justice?"

"We feel the anger, little brother," Rabbaneh said from behind Nijiri. A hand came to rest on his shoulder, squeezing gently. "Dreamblood silences nothing. It merely...softens." He paused, then said thoughtfully, "Perhaps if you were to share our peace—"

Nijiri pulled away. He took care to keep the movement smooth and minimal, polite aversion rather than vehement rejection. "I would prefer to find peace on my own."

Rabbaneh sighed and dropped his hand. "The choice is always yours. But please try to remember, little brother, that Ehiru went *willingly*."

"Yes." Nijiri saw the scene again in his mind: the shame in the Superior's eyes, and the aching grief in Ehiru's. "He went because the Hetawa betrayed him and he could not bear to be among the corrupt any longer."

"You trespass," Sonta-i warned.

Nijiri got to his feet and turned to face them, his fists clenched at his sides. "I speak the truth, Sonta-i-brother. I saw the beast that attacked me last night. *I suffered its touch.* And the only reason I survived is because Ehiru-brother fought it away and gave me his last dreamblood. Sharer Mni-inh saw the evidence of this and vouches for Ehiru-brother. Even the Superior acknowledged that imprisoning our brother was not justice but the will of Yanya-iyan. *Politics.*"

He spat out the last word like the poison it was, and was gratified to see Rabbaneh grimace in distaste. Sonta-i's normally impassive expression grew thoughtful, however. Sonta-i would be the key, Nijiri knew. The dreaming gift had come upon Sonta-i too young, or so went the rumors among the acolytes. He had no true emotions, though he mimicked them well enough when necessary, and he drew no distinction between the waking world and the vagaries of dream. Neither could be trusted; neither was real in his eyes. It was a disadvantage in Gathering, but there were times—like now, perhaps—when Sonta-i's view of the world made him the most flexible and pragmatic of all the Gatherers. Self-interest, not tradition or faith, drove him. If Nijiri could appeal to this, Sonta-i might prove an unexpected ally.

"We do not judge—" Rabbaneh began.

"But we traditionally have some say," Sonta-i interrupted. "Especially in the matter of our own. It *is* strange that we were not consulted."

Nijiri held his breath.

"The Superior had to make a quick decision." Rabbaneh folded his arms and began to pace—and this tension too was a sign, Nijiri realized. The Superior's decision sat poorly with both his pathbrothers.

"If Mni-inh had declared Ehiru a danger, then the Superior's quick decision would have been justified," Sonta-i said. "Mni-inh says his mind is yet whole."

"It is," Nijiri blurted. "He shows only the early signs so far, just hand-shaking and a bit of temper—"

He realized his error when they both glared at him. Sonta-i's face somehow became just a touch colder.

"The method of any Gatherer's communion with the Goddess is private, Nijiri," he said. "You will understand that better—and no doubt respect it more—when you've had to face the long night without dreamblood yourself."

Nijiri bowed over both his hands in shame. "Forgive me. It's only…" His shoulders and throat tightened. *Goddess, no, not tears. Not now.* "I can't bear this."

Rabbaneh stopped pacing, his expression strained and grim. "Nor can I." He turned to Sonta-i. "You understand what this means."

Sonta-i nodded. "We don't have enough information to make an assessment yet. Therefore we must acquire more."

"Perhaps we should take this to the Council of Paths," Rabbaneh said. "Our judgment may be impaired by our closeness to the situation—"

Sonta-i looked at him; Rabbaneh fell silent. Nijiri frowned at both in confusion.

"No," Rabbaneh said at last. He turned away, his back stiff, and sighed. "I don't really believe that."

Sonta-i regarded Rabbaneh for a moment. Then he turned to Nijiri, his gaze speculative. "How will you find him if you go?"

Only Hananja's grace prevented Nijiri from gasping aloud. Instead he took a deep breath to calm the sudden racing of his heart. "He'll be in one of the guard-stations," he said. "Yanya-iyan has no dungeon and the Sunset Guard does not control the prison."

"There are eight guard-stations, Apprentice. One for each quadrant of the city, inner and outer."

"I'll have to check them all, Sonta-i-brother. But I think he'll be at one of the inner stations, since they're closer to Yanya-iyan. I imagine the guards will want to be in range of quick reinforcements, if our brother should somehow break free."

Sonta-i's eyes, gray as stone, probed Nijiri's for several long moments—though what he sought, Nijiri could not fathom. Rabbaneh stared at Sonta-i in disbelief.

"You cannot mean this, Sonta-i."

"Neither you nor I can go," Sonta-i said. "The city has only two working Gatherers left; we are needed."

"So is Nijiri! He must replace Una-une. Bad enough we'll have one green Gatherer, but if Ehiru is lost, we have to begin training another."

"If Ehiru is lost when he *should not be*," Sonta-i said with the faintest of emphasis, "we will have lost far more than a seasoned Gatherer. We will have lost the autonomy that is absolutely essential for our proper function. We will have allowed a clear injustice to impact our actions. We, who must be purest of all."

Rabbaneh shook his head. "But Nijiri is only a boy, Sonta-i."

"He is sixteen, a man by law. In the upriver villages he might be married already, perhaps a father." Sonta-i focused on Nijiri, though his words were for Rabbaneh. "The pursuit of justice is the duty of every Gatherer, even the least of us. One of our brothers has been wrongfully imprisoned."

"This is not the way to free him!"

"Indeed. Only the truth can do that. But the truth in this case intersects with the duty of our path."

"You mean for Ehiru-brother and me to find the Reaper," Nijiri breathed, understanding at last. His head reeled with wonder. "You mean for us to kill it."

Sonta-i nodded. "You'll need proof to clear Ehiru's name. The Reaper's body should do."

"And if you don't find that proof," Rabbaneh said in a tight voice, "neither you nor Ehiru will ever be able to return to the

Hetawa. You'll both be declared corrupt and hunted down. *We* will be sent to hunt you, along with half the Sentinels. Do you understand? While you hunt the Reaper, you walk the Gatherers' path only in Hananja's eyes. No one else—not the city guard, not the Sunset Guard, not the Sentinels—will acknowledge it."

*I chose the Gatherers' path for only one reason anyhow,* Nijiri thought, and lifted his chin. "I'll serve in my heart if serving in public means swallowing injustice."

To his utter shock, Sonta-i smiled. It was a horrible expression beneath his dead gray eyes, lacking the slightest touch of amusement or pleasure, and the sight of it sent a shiver along Nijiri's every nerve.

"Rabbaneh and I do not endure injustice either, Apprentice," Sonta-i said. "We send *you* to kill it."

# 15

( ⊙ )

*Women are goddesses, like unto Hananja Herself. They birth
and shape the dreamers of the world. Love and fear them.*

(Wisdom)

It was the hottest time of the day. Sunandi had fallen asleep on
a couch in the second-floor breezeway when Etissero's son Saladronim prodded her awake. "Jeh Kalawe. A man."

She sat up, bleary from sleep and the heat. A dry, dust-laden
wind blew into the house and set the curtains a-billowing; she
yearned momentarily for the cool moist breezes of Kisua. "Tell
him I'm not interested."

"At the door, Jeh Kalawe. He said he was a merchant but he
didn't look right. He asked after the mistress of the house. I told
him we were Bromarte, we leave our women at home like sensible people. He said that was all right because he wanted to see
the *Kisuati* mistress of the house."

That woke her up. "What did this man look like?"

"Tall. Black as you. Shaven bald but for two long braids at the
nape. He didn't act like a merchant either, Jeh Kalawe. He never
smiled."

"*Bi'incha.*" She knew who it was. "Did you tell him I was here?"

Saladronim gave her a do-you-think-me-mad? look. "I told him there were no women here at all, but there was a timbalin house down the street if he was desperate. Then I closed the door on him."

"I doubt—" But she did not finish her doubt, for the curtains stirred again and the Gatherer stood there, framed in the breezeway door. Her eyes widened. Saladronim followed her gaze, caught his breath, and stumbled back.

The Gatherer inclined his head to each of them, keeping his movements slow and making no move to enter. That drove back Sunandi's terror enough for her to unclench her throat, though she still had to swallow before speaking. "Priest. You nearly scared the life out of us. Or is that your intention today?"

"The abeyance holds," he said to her. His eyes fixed on Saladronim. "Please forgive me for attempting to deceive you, but I had need to speak with this woman."

Saladronim opened his mouth and squeaked, then cleared his throat. "I won't allow you to harm Jeh Kalawe. She is a guest of my father."

Sunandi almost smiled at Saladronim's bravery. He reminded her of Lin, though Lin would never have shown such bravado unless she had a weapon hidden to back it up. To her surprise, the Gatherer's face softened for a moment as well.

*Thinking of his apprentice killer, no doubt.*

"I will not harm her," the Gatherer replied, and Sunandi almost relaxed before she remembered that he didn't consider killing her to be harmful. "May I enter?"

That calmed her at last. Gatherers never begged pardon or asked leave when they were on Hananja's business, which meant he'd come here for his own purposes and not the Gathering. She hoped. Saladronim glanced at her, querying; after a wavering instant, she nodded. Taking a deep breath, the boy nodded as well.

The Gatherer stepped over the threshold, flicking the curtain back into place behind him. As he did so, Sunandi recalled Saladronim's words: *he didn't look right.* No he did not, she agreed, noting that the Gatherer still had on the same loindrapes he'd worn two nights before. He looked more exhausted than the heat could account for, his shoulders slumped and movements noticeably sluggish. In Yanya-iyan, she had guessed his age at around forty floods—though it had been hard to tell for certain, for he and the Prince shared the same peculiar, handsome agelessness. Now he looked all of his years and then some.

Intuition sparked understanding and she said, "They've turned on you, haven't they?"

His head jerked up and he stared at her in something like hatred, but that lasted only a moment before pain replaced it. He looked away.

Answer enough. She took a deep breath and decided to try diplomacy for a change. "Your apprentice?"

He shook his head, eyes fixed on the floor. "I am alone."

"And why have you come?"

"To return to the Hetawa and my life, I must complete your Gathering."

He said it gently, yet the words sent a chill through her in defiance of the afternoon's heat. Beside her, Saladronim stiffened.

"You said I was still in abeyance," she said.

"You are. I don't accept bribes. Not even when the offer is peace, which…" The Gatherer closed his eyes and sighed. "Which I crave more than you can imagine. But it would be a false peace if I simply Gathered you and went back now. I have too many questions." He focused on her. "I require your aid to find answers."

Sunandi nodded to cover her shock. She glanced at Saladronim. "Go inform your father that he has another guest."

Saladronim stared at her in mute disbelief. She stared him down, and after a moment he shook his head and trotted out of the breezeway. She heard his feet slap against the stone steps on the way down, and bet herself three gold coins that he would creep back up to eavesdrop.

But for the moment they had the illusion of privacy, so she turned her attention back to the Gatherer. "It's not my place to offer you hospitality in this house, but I know its owner and he follows true guest-custom. He would not want you to stand when you so clearly should sit."

He hesitated; for a moment she thought he might refuse. But then he moved to the other couch in the breezeway and sat across from her, straight-backed and formal. "Thank you. My path…we sleep in the daytime."

"Civilized of you." She relaxed enough to fan herself, hoping that would encourage him to relax as well. "So you want my aid. I don't know if I can give you the answers you seek, priest. I'm woefully short on such things myself. All I can offer is information, and I have nothing new to tell you since last night. I might be able to send you more, once I reach Kisua."

"What sort of information?"

She gave him a thin smile. "Are you certain you want to know? All the information was gained through corruption."

He shook his head. "Corruption is a disease of the soul, not mere words or information."

She would have liked to argue that point, but knew better. "Kisua has a network of spies throughout this continent, the east, and in the northlands. Some are common folk. Some have rank, like myself. All that we know, we send back to the Protectors."

"And you believe they would therefore know something of Gujaareh's Reaper? Why would they care?"

She stared at him in frank surprise. "Every nation from the icy reaches to the southern forest watches your land, priest. Some watch to imitate or compete, but most watch out of fear. Gujaareh is too powerful and too rich and too strange. Those who live in the shadow of a volcano would be fools not to watch closer, when it starts to smoke."

He frowned. "There's nothing strange about Gujaareh. If we have prosperity and strength, that is only Hananja's blessing."

"So you say, priest. Those of us from lands not so blessed see it differently. And the warning smoke is hard to ignore: Gujaareh's army swollen to greater numbers than ever before, Gujaareen ambassadors weaving secret alliances with the northernmost lands. We notice when our ambassadors die mysterious sudden deaths as soon as they have something to warn us about."

The Gatherer shook his head again—not in denial this time, she guessed, but in confusion. "I know nothing of these things." *Nor do I care*, he did not say, but Sunandi read it in his face. "What have they to do with the Reaper?"

165

*Perhaps everything,* she did not say, and hoped he could not see that in her face. "I don't know for certain. But I know your Prince is behind it."

His eyes narrowed. "Not the Hetawa?"

"Why would the Hetawa keep a monster as a pet?"

"Why would the Prince?"

She hesitated, then decided to risk trusting him a bit further. "There are rumors. *Only* rumors, mind you."

"Of what sort?"

"Of the sort that keep Kisuati children awake at night, priest. We tell them stories about your kind, you know. 'Be good, or a Gatherer will get you.'"

His face twisted in disgust. "That's a perversion of everything we are."

"You kill, priest. You do it for mercy and a whole host of other reasons that you claim are good, but at the heart of it you sneak into people's homes in the dead of night and kill them in their sleep. This is why we think you strange—you do this *and you see nothing wrong with it.*"

The Gatherer's expression became stony, and Sunandi caught herself before she might have launched into another denunciation. She dared not attack his beliefs any further. Much as it might disgust her, his rigid orthodoxy was the only thing keeping her alive.

"Why would the Prince allow a Reaper to roam the city?" he asked again, his voice flat.

She took a deep breath and let it out slowly. "Centuries ago, when your Inunru founded the Hananjan faith in Kisua, there were none of the rules and rituals you use now to control the magic. No one knew what a rogue Gatherer could do until the first Gatherers did it—and the horrors they inflicted on Kisua are the reason narcomancy was outlawed there. They say a Reaper can breathe death through the very air. They say they *devour* souls rather than sending them elsewhere. There are stories of them draining the life from dozens, even hundreds at a time without sating themselves..."

He was shaking his head even before she finished. "Impossible. I can carry the dreamblood of two, perhaps three souls within me. It's taken me twenty years to build up to that."

"I only repeat the stories, priest. In the early days, the Hananjans in Kisua recorded many examples of what Reapers could do, and the 'uses' of their terrible magic. Those records were outlawed along with the rest of dream magic, but the *stories* are told to this day. We use them to frighten children—but what if someone heard those tales and believed? What if someone with power, who wanted more of it, decided to see for himself whether the tales of Reapers' magic were true?"

The Gatherer said nothing to this. Sunandi saw that his posture had become even more rigid, his brow furrowed in clear disquiet. Abruptly he stood, startling her, and began pacing back and forth in the narrow breezeway. "That would be insanity. The creature is a walking pestilence, hunger without a soul. No one could control it." He almost spat the words, speaking so harshly and quickly that the words almost tumbled over each other. "There was no one around to direct its attack. It acted on its own madness."

It took her a moment to understand what he meant, and then Sunandi caught her breath. "You've seen it!"

The Gatherer nodded absently, still pacing. She noticed, with some concern, that his hands shook like those of a sick elder when he wasn't clenching them in agitation.

"Last night," he said. "It attacked us in an alleyway after we left Yanya-iyan—" He stopped pacing and looked at her in sudden horror, as if he'd only just remembered something. "*Indethe etun'n ut Hananja*," he whispered. Sua, though with an archaic flavor Sunandi had seen only in the oldest poems and tales. *May the gaze of Hananja turn outward upon thee.* Their version of a blessing, though Sunandi preferred Hananja keep Her gaze to Herself.

But it was the pity in the Gatherer's eyes that troubled her most. "What is it?"

"The Reaper," the Gatherer said. He spoke as softly as he had the night before, compassionate even with death in his eyes. "When we encountered it, it had already killed. Your north-blooded child—"

Sunandi's heart shattered.

Through a dim roaring in her ears she heard the rest of his words. "The alley was dark, but I did see the body clearly. Please forgive me. I would have given her peace, seen her safely to Ina-Karekh, if..."

If there had been anything left to Gather.

Sunandi was not aware of screaming at first. It was only when hands caught her wrists that she realized she had lifted them to claw at her scalp. And it was only when something scraped in her throat that she noticed the strangled, anguished cries echoing from Etissero's walls. Through a haze she saw Etissero at the top of the stairs with a knife in his hand, staring uncertainly at the scene before him. Then the Gatherer's arms folded about her and she crumpled into them, too lost in anguish to care that she wept on her sworn killer's shoulder.

"I would ease this for you if I could," the Gatherer whispered to her through the roaring, "but I have no peace left to share. I still have love, though. Take it, daughter of Kalawe. As much as you need."

*There will never be enough*, she thought bitterly, and let the grief close about her like a fist.

# 16

(◦⊙◦)

*Four are the tributaries of the great river. Four are the*
*harvests from floodseason to dust. Four are the great*
*treasures: timbalin, myrrh, lapis, and jungissa. Four bands of*
*color mark the face of the Dreaming Moon.*
*Red for blood.*
*White for seed.*
*Yellow for ichor.*
*Black for bile.*
(Wisdom)

Nijiri had seen six floods by the time of his adoption into the House of Children. Long before that, however, he'd begun learning the ways of the servant caste into which he'd been born. He still remembered his mother's first lessons in the proper way to walk: back bent, strides short but brisk to convey humility and purpose. Never look a higher-caste in the eyes. When waiting, keep eyes forward but see nothing, show nothing—neither impatience nor weariness—no matter how long one has been standing. "They will see you, but not see you," she had told him. "When they need you, you will have already come. What they need, you will have already done. If they no longer need you, you will not exist. Do these things, and you may have what freedom our caste allows."

Those lessons had served him well in his quest to become a Gatherer. Servants were servants, after all. And today he'd had no trouble getting into the first guard-station by pretending to be a wine-seller's boy. So convincingly did he stammer and stoop that the guardsmen did not question his shorn hair or the pouch on his hipstrap, and not once did they look into his face as he spun his tale. His master had too much left of sweetwine chilled with fruit juices; would they not buy it to give to their prisoners? He would discount the price if so. The guards had been too interested in cheap wine to watch their tongues, laughingly telling him that they had no prisoners but would buy his wine for themselves. Nijiri left promising to bring it and never returned.

The ruse had worked on the second guard-station as well, though they'd actually had a prisoner. After noting the number of guards and the location of the exits, it had been a simple enough matter for Nijiri to pass through the alley beside the building, where he stood on a storage urn to peer through the slotted window. The man within had the filthy, half-starved look of an unclaimed or mistreated servant who had probably turned thief to survive; he was not Ehiru.

But this discovery troubled Nijiri deeply, for it meant that his first two guesses as to Ehiru's location had been wrong. Neither of the stations' men had been of the Sunset Guard, either. If Ehiru had been in either place, he was now gone.

*What if I've lost him? What if they have taken him to the prison—or had him killed?*

171

No. He could not allow himself to think such things.

The worst of the afternoon heat had faded by the time Nijiri stopped at a public cistern to drink. So dispirited was he that he did not, at first, sense the pressure of a gaze against his back. A handful of people loitered in the cistern-square, drinking from the provided cups or watering horses at the animal trough. It was only when the soldier touched his shoulder that Nijiri became aware of the man's proximity. He jumped and whirled, spilling his cup and exerting every ounce of will not to drive his fist through the man's throat in reflex.

"Jumpy," the man said with a chuckle. He was tall, handsome, tawny-skinned, with neatly woven braids—probably from a well-to-do family of the military caste. And he wore the rust and gold of the Sunset Guard.

Nijiri's heart sped up.

Then he remembered to be a servant. He dropped the cup and bowed deeply. "Please forgive me, lord. Did I wet you? Forgive me."

"You didn't wet me, boy. And even if you had, it's only water."

"Yes, lord. How may I serve? Will you have water?" This earned him a foul look from the cistern servant, who'd probably been hoping for tips.

The Guardsman laughed. "No, no, boy. Will your master be needing you back soon? Does he object to you lending out your service?"

Nijiri straightened a bit from his bow, keeping his shoulders hunched. His mind raced; he could not let this chance slip past. There had to be some way to probe the Guardsman for information, if Nijiri could only hold his interest. "Er, no, lord," he said.

Vague memory prompted him to add, "So long as there is no loss in it for him, lord."

"Of course." The Guardsman reached into his belt pouch and drew out a thick silver coin, flashing it and then putting it away. "For your master. I won't keep you long." He inclined his head toward a nearby alley, narrow and shadowed.

Forgetting humility for an instant, Nijiri stared at him in confusion. But abruptly a memory of Hamyan Night returned to him, and with it the Prince's words. *Someone would have made a pleasure-servant of you.*

Grace of the Goddess and all Her divine brethren. Here too? For a moment he fought back fury.

He was opening his mouth to mutter some excuse when the rhythmic tinkle of bells caught his attention. Across the cistern-square, a small party entered from a side street: four figures robed in gauzy yellow hekeh surrounding a fourth in pale green. Sisters of Hananja.

The folk gathered in the square drew back in reverence, making a path. The Guardsman inhaled and backed away in a respectful bow as the party approached the cistern. The cistern servant did the same, and belatedly Nijiri remembered to bow as well.

"Hold, child." The green-robed woman at the center of the party held up a hand to point at him. The veil obscured all but the faintest outline of her face, but Nijiri's pulse quickened anyhow at the sound of her voice. Could it be?

He straightened, pointing at himself in disbelief as a meek servant boy should; she nodded. "Come," she said. She and her acolytes turned away, and he followed quickly.

The acolytes moved to surround him, letting him walk beside

the Sister. No one followed them as they left the square. Nijiri glanced back and caught a glimpse of annoyance warring with awe on the Guardsman's face; the awe won out and the man flashed a rueful but good-natured smile at Nijiri before turning away. Then the Sisters turned down a different street, heading into the crafter's district. The shops and smithies here had already closed for the day; most crafters worked at night. Only a few people were still about. Some of these glanced at Nijiri and the Sisters, then quickly looked away; most did not even look. They might envy him for being chosen as a dreamseed tithe-bearer, but no one would show that envy openly. To do so invited Hananja's displeasure—and the Sisters'.

"Unwise, Gatherer-Apprentice," said the Sister. Her voice was low and did not carry. She walked at a stately pace, the bells lining the fringe of her robes and veil tinkling in time. "A man intent on pleasure rarely offers much in the way of information, before or after."

Nijiri felt his cheeks heat. "Sister Meliatua?"

He could not see her face clearly, but he thought she smiled. "You remember."

He could hardly have forgotten. "It was the only way, Sister. I—" He hesitated then, unsure of how much to tell her.

She did not look at him as they walked. "Ehiru is no longer in custody. He was released just after sun-zenith, whereafter he left the city through the south gate. He had a token of hers, so a guard there told him how to find the Kisuati ambassador. I do not know why he was released."

So stunned was Nijiri that it took him several breaths to find his tongue. "You . . . how did you . . ."

Another possible smile. "I listened, Gatherer-Apprentice, just as I taught you to listen on Hamyan. We of the Sisterhood have contacts both in and beyond Gujaareh who are willing to provide us with useful information."

Nijiri frowned, making a guess. "Kisuati contacts?"

"And Soreni, and Jellevy, and many others, including some of your brethren. Rabbaneh asked me to assist you. He said you might be in the vicinity of the guard-stations."

So it was more than luck that she had come along when she did. "Then do you know where I can find my mentor, Sister?"

"No, but the guard at the south gate might, if you can convince him to tell you. You should move quickly, though. I imagine Ehiru will get information from the Kisuati woman and then kill her. After that, who can say where he will go?"

Nijiri frowned. "Gatherers do not 'kill,' Sister."

She smiled again. "I do not actually share my body with tithebearers, Apprentice. I merely give them dreams. Yet when they wake they are spent and sated, their bodies quivering with remembered ecstasy. Do you think the distinction matters to them much, if at all?"

Nijiri flushed. "I suppose not."

"You must learn to see things from many angles, Nijiri. If anything, that has always been your mentor's one failing. He sees only Hananja's Law." She sighed; bells sang around her veil. "That narrowness of purpose makes him the greatest of your brethren, but it also leaves him ill equipped to handle the schemes of the corrupt."

Nijiri tried not to think of the look of utter loss that had been on Ehiru's face when the Sunset Guardsmen took him away. "Then it's my task to bear that burden for him, Sister."

She glanced at him, then away. "I see. You know something of corruption yourself. But you're so young..." It was a question.

He hesitated, but there was something about her that encouraged candor. "I was servant-caste before the Hetawa adopted me. My mother taught me how to satisfy an adult's lust almost before I learned to walk. It's something most servant-caste parents teach their children—something they hope the child will never need, but which could spell survival if the time ever comes." He shrugged, then sobered further. "But I had no trouble as a servant. Only as an acolyte, in the Hetawa."

She said nothing, though Nijiri paused, fearing her censure. Her silence helped; after a moment he was able to relax and continue.

"All acolytes go on the list," he explained. "To serve as pranje attendants, I mean, whenever a Gatherer or Sharer goes through the ritual. It's supposed to be impossible to escape this duty— but there are ways. And *which* list one ends up on is often a matter of earning the favor of the Teacher who controls that list."

"You wanted to be on Ehiru's list?"

Nijiri's step faltered for a moment. Flustered, he fell silent; Meliatua sighed and touched his hand in reassurance.

"I had a mentor, too," she said, softly. "If we had such rituals, I would've wanted to serve her, and no one else. No matter how wrong or selfish that might have been considered by my peers."

Slowly Nijiri nodded. "Yes. It was like that."

"You love him. Ehiru."

Nijiri stopped in his tracks, his blood running cold, and

Meliatua stopped too. Before he could stammer some excuse, however, she stepped close, like a lover, resting her palms on his chest. "I was servant-caste, too," she said gently. "I remember the same lessons as you—but I remember, too, that some of those lessons were wrong, Gatherer-Apprentice. They were all about protecting yourself, making yourself strong enough to survive a servant's life. There were no lessons about how to love safely, or what to do if you did not."

Nijiri stared at her, forgetting for the moment that they stood in the middle of an open street, surrounded by her attendants and gods knew who else. He remembered his initial thought that she had, somehow, read his mind, on Hamyan Night—but no. Perhaps it was simply the fact that she understood him.

"I . . ." He faltered, licked his lips. "I don't know what to do."

She shrugged. "You've done what you can—put yourself close to him, aided him, let him aid you. In the end, that's all any of us can do for the ones we love. And he needs you, Nijiri. More than he realizes. Perhaps even more than you do."

Her hands stroked his chest; inadvertently he put his hands on her waist, since that seemed the only proper way to respond to her touch. "You know, though: being a Gatherer is everything to him. Can you love him, knowing that you'll always be second in his heart?"

"I have always known that." Nijiri closed his eyes, remembering nights he'd lain awake, wanting. Knowing he could never have what he wanted. "I'll take what he can give me, and be satisfied with that. It's just that . . ."

A Gatherer belonged wholly to Hananja, the Teachers said. It was true for all four of the paths of Hananja's service—but the Gatherers were special even among those. No one cared if Teachers or Sharers slipped into each others' rooms at night, so long as they were discreet about it. Even Sentinels took watchbrothers, and fought harder for them than any others. But among the Gatherers, it was different. Respect, admiration, brotherly love—those were right, acceptable, even encouraged. Only selfish, singular desire was forbidden.

"It's very hard, Sister," he whispered, unable to meet her eyes. "I became a Gatherer because I wanted to be strong. Because then I would not need others, and grief would no longer have the power to hurt me. I wanted to be with Ehiru; I wanted to *be* Ehiru. And now…"

She smiled through her veil—and then very, very gently, pushed him away.

"Now, you're not a child anymore," she said. "Now you see: Gatherers are only as strong as other men. Now you know you cannot be Ehiru… but you can be worthy of him. And now you know: there's no shame in love."

He could not help a small, bitter smile. "No. But there's more pain than I expected. And it takes more strength than I realized it would, to endure."

She watched him a bit longer before inclining her veiled head. "Forgive me for disrupting your peace, then, Gatherer-Apprentice." She resumed walking and after a moment he forced his legs to move again. His heart took longer to settle, but she remained quiet as they walked, and gradually, it steadied.

"There's a taxmaster in the Unbelievers' District who is known to me," Meliatua said at length. "His booth is just beyond the gate, on the third corner; ask for a half-Jellevite named

Caiyera. Tell him you're my friend, and he'll tell you the Kisuati woman's location. But do this soon; his shift ends not long after sunset."

Nijiri glanced up at the already-reddening sky. "Yes, Sister."

They had reached another intersection. The street-market here was brisk with people and business; many shoppers came out only once the day's worst heat had faded. Across the square was a broad street marked by an arch, and some ways beyond that Nijiri could see the south gate, which led to the Unbelievers' District.

"Don't linger after dark, Gatherer-Apprentice," Meliatua said, and he looked at her in surprise. "The beast that stalks the nighttime streets has tasted your soul once already and may crave more. You don't yet have the skill to fight it."

Unease warred with pride; Nijiri squared his shoulders. "I was caught by surprise, Sister."

She smiled again, but something about that smile let him know he was not being mocked. "Of course." She stepped close again, lifted a hand, and touched his cheek to the tinkle of bells. "Go with Hananja's blessing, Nijiri, and remember that there is no *corruption* in love, either."

She turned away, her acolytes following, and it was only after she'd left him that he comprehended her words. They made him feel—not better. But more sure of himself.

With his sense of purpose renewed, he started toward the gate to go and find Ehiru.

# 17

(•⊙•)

The Gatherer had meditated, he had prayed, but it was not enough. It was never enough. In the end, when the mind forgot prayers and lost the ability to meditate, all that remained was the terrible, ceaseless gibber of raw need. Only one thing could silence that need. In the morning they would come, in the morning they would come; this became his reason for existence. Until then, nothing to do but endure. Distract himself. A boy lay pinned beneath him with eyes shut. An offering. The Gatherer lifted his free hand to stroke one of the boy's cheeks, marveling at the beauty and innocence of youth. He could devour that beauty, paint himself with that innocence. Would that erase the sins of his life? Perhaps he could find out.

He felt no rage when he first drove his fist into the boy's belly. It had been a way to distract himself, nothing more. But as the boy's eyes opened wide, filling with shock and agony and the horrible sick awareness of what death might feel like when it came, something replaced the drumming, churning need: relief. The boy had never experienced such pain before. He was terrified. And at the sight of another's fear and agony, the Gatherer's own diminished. Just a little, but even that helped.

Oh, yes. And such lovely eyes the boy had. Like desert jasper.

So he lifted his fist and brought it down again, and again, soon *finding himself delighted by the boy's cringing, his whimpers, his hoarse garbled pleas. Eventually there was blood too, and that gave him the greatest pleasure of all.*

\*     \*     \*

Ehiru came awake with a gasp, his heart pounding in the cool darkness of Etissero's house.

It could not have been a dream. He had hardly enough dreamblood to sustain his life at the moment, and even if he'd had more, it could not have been a dream. He had not dreamed in twenty years.

A vision, then—but a horrible, sickening one. Ehiru sat up, putting his forehead in his hands to dull the ache that was caused by exhaustion, sleeping outside of his normal pattern, and his soul's growing need. He could barely think around that ache, but he knew his basic narcomancy well enough. Most visions were born from memories. Nijiri had never served him in the pranje, and therefore Ehiru had never beaten Nijiri. He couldn't have. To deliberately inflict such pain on another was not just corrupt, it was alien to his very being.

Unless his memories were not so clear as he believed. Or unless the images plaguing his rest had been not a vision of the past, but a true-seeing of the future.

He moaned, too empty of peace even to pray.

"Ehiru-brother."

His hands formed fists and his body swung upright, coiling itself to attack. But the figure that sat on the couch opposite Ehiru in the breezeway did not move, waiting for him to calm. That consideration cleared the sluggishness from his mind so that he could think at last. Nijiri.

Ehiru's belly clenched. *Did I ever hurt you?* he wanted to ask, but he could not muster the courage to face the answer.

Nijiri's dim form stirred and came over, crouching beside his couch in a pool of Waking Moon's light. Ehiru's fear eased at the naked concern on the boy's face. Could someone he had used so cruelly still love him? Surely that was his proof.

"You're not well, Brother," Nijiri said. He spoke in the softest of whispers, as on a Gathering. "You need an infusion."

"I need *peace*," Ehiru replied, and winced as his voice cut the silence, hoarse and louder than usual. "But She denies me that even in sleep."

Nijiri took Ehiru's hand, fumbled with it, and lifted it to his face. He held the fore and middle fingers apart, trying to lay them on his own closed eyelids. An offering—

"No!" He jerked away; Nijiri frowned. "My control is weakening, Nijiri. I might not stop with just a little."

"Then take it all, Brother." Nijiri gazed up at him steadily. So trusting! "You know I'm not afraid."

The words teased forth a memory of their first meeting: the bringer of death and the child who welcomed it. That memory had always brought Ehiru peace and it did not fail to do so now, pushing back the confusion and misery that the false-seeing had caused. He exhaled. "Hananja hasn't chosen you yet, and I will not risk your death. I can hold for a few days more. There will be others who need Gathering. There always are."

The boy scowled. "I don't like that plan, Ehiru-brother."

"Nor do I. But the only alternative is to return to the Hetawa, which we cannot do yet." He paused as the implication of the boy's presence finally sank in. "*You* should be there, though. Why aren't you?"

"Sonta-i-brother and Rabbaneh-brother sent me to help you escape the Sunset Guard."

"*What?*"

Nijiri squeezed his hand to silence him; Ehiru had been too shocked to keep his voice down.

"The Reaper is an abomination against the Goddess," the boy whispered. "The Superior and the Prince have not done their duty in destroying it, therefore we—you and I—must hunt the creature down." He hesitated, then added, "Doing so will also prove your purity, Brother. We'll be able to return to the Hetawa then."

*Blessed Hananja, was I such a fool at sixteen? If so, thank you for letting me see forty.* "Rabbaneh and Sonta-i should have known better than this. Even if we destroy the Reaper, we can no longer trust the Hetawa. Someone there *created* that monster."

"And once we return to the Hetawa we will find that person, or persons," Nijiri said, doggedly. "Easier from within the Hetawa than without. We can seek aid from the Council of Paths—"

"Whose members may themselves be involved in this nightmare—"

"Then we'll purge them, too!" Startled, Ehiru looked at Nijiri and saw that his expression had gone fierce and cold. It was a fleeting glimpse of the Gatherer that Nijiri would one day become, and in spite of everything Ehiru felt his heart swell with pride.

"Sonta-i-brother reminded me of our path's role," the boy continued. "Must I remind you? If the Hetawa has become corrupt then it is our *duty* to purify it, under Hananja's Law. It is that simple, Brother."

That simple.

Ehiru sat back against the wall, feeling his world invert once more. Could it really be? He took back his earlier prayer, instead thanking Hananja for once more granting him the clear vision of sixteen, if indirectly through Nijiri's eyes. Two days' worth of unhappiness and confusion faded from his heart, and for the first time in what felt like ages, he smiled.

"Sometimes it's wise for the mentor to listen to his apprentice rather than the other way around." Ehiru squeezed Nijiri's hand, then waved toward the other couch in the breezeway. "Rest. In the morning we leave with the Kisuati woman. We're going to Kisua."

"Kisua? But the Reaper is here."

It was, but the answers that Ehiru needed—the who and the how and the why of it—were not. Killing the creature would not eliminate the corruption underlying the whole affair; he could trust no one in Gujaareh. But the woman Sunandi sought the same truth as he, and in her homeland she had the resources to perhaps uncover it. Corrupt or no, she would be useful to his cause.

"We'll return here afterward," he told Nijiri, "but first we resolve the matter of the woman's abeyance. If what she says is true, then the Reaper may be only a symptom of much greater sickness."

"In what way?"

Ehiru sighed as some of his peace faded. He had known it could only be fleeting. "A purge may be needed throughout all Gujaareh."

*By the time we finish, the Hetawa's stores of dreamblood will overflow.*

# SECOND INTERLUDE

(•☉•)

*This truth Gujaareh has never liked to acknowledge: our Hananja is not the greatest of the Dreaming Moon's children. She is not artful like Dane-inge, who dances rainbows across the sky to mark the end of floodseason. Nor is She industrious like Merik, who grinds down the mountains and fills up the valleys left by his father's rutting. Yet it was given to Hananja to see to Her family's health and happiness—an important task in any lineage, to be sure, but even more so among immortals. Thus did She create the place we call Ina-Karekh, where Her fellow gods might entertain themselves with every wonder in imagination. But because there was nowhere to put this place—for Ina-Karekh is vaster than both the heavens and earth—She kept it within herself. She taught Her brothers and sisters to separate out their innermost selves and send only that to Ina-Karekh, leaving the rest behind. And because the gods found our kind entertaining, She shared this gift with mortals too.*

*One might say this was a kind of madness, however. Consider: our Goddess has invited so many to dwell within Her mind. How does She think Her own thoughts? Where in all of Ina-Karekh are Her own dreams hidden—if She permits Herself anything at all?*

*Then consider the following.*

*When the Gatherer Sekhmen was a child, he could not sleep unless the Moon Sisters sang to him at night. He tried to sing their songs to his siblings in the House of Children, but they heard only silence.*

*As an acolyte, the Gatherer Adjes conversed most earnestly with Gujaareh's Kings on their Thrones of Dreams.*

*The Gatherer Me-ithor showed signs of the dreaming gift early, but his parents were faithless and tried to keep him from the Hetawa. At seven floods he slew his mother in her bed, thinking her a monster.*

*In the Gatherer Samise's times of pranje—of which I speak only to illustrate my tale—it was necessary that his nails be wrapped in hekeh strips, with a wooden bit strapped into his mouth, or he would bite and claw himself to free the insects beneath his skin.*

*Do you think I malign their names in saying these things? Did I malign the Goddess, by suggesting that Her madness infects her Servants? I mean only for you to understand this: the dreaming gift has always been a two-edged blade. But as She taught us—is it not wisdom to seek the treasure in what others might scorn as a curse? Is it not civilized of us to make of madness, magic?*

# 18

( ⊙ )

*When death comes unheralded, preserve the flesh.*
*Summon chanters and singers, burn sachets*
*and call ancestors. Beat drums to drive the dead*
*from Hona-Karekh, and make prayers to the gods*
*to guide the soul's direction. Make tithe to the Hetawa,*
*so that no loved one's soul might be risked again.*

(Wisdom)

Sunandi awakened just after dawn to the sound of Etissero's angry shouts. Rising from the bed where she'd cried herself to sleep, she pulled on a gown and went upstairs to find Etissero in full form, yelling in three trade-languages. She was unsurprised to see the cause of Etissero's anger: the Gatherer's young apprentice had arrived. The boy stood in front of the Gatherer now, radiating that peculiar combination of determination and protectiveness that Sunandi had noted the night before last.

The night before last. Had it really only been such a short time since she'd sent Lin to her death?

The Gatherer-child's eyes shifted to her. Etissero followed his gaze and broke off in the middle of insulting their mothers in

Soreni. Looking abashed, Etissero switched to halting Sua. "Please forgive, Speaker-Voice. I did not mean to wake."

"It's all right," she replied in equally poor Bromarte, then focused on the Gatherers. Ehiru stood with eyes downcast, showing the shame to be expected of anyone who had violated guest-custom. He looked better than he had the day before, but still not quite well. The boy...when she looked at him he narrowed his eyes, searching her face. Gujaareen could read death, Etissero had said, so she gazed back and let him see her grief. He blinked in surprise, then grew solemn; after a moment he nodded to her in understanding. Yes, and Gatherers read death best of all.

"You're coming with us, then?" she asked the boy.

"Yes," he answered.

"Fine," she said, and turned to Etissero. "Do you think Gehanu's band can accommodate three instead of one?"

Etissero looked ready to protest, but he settled instead for folding his arms and throwing a resentful glare at the Gatherers. "Yes, yes, the number doesn't matter. But *look* matters, and neither of these two will be able to pass as anything other than the murderers they are."

"We do not—" the apprentice began, but the Gatherer put a hand on his shoulder and he subsided immediately.

"With the right clothing, we can blend in well enough," Ehiru said. "Under what guise will we travel?"

"Part of a minstrel caravan." Etissero smiled, daring them to look horrified.

Ehiru smiled as well. "Such caravans have many members. Guardians, those who perform, workers who care for the group's animals and properties. Nijiri and I shall be the lattermost. I shall be Kisuati, he Gujaareen."

"Kisuati speak Sua!"

"As do I, sir, ceremonially and the common speech," Ehiru replied in that tongue. He spoke with no trace of a Gujaareen accent, Sunandi noted, though there was a touch of highcaste in his inflections.

"You're a Kisuati who was once wealthy and respectable," she said, and he nodded understanding. She turned to Etissero and switched back to Gujaareen so he could understand.

"Will you gift us with suitable clothes and traveling supplies? I won't offend you by offering reimbursement, especially when you shall be family in my own house whenever you next visit Kisua." And, of course, she would also steer as much lucrative sonha business his way as she could.

The gesture seemed to mollify Etissero. "Of course. I'll have Saladronim find clothes for the boy; they're almost of a size."

He moved to pass her on the stair, but paused and touched her arm. "Are you certain of this, 'Nandi?" He glanced back at the Gatherers, not bothering to hide his dislike or lower his voice. "If that black one harms you, I'll kill him."

"You will do nothing of the sort," she snapped, darting a glance at Ehiru. The older Gatherer turned away and went to the breezeway curtain, affording them what privacy he could. The apprentice, however, eyed them coldly for a moment before turning to follow his master.

"Guest-custom—"

"*Does not apply* once I leave your house, Etissero. And much as you love me, you told me yourself: I'm all but dead already.

Unless I can convince these two that my apparent corruption is the scheme of even more corrupt people, with more corrupt purposes." She smiled in resignation. "And even then they may kill me. They might even be right to do so."

He stared at her for a moment. "You didn't kill the scamp, Sunandi."

"I sent Lin forth. I knew our enemies would stop at nothing to keep the secrets she carried. An army captain who did the same in wartime would accept responsibility for a subordinate's death, would he not?"

"You're no army captain and the girl wasn't a soldier, and we're not at war."

"But we are, Etissero—or we may be, as soon as I tell the Protectors what's going on in this city. Lin wasn't even the first victim of that war." She closed her eyes and touched her breast. If a Reaper had not been involved, she could have at least hoped that Lin would find Kinja, somewhere in the vastness of Ina-Karekh. Then they could have been father and daughter in death as they had not been able, in life. But Reapers left nothing in either world when they were done with a victim: no waking life, no soul to dream. She had not even hope for comfort.

Etissero took her hand. "If not for these"—he jerked his head at the Gatherers—"I would order you to stay here until your grief is spent, 'Nandi. You should be among friends at this time, not enemies."

"The enemies are better. They'll help me to remember why Lin died." She smiled a smile she did not feel and gently disengaged her hand from his. "And I have endangered your family enough by remaining here."

His face fell but he said nothing, for he knew she spoke the truth. She smiled, leaned close, and kissed him on the cheek. "Now hurry," she said. "The caravan will surely leave before the afternoon rest hour."

\*     \*     \*

The market square of the Unbelievers' District was crowded when they arrived, the air thick with dust and the smells of fried food and animal dung. Shoppers and traders hawking their wares mingled in a cheerfully chaotic mass that made the more orderly markets of Gujaareh seem funereal by comparison. Then too Sunandi saw less pleasant reminders that they were no longer in Hananja's City: pickpockets roamed the crowd, a shopkeeper shouted insults at a recalcitrant customer, and dealers in shadier wares did brisk business on the fringes. Surreptitiously she tucked her wrist purse into her travel-robes.

She worried at first that the two Gujaareen, unused to the rough ways beyond their city's walls, might not be so careful. Yet Ehiru had already tucked his purse out of sight, and as usual the boy had taken cues from his master. To a point: Ehiru moved through the crowd with such calm and ease that no one could mistake him for the pious monster he truly was, but Nijiri gaped openmouthed at everything around him. He looked exactly like a runaway servant-caste boy getting his first glimpse of life beyond Gujaareh's walls, but she didn't think it was an act.

She slowed as they came to an area where the crowds thinned to flow around a knot of camels, piles of packaged goods, and small animals in cages. A menagerie of folk—she noted Gujaareen, Kisuati, Bromarte, Kasutsen, Soreni, and what looked like a Jellevy dancer—swarmed around and over the caravan like ants, checking harnesses and loading the camels. Sunandi spied a tall, broad woman with the fierce features of a far-southerner standing at the epicenter of the chaos. Before Sunandi could call out, the woman turned and noticed her.

"Nefe!" she cried, opening her arms and beaming. "How long has it been, you brat? Come here and take your punishment."

Sunandi smiled and went to the woman, who wrapped big arms around her in a mighty hug that picked her up several inches off the ground. She *oof*ed but endured the hug, chuckling in spite of herself as the woman finally released her and gave her a narrow-eyed look, still gripping her by the shoulders. From the corner of her eye she could see the Gatherers staring.

"You need something again. Ah-che." The woman made a face. "You never come around unless you do."

"Because you haven't run me off yet." Sunandi gestured toward the two Gujaareen. "My companions and I need passage to Kisua. Quickly, and quietly."

The woman glanced at the men and grunted in disinterest before turning her attention back to Sunandi. "You know I'll take you, Nefe, but it won't be a comfortable journey. We're going the desert route, not the river way. Nothing along the river but poor villages that can't afford to pay us. At least in Tesa we'll make a profit."

Sunandi grimaced. "I'd actually hoped to hear you say that. The desert route is faster."

"You hate the high desert, you spoiled soft thing."

"I won't complain. Haste is more important than comfort this time."

The woman's smile faded; she examined Sunandi closely. "You're in real trouble."

"I am, 'Anu."

Gehanu did not ask further, though she gave Sunandi's shoulders a firm, reassuring squeeze. "Then we'll get you there. Should take only seven days by the oasis road. Where's that pale girl of yours? She complains more than you do."

Sunandi lowered her eyes, and the woman caught her breath. "Moon's Madlight. So that's it. Then we need to go now, I'm thinking."

She finally turned to the two Gujaareen. "I'm Gehanu. You?"

Sunandi saw the boy glance uncertainly at Ehiru; Ehiru bowed over one hand and the boy quickly imitated him. He spoke in Sua. "I am Eru, and this boy is Niri. We will work for our passage, mistress."

Sunandi blinked in surprise. Ehiru had hunched his shoulders and raised the pitch of his voice, making it slightly nasal; he kept his eyes lowered in the manner of a humble lowcasteman. Together with his highcaste accent, it was perfect for the role they'd given him: a once-wealthy Kisuati, now disinherited and humbled for some youthful indiscretion. She could see Gehanu assessing and dismissing him all at once.

"Of course you will, che," Gehanu snapped. "We all work here. What can you do, boy?"

Nijiri bowed deeper—a perfect Gujaareen servant-caste bow with a hand-inflection indicating that he was unclaimed and willing to accept a new master. When he straightened, he looked at Gehanu with an ingenuous blend of shy hope and fear that was completely at odds with his true manner. "I clean very well, mistress," he said. "I can do anything else if you show me but once. Except...except cooking." He looked so crestfallen by this that Sunandi almost laughed.

Gehanu did laugh—once and loudly, but it was clear the boy had charmed her. "We'll make sure you get nowhere near the cookfire, then." She glanced around at the caravanners and raised her voice in a thunderous shout. "Move yourselves, you lazy stones, we're striking out before sun-zenith!" The caravanners ignored her with the air of long practice.

Ehiru nodded toward a group loading sacks into a wagon. "Shall I help, mistress?"

"If you think you can do it without cocking things up." Gehanu jerked her head toward the wagon, and Ehiru nodded and went to join the loaders. She watched him go, a look of approval on her face. "You, boy; can you sing?"

Nijiri looked startled. "Sing, mistress?"

"Yes. Open your mouth, let sounds come out, occasionally with words."

The boy's complexion, almost as pale as a northerner's, turned a startling pink. "Not well, mistress."

"Dance?"

"Only prayer dances, mistress. Same as any Gujaareen."

"It's a start, and in the south you might actually be a novelty." She glanced at Sunandi. "You're a friend. Your pretty-speaking man isn't, but taking on passengers isn't something the others would question—if those passengers look like they can pay. Gujaareen servant-castes aren't permitted to accumulate money. So our young friend here will be a dancer I'm considering for apprenticeship and permanent hire. Che?"

Nijiri looked startled. A sharp needle of cold threaded Sunandi's spine. She hadn't made such a stupid, amateur mistake in years. Kinja would have swatted her for it. Lin would have been shocked. It took only one minor inconsistency, any error of logic, to arouse suspicions. There were many among a minstrel band who would gladly earn extra money reporting suspicious strangers to gate guards or tradepost officials. She could have gotten them all killed.

Gehanu saw her horror and took her by the arm, leading her toward the camels and beckoning for Nijiri to follow. "Sowu-sowu, Nefe, don't worry. I'll take care of you like I always do. We'll get you back home fast as skyrers, and then all will be well. Che?"

It was said that the gods favored fools because they were entertaining to watch. Privately thanking whichever god had found her amusing for the time being, Sunandi leaned gratefully against Gehanu. "Ah-che."

The caravan line had already formed. Six unladen camels trailed at the rear to be sold along the journey. Gehanu ordered three of these saddled for Sunandi and her companions, and as the sun peaked overhead they set off along the dusty, heat-hazed road.

# 19

( ⊙ )

*A Gatherer shall, under the guidance of the Sentinel path, strengthen body and mind for the rigors of Her service. He shall strike quickly and decisively in Her name, that peace may follow just as swiftly.*

(Law)

Rabbaneh landed on a rooftop near the Hetawa plaza, panting and shivering. Too much dreamblood. He'd been Gathering nearly every night since Una-une's death, and twice on some nights since Ehiru had begun his penance. So many in the city called for a Gatherer's services; it was cruel to make them wait. He sat down behind a storage shed and leaned his head against its wall, waiting for the giddiness to pass. He was not Ehiru. His dreaming gift had never been strong. It would be good—*very* good—when things finally returned to normal in the Hetawa.

The sound of footsteps on the stones of the plaza below did not disturb Rabbaneh at first. Dreamblood still sang in his soul, suffusing his mind with its warm glow. Servants heading home after late-night labors, maybe; what did it matter? But gradually awareness penetrated the haze, and he noticed that the walkers were moving briskly, staying close together. Occasionally the rhythm of the steps jarred as one or another jogged a little to keep up. And one set of steps lagged from time to time, its emphasis shifting from one foot to the other and back again. In his mind's eye Rabbaneh saw the owner of these steps trotting along with his fellows, but periodically glancing around as if to check for observers.

Rabbaneh opened his eyes.

Another Gathering was beyond his capacity at the moment, but he could certainly mark a new tithebearer for a later visit. Rolling to a crouch, he crept to the edge of the rooftop and peered over, hoping to glimpse the culprit's face.

They were almost across the plaza, headed for a street two blocks to Rabbaneh's right. He counted three men: two acting as guards for another between them. They were too far away to see clearly. The Dreamer had set, leaving the streets dim and dull beneath Waking Moon's paltry light, but their noisy footfalls might as well have been a lantern to a Gatherer.

Quietly, along the rooftops, Rabbaneh followed.

The artisans' district blended into a higher-caste area that lined the most beautiful part of the river. A zhinha neighborhood: the houses here varied wildly from the traditional Gujaareen style, incorporating architecture from a dozen foreign cultures with little care for practicality, only aesthetic distinctiveness. Here Rabbaneh was forced to slow down, for one building had a rooftop of flat sloping plates that was maddeningly difficult to navigate, and another bore so many elaborately carved statues of monsters around its edge that he could find no easy access. Privately cursing fools with more money than taste, he finally found one roof with neat overlapping shells of baked brick. He had to go on hands and toes to distribute his weight and avoid breaking them, but he made it across and onto the proper Gujaareen roof beyond that, which allowed him to catch up. When his quarry stopped, so did he.

The three men stood at the side door of a sprawling house. The size meant the house was surely owned by one of the older zhinha lineages, but Rabbaneh did not recognize the family pictorals decorating the lintel. When the door opened neither did he recognize the man who beckoned the three guests in. Likely just a servant anyhow.

But he *did* finally recognize the three men when the light from the doorway illuminated their faces. The Superior, and the Sentinels Dinyeru and Jehket.

*In Her name and inward sight.* Rabbaneh caught his breath.

The door closed behind them. Rabbaneh began searching for a way onto that roof. If he could swing down into a window, or hang from a balcony—

He spotted the danger and froze. Another man stood on the roof of the zhinha house, scratching himself in the shadows of a chimney. Short-shorn hair, short sword on one hip, bronze half-torso armor whose gleam was obscured by a rust-colored evening drape.

*A Sunset Guard?* That meant the Superior was meeting with someone from Yanya-iyan. Someone who held the sanction of the Prince himself.

Looking around, Rabbaneh's eyes sifted seven guards from the predawn shadows: a total of three on the rooftop of the house, another three scattered around the rooftops of nearby buildings, a seventh on the ground and standing quietly near the house's stable.

Not enough. The Guard moved in fours. Where was the eighth?

The faint grit of a footstep behind made Rabbaneh's skin prickle. He forced himself not to react even though he imagined a fiery line along the center of his back where the Guardsman's impending stab was doubtless aimed. When instinct told him his enemy was close enough, he struck, twisting about to slap at the flat of the blade. The Guardsman jerked in surprise and struggled to bring the blade around again, but by then Rabbaneh was on him, tackling him to the ground so that the other guards wouldn't see the struggle. Before the man could cry out, Rabbaneh slapped one hand over his mouth and used the other to set his scarab jungissa humming and lay it on the man's forehead. He stiffened, paralyzed but still awake; his terror and fury fought the magic. Rabbaneh smiled and forked two fingers toward the man's eyes. They closed reflexively and Rabbaneh laid his fingers on them, reinforcing the jungissa's magic with a powerful narcomantic command. It took long, taut breaths, but at last the rigidity went out of the guard's body; he sagged into sleep.

Leaving the jungissa in place—it would hold the sleep-spell—Rabbaneh returned to the edge of the roof. Six figures still patrolled calmly on the rooftops, the seventh on the ground. He had not been seen.

Grinning to himself, Rabbaneh headed across the roof, moving on fingers and toes again. Carefully he swung himself over the edge and dropped to a window, bracing his toes on the sill.

Inside he could hear someone snoring enthusiastically. He dropped again, catching the sill with his hands, grunting just a bit as his knuckles scraped against the wall. He grunted a second time when he dropped to the ground, this time landing in a crouch. Sonta-i, his former mentor, would *tsk* at all the noise he was making, but it could not be helped. He was not as young, nor as lean, as he had once been, alas.

And this was not a mission to share Hananja's peace. The rules for spying were surely different.

He went to the corner of the building he'd just descended, and flicked a glance around. One guard still stood near the stables, pacing back and forth. Doubtless the house's servant-entrance was in there. The main entrance was also within his sight. But Rabbaneh did not need an entrance; a window would do for his purposes. He glanced up and watched awhile, noting that the roof-guards peered down at the ground only occasionally. There was an alley directly across the street that ran behind the zhinha house. If any of the guards happened to glance down while he was crossing, or if the stable-guard turned his way...

Nothing to be done but trust in Hananja. Whispering a quick prayer, Rabbaneh waited until the stable guard paced in the other direction, then darted across the street.

There was no outcry, so he slipped deeper into the shadows and began making a circuit of the house. The first set of windows were useless—bedrooms, with someone sleeping in each. The second set were another matter, for they opened onto the kitchens. Warm, spice-scented air wafted out through the hangings; he could hear servants within preparing food to serve to the guests. Perfect.

He climbed the side of the building quickly, using the window as his starting point and then shifting to a ceramic gutter-pipe that ran from the roof. When he reached the upper set of windows he stopped, finding toeholds along the bracers of the pipe, for he had found what he sought: the Superior's voice could be heard clearly from inside.

"—No *right*," the voice said. Rabbaneh raised his eyebrows; it was nearly a snarl. The Superior rarely displayed such anger in the Hetawa.

"I have every right," replied a different voice in a venomous tone—also familiar, though Rabbaneh could not place it. "You did no less to my father, and if I hadn't taken matters into my own hands, you'd be doing the same to me. I consider the return of my brother a step toward repayment for those crimes."

"You don't understand him!" said the Superior. "He *believes*. Her Law is in his blood, in his very soul. Manipulate him like this and he won't bend to become your tool, he will *break*."

"That is possible. But when he breaks, it will be in your direction. He'll spend his fury on the Hetawa, then turn to me for comfort. And I shall offer it to him gladly, because blood is still stronger than any oath."

Ehiru, Rabbaneh realized with a chill. They spoke of Ehiru. And that meant the other speaker was not some spokesman, but the Prince himself.

"He doesn't know what you are." The Superior's voice dripped loathing. "If he did, he'd Gather you himself."

"I am only what you made me," the Prince said. He spoke so softly that Rabbaneh strained to hear his voice. "What do you think he'll do to *you* when he learns that?"

The Superior did not respond, and when the Prince spoke again, his tone had changed. "And my brother is what you made him, so unfortunately I realize he cannot be trusted. Are you certain it was her?"

"Absolutely," said a third voice. Rabbaneh did not recognize this one at all. "One of my men spotted her in the market. She joined a minstrel caravan that left the city at sun-zenith yesterday. I've had the gate men dismissed for failing to detain them."

"And Ehiru was with her." The Prince sighed. "I thought Gatherers were honorable."

"You dare!" The Superior sounded apoplectic. "If Ehiru judges the woman corrupt, he'll take her. He—"

"I can't wait for him to make up his mind," the Prince snapped. "If the woman reaches Kisua, there's no telling what the Protectors will do. I need them surprised, frightened. *Predictable.*" He sighed. "Charris, send a messenger pigeon south. Can our troops there overtake the caravan?"

"If the minstrels took the river route, easily. If they went through the desert, it will be more difficult. Every caravan follows its own route. But if they pass through Tesa, my men can catch them."

"See that they do." The Prince's voice had the edge of command.

"Will you kill her right before Ehiru's eyes?" asked the Superior. "Will you rub his nose in your corruption, and still expect him to serve you?"

There was a moment of silence. "He'll see it eventually, Superior," the Prince said, his voice heavy with meaning. "Corruption is all around him, after all."

The Superior said nothing to this. The third man—Charris—cleared his throat in the uncomfortable silence that fell.

"What of the Gatherer after the woman is dead?" Charris finally asked. "Or if he has already killed her?"

"I keep my promises to my brother," said the Prince. "If he's killed her, then escort him back here and allow him to return to the Hetawa. All charges against him will be dropped. Won't they, Superior?"

In a low voice the Superior replied, "Yes."

"If he has not killed her," the Prince continued, "then our bargain is forfeit. Capture him and bring him back, but to Yanya-iyan. Unharmed, please. I'll have another use for him."

"You dare not." That from the Superior, seething with fury—and fear, Rabbaneh sensed. "You *dare* not."

"I dare far more than you could ever imagine, Superior." There was a pause; ceramic clinked against ceramic as liquid poured. "Now go scurry back to your little hole, and cower there until I have need of you."

To Rabbaneh's amazement the Superior did not react to this contempt. Cloth shifted and sandals shuffled; the meeting was over.

Quickly Rabbaneh climbed down the pipe and dashed back through the alley and across the street to the building next door. The shadows engulfed him just as the door of the zhinha house opened. The Superior emerged, gesturing curtly for his Sentinel attendants to follow, and they headed away into the night.

Climbing up to the roof, Rabbaneh returned to where the

guard lay sleeping, the scarab-jungissa still humming faintly on his forehead.

"You're a fortunate man," Rabbaneh whispered, removing the stone and laying fingers over the man's eyes. "You'll have a pleasant dream of shirking your duty and taking a nap. Your captain will likely punish you, but not with your life. That is because you won't remember seeing me up here, except as a fragment of a dream."

He wove the dream into the man's mind as he spoke. It was not the most ethical application of narcomancy, but perhaps Hananja would forgive the misuse because his intentions were pure. And because the life of a pathbrother was at stake—though only the gods knew what could be done about it at this point.

It was enough that they knew, Rabbaneh decided, and he hurried home to share the knowledge with Sonta-i.

# 20

( ⊙ )

*Tell me, Mother Moon O tell me*
*Ai-yeh, yai-yeh, e-yeh*
*When will Brother Sleep come calling?*
*Ai-yeh, an-yeh, e-yeh*
*On the night of river-dancing?*
*Ai-yeh, o-yeh, e-yeh*
*In the peace of Moonlight-dreaming?*
*Ai-yeh, hai-yeh, e-yeh*
*Tell me, Mother Moon O tell me*
*Ai-yeh, kuh-yeh, e-yeh*
*Who will bring my brother home?*
*Ai-yeh, si-yeh, e-yeh*
*Though I welcome him with singing*
*Ai-yeh, nai-yeh, e-yeh*
*Must I sing my song alone?*
(Wisdom)

On the first day out of the city, the caravan crossed a tributary of the Goddess's Blood, passing through a village called Ketuyae. There Nijiri had gotten his first glimpse of how the folk of the upriver towns lived. The rhythmic work songs of the washing women lingered in his mind, as did less pleasant memories of human wretchedness. Some of the structures used as homes in Ketuyae were little more than lean-tos made of mud and sticks and palm leaves. The village was too tiny to merit a satellite temple of Hananja; Nijiri saw only a single overworked Sharer whose hut was barely finer than the lean-tos. There were no public crypts for the dead, just patches of ground where bodies— not even burned!—had been crudely shoveled into the earth. He saw no clean well, no bathhouse. He couldn't tell the high-castes from the servants. When he asked a fellow member of the caravan how children in the village were schooled, he got only a shrug in response.

Now Ketuyae was a fond memory. They had been traveling hard for two days since, passing first through arid rocky foothills and then into the vast, windswept dunes of the Empty Thousand. The desert was not actually a thousand miles wide, Nijiri understood, but it was hard to believe otherwise when from the back of his camel he could see nothing but sand and heat-haze in every direction. The remaining four days of the journey felt as though they might as well be a thousand years.

He had lost himself in unhappy contemplation of the grit in his eyes, the heat, and the rivulets of sweat tickling his back when he was shocked out of misery by cold water splashing onto his face and neck. He yelped and glanced around to see Kanek, one of Gehanu's sons, grinning at him from another camel with an open canteen in his hands.

"Wake up, city boy." Kanek was grinning. "We're almost there."

"There…?" Nijiri blinked away water, trying to comprehend. They couldn't be at Kisua yet. And why was Kanek wasting water?

"The oasis at Tesa, city boy. See?"

He pointed ahead. Nijiri followed the arm and saw what at first seemed to be just another mirage glinting against the horizon. Then he noticed the palm trees spiking toward the sky, and buildings squatting around their trunks.

Kanek splashed more water at him. "We'll get to bathe soon, and drink all we want, and wash our clothes so we no longer smell like dungheaps. So wake up!"

His good humor was infectious and Nijiri started splashing water at Kanek in return, giving him a good wetting before Gehanu turned and glared them back to discipline from several camels ahead. Still, the spirits of the whole caravan seemed to lift as the news spread. Nijiri glanced around for Ehiru, wondering if he dared splash his brother—and his fine mood dissipated at once. Ehiru's camel plodded along near the rear of the caravan, moving more slowly than its fellows. Atop it, Ehiru rode with his head down and headcloth hanging 'round his face, giving no sign that he had heard the news.

"Go wake your friend," Kanek said, following Nijiri's gaze. "I think he's still in the desert."

Nijiri nodded and reined in his camel, dropping back through the caravan column until he rode abreast with Ehiru. "Brother?" he said. He kept his voice low, though none of the other caravanners were close enough to overhear anyhow.

Ehiru's head lifted slowly; he focused on Nijiri as if from a great distance. "Nijiri. All is well?"

*Obviously not, Brother.* "Have you not heard? We will reach Tesa soon."

"So soon? Good."

He spoke softly, but Nijiri heard the detachment in his voice. This was how the change always began, with the pranje; the Gatherer's attention gradually turned inward to focus on the coming struggle, sparing little for the nonessentials of personality or emotion. That would be the only sign on the surface, at first. But somewhere within Ehiru, in the formless space between flesh and soul, the umblikeh that kept him whole was dry and cracking. Without dreamblood to nourish it, that tether would fray, loosening his soul to swing uncontrollably between waking and dreaming. Eventually the tether would snap and Ehiru's soul would fly free into death—but not before he had lost all ability to tell vision from reality.

And while Ehiru struggled to keep his mind intact, his soul would be hungry, so hungry, for the peace that dreamblood could give him. If his control faltered even once—

*If he falters, I must Gather him.*

Was he ready for that? Barely trained as he was, far from home, under the duress of time? No, of course he wasn't. And even if he could somehow make himself ready, could he then keep perfect peace in his heart, as a Gatherer should?

More heavily than he needed to, Nijiri put a hand on Ehiru's.

"It may be some hours yet before we reach the oasis, Brother," he said, to distract himself. "Are you hungry?" He rummaged among his robes and found one of the cloth sachets of food that had been given out at the last rest hour. "I have a hekeh-seed

cake left over from breakfast. Gehanu soaks them in honey…"
He peeled the sticky treat free and held it out.

Ehiru glanced at it, shuddered as if the sight made him queasy, and looked away. Nijiri frowned. "What is it, Brother?"

Ehiru said nothing.

A vision, then. Too soon; it had been only three fourdays since Ehiru had given his last tithe to the Sharers. Nijiri kept his tone even and said, "Tell me what you saw, Brother, please."

Ehiru sighed. "Insects."

Nijiri grimaced and began to rewrap the cake. Most visions were harmless. But like pain with the body, unpleasant visions served as a warning for the mind, indicating imbalance or injury. It was a thing that Sharers could deal with on a temporary basis—siphoning off the excess dreambile, adding sufficient dreamichor to restore the inner equilibrium, perhaps other things; Nijiri had never learned much more than basic healing techniques. But only dreamblood could cure it. "There aren't any. But I'll hold this until the vision has passed, if you like."

"No," Ehiru said. He reached over and broke off a piece of the cake, lifted it to his mouth without looking, and ate it, chewing grimly. "It was only a vision. Eat the rest yourself."

Nijiri obeyed, shifting to ease the ache in his buttocks. If he never rode another camel, he would die in peace. "We can rest properly tonight, Brother," Nijiri said. He hesitated and then added, "And you can draw dreamblood from me, just enough to stave off—"

"No."

Nijiri opened his mouth to protest, but Ehiru forestalled him with a small pained smile. "My control was weak the last time you offered; now it is gone altogether. I have no wish to kill you, my apprentice."

His choice of words chilled Nijiri despite the desert heat. "Gathering is not *killing*, Brother."

"Either way, you would be dead." Ehiru sighed, lifting his head to gaze toward the distant oasis. "In any case, there may be another way."

"What?"

Ehiru nodded toward the middle of the caravan. A light palanquin of balsawood and linen bobbed amid the river of cloth-wrapped heads, carried by sturdy young men on the smoothest-gaited of the camels. From within the palanquin came the sound of a racking, weary cough.

"Their matriarch," Ehiru said very softly. "I have heard such a cough before. I would guess she suffers hardened lungs, or perhaps the sickness-of-tumors."

"Dreambile could cure the latter if she has the strength to bear it," Nijiri said, trying to recall his Sharer-lessons. He had seen the old woman during their rest hours. She was a cheerful little creature who had probably been spry before her illness, seventy floods at least. Her old body would be slower to respond to the healing power of the humors, but the effort wasn't hopeless. "I know nothing of hardened lungs, though..." He trailed off, seeing suddenly what Ehiru meant. "...Oh."

Ehiru nodded, watching the palanquin. "She could have visited the Hetawa before the minstrels left Gujaareh, but she didn't."

*She does not want to be healed!* Nijiri stifled excitement. It was the best of all possible circumstances. And yet Ehiru's angry

211

words from a few nights before, after Nijiri had recovered from the Reaper attack, lingered in his mind. "So...you've changed your mind about testing yourself?" He did not say *facing the pranje*, for one did not speak of such things while among layfolk, even quietly.

"No. I still intend to submit myself to Her judgment. But I must seek dreamblood now, or become dangerous to our companions." He sighed. "Once I settle the matter of the Hetawa's corruption, then I can contemplate my own."

"Yes, Brother." Nijiri tried to feel glad for that respite.

"Of course, there is one blessing in this. You'll finally have the chance to assist in a Gathering."

Nijiri caught his breath; he had not considered that at all. "Will you speak with her, Brother? Tonight? May I attend?"

Ehiru mustered a rough chuckle, which drove back some of Nijiri's worry. If Ehiru was still capable of humor, he was not as far gone as Nijiri had feared. "Tonight, yes, I shall assay. You may attend if she wishes it, my greedy apprentice." Then he sobered. "This serves our purposes, Nijiri, but we must never forget that the *tithebearer's* needs come first."

"Yes, Brother." They fell silent for the rest of the ride into Tesa.

Palm trees rose out of the sand until they loomed more and more like mountains, the closer they drew. The town beneath was clearly far more prosperous than Ketuyae had been. Narrow fields ran between the houses, taking advantage of an irrigation system that appeared to have been haphazardly rigged throughout the town with fired-clay pipes. Potted plants grew wherever the pipes wouldn't go, on balconies and rooftops and street corners. The sight of so much green lifted Nijiri's spirits again. He darted a glance at Ehiru and was pleased to see that his mentor seemed to have regained a measure of alertness as well, sitting straighter on his camel and looking about with interest.

Children came forth at once to surround the caravan, chattering in a syrupy dialect of Gujaareen that Nijiri found barely comprehensible; they offered sweets, flasks of water, flowers and other welcoming trinkets. Adults came out of their houses or looked up from their work, waving. Gehanu, apparently well known to the townsfolk, waved back and called greetings as they rode along. The caravan kept moving forward until the street widened and they faced the oasis itself: a circular pond surrounded on all sides by a low wall, only a few dozen feet across but clearly the heart of the village. All the roads ran to it; irrigation lines radiated from its walls like the spokes of a wheel.

Here the troop stopped and dismounted, tethering the camels near troughs that had been set aside for watering animals. Gehanu walked through the group calling out instructions and the rules of the town: guard the caravan's goods in shifts, disputes weren't allowed at the water's edge, and everyone was required to pay at least one visit to the village baths. "Or none of the maidens or lads here will look twice at you," she said. A group of passing Tesa-girls giggled to emphasize her point.

Nijiri spent a while unloading and feeding the camels along with all the others. He spied the palanquin on the ground and surreptitiously watched as a young man helped the old woman walk around to ease the stiffness of her legs. She stopped every few steps to let out a series of hollow, wheezing coughs. Each one left her visibly drained, leaning harder on the young man's arm. She was thin and weak and had probably been ill for months. Nijiri's heart tightened in sympathy and anger.

"Thinking killing thoughts, boy?"

Nijiri started and turned to see Sunandi nearby, pouring a vase of water into the animals' trough. She looked every inch the rough caravanner; her full lips were now chapped, her skin was dry, and gone were the brightly colored wraps she'd worn at Etissero's, along with the earrings and the looping necklaces. Here she wore only shapeless layered robes in earthen tones, same as the rest of them; the only sensible attire for the high desert. The headcloth with which she'd covered her short-shorn hair did accent her angular, large-eyed face nicely—Nijiri reluctantly had to admit that she was quite beautiful—but aside from that, she might as well have been just another juggler or dancer with the caravan troop.

She did not look at him as she worked, and she kept her voice down, but he heard the edge in her tone.

"You believe it better for her to suffer like that?" he asked. "A Sharer could have eased her pain."

"For a price."

"A few dreams! From such an old one they would have been rich. All Gujaareh could benefit from the power within her."

She straightened and mopped her brow with one sleeve, then glared at him. "You sound like a vulture," she said. "Circling 'round the weak, waiting for your chance to feed. All your kind—pious, well-meaning scavengers."

Nijiri felt heat, then cold, run through him. He set down the saddlebag he'd been carrying and turned to face her. "You grieve for your northblooded girl," he said, keeping his voice low. "No one has eased the pain for you, so I'll forgive that insult. But you, with your life steeped in lies and corruption, can comprehend none of Hananja's blessings. For that I pity you."

She stared back at him. Not trusting himself to be civil any longer, Nijiri turned and headed toward the oasis, where Ehiru was helping some of the others distribute water to the animal troughs. Nijiri joined him and wordlessly helped until the task was done. Then Ehiru, who of course had noticed his mood, took his arm and pulled him to a quiet spot beside a feed-seller's stall. "Tell me," was all he said, and Nijiri did.

By the time he'd finished telling the tale, his anger had been replaced by shame. Ehiru said nothing for a long while, watching him, and Nijiri finally blurted, "I shouldn't have gotten angry. She was in pain. I should have comforted her."

"Yes," Ehiru said, "but I suspect she wanted no comfort from one she blames for the death of her girl."

"I didn't kill her girl! The abomination did that!"

"To her, you and the Reaper—and I—are one and the same."

Nijiri folded his arms over his chest, shifting from foot to foot. "I've never understood why anyone fears Gathering," he said. "Barbarians know no better. But the Kisuati worship Hananja, if not in the same way as us. They're civilized." He glanced at Ehiru and saw a rueful smile on his mentor's lips.

"Civilization may not be all you think, Nijiri." Ehiru took Nijiri's shoulder in a comforting grip for a moment, then pulled Nijiri to walk with him toward the caravan. "But in the future, when a tithebearer attacks with anger and you feel anger in response, think of your mother."

Nijiri stopped walking, startled. "My mother? But she died in peace. The northblooded girl did not."

"My mother died in peace too," Ehiru said. "Not with a Gatherer's aid, but through her own goddess strength. Yet still I wished for years afterward that she had not died. Even knowing that I would see her again in Ina-Karekh, I thought only of the fact that I could never talk to her, never feel her arms around me, never breathe her scent... not while I yet lived. Sometimes I feel that pain still. Do you?"

And suddenly the old ache was there in Nijiri's heart, sharper than it had been for years. "Yes." And as he said it, he understood. If *he* still felt such pain years later, knowing that his mother had died well, how much worse must the pain be for Sunandi, whose agony was still raw and exacerbated by the horrible circumstances of the child's death?

"You see," Ehiru said. He stopped then and they both looked up. The caravan was beginning to settle, pitching tents in a paved square set aside for that purpose by the village folk. On the other side of the square a little girl helped the old woman into a large, ornately decorated round tent.

"Those in pain deserve our compassion," Nijiri said, his thoughts on that long-ago day in a servants' hovel. "I won't forget again, Brother."

Ehiru nodded, and together they returned to the tents to prepare for the Gathering.

# 21

(◦⊙◦)

*A Gatherer shall immediately bring all tithes collected to the
Hetawa, to be entrusted to his brethren of the Sharer path.
Only the merest portion is to be kept by the Gatherer himself.*

(Law)

Ehiru resumed his fallen aristocrat's guise and found Gehanu in
her tent. "Have you any eathir root, mistress? In some lands
they call it ghete."

Gehanu paused in the middle of chewing some sort of spiced
meat on a skewer. Village women had come among the minstrel
band during the unpacking, selling food and drink. "You plan-
ning to put someone to sleep?"

Ehiru smiled and touched his own torso, just below his rib
cage. "Ghete can ease spasms here. It sometimes stops a cough."

Her eyebrows rose. "Ah. For Talithele, che?"

"Is that the name of your elder? Yes, mistress."

"You don't look like a healer."

"There are healers in my family, mistress. Some even serve
the Hetawa in Gujaareh. I picked up a few tricks."

"Mmm. Hold on. Kanek!" Her bellow almost caught Ehiru by

surprise, but he had grown used to the woman's rough manner-isms over the past few days. There was a shuffle outside and then Kanek poked his head into the tent, scowling. "Go find the village headman and ask for ghete root," Gehanu told him.

"Ghete? Palm wine tastes better, Mother."

"Just do it, you disrespectful shiffa." She glared until the boy disappeared. They heard his grumbles as his footsteps faded.

"Thank you, mistress." Ehiru flattened both his hands and bowed over them.

"Ete sowu-sowu." Ehiru thought the language might have been Penko, but he could not be certain. Her Gujaareen was fluent, at least, though she tended to speak too fast; it took time for him to sift out the words from her accent. "If you can make Talithele more comfortable, it will be worth getting in debt with the greedy old bastard who runs this town." She set down the skewer and rummaged among her robes for a moment, finally coming up with a long pipe. She raised her voice again. "And an ember from the fire!" A faint annoyed sound was the only reply.

Ehiru smiled. "It's good to have dependable sons."

"Ah-che. Like that boy of yours, hmm? I see him hovering always, making sure no one bothers you much, taking care of problems before you notice." She did not see Ehiru's look of sur-prise as she rummaged again and came up with dried leaves, which she began to pack into the pipe. "If only my sons were as clever and thoughtful. Though of course Niri isn't your son." She glanced up at him, her big southerner eyes bright and sharp.

"No, mistress, he is not."

She grunted and bit another piece of meat off the skewer. "Bed-warmer?"

Ehiru smiled at the notion. "Protégé. I'm teaching him about life."

Gehanu grunted in amusement. "And he listens? Motro sani'i—a miracle to amaze even the gods."

"He listens when it suits him." Ehiru smiled. "Young men."

"Mmm. Too young for sense, too old to beat. But young women are worse, trust me. Three daughters back home, along with my other three sons. Should probably beat my husband for inflicting all of them on me, but he's pretty and he doesn't eat much, so I keep him around." She cocked her head, examining him. "*You're* pretty. You have a wife?"

Ehiru heartily wished that Kanek would hurry back. "No, mistress."

"You looking?" She grinned, flashing a substantial gap between her front teeth. In the southern lands this marked a woman of great passion, or so Ehiru had heard.

"No, mistress."

"Why not?"

"I'm a servant, mistress." He and Nijiri had decided to keep up their guise at all times, though Gehanu had already guessed that they were not what they seemed. She didn't know the whole truth, and there was no way of knowing who might be listening, through thin tent walls.

"Got to make more servants somehow, che? Nefe is pretty."

Ehiru forced a laugh. "True. But she is of a different world, mistress."

"Hn, yes. No time for children anyway, that one. Always busy she is, always worried about something. She needs a nice mellow man like you, but she'll never slow down enough for that."

The flap lifted again—much to Ehiru's relief—and Kanek slipped inside. "Ghete." He set a small bladder, tied with a leather cord, down on the tent-rug.

"What did the headman want for it?" Gehanu asked.

"Nothing. He was so surprised that we wanted it that he gave it to me without asking anything in trade."

"Ha! He must be getting senile. Good. I'll trade more with him tomorrow. Now go bathe; you reek."

Kanek rolled his eyes behind Gehanu's back, winked and grinned at Ehiru, and left. Ehiru bowed humbly in thanks and reached for the bladder. Gehanu's hand fell on his own, forestalling him.

"You understand our ways are different from yours, che?" Her mouth stretched in something that was not quite a smile; her eyes were serious. "I know her time will come soon; I'm not a fool. But remember: she did not ask for you."

Ehiru froze, realizing all at once what she meant and wondering how she'd figured it out and deciding at last that it made no difference. Such things were Hananja's will.

"I shall respect her wishes," he said, discarding the affected manner of speech he'd used before. "Her life does no harm, so her death is her choice."

Gehanu gave him a long and assessing look, but finally nodded and let his hand go. "I met one of your kind once, long ago," she said. "Came to take a Gujaareen in our troop whose appendix had burst. He was quiet and strange like you, but there was great kindness in his eyes."

Ehiru let go of the bladder of eathir, now that they both knew he didn't need it. If the old woman refused him, Gehanu's people could give it to her in a tea. "Is that how you knew me?"

"I suspected, but I wasn't certain. He wasn't sad like you. I didn't think your kind got sad, or mad, or anything else." She narrowed her eyes at him. "And you aren't *supposed* to, are you? What's wrong with you?"

"I am preparing myself to die."

"What in the gods' names for?"

He could not bring himself to lie, though he knew the truth would make her uneasy. "I destroyed a man's soul."

Gehanu caught her breath and drew back, horror plain on her face. Then it faded, replaced by concern. "Was it an accident?"

So few others had asked that question. It was a relief to not be assumed evil. "Yes." He gazed down at his hands. "And no. It was incompetence. I forgot my duty and let fear and prejudice dictate my actions. Only for a moment, but that was enough."

She frowned. "Do you intend to do it again?"

"Of course not. But there are—"

"Then stop your moaning and move on." She gestured with one hand and abruptly noticed the unlit pipe in it. "Damn forgetful brat." She set the pipe down. "My grandmother needs you, Gatherer, so wake up and do your job. Go on now."

He blinked in surprise. "You trust me to complete this task properly?"

"Are you deaf?"

Ehiru opened his mouth, then closed it. She had given him her answer already. For a moment he was overwhelmed, his heart feeling as if it would burst from gratitude—and terror too, for what if he should mishandle this Gathering like the last one?

No. Gehanu was right. Talithele needed the Gatherer Ehiru, not the miserable penitent of the past few days. He took a deep breath and straightened. "I accept your commission. I shall prepare myself and then speak with Talithele-elder, to make an Assay of Truth."

She inclined her head in approval as he got to his feet and left.

Nijiri was hovering nearby, of course. "A bath first," Ehiru said, and wordlessly the boy followed him to the village's bathhouse. Ehiru paid for both of them and a village man led them into the washing chamber, where they undressed and sat while the man scrubbed them both with palm fronds and acrid soap. After the rinse, they were led to the bathing chamber and left there to soak in the warm, oiled, and scented water. Nijiri kept a respectful silence the whole time, allowing Ehiru a precious few moments to pray. When Ehiru had soaked enough, he was surprised to find that his mind was quiescent, his heart at peace. He lifted his head. Nijiri had been watching him; when he saw Ehiru's eyes he smiled.

"Come," Ehiru said. They left the pool, dried themselves, dressed in clean clothes, and then headed to Talithele's tent. "Wait outside," he told Nijiri, and the boy nodded and slipped into the shadows behind the tent. He would come if and when

Ehiru called him, and that would happen only if Talithele wanted him there.

The minstrel encampment had mostly settled for the evening, though some of the younger members had started an impromptu performance, playing lyre and cymbals at the water's edge. From within the tent Ehiru heard silence; Talithele's attendant either had gone, or slept along with her. If they had been Gujaareen he would have gone in without asking. Instead he drummed his fingers against the taut hide of the tent wall. "Elder? May we speak?"

There was a stir from within, followed by another of the old woman's racking coughs. After the cough stopped he heard, "As much as speech is possible, whoever you are. Come."

Ehiru slipped in through the tent-flap. Within, the tent was spacious and comfortable, lit by a beeswax lantern that hung from the smokehole. The honey scent did not quite disguise the smell of age and sickness, but Ehiru paid that no mind. Thick fur rugs covered the floor and cushioned the hard stone. The inner tent walls had been painted in brightly colored geometric patterns of some southern style he did not recognize. At the center of the chamber lay two pallets, but only one was occupied at the moment. The old woman was there, struggling to sit up and greet her visitor.

Ehiru moved quickly to crouch at her side and prop her against a stack of cushions nearby. "Forgive me, Talithele-elder. I did not mean to interrupt your rest."

"Couldn't rest with this damn cough," she muttered. He heard Gehanu's choppy accent in her words. She narrowed her eyes at him then, looking him up and down. "Ah-che. The handsome boy who joined us in Gujaareh. They give you 'take care of the old woman' duty for the night?"

Ehiru smiled. "It would be an honor if they had, Elder, but no. I have come for a different purpose." He paused while she coughed again, harshly and with obvious pain. A flask of water and a cup sat on a tray nearby. When the spasm passed, he poured water for her and lifted this to her lips, holding it while she sipped. She nodded thanks when she was done.

Setting the cup down, he paused for a moment and then reached into his robes for his waist-pouch. Pulling it out, he opened it and poured his Gatherer ornaments into his palm.

She peered at the polished stones with bright-eyed curiosity. He picked up the cicada and held it up for her to see. "Do you know what this is?"

There was no mistaking the blue-black gleam of jungissa, or its characteristic hum when he tapped the cicada's back. Talithele's eyes widened. "Kilefe, che? What we call the living stone. I heard that it hummed, but never saw it for myself."

He smiled. "We call it jungissa. The hum is not life, but magic. The stones fall from the sky, now and again; we believe they are remnants of the Sun's seed, scattered across the heavens. It took ten years to carve this one, and it took me five years to master its use." He turned the cicada in his fingers, thoughtful. "There are only a handful of jungissa in all the world."

She nodded, fascinated—but then her rheumy eyes narrowed at him. "In my land, we tell stories of the kilefe stones and what the priest-warriors of the river kingdoms do with them."

Ehiru nodded, gazing into her eyes. "We use them to hold

spells of sleep in place, while we travel with the sleeper into Ina-Karekh—what we call the realm of dreams."

"Ah-che." She sat back, thoughtful. "You've come to kill me."

"Death is only part of what I bring." He lifted a hand and touched her cheek. She was old, weak; he could feel the hair-thinness of her tether. With the barest brush of his will he pushed her into the edges of Ina-Karekh, carefully steering her into a dream of pleasant memory. A vision of her home village bloomed in both their minds. Around him were huts with grass-thatched roofs, goats being chased by children, guinea fowl scratching in the dust. He smelled animal dung and grain-dust from the storage house nearby. He saw the tall, handsome youth she'd loved so long ago, and for a moment he loved along with her.

With a sigh of regret he ended the dream there, pulling her very gently back to Hona-Karekh. So near death was she that he hadn't even needed to put her to sleep for that brief journey; she blinked once or twice and then stared at him.

"In Gujaareh, my task is to help guide others into Ina-Karekh in the manner that I have shown you," he said. He caressed her cheek, admiring the beauty in every sun-weathered seam of her skin before finally dropping his hand to rest on hers. "I have not the skill to heal you, but I can at least see that your afterlife is peaceful and filled with your loved ones and favorite places."

She stared at him, then let out a long sigh. "What a seducer you are. I never dreamed I would be courted again at my age, or that I would be so tempted to give in. How many women have you had with that silver tongue?"

Ehiru smiled. "None, Elder. Women are forbidden to my

kind. But…" he ducked his eyes, feeling his face heat beneath her knowing gaze. "I have loved many in the course of my duty."

"Ti-sowu? Loved them, you say?" She cocked her head coquettishly. "Do you love me?"

He could not help but chuckle, though he kept it soft so as not to break the spell of peace. "I believe I could, Elder. When I share the dreams of another it is difficult not to love them…"

As he said the words, he faltered to silence and nearly flinched from the sharpness of the chill that moved through him. Was that it, then? Had he perverted the Bromarte's Gathering because, in the moment after that eerie true-seeing, he had failed to love the bearer of Hananja's tithe? He had disliked the man already—without cause, simply because he was a barbarian. And then he had allowed that prejudice to overwhelm his sense of duty. He had failed to master his own disgust and fear as he might have done for another.

So lost was he in the revelation that his attention wandered; Talithele uttered another harsh cough which drew him back. Privately he cursed and thrust his inappropriate thoughts aside. He had meant to keep her calm and relaxed to ease the coughing.

But as she recovered, her sharp eyes laid his soul bare. "You are troubled, priest."

He bowed his head. "Forgive me, old mother. My mind wandered."

"Nothing to forgive. A mistake is a small matter." She smiled again. "But you would not know that, would you? Poor man."

"Eh?"

She turned her hand under his and grasped it, patting the

back of it with her other hand. "I can see how they made you," she said, her voice soft despite its hoarseness. "They took away everything that mattered to you, che? Upended your whole world and left you alone. And now you think love blooms in a breath and silencing pain is a kindness. Ah, but you're young."

He frowned, so startled that he forgot the spell he'd been weaving. "Easing pain *is* kindness, old mother. And my feelings for the people I help—"

"I don't doubt your love," she said. "You are a man made for love, I think. Your eyes make me *want* to die, there's so much love in them. But it isn't real. Real love lasts years. It causes pain, and endures through it."

He was too stunned to respond for several breaths. When he finally found his tongue he could barely stammer out words. "That pain comes with love…that I can accept, old mother. I have lost loved ones—family. But they died quickly, and I pray thanks to my Goddess every day for that blessing. Are you saying it would have been better to let them suffer?"

She snorted aloud. "Suffering is part of life," she said. "All the parts of life are jumbled up together; you can't separate out just the one thing." She patted his hand again, kindly. "I could let you kill me now, lovely man, and have peace and good dreams forever. But who knows what I get instead, if I stay? Maybe time to see a new grandchild. Maybe a good joke that sets me laughing for days. Maybe another handsome young fellow flirting with me." She grinned toothlessly, then let loose another horrible, racking cough. Ehiru steadied her with shaking hands. "I want every moment of my life, pretty man, the painful and the sweet alike. Until the very end. If these are all the memories I get for eternity, I want to take as many of them with me as I can."

He could not accept her words. In his mind he saw again his mother's face, aristocratic and beautiful, marred by streaks of blood. He could smell that blood, and bile and the reek of broken bowel; he saw his mother's eyes, staring outward with no one to shut them. Women were goddesses who needed no assistance to reach the best of Ina-Karekh—but her death had still been horrific, not at all the queen's death she'd deserved.

He looked up at Talithele and in that moment could see the same ugly ignominy awaiting her. She would cough until her lungs tore to pieces, and die drowning in her own blood. How could he leave her to suffer so? No, worse—stand by and watch?

*I could take her anyhow,* came the thought. *Gehanu would never know.*

And on the heels of that thought came a chill of purest horror.

Swallowing against the dryness of his throat, Ehiru pulled his hands away from hers. "It is your right to refuse the tithe," he whispered. The words came more by rote than conscious effort. "Your soul is healthy and your life does no harm. Remain in Hona-Karekh with Hananja's blessing."

He pushed himself up from the rugs and would have fled the tent then, but he stopped when she said, "Priest. I may accept the pain, but I'm not a goddess, whatever your people might think. My last days will be easier to bear if I am not alone. Che?"

He heard the plaintive hope in her voice and nearly wept. In a thick voice he replied, "Then I'll visit again, old mother."

She smiled. "So you love me after all. Rest well."

"Rest well, old mother."

He left the tent and kept walking forward, his strides brisk, his fists clenched at his sides. Almost immediately he heard the scuffle of feet behind him as Nijiri recovered from surprise and followed. The boy asked no questions, for which Ehiru was supremely grateful as he reached the wall of the oasis, dropped to his knees, and gripped the lip of smooth stone as if for life. Perhaps he could dance. Perhaps he should weep. Anything— so long as it took his mind away from the terrible sin he'd almost committed, and the sour taste of dreamblood-lust in his mouth.

He did nothing but tremble there in the dust until Nijiri took his hand. "*Tatunep niweh Hananja*," the boy said—the opening phrase of a prayer. All at once Ehiru's anguish began to fade. Again the boy had proven his worth.

*There's no more time. I must make him ready to serve Her now, for I can do so no longer.*

Then he bowed over his hands and lost himself in prayer.

# 22

⟨·⊙·⟩

*Jungissa stones may be touched only by those
in the service of Hananja.*

(Law)

The Reaper does not serve Hananja. It no longer needs a stone.

*       *       *

*Niyes was a fool to think he could escape this nightmare,* thought
Charris.

Now *General* Charris, elevated to Niyes's place. Once Charris might have been pleased with the appointment and with the
oblique victory over his old rival, but no longer. Now he would
have given anything to be able to hand the title back to Niyes,
and the foul duty that came with it.

The prisoners knew they were to die. They moved reluctantly, only after much shoving and shouting on the guards'
parts; Charris could see the despair in their eyes. They could
not have seen the heavy-walled, locked wagon that Charris had
brought with him to the prison, and which now stood in an
adjoining courtyard. They could not have known about the
monster locked inside it—yet still they seemed to sense the

imminence of death. Criminals they might be, but they were true Gujaareen as well.

Because of that, Charris—normally more pragmatic than devout—prayed for them. *May Hananja watch over you in the dark places you'll inhabit for eternity*, he whispered in his mind. *And may you die better than Niyes did, for I saw his body when that thing was done with him.*

"Sir." Charris turned to see one of his message-riders standing at attention, escorted by one of the prison guards. The rider was sweaty and filthy, all but swaying with exhaustion. Charris narrowed his eyes and ordered the guard to go fetch lemonwater and salt. Then he pointed toward the floor, and the rider gratefully sat.

"Report."

"Orders were delivered to the southeast garrison by messenger bird two days ago," the rider said. "Another bird was dispatched from there to the southwest. The southeast commander distrusts birds for critical information, so he sent me to deliver the message to—" He hesitated. "To the high desert. I killed a horse getting there, but delivered the message successfully. On the return journey I passed through the border town of Ketuyae. The minstrel caravan crossed the river there a fourday ago."

"Just four days? You're sure?" Barring storms or accidents, the fastest desert route to the Kisuati Protectorate's northernmost trade-town was usually seven days. Ketuyae was a day out of Gujaareh. They would be past Tesa by now, half their journey completed.

"Yes, sir. But the desert commander assured me that his troop would be able to catch up to the caravan. They have good trackers.

And they have Shadoun horses, bred and trained for the high desert and twice as fast as any camel."

Which meant that it would take another day, perhaps two, for the garrison troop to find and catch up with the minstrel caravan. Right at the border. Charris could only pray that Sesshotenap, the commander of the desert force, would have enough sense to send his men without Gujaareen livery. All they needed was for a Kisuati patrol to catch a party of Gujaareen soldiers where they weren't supposed to be, dispatched from a garrison that wasn't supposed to exist, trying to kill a Kisuati ambassador. War was coming—Charris wasn't blind—but an incident like that could precipitate it sooner than the Prince wanted.

*And if that happens, I'll be lucky if he only beheads me.* Which reminded him of the task at hand.

The guard returned with a salt biscuit and a cup of lemon-water, which he held for the messenger, as the man's hands would not stop shaking. "Take a fourday's rest," Charris said, "but you must leave this place to do it. Guard, help him to the stables."

The messenger started and spilled a little of the water down his chin; out of habit he wiped his chin and licked the moisture from that hand. "Sir? Begging your pardon, but my horse is half dead, and I'm not much better—"

"You may have a fresh mount from our stable. But you should go quickly."

"It's a whole extra day to the city from here, sir!"

Charris scowled. "Stay, then," he snapped. "But when you hear what's about to happen and the sound haunts your night-mares for the rest of your life, remember that I tried to spare you."

He turned on his heel, ignoring the messenger's confused

"Sir?" behind him. As he walked off the parapet into the tower stairwell, he heard the prison guard telling the messenger to leave and not be a fool. Ah, but of course; the prison guards had witnessed this horror before, though on a lesser scale. They knew what was to come better than Charris himself did.

On the ground level the warden of the prison met him, his craggy face tight with nervousness. "Your, ah, guest has been restless, sir," the man said, turning to walk with Charris. "We tried to put food through the window-bars, but he growled at us and flung it out. We could try again—"

"No," Charris said. He reached for his hip-pouch and took out the rough chunk of jungissa-stone that the Prince had given him. "Food isn't what he hungers for right now. Make certain your men are out of the courtyard, and then wait."

He walked through the arched corridor that led to the other courtyard. Normally prisoners were let out to exercise here, but at the moment the dusty yard held only the reinforced wagon. The horses had been unhitched to stop them from chafing against the harness; they kept trying to get away from the wagon. As Charris walked toward it he heard nothing from within, though he sensed the attention of the thing inside. The window-shutters had been nailed closed save for the one used to feed its occupant. This one was barred, but as Niyes drew close he saw only darkness within.

He stopped just beyond the range of any arm that might extend through the bars and took a deep breath to school his thoughts. The Prince had given him explicit instructions, but between the pounding of his heart and the knowledge of what was to happen, he could barely remember them.

Then he heard something stir within the wagon. A halting voice, thick and clotted, spoke from the darkness. "Is it sunset, Brother? Will...will we go out tonight?"

Charris swallowed and tapped the back of the jungissa to set it humming. "Not tonight," he said, keeping his voice soft, no louder than the stone's hum. "But there is work for you here. Can you feel them? Gath—" He faltered, sought another word. "Assembled nearby. One hundred men in the next courtyard over. They have been judged corrupt and require your aid."

There was a shifting sound from within the wagon; the faint clink of chains. "I feel them. So many..." Then the voice hardened. "So many *corrupt*."

Charris swallowed. "Yes. You must take them, Brother—all of them at once. Do you understand? From where you are, without touching them. Can you do that?"

*The scrolls were explicit*, the Prince had told him. *In every account, Reapers could do this and more, Charris—see without eyes, kill without hands, drink life like wine and spit back wonders. Magic to rival the gods themselves. Don't you want to see that for yourself?*

*Not for all the riches in existence*, Charris had thought, though he'd known better than to give that answer aloud.

Within the wagon, Charris heard a long slow breath as though the creature tested the air through the barred window. "Filth and hatred. Do you feel it, Brother? Their fear?"

"Yes." That one Charris didn't have to feign. "I feel it."

"Filth." The Reaper's voice was hard again, almost angry. "They always fear us. No faith...blasphemy. I must purify them all. I must...I must..."

The first screams caught Charris by surprise. He'd thought there would be some warning. But Charris could still hear the creature muttering to himself within the wagon even as the individual screams blended into dozens, then a great chorus of anguish—which then began, voice by voice, to fall silent.

Then the chorus resumed, closer by.

Charris turned toward the archway and froze in shock. The warden stood there, his body rigid, his face twisting into an expression like nothing Charris had ever seen before—though his eyes were shut tight. Asleep. It was the guards who were screaming at the sight of him; the warden himself was silent. As Charris watched, the warden began to shake all over, his hands clenching and unclenching in rapid spasm, urine splattering the dusty ground beneath his loindrapes. His eyes snapped open suddenly, awake but not awake, white as cowrie shells. The muscles of his neck stood out in taut cords as his teeth ground audibly.

"No," Charris whispered.

"*No faith,*" snarled the Reaper.

It was happening all around now, throughout the prison fortress. The prisoners were dead. The guards were dying.

"No!" Horror woke Charris from his stupor at last. He ran to the wagon and banged on the bars. "Stop it! Not them! They—they are your brothers, you shouldn't, not them—"

"My brothers would not fear," came the voice from within, sounding more lucid now. More than lucid; there was a fierce, gleeful undercurrent in its voice.

"Stop it, gods damn you! You're killing everyone!"

Something moved in the shadows and then suddenly the

Reaper was at the bars. His eyes, the color of pitted iron surrounded by bloodshot whites, saw beyond the world into some nightmarish place Charris prayed he would never visit. Housing them was a painfully gaunt face, skin stretched so tightly over the bones that it shone like leather. That skin crinkled now—he expected to hear the sound of its flexing and folding, like dead leaves—in a rictus that Charris realized hours later was the Reaper's attempt to smile.

"I do not 'kill,'" the Reaper said.

Nearby, the last of the guards fell silent. Staring into those eyes, wishing he could close his own, Charris abruptly became aware that the only sound he could hear other than the wind was the jungissa's soft hum. Everyone else in the prison was dead.

Everyone but him.

*Only the jungissa protects me*, he realized.

And as that understanding came, his hand began, treacherously, to shake.

He whimpered, sensing with instinctive certainty that if he dropped the stone, the Reaper would take him. He could see that in the thing's mad eyes. It—for Charris could no longer think of the Reaper as a man—would burrow into his mind and rip loose his tether and drag him into the dank, shadowed cavern at its own core. There it would devour him mind and soul, leaving his flesh behind to rot.

As if hearing his thought, the Reaper nodded slowly. Then it moved back from the bars, fading once more into the shadows. By then trembling uncontrollably, Charris dropped the jungissa. It fell into the dust and stopped humming, leaving only the low sigh of the wind.

Some time passed.

Later, Charris could not have said how long. He had no thoughts during that time, as he waited for the first cold, invisible caress of death. But as his mind gradually resumed functioning, he became aware of slow, heavy breaths from within the wagon. The monster, having fed, now slept.

Charris looked up and saw that the stars had come out, framing the massive hemisphere of the rising Dreamer. By its multi-hued light he bent, stiffly, and picked up the jungissa. After a moment's thought he set it humming again and attached it to the gold-and-lapis collar his wife had given him at their marriage. The stone's faint whine resonated against the metal in a monotone song. That song comforted him as he finally turned to make his way out of the courtyard, heading to the stable to find the horses. For a moment the prospect of riding through the night with that *thing* hitched behind him almost made him stop thinking again, but the jungissa's song gradually lulled away his fears. It would keep him safe. Even monsters respected some boundaries.

He stepped carefully over the messenger's body as he prepared to return to Yanya-iyan.

# 23

(˙ʘ˙)

*A Gatherer shall carry with him always the mark of the Hetawa: Her sacred flower, the moontear. As well he shall leave his own mark in the form of a lesser flower, for in the execution of Her blessing a Gatherer is like unto divine.*

(Law)

When Sunandi saw the Gatherer go into the old woman's tent, she decided to act. Clenching her fists, she marched after him, intending to denounce him in front of the whole caravan if she had to—and then the boy stepped out of the shadows beside the tent. She stopped dead, suddenly uneasy. Were Gatherer-Apprentices permitted to kill? She couldn't recall, but something told her this one wouldn't care about permission.

But then the boy startled her by speaking. "He has sanction. That of the Goddess is all he needs, but he also spoke with Gehanu."

That shattered Sunandi's rising anger. Her fists unclenched and she stared at him. "I don't believe you."

"Not everyone fears death the way you do." There was no scorn in the boy's manner this time. His anger from their earlier altercation seemed to have faded completely. "Go speak to Gehanu if you doubt me."

"I will." She pivoted on her heel before she could question herself. Logic told her that in the time it took her to speak to Gehanu, the Gatherer could kill the old woman, but suddenly her courage seemed to have deserted her. The boy's manner had unnerved her too much. In that brief exchange he'd seemed far too much like his mentor, exuding the same perverse mingling of menace and compassion. That had been an unpleasant reminder of her own status of "abeyance," and the even less pleasant knowledge that they could revoke that status whenever they pleased.

It had been an error of judgment to discount the boy as a threat, she decided, trying to get a grip on her fear as she crossed the encampment and drummed on Gehanu's tent. Whatever the Hetawa did to train its killers had already set its mark deep in his soul.

Gehanu called for Sunandi to enter in her own tongue and grinned when she saw who it was, switching languages with the ease of a veteran trader. "Ah, Nefe. I would have thought you'd still be in the baths, enjoying a taste of civilization. Spoiled city woman."

Sunandi forced a smile, moving to sit opposite Gehanu's pallet. "I had a good soak earlier. 'Anu—about my companions—"

"The priest, you mean?" Gehanu smiled at Sunandi's startled nod. "You have so many secrets, some of them break loose when you aren't looking."

"So it seems. Then he *does* have your sanction? The boy said so. I didn't believe him."

"The boy was a surprise. Never saw a young one before, though I suppose they can't spring whole from gourds. Yes, I told him he could talk to Talithele."

"You—" She struggled to keep her tone polite and not accusatory. "You are aware of what he might do to her?"

"If she wants it."

"His kind don't care whether you want it or not."

Gehanu raised an eyebrow. "Aren't you the one who brought him here?"

"Under duress. I don't trust him. I don't even like him."

"A shame. He seems decent enough."

"For a killer! One of his 'brothers'..." She faltered as the grief rose again to mingle with her anger, nearly choking her. She pushed the word out around it. "Lin."

"The scamp? She was Gathered?"

"No, murdered. That thing that's been running around the city—"

"Ah!" Gehanu uttered a soft wail. "Not that! Tell me not!" She caught her breath when Sunandi nodded. "Oh gods of earth and sky."

"That monster started out as a Servant of Hananja, like him," Sunandi said, nodding in the direction of Talithele's tent. "That's why you should stop him."

But to her surprise, Gehanu shook her head. "Not my place. The choice belongs to Talithele."

"I told you—"

"He said he'd ask her permission. I believe him."

"You can't believe anything he says! Even he doesn't realize how evil he is!"

Gehanu's face became stony, and it was only then that Sunandi realized she'd raised her voice in her host's tent. "*Bi'incha.* Gehanu, forgive me." She sighed, rubbing her eyes. "I'm going mad. I miss Lin so much, I can't even think anymore."

"Forgiven," Gehanu said at once, her face softening. She reached over to take Sunandi's shoulder. "My heart aches with you, Nefe. But Talithele is dying. In my land she would be surrounded by dozens of her offspring, welcomed by all the ancestors buried beneath our soil. Here she is virtually alone and cut off from the land of her birth. The priest gives her another choice. I have no right to take it from her." Gehanu lifted her pipe, took a long inhalation, and sighed out smoke. "At least with the priest she will have no pain."

Sunandi lowered her eyes, feeling her own grief resonate with Gehanu's. If she could have given Lin this choice—Gathering, or the terrible death the girl had suffered instead—would she have done so? She refused to contemplate that question.

Instead she said, "Forgive me for questioning your decision."

Gehanu shrugged. "If it comforts you, I doubt she'll accept his offer. We asked her if she wanted to go to the Hetawa while we were in Gujaareh, and she said no. Didn't want to be healed—just wants to let life happen as it may. I can't imagine an eightday would have changed her mind. She'll stay around for as long as she can, just to plague me."

Sunandi smiled in spite of herself. "That would be good."

"Good? You don't know the woman. Enough about that. I'm glad you came, because I had something else to tell you."

"Oh?"

Gehanu nodded, setting the pipe down on its stand. She

241

began to rummage in her robes. "The village headman had a message that he wanted sent to Kisua. Since you speak for Kisua..." She pulled her hand out of a fold and opened it to reveal a tiny scroll. Sunandi caught her breath; it was the same type of scroll that Kinja had always used in communicating with Kisua's network of spies. She hadn't realized that network extended to Tesa. Kinja must have cultivated the village headman on his own.

She took the scroll and opened it, scanning the coded hieratics quickly. "Strange."

"Another stray secret?"

"I'm not certain. It says that some of the Shadoun have seen odd things some ways east of Tesa, in the high desert. Tracks where there should be none—camels and horses, many in number and carrying heavy enough to leave lasting marks. Two trackers went east to follow, but never returned. I don't understand why the headman thought this was significant."

Gehanu frowned. "The Shadoun tribe have lived in the high desert for generations. For one tracker to go astray is unusual. Two is bad."

"They could have been tracking a trade caravan too poor to pass through Tesa. Some poor fools who got lost. A marauder band that killed them, maybe."

"A lot of marauders, if so. And with a lot of provisions; you can't bring that many horses into the high desert without a reliable source of water and feed. That doesn't sound like poor lost caravanners."

"Soldiers, then?" Sunandi shook her head. "No. The Empty Thousand is neutral territory between the Protectorate and the

Gujaareen Territories. It belongs to the desert tribes, really, though mostly because no one else wants it. Neither land is permitted to send soldiers into it. Neither land *could*—there's nothing out there but sand. Soldiers need barracks, horses need stables…"

She trailed off even as Gehanu's eyes widened, both of them realizing the truth in the same moment.

"And a means of resupply," Gehanu said.

Sunandi nodded, her mind numbed by the implications. "A garrison. Near one of the smaller oases, most likely. But how big a garrison, housing how large a force? There can't be many. A force of any great size would have left permanent tracks as it moved through the desert. But then…" She drummed her hands on her legs, thinking. "It doesn't have to be a large force. Just enough to strike Kisua's defenses from an unexpected direction in advance of Gujaareh's real armies. With such surprise they could take the northernmost cities of the Protectorate, establish a foothold before our army could get back to fight them." Her hand trembled and she clenched it around the scroll. "Even with Kinja's warning, I never dreamed the Prince was this mad."

Gehanu watched her, nibbling her bottom lip a bit. "I'll send word around the camp. We'll leave well before dawn, and move with as much speed as possible."

Sunandi nodded. "The sooner we can get this news to Kisua, the better."

"Not only that." Gehanu gave her a small pained smile. "Those trackers went missing because there's an army out there trying not to be noticed, killing anyone it finds. If some of those recent tracks came from messengers bringing orders to that army from the city—the city where someone tried to kill you— I think maybe they will be trying hard to find *us*. Che?"

The evening desert chill had set in, but that had nothing to do with Sunandi's shiver. "Ah-che," she whispered.

"Ti-sowu." Gehanu smiled again, turning to a saddlebag that sat nearby. She flipped it open and pulled out two cups, followed by a polished gourd engraved with decorative carvings. "Here. You need to sleep tonight."

Sunandi raised her eyebrows as Gehanu gave her a cup and poured a generous amount from the gourd into it. Paniraeh wine, a potent spirit made only in the far southern countries. In spite of herself, she smiled down at the little cup. "I'll need more than this if I'm to sleep anytime soon."

"I promised I'd take care of you, didn't I?" Grinning, Gehanu produced a second bottle from the bag, then nodded toward the already-opened one. "That one is yours."

# THIRD INTERLUDE

( ⊙ )

*Now that you have heard the greater stories I must begin the lesser—
for I see that you have grown weary and distracted. No, don't apologize.
We are men of the Hetawa, after all; sleep is no hindrance. There, take
the couch. Sleep if you wish. I'll weave the tale into your dreams.*

*It began with a madman. In the days when Gujaareh was new—we
had only flesh healing in those days—the castes of the city began to take
shape. Those sonha nobles who had settled here from Kisua split into
two groups: the shunha, who wished to uphold the ways of Kisua as
much as possible, and the zhinha, who wished to make Gujaareh something new. The former kept to themselves and preserved the most
important lore of our motherland, while the latter mingled with outlanders and adopted many of their ways. Each group needed the other,
for without this mingling of tradition and progression Gujaareh could
never have established herself as a powerful trading nation so quickly.
Yet each group scorned the other too, for the divisions between them
were deep.*

*Two things kept them together: love of Hananja, and hatred of our enemies. In those days Gujaareh was threatened by the Shadoun, a proud tribe from the desert who beheld Gujaareh's growing wealth and coveted it for themselves. They believed us soft because of our civilized ways, and our belief in a sleeping goddess. But time and again we drove them back when they sent their raiding parties to test our defenses. It was the great general Mahanasset who led our army in those days—a man born pure shunha, yet also learned in the ways of foreign lands. His victories were brilliant, his strength in battle legendary; all loved him, from soldiers to the most rigid elders.*

*Yet as time passed, his leadership began to falter. First he lost one battle, then another. Rumors drifted back from the battle lines of strange behavior. Mahanasset gave orders to soldiers long dead, charged screaming at phantoms no one else could see. The Protectors of the city, for we did things like Kisua in those days, began to worry that it would be necessary to replace him, which would be a terrible blow to the people. If Mahanasset fell in battle, the city would revere him and the armies fight harder to avenge his name. But if he were set aside, the city would be wounded by sorrow. With the Shadoun hovering near like scavengers, we dared not weaken ourselves.*

*Thus did Inunru, the founder of our faith and head of the Hetawa at that time, intervene with a possible solution. In the ancient knowledge of narcomancy brought out of Kisua, there existed a secret form of healing that had been forbidden in the motherland because it brought death as well as life. Yet applied properly, this secret art might have the power to do what the Hetawa's healers otherwise could not—restore a broken soul to peace.*

*Yes, you understand now. It seems strange to think that something so valued in our society today was once feared and misunderstood then . . .*

but this was the beginning of the change. Mahanasset was brought to the Hetawa—raving, sick, unable to tell reality from phantasm. One of the Hetawa's priests, a dying old man, offered himself as the donor of the dream. Inunru himself performed the transfer from one to the other—and in the process the city beheld not one but two miracles. The first was the restoration of Mahanasset's sanity. He leaped up from his sickbed whole and healed in every way. The second, unexpected, miracle was the joy with which the old priest died. "Hananja, I come!" he is said to have cried in his sleep before the end. And there was no doubt that the old man had died happy, for Inunru shared his joy with everyone present. Many wept to know that he had experienced such peace.

The rest you can guess. Mahanasset resumed control of his army and led them in a devastating strike against the Shadoun, forcing them to pay tribute, barring them from the local trade, and assuring the world of Gujaareh's strength. The dying began to come to the Hetawa in fours, then in hordes, choosing peace over misery and pain. The afflicted were brought to the Hetawa as well, and sent away sane or healed in body. When Mahanasset returned from his victorious campaigns, the people were so joyful that they made him their ruler in place of the Protectors, naming him 'King' as barbarians do their lords. But he refused this.

"This is Hananja's city, as I am Hananja's servant," he said. "She can be the only true ruler here. I will rule in Her name as Prince, and claim 'King' only when I can take my place at Her side in Ina-Karekh. And I will rule with the guidance of the Hetawa, without whose wisdom Gujaareh might have fallen."

And so it was. Under Mahanasset the Hetawa's law became Gujaareh's law, and Hananja's peace became the Prince's gift to the people. And thus did it begin that we honor Hananja above all others.

# 24

(˙⊙˙)

*Members of the four paths to Hananja's wisdom are
permitted to put aside propriety and the order of command,
so long as this is done in service of peace.*

(Law)

The Superior of the Hetawa sat in his office, enjoying the
sounds of early morning, and wondering again how long it
would be before his Gatherers came for him.

A day and a night had passed since the meeting with the
Prince, and its aftermath. Usually when he returned from such
meetings in the small hours of the morning, few of the Hetawa's
denizens were about—only the two Sentinels who served as his
bodyguards, the ones on guard duty, and the handful of Sharers
on night duty. Sometimes a few sleepy acolytes accompanied
the latter, in their contemplation of the Sentinels' or Sharers'
paths, and a few apprentices assisted their older brethren. But as
the Superior had passed through the Hall of Blessings that
morning, Rabbaneh had been there, kneeling at Hananja's
feet—but not praying. The Gatherer instead faced the Hall's
entrance, and he had not donned his hooded robe; he was still

on duty. Shocking to see him like that, the Superior reflected, with his back to the statue. A snub to Hananja, though a mild one since after all the statue was only a statue.

But Rabbaneh's gaze had been fixed on the Superior, his face unsmiling, his gaze a condemnation. *There is only one affront to Hananja here,* those eyes had said. And with that, the Superior had known his Final Tithe had come due.

He had spent the time since confined to his rooms, ordering no visitors so he could pray and contemplate and prepare himself for Hananja's peace. During the night he had inadvertently fallen asleep, and been astonished to wake up alive. There would be no time to brief Teacher Maatan, his chosen successor, in the secrets that came with the mantle of Superior. Those secrets had all gone wrong anyhow. Perhaps if they died with him, the Hetawa might survive the coming storm.

The beaded front hanging rattled to announce that someone had entered his quarters. The Superior tensed, then forced himself to relax. Only a Council messenger or a Sharer responding to an emergency could violate the Superior's privacy when he requested it. And Gatherers, of course. They went wherever they pleased. He opened his eyes.

They stood on the other side of his desk, solemn, still dressed in their sleeveless formal robes after the morning's Tithing Ceremony. Not a Gathering, then. The Superior wasn't certain whether to feel relief or annoyance.

"We would speak with you, Brother Superior." Sonta-i, sounding as though he'd come to discuss the weather. And perhaps this meant no more than that to him, with his peculiar sense of right and wrong. Doubtless it was Rabbaneh who needed the explanations and details; for Sonta-i it was a simple matter. If the Superior was corrupt, then the Superior would die.

"Yes," the Superior said. "I've been waiting."

"We come to speak only," Rabbaneh said. He sat in the chair on the other side of the Superior's desk. Sonta-i remained standing.

"An Assay of Truth, then. I should thank you for your consideration." The Superior sighed. "Though a part of me would prefer you get this over with."

"Explain," Sonta-i said. "Perhaps we shall oblige you."

The Superior rose, going to a nearby cupboard. He opened it and took out a red bottle, wrought of glass by one of the greatest craftsmen in the city. Gatherers shunned drink for their own pleasure, but sometimes they would partake on a tithebearer's behalf. "Drink with me, Brothers. I'm not quite an elder yet. I'm not ready to spend my last hours alone."

"Is this a confession?" Rabbaneh watched his face intently as the Superior took three red glasses from the cupboard and set them down on his desk. "Are you *asking* for Hananja's blessing?"

The Superior paused for a moment, considering, then sighed and began to pour. "Yes to the first question, no to the second. I would like very much to live. But I know the law of this land as well as you and by that law, Her Law, I am corrupt. Whatever you may think of me, I have never *wanted* to be a hypocrite." He paused, taking his glass and nodding for them to take the others. Rabbaneh hesitated but then took one. Sonta-i did not.

Instead Sonta-i said, "Whether you wanted it or not, you have become one. Only a hypocrite would decry our brother as a rogue, then allow the Prince to take him away. If you believed him dangerous, he should never have left this Hetawa and the care of his brethren. But Rabbaneh says you acted on the Prince's orders." For just an instant something flashed across Sonta-i's weathered face: curiosity. "How is it that the Superior of the Hetawa, Hananja's foremost Servant, follows any orders save Hers?"

The Superior lifted his glass and took a sip, savoring the sweet, clear taste. A Giyaroo liqueur; one of the few northland delicacies he had ever liked. "You must understand I did not know everything at first. The Prince is a master at concealing his plans. For three years even I was fooled. Now I know the truth: the Prince is quite mad."

Rabbaneh's face was implacable. Good-humored Rabbaneh, who had been hot-tempered Rabbaneh in the years before he'd become a Gatherer. Fascinating to see that something of their old selves could surface at times like this. "Then he should be given dreamblood and healed."

The Superior fought the urge to laugh. He covered it by taking a long swallow from the glass instead. "He *was* given dreamblood. That was how this nightmare began." Ah, but it had begun long before that, in the birth throes of Gujaareh and even before that in Kisua. He should confess it all to them, tell the whole truth so that they could experience the same shock and horror and disillusionment that had afflicted him since he'd found out—

No. The words of his predecessor drifted back to him, full of loathsome wisdom: *A Servant of Hananja exists to ease Gujaareh's pain. The role of the Superior is to ease the pain of his fellow Servants. There are secrets that would destroy your brethren; it is your duty to bear them alone.*

Bear them and be crushed beneath them, it seemed.

"The Prince killed his father to gain the throne," the Superior said, gazing into the red glass. "Such things happen. But when Eninket—our Prince, pardon—took the Aureole, he immediately began to show signs of a dangerous instability. Among other curious acts, he sent a force to Kite-iyan and had slaughtered every one of his father's wives and other children, down to the newborns. Including his own mother. Only Ehiru survived, because the Hetawa had laid claim to him by that point." He paused, thoughtful. "Some say Ehiru's mother had the gift of true-seeing and knew the slaughter would come. We shall never know for certain, as Ehiru does not speak of his past."

"Perhaps because it has nothing to do with the current situation," Sonta-i said.

The Superior smiled. He envied Gatherers their ability to see the world in simple terms: peace and corruption, good and evil. A Superior had no such luxury.

"It has everything to do with the situation, Brother Sonta-i, but I appreciate your impatience." He took another sip of the liqueur. "The Hetawa's duty seemed clear. We offered the Prince dreamblood—as a privilege of power, you see. The upper castes of the city whisper that it far surpasses timbalin or any other pleasure drug. The fact that it heals the mind is something they neither understand nor care about, but it suits our purposes. So a Sharer was dispatched to provide the dreamblood and perform the healing. But the Sharer found there was no madness to heal—not in the physical sense, at least. His humors were in balance; his head had suffered no injury. The Prince's... excesses... were committed in perfect sanity."

"Corruption," Rabbaneh said. He scowled. "On the *Sunset Throne*."

"It has happened before," the Superior said, taking care to keep irony out of his voice. They were already angry enough. "A certain amount of corruption is inherent in any position of power. For the peace of the city we tolerate it. But what is relevant in this case is that the Prince, as a result of our attempt, tasted dreamblood. He demanded more."

Sonta-i was staring at him with narrowed eyes, perhaps sensing his prevarication. To avoid the Gatherer's probing gaze, the Superior drank the last of the liqueur, which delved a pleasant fiery trail down his throat.

"You didn't give it to him?" Rabbaneh's eyes were wide as he understood—or thought that he understood—the danger. "In quantities sufficient to heal..."

The Superior sighed. "A Prince who can slay his own mother is capable of many things, Gatherer Rabbaneh."

It took a moment for understanding to sink in for Rabbaneh. When it did he caught his breath. "He would not dare threaten the Hetawa! All Gujaareh would rise up against him."

"He would never threaten *openly*. But make no mistake; though the Hetawa and the Sunset Throne purport to share power in the city, along with the highcastes and the military, the Prince is stronger than any one of those groups alone. Ordinarily we have the support of the people to balance this weakness in our favor; any attempt to control the Hetawa, by any power of the city, would be seen as an affront to Hananja Herself. Even the servant-castes would take up arms on our behalf. But in this case, the Prince had a weapon to counter that as well—the weapon we had given him. He would claim that the healing marked the Hetawa's attempt to control the Throne."

He saw the quintessential horror of that sink in for both of them. The Hetawa, publicly accused of corruption? Unthinkable. Intolerable. They were both so very, very pure.

"So now the Sunset controls the Hetawa of Hananja." Sonta-i folded his arms. "Foul as this circumstance is, it doesn't explain your secret meeting with the Prince in the small hours of the night, like some skulking criminal. Or the fact that the subject of conversation was our brother. You will explain."

The Superior's fingers tightened on the glass. Clever Rabbaneh, not just following him but eavesdropping as well. So much for protecting them, then. He prayed their faith would survive the truth. It had taken many years for his own to recover.

"It is in part that Ehiru is his last living brother," the Superior said. "I believe he enjoys having his brother's life in his hands at last. The rest of it…Understand, my Gatherer brothers, that even I didn't realize the lengths to which the Prince was willing to go. I thought if we kept him in dreamblood that would be enough. As Superior, I have all but bathed in corruption—yet always I have tried to keep it from soaking through my own skin. The good of the people, the will of Hananja; these things I have kept foremost in my mind."

"Corruption is a disease of the *soul*," Sonta-i said. The Superior had expected no mercy from him. But when he looked at Rabbaneh and saw the same hardness in the younger Gatherer's eyes, he knew Hananja's judgment had fallen upon him at last.

So be it.

"Tell us the rest of it, Superior," Rabbaneh said, very softly. "Tell it all."

"Dreamblood," the Superior said. "In the end, it all comes down to that."

*May Her blessing wash me clean*, he thought as he began his final confession, *and the Hetawa along with me. May I find the peace in Ina-Karekh that I have never deserved. And may you, my Gatherers, my brothers, find the strength to save us all.*

# 25

(◦ ⊙ ◦)

*The shadows of Ina-Karekh are the place where nightmares dwell, but not their source. Never forget: the shadowlands are not elsewhere. We create them. They are within.*

(Wisdom)

The first half of the journey to Kisua had been filled with routine—dawn waking and breakfast followed by twelve sweltering, mind- and body-numbing hours on camelback as they forged their way across the golden dune sea. But then had come Tesa, the halfway point, and after that the routine changed. A new sense of urgency seemed to have gripped Gehanu. She drove the caravan across the desert at a pace that left even the most experienced of the minstrels complaining at the end of the day. They began before dawn and finished well after sunset, stopping only when continuing would have threatened the camels' health.

Nijiri was thankful, despite his own exhaustion and soreness. Because of the brutal pace, few of the minstrels noticed Ehiru's shivering despite the day's heat, or his unfocused stare. Or the prayers that he continually murmured under his breath, a litany against the swirling chaos of sound and vision that had surely begun to overtake his mind. It was the beginning of the pranje—out here in the wild desert, miles from any center of civilization where a suitable tithebearer might be found, with no hope of privacy or solitude to ease the Gatherer's suffering during Hananja's test. And surrounded by unbelievers, for even the Gujaareen among the minstrels were the sort who worshipped Hananja only in word and not heart. They would not offer themselves to a Gatherer's need, no matter how much they revered Hananja's highest Servants. So what could Nijiri do but lie beside Ehiru at night, whispering prayers to help him focus on reality? By day he rode alongside Ehiru, assisting his brother when he could and using all his guile to turn aside the chance attentions of the minstrels.

But as he'd feared, one among their party had already noticed.

The Kisuati woman confronted him at the midday rest break. "What's wrong with him?" she demanded. They had begun to enter the scrublands that presaged Kisua's northern border. The track of the Goddess's Blood meandered in lazy east-west loops at this point, which—along with the fact that travel south was against the current—was what had made the desert route the faster option. In another day they would cross the river at the Imsa Narrows, which marked the northern border of Sunandi's homeland.

*She will have power then.* Nijiri reminded himself of this as he accepted the canteen that she offered, her excuse for speaking privately to him. Since they would reach the river soon, he drank deeply before replying, grimacing at the brackish taste.

"Too much time has passed since his last Gathering," Nijiri

said, speaking quietly. He sat in the shadow of his camel, close enough to watch Ehiru but not so close that the other caravanners would notice.

She crouched across from him. "When will he become one of those *things?*"

"We do not speak of this to layfolk—"

She spat a stream of Sua at him, too fast for him to follow although its gutter content was obvious. "You will speak of it to *me*," she finished in Gujaareen. Of course. She too had seen that the balance of power between them was shifting. They could still kill her, and would if Ehiru deemed her corrupt—but in her land that would bring the wrath of the Protectors down on their heads.

Nijiri sighed. "Gatherers are not like other men. The tithes we collect for the Goddess...change us. Surely you have heard of this in tales about our kind."

"Yes. You go mad if you don't kill. Why aren't you mad yet?"

Nijiri felt his cheeks heat in a mingling of anger and shame. "I'm only an apprentice. I've never collected dreamblood."

"Ah. Then answer my question: when does he change?"

"He will not."

Another Sua curse. "Clearly it has already begun."

"He would never permit himself to become such an abomination. He would die first." Nijiri fought the tears that suddenly stung his eyes. "He's dying *now*. If he were the monster you imagined, half this caravan would be dead already. Instead he waits, enduring nightmares you cannot possibly imagine. Can you not see his suffering?"

She rocked back on her heels at his anguish; Nijiri could read consternation in her eyes. "What I see looks like madness. What does he wait for?"

Nijiri bowed his head, telling himself fiercely that he would not weep before this unbeliever. "Me," he whispered.

"You!"

"I'm the only one here who can give him death in the proper manner. If I can manage it. My training is complete but I have never...my narcomancy is..." He was breathing too hard, his fists clenching. He took a deep breath to get control of himself. "There's no way to practice Gathering. When the time comes, the apprentice must simply *do* it. But to Gather my mentor..."

Sunandi stared at him as he faltered and let the words fall away. Several breaths passed. In Gujaareh it was considered proper to allow such silences in conversation, but Nijiri had already realized this was not something foreigners did. If Sunandi was silent, it never indicated peaceful thoughts.

"I should attend him," Nijiri said at last. He handed the canteen back to her and got to his feet. "Tonight I'll...After tonight, I will be the one who goes with you to learn whatever your Protectors can share of the Prince's plans. Then I'll return to Gujaareh and destroy the Reaper." Hollow words. The monster would kill him and they both knew it. But he could say nothing else with grief still thick in his throat.

She watched him, frowning, her anger visibly lessened. "Why did he come on this journey?" she asked. "It seems foolish if he knew he wouldn't survive it."

Nijiri shook his head. "A Gatherer can endure without dreamblood for several eightdays—as much as a full turn of the Waking Moon. But that's amid the peace and order of the

259

Hetawa, where the Gatherer may pray and calm himself amid the Contemplation Gardens. Fear and danger devour dream-blood faster." He sighed, unhappily. "Ehiru's heart lacked peace to begin with because of his last Gathering, which went badly. And then he met you, with your accusations against the Het-awa. And then the Reaper attacked and forced him to use his last reserve to save me..." He sighed, bowing his head. "Gather-ers need peace, to thrive. In more ways than one."

She stared at him for a long moment. Then she did some-thing odd: she got to her feet, paced a few steps away, then paused and turned back. "What does he need?"

"What?"

"To survive." Her lip curled as if the very words offended her, but she said, "Can he be saved at this point?"

Nijiri scowled. "Do you expect me to believe you care?"

"I care that making my case to the Protectors will be easier if he stands at my side." She smiled thinly at Nijiri's look of affront. "One of the dreaded Gatherers of Gujaareh—the famous Ehiru himself—petitioning the Kisuati Protectorate for aid because he can no longer trust his own rulers? That will appeal to their vanity as well as their reason. And add to my prestige."

"How dare you use him for your...your..." He groped for the words, almost too outraged to speak. "Your filthy, *corrupt* games—"

"Lower your voice, little fool!"

He did so immediately, his anger chilling as he noticed the curious glances of the other caravanners and realized his out-burst had been overheard. But he let his gaze show his loathing, glaring at the woman as he would never have done at a Sister.

"If only he would revoke your abeyance," he said. He kept his tone gentle, though the words were vicious. "*That* would save him. But he's too honorable to take even the likes of you without being sure of your corruption."

She smiled, and in spite of himself he was amazed by her steel. "And I appreciate that consideration," she said, "which is why I'm willing to help you save him. He needs death, yes? There's a hospital—think of it as a temple, but only for healing and not worship—in the town of Tenasucheh, just on the other side of the Kisuati border. I can bring him there, speak to the healers. If he kills someone already dying I may be able to justify that to the Protectors."

*To save Ehiru-brother*— Hope, after so many days without it, struck so fiercely that it seemed to burn in Nijiri's belly. "It must be someone willing to die. Otherwise he may refuse."

Her eyes rolled. "Willing, then. Though a dying man should not be so picky."

"He's not like you. To a Gatherer, death is a blessing."

"But not to you." She gave him a cold, knowing smile; he flinched. "I've seen the way you look at him. You would do anything to keep him alive—so you shall take this chance, even though you despise me. And then you shall stand beside him in the Protectors' Hall and beg them for help, knowing that your every word increases my power. Then they will listen to me even though I'm only Kinja's too-young, unseasoned daughter. We must use one another now, little killer, if we are both to achieve our goals."

Nijiri flinched at her words and their implications—far beyond the petty schemes she imagined. It was as the Teachers, even lecherous Omin, had warned him: *those who consort with the corrupt eventually become corrupt themselves.* Evil was the most contagious of diseases, so virulent that no herb, surgery, or dream-humor could cure it. One's sense of what was normal, acceptable, became distorted by proximity to wrongness; entire nations had succumbed this way, first to decadence, then collapse. Sunandi, and perhaps all Kisua, was well advanced in the throes—and now she had spat this sickness onto Nijiri. Only his will would determine whether the sickness passed and left him stronger, or consumed him wholly.

But he would keep others' needs foremost in his thoughts, as Gatherer Rabbaneh had taught him. He would risk corruption, if that was what it took, to see that peace was restored and justice done. Because that was what a Gatherer did. And if it cost his soul to do so... well, at least he might save Ehiru. That, alone, would be worth it.

"So be it." He turned away to go tell Ehiru the news. Perhaps, knowing that this hospital was near, his brother could hold out a little longer. But then he stopped.

Ehiru was on his feet. He had stepped out of the makeshift lean-to that the minstrels used to shield themselves from sun at the midday rest, and stood now facing north. To Nijiri's eye the deterioration was obvious in the way that Ehiru swayed slightly as he stood, and in the hollows of his face; he had no appetite these days. But his back was straight and his eyes—though dimmed at the moment by a slight confusion, as though he doubted something he saw—were for the moment lucid. Nijiri felt hope rise a notch higher. Surely Ehiru could last another day or two.

"Something is out there," Ehiru said suddenly. The minstrels glanced around at him in surprise. He took another step onto the hot, rocky sand. "Someone is coming."

Nijiri went to him, Sunandi forgotten as he touched his brother's arm and spoke in a low voice. "Is it a vision, Brother? Tell me what you see."

"Evil," Ehiru said, and for a sick instant Nijiri wondered if Ehiru spoke of him. But the Gatherer's eyes were fixed on the horizon.

"No. Gods, no." The Kisuati woman stood nearby; Nijiri saw that her eyes too had fixed on the horizon. Puzzled, Nijiri followed their gazes and finally saw for himself: a row of dust-shrouded specks amid the wavering heat-lines, flickering and solidifying and flickering again—but growing closer.

"Evil, and blood," Ehiru said, and then he turned to Nijiri. "We should run."

# 26

**( ⊙ )**

*A Gatherer shall submit himself to Her test once per year. He shall purge himself of all tithes, and travel between dreaming and waking with only Her favor to guide him. He shall endure in this state for three nights, or until death draws nigh. At the height of this test, he shall be attended by one who does not begrudge Hananja's tithe. If even once the Gatherer claims Her tithe for his own selfish desires, he shall fail.*

(Law)

In the borderlands between Ina-Karekh and Hona-Karekh, a voice whispers.

For a time Ehiru could ignore the voice, as he had long ago learned to do. Deny a vision and it has no power. This one is easy to deny. It is soft, sometimes inaudible, rambling and gibbering when he can hear it. But it never stops, and every so often it says something so provocative that he cannot help responding.

*His words were full of lies. "Remember that I freed you"* love me *forgive me serve me.*

Eninket? thinks Ehiru. Perhaps.

*One lie, another lie. The Superior. The Kisuati woman. The Law and Wisdom of your faith. Your brothers, all your brothers.*

No. I do not believe that.

*All your brothers. Even the boy. Brother protector lover son.*

Nijiri would never lie to me. I will listen to no more of this.

\*    \*    \*

A vision:

He walks along the banks of the Blood at sunset, Kite-iyan gleaming atop its hill in the near distance. He is small. His mother holds his hand. He looks up at the woman he can no longer remember clearly, though parts of her linger in his mind: skin smooth as polished nightstone, a laugh rich like cattail wine, eyes that are pools on a Dreamer-less night. Is she beautiful? She must be, for she is a foreigner and yet has become the firstwife of a king. He wishes he could remember more of her.

"Soon," he says to her, a man's voice coming from his childish throat. "I will see you again very soon."

She looks at him, dark lips and graceful brows and blurred perfection, and he knows that she is sad. This troubles him for reasons he cannot remember. But when he opens his mouth to speak to her again, the words flee and the thoughts jumble and the vision is

\*    \*    \*

"It is not real, Brother."

Ehiru blinks and sees darkness. Cold air goosebumps his skin. The Dreamer's shifting light makes the dunes seem to roll like water in the distance. A warm body presses against his on the pallet. Nijiri.

"I know," Ehiru says, though he is beginning to doubt that

265

what he sees is not real. His mind has begun to wander toward Ina-Karekh, and he knows better than anyone that the land of dreams is a real place with real power.

"I want to be with my mother," he says, and the boy flinches. Ehiru regrets inflicting pain in this manner, but Nijiri is a man by the laws of their people, a sworn Servant of the Goddess. It is time for him to face the responsibility of his role. "At Kite-iyan. You have never seen that palace, so I will describe it to you." And he does so, drawing on a hundred memories from his childhood, embellishing its beauty unnecessarily. "I can shape the rest, but it must be that place. She will be there, and I want to see her again."

The boy's tears wet his skin. "Do not ask this of me, Brother. Please."

But there is no one else and they both know it. And even if their other brothers were available he would choose Nijiri, for the boy loves him. That is the key, Ehiru understands now. Gathering is an act of love; without that, it becomes something perverse. When Nijiri Gathers him there will be beauty more sublime than he has ever known, because the boy has loved him for years, loved him through pain and beyond, loved him with a strength that pales the Sun's love for the Dreamer.

He feels no shame at the thought of using that love for his own ends. It has always been a gift freely given between them.

*       *       *

The voice returns at mid-morning, when they resume their ride and monotony weakens the wall he has built to contain the madness. He ignores most of its ravings until it says,

*The Kisuati woman is beautiful, is she not?*

He is prepared for this. Lust is one of the first emotions to break free once a Gatherer's dreamblood reserves are drained. He ignores the voice and the image it plants in his mind: Sunandi lying on a red cloth, her long neck bent back for his lips, her full breasts ready for his hands, desire in her long-lashed eyes. There is a powerful stir in his loins, but this too he ignores out of long habit.

*Never once with a woman in your whole life. Why? Kisuati women know ways of preventing children.*

Children are the least of the prohibition, he thinks back, irritably. There is also the danger of corruption—even greater with her. She lies for a living.

The voice sounds triumphant, as if getting him to respond has been its private battle.

*No need for lies in bed,* it whispers slyly. *No need for speech. Just lay her down and spread her thighs and bury your troubles in her flesh.*

No.

The voice bursts into laughter, harsh and mocking, because it knows that his refusal is not for lack of interest. It will try again later when his will has weakened further and he has become more susceptible to its suggestions. That is only a matter of time.

\* \* \*

Another vision. Fire dances along the horizon. The earth itself is burning. Inhumanly tall figures stride toward him amid the flames. Gods? But their faces are familiar. He gasps as he recognizes his brothers, Sonta-i and Rabbaneh and Una-une.

But Una-une is dead—

As he recalls this, he sees that his old mentor is smiling at him. But there is no affection in the smile, though they were all but father and son during the months of his apprenticeship. Instead the smile is cold, cruel. Una-une turns his eyes downward and when Ehiru looks he sees that the god-Gatherers walk upon not sand or rock, but bodies. The corpses lie sprawled and ugly, utterly without dignity, though to Ehiru's horror he sees sigils pressed into their flesh. Rabbaneh's poppy. Sonta-i's nightshade. Una-une's green orchid. His own oasis rose, stark and black. As he stares at the last, which rests upon the breast of a beautiful lowcaste woman, *Nijiri's mother oh Hananja*, Una-une's foot comes down and crushes her chest. He hears bones breaking, sees clotted blood welling around his mentor's sandal, smells and tastes its stench. It is desecration of the most obscene kind and he screams for them to stop.

"They cannot," says a voice at his side, and he looks down into Nijiri's solemn eyes. "This is the Gatherer way."

\*     \*     \*

Ehiru jerks free of the vision quietly, some part of him recalling in time that he is surrounded by unbelieving strangers who will look askance at a man who starts screaming for no apparent reason. An overabundance of dreambile, he diagnoses as his pounding heart slows. A Gatherer no longer produces dreamblood on his own. When his reserves are empty, the mind increases the production of other humors in a hopeless attempt to compensate. The scholarly recitation helps him focus on reality even as the sound of snapping bones still echoes in his ears.

"Rest break, Brother," Nijiri says. Ever the devoted attendant.

Ehiru nods, too hollow and numb to speak. He remembers to rein in the camel so that he can dismount; he goes through the motions of setting up his lean-to by rote. When he sits down in the shade the shivers set in. He pulls his robes more closely about himself and concentrates on opening his canteen, praying that no one notices his shaking hands.

*I cannot bear this much longer,* he thinks, and looks up at Nijiri as the boy comes to assist him with the canteen. He will not plead; the boy must accept the duty on his own. *But soon, Nijiri. Please, soon.*

Nijiri looks into his face, and his own twists in anguish. Ehiru reaches up to touch his cheek, perversely wishing he had dreamblood to soothe the boy's pain. But Nijiri pulls away, and though his heart aches, Ehiru knows that this is necessary. Perhaps by putting distance between them Nijiri will find the strength to do his duty. It is an exceptionally cruel apprenticeship trial, but Hananja's will cannot be denied. Nijiri is strong enough for it, Ehiru thinks with pride. The boy has always had a Gatherer's soul.

The boy goes over to crouch in the shadow of his camel, rocking back and forth a little as he wrestles with his conscience. Then the Kisuati woman goes over to Nijiri with a canteen and Ehiru wants to watch them, see if the boy manages to keep his temper this time, but he cannot because another vision comes upon him and it is so fierce that he cannot resist and he sees

\* \* \*

Blood and death blood on the sand blood and fire blood upon blood upon blood. Kill the Kisuati woman kill the witnesses kill them all except Ehiru, bring him back in chains in chains in chains.

Slyly the voice says, *Eninket knows you have betrayed him.*

I betrayed no one. When the abeyance ends—

*Delay, disobedience. HeShe is the Avatar; his word is Her word, which is Law. But there's still time. Kill the woman now and Shehe will be merciful. You can go back to the Hetawa. You can have peace again. The woman is young but her life has been rich. Her dreamblood will be sweet as you swallow it into your soul.*

No! I cannot Gather for selfish gain! That is an atrocity—

*The atrocity is what will happen now. Because of you. Do not forget this, fool, beloved of Hananja. Real blood will flow because of you.*

He looks up and sees death coming. A true-seeing—

\* \* \*

Reality returned, hard as a blow.

"Something is out there," he said. He felt no particular urgency as the words came. "Someone is coming."

Nijiri was at his side immediately. "What do you see?"

The figures strode toward him from the horizon, immense, smiling, cold-eyed. They were evil, and he told Nijiri so. Flight was the only option—though he sensed already that flight would be hopeless.

"Break camp!" Gehanu cried. She ran through the milling minstrelfolk, swift despite her bulk. "Quickly, we must go! Soldiers of Gujaareh!"

The minstrels' confusion beat against Ehiru's mind, their questions against his ears. Why would soldiers of Gujaareh threaten them? Where had those soldiers come from? Ehiru did not know either, but someone did. There was no confusion in the Kisuati woman as she turned toward her mount—but as she did, her eyes met his and revealed her fear.

"They mean to kill you this time," Ehiru told her.

She flinched, then her lips quirked in a bitter smile. "I seem to hear nothing else from you Gujaareen these days." Then she was gone, heading for her camel, and Nijiri was tugging him toward his.

Ehiru gripped the boy's arm. "I'll be fine," he said, and saw the boy's eyes widen at his sudden lucidity. He smiled tightly in response; a Gatherer's will was a formidable thing. Nijiri smiled back before nodding and sprinting toward his own beast.

They mounted and whipped their camels to the loping canter that was their fastest run. The camels smelled their fear and obliged without protest. The Kisuati border was only a half-day's ride away. There was no way to tell how far back the Gujaareen were through the heat-haze, or even whether they had spotted the caravan. There was hope.

*No there isn't*, laughed the voice in Ehiru's mind.

When he glanced back again, the wavering specks on the horizon had resolved into clear shapes: men on horseback, four fours or more, riding hard to catch up to them. The minstrels called out to one another in polyglot urgency and all around Ehiru daggers and camelwhips and the occasional short sword appeared. Then Gehanu called out something else and the leaders of the caravan turned, dragging the rest to a halt. Instantly they began circling, backs to one another, weapons at the ready. Talithele's palanquin they set down at the center, along with the heavier of the trade goods so as to make their mounts more maneuverable.

To Sunandi, Ehiru heard Gehanu shout, "Go!"

To which Sunandi replied, "I'll never make it."

"Try, damn you! We will hold them here."

But already Ehiru could see that the double-line of horses had split, some veering to the east and the others west to flank them. The minstrels would never be able to hold all of the soldiers, and it would take only one to break off from the two-pronged attack and run Sunandi down.

"Merik's Fires, they're not slowing at all—" Ehiru heard one of the minstrels gasp, and then the soldiers were upon them.

Somewhere in the chaos that followed, Ehiru flung himself off the camel and rolled to his feet in the sand. He could fight better on the ground. A soldier rode at him with sword drawn; he braced himself. It took all his strength and skill to capture the flat of the blade between his hands when the soldier swung at his head. He threw his weight to one side and twisted the sword sharply; surprise and momentum made the soldier lose his grip on the hilt as the horse rode past. Ehiru threw the blade aside—and then gasped as his sight blurred, another landscape superimposing itself on the present. A forest out of nightmare: ferns whose tendrils reached for him, palm fronds dripping poison...

*No! Not now! Not—*

"—That one, damn you!" Ehiru pulled himself out of the vision to see a soldier on the other side of the chaos, reining in his horse to shout at the man who'd just tried to decapitate

Ehiru. This one wore no livery—none of them did—but the stamp of the Gujaareen military caste was plain in his sharp features and heavy jaw. Something in his manner hinted at command. "Orders are to bring him back alive!"

Then Ehiru had no more time for thought. Dust and cacophony filled the air, human cries mingling with animal panic and the clang of metal. Around him life and death flickered in vignettes: Gehanu's son Kanek struggling to control his frightened mount while a soldier bore down on him from behind. The singer Annon desperately using her precious harp as a shield while a soldier hacked at it with his sword. A dancer whose name Ehiru did not know screaming on the ground with his belly open and intestines laid out before him.

His sight locked on the last. A Gathering would be more merciful than the death the dancer faced now. Pivoting on his toes Ehiru stalked toward the man, the battle around him fading into so much background noise. "There are no Sharers here," he whispered to himself. The words rang hollow despite their truth. He pushed aside guilt and tried to focus on his duty. "It must be done."

But before he could reach the man there was a flurry of something at the edge of his vision. A distraction; he ignored it. But then it moved into view and he saw a soldier, horse wheeling away from a minstrel with a whip—

*NO!*

—And the dancer made no sound as the horse's hoof came down on his head. Brain and bone sprayed the ground, the essence of a man's whole self scattered to the dust.

Ehiru was not prepared for the rage, a flood of hatred so

savage that his head pounded with it. But the soldier who had stolen his tithebearer had ridden off into the fray already.

*Kill him*, said the voice.

And Ehiru replied, "Yes, I shall."

He ran after the soldier, silent, intent. Something moved across his vision and blocked his path, a different soldier brandishing a sword, words about surrender. He batted the sword aside and took hold of the arm that held it, ramming the heel of his free hand into the elbow. The wet pop of the breaking joint sounded like the head of the dancer, who might have been sentenced to an eternity in the shadowlands by a soldier's carelessness. "I shall avenge you," he whispered to the dancer's soul, yanking the screaming, broken-armed soldier off the horse. The soldier kept screaming, writhing on the ground and holding the flopping ruin of his arm. Ehiru contemplated him for a moment, then remembered that this was not the soldier he wanted. He stepped around the riderless horse and continued after his prey.

Another soldier fell to the ground at his feet, choking and spitting blood. Nijiri ran into view, poised to strike again, though he held the blow when he saw that the soldier was disabled. Ehiru smiled at the sight.

"Brother!" The boy was wild-eyed. "There are more soldiers approaching from the south, a Kisuati patrol. If we can hold out a bit longer—" He caught his breath and whirled away as another soldier rode at him.

"Good," Ehiru said, gliding onward. The boy was a Gatherer; he could take care of himself.

He spotted the soldier he'd marked near the center of the madness—perilously near Talithele's palanquin. "You shall *not*," he whispered, and charged past a riderless camel to grab the man's leather half-torso under the arm. He hauled with all his weight and the startled soldier tumbled to the ground, confused but still trying to raise his sword. Ehiru stepped on the sword and put one knee on the man's chest to pin him down. Then he took hold of the man's hair and chin to break his neck—

*Take him.*

He frowned, pausing.

*For the Goddess. A tithe was lost; here is another.*

Around Ehiru the world was chaos. The soldiers had spotted the Kisuati patrol and were beginning to withdraw, harried by the surviving minstrels. Gehanu was on the ground, holding Kanek's body and screaming her grief.

*So much death and waste. The woman's corruption and the Superior's lies and Eninket he is Eninket.*

"You should have trusted me," Ehiru snarled at the face below him. The soldier's eyes widened. Then Ehiru put his hand on the man's face—

*mother*

—and forced his eyelids shut—

*Hananja I beg you for peace*

—and then he was inside the soldier and the taste of dream-blood was a sweet shock, like the first splatter of rain after a long drought. And after the taste, a torrent. He threw back his head and shouted in ecstasy as the self of the soldier poured into the aching hollowness within him, sending life surging from his core out to the very tips of his fingers and toes. So delicious it was, so powerful that his head reeled and his groin throbbed and his scalp tingled and OH GODDESS YES he needed more, so much more that he shoved aside the soul to look for it. There was nothing left save what little the soul needed to remain intact but what did that matter? He snapped the tether and sucked what spilled and crushed the soul and swallowed that too, and when nothing remained but tatters of mortal anguish, only then was he satisfied.

And then horror smashed up from the depths of Ehiru's consciousness and shattered the bliss with a single word. The name for his sin:

*Reaper.*

# 27

(•⊙•)

*Inunru, first Gatherer and founder of Gujaareh, creator of*
*narcomancy, father of healing: the details of his murder have*
*been lost, like patterns in sand.*
(Wisdom)

As the soldiers bore down on them, Gehanu grabbed Sunandi's
arm. "Into the palanquin."

Sunandi struggled to force her camel to turn; the anxious
beast still wanted to run. "Hide with a sick old woman? I'm not
a coward—"

"Don't argue with me, fool woman! Get in there and maybe
you'll survive to warn your land!"

There was no arguing with that. Swallowing her pride, Sunandi dismounted and ran to the palanquin. Two of the minstrels
were helping Talithele inside, piling saddlebags around the
palanquin to help shield it. She joined them and climbed inside
the flimsy cloth-and-balsa enclosure with the old woman. An
instant later the sounds of chaos erupted around them, shouts
and clanging metal and the whistling of frightened camels. The

palanquin shuddered with the vibrations of hooves and bodies against the ground.

Talithele caught her breath in fright, which turned into a racking cough. Sunandi helped her hold a cloth to her mouth, wrapping an arm around her for comfort and willing the pounding of her own heart to slow. But the sounds from without were too terrible to assuage her fears. Finally—for not knowing made the waiting worse—she pulled aside one of the palanquin's drapes to expose a sliver of outside, and peeked through.

*Guidance of the Protectors!*

Only a few moments could have passed since the beginning of the attack, but already the air was thick with dust and the stench of blood and worse. Just beyond the tent lay the body of one of the men who'd helped them into the palanquin. Beyond that she saw another minstrel fall from his camel, screaming; an instant later she gasped in horror as a soldier ran him down. Gehanu ran past, screaming like a madwoman and brandishing a short sword with both hands. Then Sunandi's heart leaped into her throat as a soldier swung his horse about and narrowed his eyes at the palanquin, spotting her as she peered through the curtain.

"We must go!" Hooking an arm around Talithele, she put her shoulder under the old woman's arm—she was light as a child—and hauled her out of the palanquin's other side, struggling to climb over the saddlebags. Behind them she could hear the beat of hooves, all but sense the soldier's malice directed at her back as he drew closer, closer yet, close enough to run her through—

There was a horse's sharp squeal of protest from behind her. She put her hand on the ground to brace herself and haul

Talithele over a sack of fruit; the earth gave a hard shudder against her palm as something heavy landed nearby. She struggled to her feet and saw:

The soldier's horse was dead. So was the soldier, lying sprawled across the now-smashed palanquin, his neck broken. Above the soldier, his fists still clenched, Nijiri stared down at the body with something like shock on his face.

Sunandi helped Talithele upright and tried to catch her breath. "Little killer," she said between pants. "How fortunate for me that you are."

He flinched and glared up at her, anger displacing the shock in his diluted brown eyes. Then his face hardened, turning as cold as his mentor's. "Stay with me," he told her. "Carry the elder and I'll protect you both."

She wanted to refuse him, but pragmatism—and the scream of another horse as it went down nearby—outweighed pettiness. Nodding, she lifted Talithele in her arms and moved behind him, trying not to crowd against him in her terror. He stayed where he was, keeping the palanquin debris and piled baggage at their backs, crouching in some sort of defensive stance. But when Sunandi looked around, she was relieved to see there would be little need of the boy's skills. Although the caravan clearly had been on the losing side of the battle, their attackers were beginning to withdraw, calling alarms to one another and looking southward in visible agitation. Sunandi followed their sight and spied another party of riders drawing near, trailing a dust-plume in their wake and bracing the green-and-gold wooden shields of the Protectorate to the fore. Relief nearly brought tears to her eyes.

Abruptly Nijiri stiffened and whirled, looking not toward the Kisuati riders but off in a completely different direction. "Stay here," he told her, and before she could protest he went running off. She saw him halt beside Ehiru, who sat slumped on his knees beside the sprawled body of another soldier. But she had no more time to puzzle this out as the rescue party arrived.

The Kisuati riders split, the bulk of the troop continuing on in pursuit of the Gujaareen while a four veered off and slowed to ride among the minstrels. Sunandi glanced down at Talithele, torn.

"Put me down," the old woman whispered. Her voice had gone hoarse. "I will be fine."

After another moment's hesitation, Sunandi crouched and helped Talithele to lie down amid some sacks of northern herbs, whose savory fragrance did little to cover the smell of death around them. They had left all their lean-tos behind when they broke camp, so she pulled some of the mangled palanquin debris over the pile and jammed one broken pole into the ground, hooking a cloth over its end to give the old woman some shade. Then she turned and raised her fists. One of the Kisuati riders, a lean, large-eyed man with a slashing scar across his face, spurred his horse over to her.

"I am Sunandi Jeh Kalawe, First Voice of the Protectors assigned to Gujaareh," she called as he drew to a halt. She lifted the sleeve of her robe to reveal the gold band around her bicep, detaching the polished half-orb of agate set into it as a decoration. Its flat side was inscribed with a formal pictoral of a stylized double moon above four trees: the mark of passage granted to all Kisuati high officials.

He raised his eyebrows and said, "You're a long way from your assignment, Speaker. What happened here? These aren't the usual bandit scum."

"Gujaareen soldiers."

"Gujaareen! But how...?"

"I believe there may be a garrison hidden somewhere in the desert." She stepped closer, reaching up to put a hand on his saddle. "They attacked to stop me from bringing that secret back to the Protectors, but I have more secrets to deliver, all equally important."

His eyes widened, then hardened. "You shall deliver them, Speaker. When my captain returns I'll tell him, and we will escort you to make certain of it."

"These people need help first. They—" Grief and guilt struck then and she bowed her head. "They have suffered much because of me."

The lieutenant nodded and signaled his three riders to begin aiding the wounded. Sunandi assisted as much as she could, moving among the minstrels to perform the unpleasant task of sorting the all-but-dead from those who could still be saved.

"You're not to blame, Nefe." Gehanu's voice drew Sunandi out of the numbness. Kanek lay dead across Gehanu's knees, his chest a mass of red. Tear-tracks had dried on Gehanu's cheeks. "The people behind this don't care what they unleash to get what they want. We were just in their way."

Sunandi sighed and turned away.

*     *     *

Barely two fours of their party survived—a third of the number that had started out from Gujaareh. Like a pittance from the gods in compensation for their earlier cruelty, many of the wounded would survive thanks to the Gujaareen in their party. Nijiri revealed to the others that he was a Servant of Hananja and asked for tithes of humors to help heal the wounded. He could perform only simple healing—closing wounds, easing shock—but even that much helped greatly. The three Gujaareen minstrels who'd survived immediately let him put them to sleep and siphon whatever he needed from their dreams. He did not tell them what sort of Servant he was, Sunandi noted, and they did not ask. Nor did they censure him for lying to them, for Servants of Hananja often went in disguise for various reasons. The power of faith, even in Gujaareh's expatriate children, was strong.

The Kisuati troop returned to report that the Gujaareen soldiers, after a pitched battle, began to turn their swords on themselves when it became clear they would lose. Those who hesitated were cut down or shot by their captain, who managed to mortally wound himself before they disarmed him. He'd died as they tried to question him.

"Those two will be accompanying me as well," Sunandi said, nodding toward Ehiru and Nijiri. Ehiru sat on some baggage nearby, slumped in apparent exhaustion; Nijiri crouched near him, offering him water. The boy glanced around as they spoke, listening.

The captain assessed them in a glance and narrowed his eyes in suspicion. "Gujaareen?"

"Yes. I have promised to present them to the Protectors."

"They might be assassins."

Sunandi smiled thinly. "I assure you they are not."

The captain looked at her for a long moment, then nodded. "There are plenty of extra horses from the Gujaareen troop. We'll need some to carry the bodies, but you and your companions may have one each. The rest I'm giving to this caravan to compensate them for their losses."

"I thank you," said Gehanu, overhearing and coming over. Her face was dry now, but its lines had deepened. She looked old and tired. "That will help."

"Gehanu…" Sunandi groped for something to say. Gehanu gave her a weary smile, reaching out to grip her shoulder.

"Go," she said. "Suffering and death are part of life. We'll be fine."

Sunandi's throat tightened. *My fault.* She began to turn away, mourning Kanek, and mourning her friendship with Gehanu since it could hardly survive such a blow. But Gehanu made a sound of irritation and abruptly pulled her into a tight embrace. Sunandi stiffened, then could not help bursting into tears, as the captain tactfully withdrew behind them.

"You're still the daughter of my heart," whispered Gehanu. She was trembling, Sunandi noticed; trying very hard not to cry herself. "That will never change."

When Gehanu finally released Sunandi, she pulled away reluctantly, remembering the night when a foreign trader had given shelter to a street child whose incompetence at thievery had gotten her beaten nearly to death. That trader had brought the child, a bright and pretty girl with no future, to the notice of an old sonha nobleman with no heirs. He had renamed her and raised her to do battle with kings—but the street child had never forgotten that first kindness.

"You're still a meddling old bat," Sunandi said back.

Gehanu gave a rusty chuckle and shook her head. "Kinja never could tame you, wild child. Go on now."

Reluctantly, Sunandi turned away. Not far off, Ehiru had mounted his horse, and Nijiri stood near his. Another horse had been saddled for her and she pulled herself onto it now, feeling a moment's pang as she gazed southward. That way lay home, and a storm of trouble when the Protectors learned of Gujaareh's plotting.

*Trouble? Say "war" and be truer.*

She glanced over at Nijiri. It took him a moment to notice her gaze; he was staring at his mentor. When he finally did turn she was stunned at the bleak despair in his face. Then he noticed her gaze and his expression became a cool professional mask.

"We must see this through, Jeh Kalawe," he said.

Sunandi frowned, wondering what troubled him. The soldier he'd killed? He was trained to kill, but not so brutally. Then she looked beyond him at the slumped, hooded, too-still frame of Ehiru, and guessed.

*Well. At least we won't have to waste time going to the hospital now.*

After the long, bloody day, and facing a far uglier future, that was the most comforting thought her tired mind could dredge up.

The captain called the march, and they spurred their horses toward Kisua.

# 28

(◦ ⊙ ◦)

*The Prince protects Hona-Karekh, as the*
*Hetawa protects Ina-Karekh.*

(Law)

Yanya-iyan's audience chamber was nearly empty when Charris entered through its bronze doors. The dais at the far end, a mounting series of steps leading up to the throne, was normally thronged with courtiers and worshippers. Now it held only the Prince, who stood with arms extended as two of his attendants dressed him in the full-torso armor that was the Sunset's traditional wartime garb. A third servant held the Aureole in place behind him, shifting it as he turned. "Ah, Charris. Please report."

Charris knelt at the foot of the steps. "No word from the south yet, my lord. The attack would only have occurred yesterday evening. It would take time for the troops to return and send a bird or runner."

"Hmm. Well, whether the woman is dead or not, she may have sent a message. We shall have to assume the Kisuati forewarned." He turned, the bronze scales of his breastplate gleaming, his arms still held out from his sides. "Do I look suitably martial, Charris? Not military-caste, of course, but acceptable?"

"More than acceptable, my lord. You will inspire our soldiers to fight to their utmost."

"Spoken like a true highcaste." The Prince lowered his arms, gave himself one final look before the mirror that a fourth attendant held, and nodded in satisfaction. Dismissed, the servants quickly left the chamber, save the Aureole-holder. "I have no need of flattery, Charris. Niyes understood that. In time I hope you will as well."

Charris took a deep breath to school his churning emotions. "Yes, my lord."

"Of course, there are benefits to having a general like you, too, Charris. You ask no awkward questions, give me no disapproving looks. I suppose that's refreshing." Walking down the steps with the Aureole-holder in tow, the Prince gave a curt signal for Charris to rise and follow. They passed through the back of the hall, Charris nodding to the Sunset Guardsmen who fell in behind them as the Prince left the chamber.

"In the end, loyalty is what matters most," the Prince continued. "Take our mad, murderous friend, who is currently chained and resting in the catacombs beneath the palace. He doesn't think—not anymore. He doesn't act unless I tell him to, or unless he's hungry and prey comes near. In many ways this limits his usefulness, but at the same time I never need fear his betrayal. There are kings who struggle all their lives to earn that kind of loyalty, and here I have created it at will." He chuckled. "True power, Charris. My father and all the Princes before me never had it, but I shall."

The audience chamber was on the highest story of Yanya-iyan. When the Prince led him onto the royal family's private balcony, Charris caught his breath at the sight of the whole city spread before them, the ground so far below that the people milling in the market plaza seemed small as dolls. To the west was the river and the fertile greenlands, source of Gujaareh's prosperity. Northward, Charris could even see the river delta and the coastal edge of the Sea of Glory. It was the whole of the Prince's kingdom, laid out as far as the eye could see.

Then he looked to the east, and stiffened.

"You must forgive me for not telling you about this," the Prince said. Charris could feel the Prince's eyes on his face, drinking in his reaction. "Admiral Akolil scorns the landed military, and I generally try to keep him appeased. But the time has come for you to know."

*Ships*, Charris thought in a daze. From their vantage he could see the eastern port, which opened to the Narrow Sea and allowed Gujaareh to trade down the continental coast as far as Kisua. The port was full of ships—*warships*—crowding in to reach the loading docks. Beyond that, he could see the expanse of the Narrow Sea spreading from Gujaareh's coast all the way to the horizon. And there he saw more ships, neatly anchored rows of them. *Hundreds* of them. They dotted the water like a pox.

"The shipbuilding five years ago on the Sea of Glory," Charris whispered. "The provisioning levies for more troops than we actually have."

"Indeed." Charris heard pride in the Prince's voice. "With aid from our allies, these ships have all made the long journey 'round the northern continent, through oceans of floating ice and other hazards too fantastic to name. We lost many, but more survived. And now nearly every one has arrived with a bellyful of fierce barbarian warriors. The Kisuati will be most surprised."

Charris struggled to make his mouth work. "When?"

"They set sail tomorrow. I'm having their resupply rushed as much as possible. Akolil assures me they can make the Iyete Straits in a single day, and be at Kisua's northeastern coast in an eightday, or perhaps a few days beyond. Much earlier than I'd intended, of course, thanks to Niyes and Kinja and lovely, treacherous Sunandi. And I'd meant to have twenty thousand troops instead of just ten; the rest won't arrive for weeks or months. But ten should be sufficient for the first wave. Kisua isn't ready either, after all."

Charris turned to stare at him, too stunned to censor himself as he normally did. "You really intend to do it. Kisua is twice our size—"

"But we have twice the wealth. And Kisua's isolationism has earned her enemies among the northern tribes, who resent the way Kisua hoards trade to the south. The northerners became eager to fight once I promised them control of that trade." The Prince smiled, turning to gaze eastward. "Though I'm not sure I'll hold to that agreement. All of their troops are going to die, after all. It will be Gujaareh's swords which ultimately subdue the Kisuati beast."

"Going to die?" Charris blurted it, trying to think through the numbness of his thoughts. War. On such a scale, war to engulf the whole eastern half of the continent and the northlands as well. Only an eightday away.

"Of course. Our mad friend has developed even faster than I expected, which is fortunate as my hand's been forced early. Everything hinges on the Reaper."

And then, suddenly, Charris knew what the Prince was going to do.

He must have gasped, because the Prince gave him a sharp look. Then smiled at his horror.

"Dreamblood," said the Prince. He clapped Charris on the shoulder, companionably. "In the end, it all comes down to that. No longer will my lineage be slave to the Hetawa. And no longer will Gujaareh be a mere crossroads for trade. We can become the center of a civilization that spans continents, bringing peace and prosperity to all. And I shall give the people a *living* god, one of flesh and not mere dreams, to worship. Do you understand?"

Charris did. And for an eternal instant as he stood there, Niyes's treachery paled before his own hunger to draw his sword and strike the Prince down.

But then the urge passed. He was zhinha, a true son of Gujaareh, and the Prince was the Avatar of Hananja. To attack him was more than treason; it was blasphemy. And so he knelt, raising his arms in proper manuflection.

"I understand, my Prince," he said. "My life is yours."

"As it has always been," said the Prince. He turned back, then, to admire the view.

# 29

( ⊙ )

*Those who honor Hananja are expected to obey Her Law.*
*However, those who dwell in the lands of unbelievers are*
*permitted to conceal their faith as needed to preserve peace.*

(Law)

Kisua.

The capital city seemed as unending as the ocean. It was easy
to see the shared history with Gujaareh in Kisua's sun-baked
white walls and narrow brick-paved streets, but there the resem-
blance ended. There were also great sprawling edifices, some
four or five stories high. There were gold-leaf lintels, brightly
colored tile inlays, and sturdy locked, ornately carved darkwood
doors. Vines grew wild over most of the buildings, their flowers
scenting the warm, humid air with perfumes so heavy that
Nijiri could breathe them blocks away. With the scents mingled
strange sounds: raucous laughter and furious arguments, the
calls of merchants hawking their wares, lullabies and love songs
long since forgotten in Gujaareh. He could taste the city's three
thousand years on his tongue, rich and thick as an elder's
dreams.

Behind him in the curtained chamber, Ehiru slept. He had not spoken since the incident in the desert; he acted only when Nijiri guided him; his eyes tracked nothing, lost in some other realm. On the way into the city, Nijiri had been able to keep Ehiru's condition hidden from the soldiers, though he suspected Sunandi had noticed. She'd made no protest when he insisted upon sharing quarters with Ehiru, even though her house was large enough to have many guest chambers. The servants had brought food and fresh clothing, then left them undisturbed, giving Nijiri the time and privacy to bathe Ehiru and attend to his own toilette.

So at sunset Nijiri had knelt on the balcony to pray and seek peace within himself. He meditated until the Dreamer rose fully, its four-hued light a comforting and familiar companion. Finally he went into the guest chamber's bedroom. Ehiru lay amid the translucent hangings, restless despite Nijiri's dragonfly jungissa on his forehead. Nijiri parted the hangings and sat down beside him, reaching up to remove the jungissa. With his fingertips he traced the frown etched into his mentor's brow. It seemed there was no peace for Hananja's favorite even in sleep. There was only one way Ehiru would have peace ever again.

Nijiri shifted his hand to lay a finger on each of Ehiru's eyelids.

Ehiru had failed the pranje's test. To Gather him now would be a kindness—far kinder than letting him wake to face the enormity of his crime. It was Nijiri's duty as Ehiru's apprentice, his duty as a Servant of Hananja. In the Hetawa Ehiru would have been sent onward already. And yet...

Nijiri's hand trembled.

In the Hetawa Ehiru would not have faced the test in the midst of a battle, surrounded by chaos and enemies. How could the test truly measure his control under such circumstances? Even Nijiri had killed—not with narcomancy, but murder was murder. And because of that, because he had been off protecting a tithebearer-in-abeyance and not attending Ehiru as he should have done, Ehiru had faced his moment of greatest trial with no one to help him. The failure was as much Nijiri's as his.

"Brother—" He snatched his hand away, overwhelmed by an anguish so intense that its weight seemed to crush him. Pressing his forehead to Ehiru's he wept helplessly, great racking sobs that echoed throughout the guest chamber and probably beyond, but he was past caring what Sunandi or her servants thought of his grief. He wanted only for Ehiru to wake and shush him and hold him, as he had on that long-ago day when they'd first met. *I would die for you*, he had thought on that day, and instead he had learned to kill, to walk in dreams, to dance his soul's joy. He had done it all to make himself worthy of this man, who was the closest thing to a father he had ever known. The closest thing to a lover he had ever wanted. There were no words for what Ehiru was to him; even Sister Meliatua had not fully grasped it. God, perhaps. Far more than Hananja had ever been.

The tears spent themselves after a time. As the tightness in his throat loosened, he pushed himself up, taking deep breaths to try and regain control. Twin streaks of wetness painted Ehiru's face. Nijiri brushed them away and then did the same to himself.

All the hard-won peace he'd achieved during the evening's meditation was gone. Sighing, Nijiri got to his feet and rubbed a hand over his hair, turning to pace—and stopping as he saw the silhouette in the doorway. Sunandi.

She walked in without asking to enter, her bare feet making no noise on the woven-grass mats, the moonlight illuminating her face in flashes as she passed near the windows. Though she had probably heard his weeping she made no mention of it, not looking at him as she passed. He was too weary to feel grateful.

When she reached the foot of the bed she stopped, gazing down at Ehiru for a long moment. "Will he die?"

Once upon a time Nijiri would have hated her for that question. Now he only looked away. "Yes."

"When?"

"When I do my duty."

"Must it be now?"

"He deliberately took a man's dreamblood and gave no peace in return. By our laws, there's no higher crime."

She sighed, folding her arms. "He sleeps well for a criminal."

"A minor sleep-spell. If he were himself, I'd never have been able to cast it on him." He looked down at the jungissa in his hands, turning it by its fragile-seeming wings. It had been owned by countless Gatherers down through the centuries—and before that, the stone from which it had been hewn had flown through the sky, spinning among the gods themselves. Perhaps it had even touched the Dreaming Moon before falling to earth as magic made solid.

"Deprivation has greatly weakened his umblikeh," he said softly. "The tether that binds a soul to its body, and to the waking world."

"And now that he is no longer...deprived?"

293

"Under ordinary circumstances, with time, the tether could heal."

She threw him a sidelong glance. "He will have no time if you Gather him."

Nijiri shook his head. "In the Hetawa he might have managed it—over months, in isolation. Out here, amid all this madness..." Nijiri gestured toward the balcony, Kisua, the world. "No. Even leaving aside the matter of his crime, it's hopeless."

He felt her eyes on him as he went to the balcony door and leaned against it, gazing out at the city and wishing it were Gujaareh. Wishing too that the Kisuati woman would leave. He had so little time left with Ehiru.

But she said nothing for so long that he finally turned back to see if she was there. And stiffened, for she had dared to sit on Ehiru's bed, stroking the fuzz of his unshorn hair with one hand.

She glanced up, saw his anger, and smiled. "Forgive my familiarity. He reminds me of someone I once knew and loved dearly." She took her hand away. "He should have the choice."

"What?"

"The choice. Of whether to die, when to die. I could accept the terrible things your kind do if you did them only to the willing."

Nijiri scowled. "You believe he is unwilling? A *Gatherer of Hananja?*"

She winced. "Perhaps he is willing. Still, his city prepares itself in secret for war, his brother schemes to use evil magic, a Reaper stalks the shadows, and he will live to see none of it resolved. That seems crueler than merely killing him outright."

Nijiri's hand clenched on the curtain. "You only want him with us when we stand before the Protectors tomorrow."

"That I cannot deny. But that serves you as well, for it will help me save both your city and mine. Whatever you might believe, I have no desire to see war between our lands. And too, it pains me to see the two of you suffering like this." Nijiri made a sound of disbelief, but she ignored him, still gazing at Ehiru. "When he told me about Lin...I hated all your kind. Everyone who uses magic. Now I begin to see that it is your Hetawa that is wicked, and not you."

He opened his mouth to curse her blasphemy, then recalled the look in the Superior's eyes when they'd taken Ehiru away in a rogue's yoke. "Not *all* the Hetawa." Oh, that was weak.

"True. You and your mentor, and even the Reaper who took my Lin...you are the victims here. The most pitiful victims of all, because you *believe*."

Nijiri stared at her, then finally sat down on a nearby chair. He rubbed his face with his hands. "Maybe you're right."

She fell silent, perhaps out of surprise at his agreement, perhaps just respectful of his pain. When she spoke again, she kept her voice soft the way a Gatherer would. "Let him live until tomorrow. Let him hear what the Protectors have to say. I don't know what sort of information they can give him, but by speaking with them, he could help to seal the breach between my land and yours. Perhaps that will give him some extra measure of peace before..." She hesitated, groping for some delicate way to say it.

"Before he dies," Nijiri finished for her. He looked her in the eye and offered a bleak smile. "Death does not trouble us, remember." He focused on Ehiru and sobered. "He will not be pleased with me when he wakes."

"Endure it," she said, getting to her feet. "Your kind make decisions about other peoples' lives—and deaths—all the time, do you not? Perhaps it's time one of you learned to face the consequences of such decisions, instead of simply killing those who object."

It was another insult—but there was a note of kindness underlying the acerbity, and he saw in her eyes that this was as near as she could come to a peace offering. He nodded to her; there was no anger left in him now, only grief. "Perhaps it is, Speaker."

He saw her eyebrows rise at his use of her proper title; after a long moment she returned the nod. "Rest well then, little killer. In the morning the Protectors will see us. Be ready." She turned and walked out, leaving Nijiri alone with Ehiru and his thoughts.

After a few moments of silence, Nijiri pushed himself up from the chair. Crossing the chamber to Ehiru's bedside, he lifted the covers and climbed in, nestling himself into the crook of his mentor's shoulder. Lulled by the steady beat of Ehiru's heart he slept for the rest of the night—not quite at peace, but blessedly without dreams.

# 30

( ⊙ )

*All who give of themselves to the Hetawa are
entitled to its care and comfort.*

(Law)

Ehiru opened his eyes to the first hint of dawn's light.

*I am still alive*, he thought, and despaired.

At his side Nijiri murmured in his sleep. There were dried
tear streaks on the boy's face, Ehiru noted, and spots on his own
chest as well. That drove back some of the anguish, for it was
selfish of him to forget that his death was also Nijiri's test. Sighing, he wiped the streaks from Nijiri's face. "Forgive me," he
whispered, and the boy sighed in response.

The empty ache inside him was gone, filled by the dead soldier's dreamblood. Yet he felt none of the usual peace or satisfaction that should have come after a Gathering—which was no
surprise, since what he had done to the soldier could in no way
be called "Gathering." He closed his eyes and saw again the soldier's face: angry at first, then terrified as he realized Ehiru's
intent. He remembered the feel of the man's soul as it struggled
to escape his hunger, as ineffectual as a moth fluttering in

hand—and that, too, had fired Ehiru's lust. Even now he shivered to recall his excitement when he'd destroyed that soul, to be rewarded by a dizzying spiral of pleasure whose peak had been more exquisite than anything he had ever experienced in his life. Mere Gathering paled beside it...and that was the proof of his irredeemable corruption. He had taken no such pleasure in killing Charleron of Wenkinsclan. In his heart he laughed, humorlessly and bitterly, at his earlier conceit; had he believed himself too soiled to serve Hananja then? What must She think of the suppurating filth he had become now?

The thought left him too anguished even to weep.

"Brother?" He opened his eyes and saw that Nijiri had woken. The boy's voice was hoarse, his face puffy. "Are you with me again?"

"Yes." He fixed his eyes on the mosaic ceiling, unable to meet his apprentice's gaze directly. Why had the Superior ever made him the boy's mentor? He had never been fit for such a responsibility.

But Nijiri lowered his eyes, and abruptly Ehiru realized the boy blamed *himself* for what had happened. "I would have done my duty last night, Brother, but I thought...today...the Protectors..." He faltered again, then took a deep breath and visibly reached for calm. "I thought perhaps you would want to see at least that part of it through."

"Few dying people have the chance to resolve their affairs," Ehiru said, keeping his tone neutral. "Gatherers should receive no special privileges in that respect."

"I know that." The boy's voice hardened suddenly and Ehiru looked at him in surprise. There was a taut, desperate sort of determination on his face—the determination of someone who knew he was doing wrong, yet did it anyhow. "But I can't fulfill the charge of our brothers without your help. I can't unravel so many secrets, and I can't find and destroy the Reaper. Not alone. I'm only an apprentice, Ehiru-brother. You can't ask so much of me."

And Ehiru sighed, for he knew Nijiri was right.

"Then I shall return with you to Gujaareh," he said at last, and shook his head at the wild flare of hope in the boy's eyes. "Only that much, Nijiri. In Gujaareh Sonta-i and Rabbaneh can aid you in tracking down the Reaper and cleansing the Hetawa. Once you take my tithe—" Nijiri's face fell; Ehiru continued ruthlessly. "You will be a Gatherer in full, then. Together the three of you will have the strength to do what must be done."

The boy bowed over his hands, trembling. After several long seconds he lifted his head, composed, though Ehiru suspected it was just a veneer over utter peacelessness. That was a start, he supposed.

"Yes, Brother," Nijiri said, his every word a grating resistance masquerading as calm. "I shall do as you ask."

Ehiru let out a slow breath. Pushing himself to sit up, he swung his legs over the edge of the bed and

*an eye of light in the darkness, glaring and gloating as he shivered in a cage and begged Hananja for death*

He froze.

"Brother?"

A vision. He was full of dreamblood, more than usual since he'd given no Sharer the surplus, and yet his soul still wandered.

"Brother." There was fear in Nijiri's voice now.

*I share it, my apprentice.*

How long before the madness claimed him again? An eight-day? Less? How long before the hunger returned, this time insatiable? His blood chilled still further as he recalled what he'd done during the battle. He had put an awake, actively resisting man to sleep without a jungissa. He had torn the dreamblood from that man's mind in mere breaths. Those were not the powers of a Gatherer.

How long before he became no different from the monster that had attacked Nijiri?

"Promise me you will do it, Nijiri," he whispered. His voice sounded hollow to his own ears. "Promise me you'll send me to Her while I am still Nsha."

He had given his soulname to the boy only once, ten years ago, but of course Nijiri remembered it. From the corner of his eye, he saw the boy inhale. Then after a moment Nijiri said, sincerely now, "I swear it, Brother." And he put his hand on Ehiru's.

*To show that he doesn't fear me. Oh but you shall, my apprentice. All shall fear me in the end if you fail. Your comfort is hollow.*

Oh, but how weak he was, that he craved it anyhow! Ehiru turned his hand up, lacing their fingers together, and they sat this way in silence until Sunandi's servants came to fetch them.

\*     \*     \*

The Meeting House of the Protectors lay at the center of Kisua's capital. It was an unassuming building, squat and wide with walls of dusty brown stone and none of Yanya-iyan's splendor, for all that it housed the rulers of a land. Small, unadorned pylons framed its wide entrance; the floors were marble but unpolished, worn dark with age. The people who stood on its steps—supplicants and influence-peddlers, he guessed, many of whom reeked of corruption—watched as Ehiru's party passed. Most were richly dressed and quiet, their eyes reflecting mingled suspicion and awe. And they marked him for what he was at once, though both he and Nijiri wore hoodless off-white robes that were the closest Sunandi had been able to come to Gatherer daywear. Mindful of Sunandi's property, they had not torn off the sleeves; no one could see their tattoos. But somehow, they knew.

Yet the austerity of the setting gave Ehiru comfort as he entered the House, behind Sunandi and with Nijiri at his side. There was a feeling to the simple architecture, and the solemnity of the people he saw inside—true wielders of power and responsibility, perhaps, not mere aspirants—that reminded him of the Hetawa in Gujaareh. Under other and better circumstances, he might have felt at home.

They passed through a dim archway and entered the House itself, a vaulted chamber lit by lattice-covered openings near the ceiling. Dust-flecked sunlight illuminated a curving stone table that stretched from one end of the House to the other. Ehiru counted seventeen people seated at this table, all of them elders and all with the look of nobility—though caste was difficult to tell, here in this land where mingling with foreigners was frowned upon. A handful of attendants lingered amid the pillars behind the Protectors; guards stood on either side of the chamber, watching Ehiru with open suspicion; otherwise the chamber was empty of all save the Protectors and the three of them.

Sunandi stopped in the space before the table and offered an elaborate bow before speaking in formal Sua. "Esteemed and wise, I come before you again in greetings. I am your voice and eyes and ears in foreign lands, and I beg you hear me now on a matter of great urgency."

The central figure, an ancient woman with thinning hair in twists, waved her hand. "We have read your initial report, Speaker Jeh Kalawe, and that of the captain whose troop rescued you in the neutral lands."

Sunandi straightened and assumed a less formal manner, though she still kept her eyes respectfully low. "Have you also read the report of Kinja Seh Kalabsha?"

"We have read your account of it, yes. We would have preferred to see the original from Kinja's own hand, Speaker." She gave Sunandi a stern look.

"My protégé Lin died trying to bring that document to you, Esteemed." She paused for only a moment, though Ehiru saw the concealed flicker of anger in her eyes. "I was unable to recover it from her remains."

"We are sorry for the loss of your slave, Jeh Kalawe," said another of the Protectors, though he did not sound sorry to Ehiru's ears. The man's casual dismissal of the northblooded girl was offensive, but it explained much of Sunandi's defensiveness about her. "You may request compensation after this audience. But I will admit to having some concerns about your report." He narrowed his eyes at her, then cast a disdainful look at Nijiri. "I have more significant concerns about your bringing these outlanders here, whoever they are."

Sunandi squared her shoulders. "They are Gatherers of

Gujaareh, Esteemed—the Hananjan priest Ehiru and his apprentice, Nijiri. I have brought them here on their request. They too seek the counsel of the Protectors."

There were murmurs of surprise at this, and several of the Protectors whispered quickly to one another. Finally the woman in the middle said, "I cannot imagine what Gujaareh's unholy priests would want of us."

"Information, Honored Elder," Ehiru said in formal Sua, his voice prompting another stir among the Protectors. He saw Sunandi glance at him in consternation as he violated some sort of protocol, but he did not care. He had too little time left to waste on propriety.

"Many disturbing events have occurred in my land of late," he said. "A Reaper walks the streets of the capital, unchecked and perhaps abetted by those in power. Twenty men—" He glanced at Sunandi. "Twenty men and the Speaker's girl are known to have died at its hands. I have been blamed for the Reaper's attacks, yet freed on the condition that I Gather Speaker Jeh Kalawe. And now your own soldiers have encountered Gujaareen troops in the Empty Thousand, again trying to kill the Speaker. I want to know why so many of my countrymen want this woman dead."

The old woman raised both eyebrows into her faded hairline. "You believe we know?"

He inclined his head to her. "I believe there must be a reason the Prince corrupts himself and risks war with Kisua to conceal the secrets this woman carries. I believe there is a reason the Hetawa aids him, and allows the Reaper to exist. And I believe, though I have nothing but my instincts for proof, that all these things are somehow connected. No one in my land who knows the truth can be trusted. Perhaps outlanders are the answer."

There was another susurrus in the chamber as the Protectors whispered among themselves. Sunandi threw Ehiru a sidelong glance. "You are a greater madman than I thought," she murmured in Gujaareen.

He nodded, unamused. Very soon it would be true.

Presently the Protectors concluded their discussion. "Very well, Gatherer of Gujaareh," said the old woman. "Half the things we have heard from our spies lately are so incredible we hardly know what to make of them. Perhaps an exchange of information will give us answers as well." Then she glanced at one of the other Protectors, who scowled mightily before finally sighing.

"I must caution you that our information is incomplete," the man said. "But it begins several years ago when our Shadoun allies found a tomb in the western desert foothills, far off the usual trails. They found it because it had been recently disturbed—robbed. The robbers fled north toward Gujaareh. We did not think this important at first, though of course we had the matter investigated. We now believe the tomb was that of Inunru—first Gatherer and founder of your faith."

Nijiri frowned in confusion and blurted, "But his tomb was lost centuries ago, and would be sacred to us now. Why would any Gujaareen desecrate—?" Sunandi threw him a glare and he subsided immediately.

"Your apprentice speaks true, Gatherer, if out of turn," the old man said, giving Nijiri an equally quelling eye before focusing on Ehiru again. "It is good to know that you at least preserve a proper reverence for the history of your faith, if not the proper manner of worship."

Ehiru lifted his chin. "Some might say we preserved both better than Kisua, Honored Elder. Magic was once used here, too."

The old man gave him a sour glare. "That was before we realized the horror of such power."

"Perhaps. But what has that to do with the present matter?"

"We did not know, until last night when we read Kinja's report as delivered to us by Jeh Kalawe." The old man sighed. "Many centuries ago, here in Kisua, the first priests who dabbled in dream magic began to go mad, or so our own lore says. Inunru—who too was at risk—studied them in hope of determining the cause and cure. A century later when magic was banned and his followers banished, most of Inunru's records were destroyed lest the knowledge they contained linger and flourish again, like a pestilence." The old man's lip curled. "But there have always been tales that some of Inunru's followers managed to smuggle several scrolls out of the city."

"We always believed," said the old woman, "that the scrolls were in Gujaareh. But apparently they were lost to your people as well...until lately." She looked at Sunandi, her expression bleak.

Sunandi nodded slowly. "I saw a locked case in the Prince's quarters. That is where he keeps them, I believe."

"Hmm." The old woman looked weary, as if she had not been sleeping well. An overabundance of dreambile, a part of Ehiru's mind catalogued, while the rest of him listened, as numbed as if by a sleep-spell. "Yes. It was the Prince's men who raided the tomb, or so we believe. All this madness began after that."

Sunandi took a deep breath. "And it explains many other things, Esteemed." She looked at Ehiru, though she continued speaking to them. "My mentor Kinja long suspected that the Prince planned a war. His contacts warned him of the Prince's negotiations with several northern tribes to forge a military alliance. And there had been a spate of unusual imports—heavy wood and iron, northern shipbuilding artisans, and the like, though all that trickled off a few years ago. But several months ago, Kinja also learned that the Prince had deliberately created a Reaper. He controls the creature using secret knowledge—doubtless from the stolen scrolls. The creature was used as an assassin, killing all who might interfere with the Prince's plans. The deaths resembled natural causes. Kinja, Kinja himself may have…" Here she faltered for just a moment, visibly fighting emotion.

"In Gujaareh, no one would question such things," Ehiru murmured, more to her than to the Protectors. He felt fresh pity for her now, hearing that both her mentor and her protégé had died at the Reaper's claws. For that, he tried to comfort her, though only with words since that was all he had. "No one but Gatherers, and we did not know. If we had, we would have helped you."

She gave a curt nod, getting control of herself, and faced the Protectors again. "Before I left Gujaareh, I also learned that the creature has been involved in a number of incidents at the capital's prison. Many prisoners have died in ways which puzzle even the Gujaareen, for these are young, healthy men who slip away in their sleep—ungently. So it would seem the Prince is not content to use his Reaper as merely a convenient assassin. He nurtures the creature's evil, helping its powers to grow for reasons known only to himself." She hesitated, glancing at Ehiru. "What I could not be certain of was the Hetawa's involvement."

And thus she'd dared not trust him with everything she knew. He heard the apology in her voice and nodded acceptance, though he marveled at it given her hatred of his kind. But somehow, over the course of recent days, her feelings toward Gatherers—no, toward *Ehiru*—had apparently changed. There was a degree of respect in her manner now, which he had never expected to see.

He glanced toward Nijiri and saw grudging compassion in the way he looked at Sunandi. Change on both sides, then; good.

"And Kinja learned, though Jeh Kalawe was the one to bring us this knowledge," said the old woman, with an approving glance at Sunandi, "that for the past five years—since the Prince found the scrolls—Gujaareh has been quietly building its fleet of ships to levels useful only for war. Other spies have confirmed this. Shipyards outside the city, along the Sea of Glory, have been producing vessels in great quantity. We do not watch the Sea of Glory closely; it has no connection to the Eastern Ocean and so poses no threat to Kisua—or so we believed. But we now know those ships were designed with thicker hulls than are needed on the Sea, built using techniques borrowed from the northern tribes. Therefore we suspect the Prince now has a fleet of ships which can sail all the way around the northern continent, through the frozen and dangerous waters at the top of the world, to reach the eastern seas." She paused. "We suspect the Prince *has sent* these ships forth already, most of them years ago. Each left its docks as soon as it was completed, never more than one at a time—but by the volume of materials involved and the guesses of our own shipmasters, we estimate some five hundred ships could have begun the northern journey by now." She heaved a long sigh. "Your Prince is as patient as an elder."

*The Kisuati woman. She cannot be permitted to reach Kisua, Ehiru, or there will be war.* Eninket's words echoed in Ehiru's mind, and he shivered at the enormity of his brother's misdirection. War had already been declared. Only its timing made any difference.

"Yes," Ehiru said. He was angry again, too angry; another mark of his corruption. He controlled it with an effort. "Patience is only one of the gifts our Goddess bestowed upon him. I hadn't realized until now just how thoroughly he has misused those gifts."

A hint of compassion seemed to flicker in the old woman's eyes for a moment. "Then perhaps you will oblige us by sharing information of your own," she said. "As I told you, we suspect the Prince has forged secret agreements with several of the far-northern tribes for military alliance, and for safe passage through their waters; these agreements have been primarily brokered through a Bromarte trader-clan. A minor member of this clan, a Bromarte named Charleron of Wenkinsclan, was one of Kinja Seh Kalabsha's contacts; he recently died. Jeh Kalawe has heard rumors that he was Gathered—or perhaps Reaped. Do you know anything of this?"

*Goddess forgive me. This madness goes so much deeper than I ever suspected.* Ehiru closed his eyes and took a long slow breath. "I was the one who collected his tithe."

The Protectors began to murmur again, though the old woman shushed them quickly. "Who commanded his death? The Prince? His own kinsmen? Did he give you any information before he died, about strife between the Prince and your Superior?"

"These things I do not know," Ehiru replied. "The commission came in the usual manner. I was told he had an incurable disease. I had no reason to suspect anything unusual..."

But even as he said this, he remembered the Bromarte's words in the dream: *they're using you.* And too, he remembered the silhouette that had been watching from a nearby rooftop.

*If I had not killed him, the Reaper would have.* He shuddered as understanding came at last, too late and tinged with a bitter irony.

The old woman looked at her fellow Protectors. "The Bromarte clans are reluctant members of the alliance, thanks to their long ties with both Gujaareh and Kisua. They have stayed as neutral as possible, only brokering deals with other clans that are more willing to fight, like the Soreni. But some of them, like Charleron, were willing to warn us of the danger."

"No troops have left Gujaareh," another man mused, picking at a spot on the table. "Their armies are at full strength, deployed a bit closer to the border than usual, but they haven't begun to move. Of that much we can be certain."

Another man said, "The Feen and the Soreni have ports along the Eastern Ocean, and they have ties to tribes with ports even along the frozen northern seas and the Windswept. Gujaareh has great wealth; they can afford to pay others to fight their wars. So if the Prince's vessels were empty, so that they could travel faster, and if they could be filled with northern warriors after making the ocean journey..."

Silence fell in the chamber. In it, Sunandi cleared her throat. "Respectfully, Esteemed...Are our warriors prepared for an attack?"

An old woman at the far end of the table leveled a hard look at Sunandi. "We have been doing nothing else since we first learned of Gujaareh's warship fleet, Speaker."

"But even so, the Prince has moved more cleverly than expected," said the woman at the center. She spoke heavily, oblivious to the quelling looks of her fellow Councillors. After a long moment she lifted her head. "I thank you for your report, Jeh Kalawe, and Gatherers of Gujaareh."

Sunandi offered her bow again. But as she straightened, she hesitated. "Esteemed and wise. Kisua has not had war for many centuries, and never with her daughter-nation of Gujaareh. Is there no hope remaining for peace?"

"That is up to the Prince," the central woman said.

"We shall of course attempt to parley with him," said another of her companions. "Though it seems unlikely he will be interested in peace after investing this much in his attack."

The central woman sighed, shaking her head. "And what will you do, Gatherer Ehiru?"

"Return to Gujaareh," Ehiru replied. "There is still the matter of the Reaper, since it seems you have uncovered no information about its connection to all this. But as for the rest...my brothers must know of the Prince's plans. There are still some in the Hetawa whom I trust, and who will help me try to stop

310

this—if it can be stopped. War is the greatest possible offense to Hananja."

The old woman considered this for a moment. "You may have horses and provisions to facilitate your journey home. But take care; by coming here, you may have made yourselves an enemy of your lord."

He bowed over one hand to her. "We serve Hananja, Elder. Our Prince is merely Her Avatar, and as such he rules only on Her sufferance."

As he straightened, he remembered Eninket's face at their last meeting: smiling, reassuring. Lying through his teeth. The rage returned—not the red, brutal rage he'd been fighting since the desert, but something cleaner and more welcome: the cold and righteous anger of a Servant of Hananja.

*Perhaps I am not wholly corrupt yet*, he decided. *Perhaps I can remain myself long enough to administer justice one last time. And for you, my birth-brother, that justice is long overdue.*

Seeing something of Ehiru's thoughts in his face, the old woman's eyes widened. But then her fear faded and she returned a slow, grim nod.

"Then I bid you good luck, Gatherer," she said, "and for all our sakes...good hunting."

# 31

(◦)

*The Hetawa shall offer healing to all, Gujaareen*
*and foreigner alike, believer and unbeliever.*
*The Goddess welcomes all who dream.*

(Law)

Nijiri heard the crowd before they walked out of the Meeting
House. At first he thought it was the river, though he had
already seen as they passed through the city that the river
curved away to the west, disappearing into the green, mist-
covered mountains in the distance. Then his ears sifted out
words and phrases and shouts, and he realized the noise was
*voices*—so many of them raised and speaking at once that the
result was a monotonous roar. He could not imagine why so
many people would assemble in such undisciplined chaos. No
public gathering in Gujaareh was ever so loud. Was it perhaps a
riot? He had heard of such things in foreign lands. Then he
stepped outside, and saw.

People: hundreds of them, possibly thousands, thronging the
steps of the Meeting House and the streets and the alleys
beyond it, men and women and children and elders, so many

that he could not see the end of them. But when he and Ehiru emerged onto the steps of the House with Sunandi, the gabble softened, then went silent altogether. Sunandi and Ehiru stopped, and Nijiri did as well, all three finding themselves the focus of countless pairs of eyes.

Breaths passed. Nijiri looked into the faces of the nearer crowd members and saw many things, from fear and curiosity to anger and adoration. More than anything else, he saw something that shocked and confused him, for though he had seen it many times in Gujaareh, he'd never expected to see it in a city that named Gatherers anathema. *Hope.* But what they wanted from Ehiru—only Ehiru, no one seemed even to notice Nijiri— he could not guess.

Then Ehiru stepped forward, turning his hands palms open at his sides. Startled, Nijiri hastened to follow, hearing Sunandi mutter something under her breath then follow as well. When he glanced at Ehiru's face he was stunned again, for the strain and misery of the past month had vanished from his brother's face. He was smiling, in fact, as he continued forward into the crowd, and his expression was the one Nijiri remembered from their first meeting, years and years ago—tenderness, sternness, warmth, detachment. *Peace.* The crowd, seeing this, murmured and parted for him, whispering to one another.

Then behind them Nijiri heard boots and the jangle of armor, jarring the aura of peace. He glanced around and saw that several Protectorate guardsmen had come out onto the steps, whispering anxiously to one another at the sight of the crowd. Nijiri dismissed them from his attention and focused on Ehiru instead, for he felt certain that what he was witnessing was no less than an intervention of the Goddess. Kisua had abandoned narcomancy centuries before—but respect for it, and faith in Hananja's power, clearly still lingered in at least some small part of her ancient soul. As Ehiru's apprentice, it was his duty to bear witness to such a momentous event.

*I do so with a glad heart. Hananja, thank You for making my brother himself again, if only for this moment.*

Then someone pushed forward from the crowd, half-dragging another figure. Ehiru stopped. Nijiri tensed, but it was only a man pulling a child along with him—a child, he realized in belated horror, who had been afflicted with some terrible crippling wrong at some point in his short life. The boy's head lolled back on his shoulders as if he lacked the strength or control to raise it, and though his legs seemed to function, they did so poorly, lurching and wavering to such an unsteady degree that without the man's aid he might have fallen. Worst of all, Nijiri saw that both his arms had withered, becoming tiny and useless beneath the elbow.

"G-Gatherer, your pardon," said the man. He wore the garb of a blacksmith and spoke such a thick dialect of Sua that Nijiri barely understood him. "My son, this is my son, will you heal him? Take my life if it will help, Gatherer, I am a loyal follower of Hananja, the healers here can do nothing for him, *please—*"

As if those words had been a signal, other voices suddenly rose around them. "My mother, Gatherer, she's dying," called a woman—and another woman's husband, and a soldier pointed to his missing eye, and a stooped elder begged to be sent to his wife in Ina-Karekh so that he would no longer be alone...so many. All of them, so hungry, pressing forward and extending hands in supplication. They even began to look at Nijiri: fingers plucked at his shoulders, at his robe. Someone caressed the back of his head and he started away, catching a glimpse of desperate yearning in a woman's eyes before the crowd surged forward again and she was lost in it.

Abruptly there were *too many* hands, too many pleading voices all around them, wanting, needing, desperate for more than any two Gatherers, any *ten* Gatherers could ever provide. Nijiri gasped as someone yanked at his robe, tearing it; on pure instinct he struck back, knocking the hand away and shifting into a guard-stance. Someone grabbed at Sunandi too, and Nijiri caught a glimpse of Sunandi's eyes widening in alarm as she pulled away—

"Let me see your son," Ehiru said to the first man who had spoken.

His voice cut across the rising din, though he had not raised it. The crowd still hushed and drew back. In the new silence, Ehiru stepped forward and took the child's chin in his fingers, pulling the lolling head upright to examine unfocused eyes.

"He is still himself," the man said. His voice was thick with unshed tears. "The withering sickness came upon him years ago and destroyed his body, but he still has a mind. He is my only child."

"I understand," Ehiru said, and sighed. "He can be healed, but not by me. Such a healing would require dreamseed to regenerate the muscles and nerves, and dreambile to stop any growth that has gone wrong. Surgery could be used to remove the parts of his body damaged beyond reclaim, and that would require dreamblood to banish his pain and dreamichor to replenish his strength. It would take many eightdays and there is a possibility it would not succeed completely. I have not the skill to do any of it."

"But you're a Gatherer—"

Ehiru looked up and the man's protests died on his lips. "A Gatherer, not a Sharer. I can help him in only one way." In the silence the words carried.

The man caught his breath—but instead of drawing back as Nijiri expected, he reached out and caught Ehiru's arm in a hard grip. "Then help him that way," the man said. "My son weeps every night knowing that he can never inherit our smithy, he can never marry or care for us, his parents; he will be like this the rest of his life. He reaches the age of manhood in two years but his mother still diapers him like a babe! He feels pain with every movement! He has begged me to kill him many times, but I, I could never...the courage..." He shuddered, bowing his head and shaking it fiercely. "But if he cannot be healed—"

Ehiru watched him for a moment, then looked at the boy. A horrible palsied movement passed through the child's flesh, tears welling in his eyes and spilling down the sides of his face, his mouth gaping open and closed and open again. It took long painful breaths for Nijiri to realize that the twitching, frenzied movement was the child's effort to nod agreement.

*Oh Goddess, how could You allow such suffering to continue? How could anyone?*

But though he had expected no answer to that prayer, he got one anyhow as Sunandi stepped forward and put a hand on Ehiru's other wrist. "I cannot permit this," she said. She spoke softly, her face subdued, but she did not take her hand away.

Ehiru merely looked at her. Nijiri heard gasps from the crowd, however, and when he turned to see what had startled them he saw two of the guards coming down the steps, spears at the ready.

"Do it, and they will kill both you and the boy's father, Gatherer," she said, raising her voice loud enough for the crowd to hear. Then she looked at the man, sighing. "I understand that your son suffers, but what you ask goes against every law we honor."

The man stared—then lunged at her, dragging the afflicted child, trying to hit her with his free hand, his face contorted with rage. The crowd cried out in collective alarm. Ehiru caught the man immediately and pulled him and the child back; Nijiri stepped in front of Sunandi to protect her. "Honor?" the man cried. "What should I honor? *Do you see my son?* What does the law do for him, highcaste bitch?"

Ehiru laid a hand on the man's chest and pushed him firmly back. "Peace," he said—and even if Nijiri had not sensed the quicksilver flow of dreamblood between them, he would have known it by what happened next. The man caught his breath and stumbled backward, clutching his son to himself in reflex. He blinked at them with no hint of his former rage, focusing on Ehiru in stunned wonder.

"Take your son to the Hetawa in Gujaareh," Ehiru told him. Then he turned to Sunandi and the guards, his eyes cold with suppressed anger. "That much is permitted, is it not? Or is even a Gatherer's advice illegal here?"

She watched him for a long moment, and with a chill Nijiri saw that she knew what Ehiru had done to the angry man. How she knew he could not guess; perhaps it was only that she was skilled at observing others. Regardless, on her word the guards could kill Ehiru for using narcomancy—and in the process free her from the threat of the abeyance, at least until matters could be settled in Gujaareh and another Gatherer dispatched to collect her tithe. Bile rose in Nijiri's mouth; he clenched his fists. *Wicked, filthy-souled woman!* he thought at her, willing her to sense his rage. *If he dies, another Gatherer is right here to take your worthless life!*

But Sunandi raised a hand, gesturing for the guards to be at ease. "Advice is permissible," she said, "though I must add that anyone who goes to Gujaareh to be healed with magic will never be permitted to return to Kisua. This has always been our law."

"I care nothing for your laws," Ehiru snapped. Then he turned and started forward into the crowd again. They parted down the middle, making a path.

Sunandi sighed, no doubt reading Ehiru's anger in the stiff set of his broad shoulders. Nijiri threw her a glare of his own and then started after Ehiru; after a moment and one last signal to the guards, she joined him.

"Whatever you might think," she said in a low voice, "I stopped him to save his life."

Nijiri snorted. "He allowed you to stop him, to save *yours*."

"What?"

He gestured around at the crowd, which had begun to murmur and shift, anguish and anger on many faces. "Look at these people, Speaker. They are Hananja's faithful and they came to see Her highest Servant. If those guards had attacked him, do you think any force short of the gods themselves could have stopped their wrath?"

She stumbled to a halt. He kept walking, too angry to care whether the crowd closed in and tore her apart in that moment. But he heard her sandals clap on the stones behind him as she jogged to catch up, and reluctantly he forced himself to think of his mother, as Ehiru had taught him. That cooled his anger, and he slowed down for her.

"It would seem I've spent too many years studying foreigners and not enough with my own people," she said, sounding chagrined. He took it for her version of an apology. "You see them more clearly than I."

"People everywhere are the same."

"All people except him." From the corner of his eye he saw her nod toward Ehiru's back.

Nijiri smiled, lifting his head proudly. "True. All people except him."

Following along in Ehiru's wake, they passed through the last of the crowd and returned to Sunandi's house.

# 32

( ⊙ )

It is the sound of screaming that wakes the child Ehiru.

For a moment he lies on his bed, listening to the chorus of his brothers' breath and wondering if the sound is the remnant of some dream. But he dismisses that thought, for he never forgets his dreams, and just a moment before he was skimming above the greenlands near Kite-iyan. There were no screams then, just the hollow rush of the wind and the pennant-flap of his loindrapes. He remembers the tickling caress of barley hairs against his skin, the fermenting smell of hot mud in the irrigation canals, the sun on his back, the sere blue sky. In the past he has dived into the mud to see what it feels like. Once it tried to drown him, but he is a proper child of Gujaareh. He proclaimed his soulname—I AM NSHA—and took hold of the dream so that the mud became like the womb he remembers only when he is asleep, harmless and enveloping and profoundly comforting.

But now the dream is gone and he lies in the real world, where he is just a little boy and his heart is full of sudden fear.

He sits up; several of his brothers do the same. This is the chamber where the youngest of the Prince's sons sleep. Tehemau has seen seven floods of the river and is oldest, but it is Ehiru to whom the other boys look. He is only five, and does not understand that they see a peculiar wisdom in him; he merely accepts it. "Goddess-touched," their tutors call it. "Blessed with the gift," said the priest who came to Kite-iyan a few days before to examine him. He gave Ehiru a necklace with an intriguing pendant: an ovoid of polished obsidian etched with a stylized moontear. "Before forty days have passed you shall join us," the priest told him then. "You are a child of the Hetawa now." Ehiru knows this is foolish. He is the child of his mother, and the father he rarely sees but loves anyhow, and perhaps this Hananja of whom he has heard so much. But he fingers the pendant now and shivers as a flicker of foreboding moves through him.

Getting out of bed, he whispers to his brothers that they should find someplace to hide. He will go to see what is happening. Tehemau insists on accompanying him, mostly to save face. Ehiru nods even though Tehemau wets the bed and sometimes, after a nightmare, weeps like an infant. Ehiru wishes one of their older brothers were here—Eninket, who is kind and knows the best stories, or perhaps the warrior Tiyesset. But Tehemau's presence will be a comfort, at least.

He and Tehemau slip into the corridor and run from one drape and flowering vase to another. Ahead is the solarium where usually they can find several of their mothers lounging on couches and cushions, chatting or playing dicing games, drawing letters or checking over figuring scrolls. A place of busy peace. Instead they find the aftermath of chaos—tables and couches overturned, cushions thrown to the floor, dice scattered. Tehemau starts to call out for his mother and Ehiru shushes him instinctively. They hear another scream nearby, followed by something stranger—sharp men's voices, deeper and rougher than those of the eunuchs who normally serve in the Prince's springtime palace. The palace guards are never allowed inside unless their father has come to visit. Is that what has happened? But if so then why do the men sound angry?

They peer around the corner and see:

Two of their mothers lie on the floor, unmoving, their fine clothing dark with spreading blood. Another cringes on a couch nearby, nearly gibbering as she asks why why why? The soldiers ignore her. They are arguing among themselves. One of them wants to spare her—"long enough to enjoy"—but the others are insisting that they follow orders. The argument ends abruptly when one of the men spits on the floor and thrusts his sword through the mother's throat. She stops gibbering and stares at him in surprise, blood bubbling over her lips. Then she sags backward.

Tehemau screams. The soldiers see them.

Tehemau gets farther than Ehiru because his legs are longer. One soldier grabs Ehiru by his sidelock and yanks him backward so hard that his vision blurs; he cries out and falls. Fear slows all that follows. Through a haze of pain-tears he sees another soldier tackle Tehemau to the ground, cursing as the boy struggles wildly. When the soldier draws his knife it catches light from the colored lanterns. So does Tehemau's blood, arcing forth and spreading over the marble after the soldier draws the knife across his throat.

Ehiru does not cry out—not even when the soldier dragging him stops and draws his own knife. It curves gracefully upward, casting blurred rainbows like the Dreaming Moon.

"Wait," says one of the other men, catching the hand that holds the knife.

"*I thought you wanted a woman?*" laughs the one that holds Ehiru.

"*No, look.*" The soldier points and another makes an exclamation of surprise and Ehiru knows that they have seen the Hetawa's pendant dangling around his neck.

"*Take him to the captain,*" says the first. The one holding him sheathes his knife and hauls Ehiru up by his hair.

"*Try to escape and I'll kill you anyway,*" he says. Ehiru hears but does not respond. His eyes are locked on Tehemau, who has stopped moving now. Tehemau has wet himself again, Ehiru notices. Through the fear he feels sorrow, for wherever his soul has gone now, Tehemau is probably ashamed.

The soldiers drag Ehiru through the corridors where his mothers' talk and music once echoed, intermingled with his siblings' chatter and play. Now the corridors are filled with the sounds and smells of death. The scenes drift past slowly, like so many minstrel plays. In the corridor he sees several of his oldest brothers dead. Tiyesset lies facedown among them with a broken lantern pole in his hands, a warrior to the end. As they pass the atrium garden Ehiru can hear strange grunting sounds; through the leaves he sees one of his mothers struggling beneath a soldier who is hurting, but not killing, her. Ehiru's soldiers see this and resume their bickering as they drag him along. They pass one of the girls' sleeping chambers and there Ehiru sees many bodies. It was their screaming that woke Ehiru and his brothers.

At last they reach the grand hall. Here the soldiers stop before a man who wears more red and gold than they do. The man stoops to examine Ehiru's pendant.

"*He is not yours!*" cries a voice, and this one wakes Ehiru from his stupor. His own mother. He turns, ignoring the pain this causes his scalp, to see her emerge from a side-corridor. She wears a brightly colored brocade wrap and the gold-amber necklace that Ehiru's father gave her; she is regal and unafraid. Soldiers immediately take her by the arms, dragging her forward. She barely seems to notice their presence. "I have given my son to the Hetawa," she declares to the captain. "Harm him and risk the Goddess's own wrath."

The captain scowls at this and orders the men to kill her.

The world slows again. Two knives go into her at breast and belly, then again at neck and side. The men step back. Ehiru lunges forward, not caring if he loses his scalp, but fortunately the soldier's grip has loosened and he slips free only a few hairs the less. He reaches her as she falls, stumbling in his effort to catch her, and failing. She lands hard enough to bounce but then lies still, her hands drifting to the floor at her sides, her eyes fixing on his. She is smiling. He skids to his knees beside her, the floor is slippery with her blood, her wrap clings to his hands when he takes hold of it in an effort to pull her upright.

"Do not weep," she whispers. Blood is on her lips. He screams something; he does not know what. "Do not weep," she commands again. She lifts her hand to touch his face, drawing a wet line down one cheek. "This is how it must be. You will be safe now; Hananja Herself will protect you. You are Her son now."

And then she stops talking. Her hand drops. Her eyes are still fixed on his, but different somehow. He is still screaming when the soldiers drag him back; they ignore him. They are upset, frightened for some reason.

"No way to know she was the firstwife," the captain says. He *sounds shaken.* "So many women here, no way to know. That's what we'll tell him."

"And the brat?"

"The Hetawa, where else? Do you want to be the one who explains to the Gatherers how he died?"

*No one answers.*

"We'll deliver him on the way back to Yanya-iyan. As far as tonight is concerned, he wasn't here."

*So they carry Ehiru outside and truss him up and strap him across a saddle like baggage, and once the killing is done they ride away with him into the desert night. And as they dump him on the Hetawa steps and leave him there for the Sentinels to collect, he recalls the old priest's words and realizes that they were not an error, but a prophecy. Now, though he would never have chosen it, he is a child of the Hetawa. Now and forevermore.*

*     *     *

Ehiru opened his eyes and lifted his head from his knee. Sunandi's garden surrounded him, wilder and thicker than Gujaareen gardens tended to be, although no less beautiful. Straightening from the awkward posture, he stretched out his leg and sighed, looking up at the Dreamer through the graceful branches of a shimanantu tree. He'd come to meditate, but the humid warmth of Kisua's nights had lulled him into sleep—and memories—instead. Not the wisest thing to sleep outdoors and without screening cloth; he scratched one leg and grimaced as he felt a four of insect bites beneath his fingers. Then he tensed, hearing a footstep behind him.

"Is your bed not to your satisfaction, Gatherer?"

He relaxed and turned to see Sunandi. She stood a few feet away on the porch that was the garden's entrance. She wore only a light shift, momentarily throwing him back to the fateful night of their meeting in Yanya-iyan that now seemed so long ago.

"The bed is fine," he replied. "Gatherers don't sleep at night."

"And yet you have the look of a man who's just woken from a fine nap."

*I'm not quite a Gatherer any longer,* he thought, but did not say. She probably knew it, anyhow.

"Where's your little killer?"

Ehiru shook his head. "In Ina-Karekh, though his body is in your guestroom with my jungissa holding him in sleep. He would be awake too, if not for that, worrying over all our troubles."

"Hmm, yes." She sighed. "I'm glad to know that Gatherers, too, have sleepless nights. Makes you seem more human."

"I could say the same of ambassadors," he said, turning to look up at the Dreamer again. Waking Moon peeked around the curve of her larger sister, a signal of the coming dawn. "Someone in your profession must see so much evil, day in and day out. It surprises me to see that you can still be troubled by anything enough that it disturbs your sleep."

"A matter of degree, Gatherer." She walked down the steps, coming to stand on the grass beside him. "Everyday evils are nothing to me, true, but this war is so much more than that." She hesitated, then added in a tone of resignation, "Perhaps I should be glad that I won't live to become so jaded."

He sighed up at the Moons. "You sought to prevent war. There's no corruption in that."

He sensed her surprise and sudden attention in the moment of silence that followed. "Even if my methods...?"

"Corruption is a disease of the soul, not the actions, Jeh Kalawe. And though the latter are often symptomatic of the former, it is a Gatherer's duty to see beyond superficialities. When I return to Gujaareh, I'll inform the Council of my judgment." He glanced back at her. "See to it that you never grow corrupt enough to accept evil *without* losing sleep, however, or it will be dangerous for you to enter Gujaareh again."

She exhaled, fourdays of tension released in that one sound, and closed her eyes for a moment—perhaps sending a prayer of thanks to whatever gods she respected, or perhaps just savoring life anew. But when she opened her eyes the old irreverence was there. "Be sure you tell your apprentice too, priest. He doesn't like me."

In spite of his mood, Ehiru smiled. "Nijiri has little experience with foreigners or women. You confuse him."

"And that which confuses must be destroyed?"

"Or understood. But you, Sunandi Jeh Kalawe, are a difficult woman to understand under the best of circumstances. You can't blame Nijiri for throwing up his hands and deciding to kill you as the simplest solution to the matter."

She laughed, low and rich. He watched her, obliquely fascinated by the sound and the long graceful lines of her neck. "He wouldn't be the first man to come to that conclusion," she said, looking up at the Moons. "The Prince seems to have felt the same way. And Kinja often joked about it." She fell silent then, abruptly, and he remembered that she was still in mourning.

"This Kinja," he said. He gazed at the Dreamer as he said it, but he caught her look from the corner of his eye, sensed her sudden tension. He kept his tone soft, trying to convey that he meant only to comfort her. "Will you tell me of him? Since, it seems, he died trying to save both our lands."

She was silent for a length of time. It was very Gujaareen of her, though Ehiru suspected she would not appreciate the description.

"He was..." she began, slowly, "Well. My father, officially, by adoption. But in truth he was more like you are to Nijiri—an older brother, a mentor, a friend. I loved him the same way that boy loves you." She paused then, glancing at him. "Perhaps not in quite the same way, though. I never wanted Kinja as a lover."

"Even if you had, he would have loved you too much to indulge your desire," Ehiru replied, evenly. "A father has power over a woman that no lover should have, after all, and vice versa." He shrugged. "This Kinja seems an honorable man, and honorable men are not so selfish."

"Perhaps you should say this to your apprentice, priest."

Ehiru shook his head, slowly, and brushed away a persistent biting insect. "I've known Nijiri since he was a child. Nothing stops him, or dissuades him, once he sets his mind on a thing. That will make him a good Gatherer." And then, because the moment seemed to demand a degree of candor, he added, "And I'm selfish enough to want his love, for whatever time I have left. I won't abuse it, but...I'm not strong enough to turn it away, either. Perhaps you'll think less of me, for that."

She sighed and hunkered down to crouch beside him, arms wrapped around her knees. "No. I don't think less of you. Embrace love while you have it, priest—from whichever direction it comes, proper or improper, for however long it lasts. Because it always, always comes to an end."

Her pain, her aching loneliness, was almost more than Ehiru could bear. He wanted so badly to touch her, stroke away her sorrow and administer peace in its wake, but he dared not. His desire for her was dangerously strong already. Then too, he realized sadly, he could not spare the dreamblood. His mind was consuming what he'd taken from the soldier far too quickly.

Well, there were other ways to share peace.

"I'm no woman," Ehiru said. "I won't have the strength to travel on my own, once I dwell permanently in Ina-Karekh. But before that, if I have the opportunity, I'll seek out this Kinja, and tell him what a lucky man he is."

A small tremor passed through her, and her face twitched. "Thank—" But she could not complete the phrase. Tears welled in her eyes, abruptly. Ehiru looked away and fell silent, to allow her that much privacy.

After a moment, she took a deep breath and said, in a calmer tone, "The boy says you mean to, er, take up permanent residence in Ina-Karekh soon."

"Yes. I must." He lowered his eyes. "I'm no longer fully in control of my mind, Jeh Kalawe. Even this moment is just an island of lucidity in the flood of madness that surrounds me. In truth, you shouldn't be alone with me. It isn't safe."

"The boy doesn't fear you."

"But you should. Even he should." He sighed, watching the garden's shadows shift in a breeze.

"No." To Ehiru's surprise, he felt Sunandi's hand cover his. "In the desert, you endured days of madness when you could easily have taken me. That's not the way of a murdering beast, no matter what you did to that soldier. And as you say, Gatherer—sometimes, no matter how horrid the outcome, we *must* judge a person by his intentions rather than his actions."

And then, to his greater shock, she leaned in and kissed him.

It lasted only a breath, just long enough for him to taste the merest hint of her berry-dark, rose petal–soft lips. He had never kissed a woman before. Later, he would recall the scent of whatever oil she'd put on after her bath, the sound of her breathing, an impression of cinnamon on the tip of his tongue. The feel of her hand on his, and the softness of her breast against his arm. Later he would imagine pulling her closer, regret that he would never know the fulfillment of such thoughts, and be glad, at least, that he'd had the chance to experience this in his last days of waking.

Then she pulled back with a small sad smile, and he stared at her, still stunned.

"May Hananja's inward sight be ever upon you," she said softly, the blessing's syllables rolling beautifully in her native tongue. Then she stroked his cheek with one hand. "I can't wish you peace, for when you return to your homeland you must fight. But good luck."

And then she got to her feet and left the garden. Ehiru stared after her for a long while, unsure of what to think, or whether to think at all. Eventually, though, it came to him that he felt better. More certain of the choices he'd made, and the path he faced. In her own way, she had given him peace.

"Peace and luck to you as well, Sunandi of Kisua," he said softly. "And farewell."

# 33

(・⊙・)

*There is the flood, once per year, which marks experience.*
*There is the full Dreamer, once per decade, which marks*
*knowledge. There is the Waking Moon each morning,*
*which marks contemplation. There is the river,*
*ever-present, which marks history.*

(Wisdom)

Traveling with the flow of the Goddess's Blood, it took nine days to reach the outskirts of the Gujaareen Territories. Nijiri spent most of those days doing his share of work on the merchant barge that bore them north toward home. When he was not working the longoar or fishing for their dinner, he whiled away the hours watching the greenlands pass on either side of the river as they drifted along. Sometimes he played tehtet, a numbering game that required one to bluff and lie to win, with the vessel's Kisuati crew. Unintentionally he endeared himself to them by losing every round.

Keeping busy helped Nijiri avoid thinking of the future, although that went only so far. Sometimes he would look up and see Ehiru, who spent most of his own free hours standing at the prow of the barge like a solemn statue, absorbed in whatever thoughts occupied his mind these days. At other times the barge would float through a village, gliding past farmers preparing their fields for second planting and children watering their beasts at the riverside. At such times Nijiri would be painfully struck by the overwhelming *normality* of what he saw. Beyond the fields, vast and terrible conspiracies were in motion: armies on the move, monsters unleashed, death on a nightmarish scale threatening to swallow all the land. Yet for the common folk of Kisua and Gujaareh, life went on as it had for centuries, unscathed by time or trouble.

*This is what we fight for*, Nijiri would think in such moments, waving and smiling at a farm child or pretty maiden. This simple, ordered life was Hananja's truest peace, which priests of the Hetawa had devoted their lives to protecting for generations. This was what it truly meant to be a Servant of Hananja.

Then he would look at Ehiru and remember what awaited them in Gujaareh, and whatever peace he had found would vanish again.

Thus did he pass the days as the villages became trade-posts, and the trade-posts became towns and smaller cities, and at last on the tenth day the towers and sprawl of Gujaareh's capital began to grow in the distance.

The barge captain—a former Kisuati army officer—was sanguine about the risks as the crew prepared for the end of its journey. "I've smuggled more than my share of contraband through Gujaareh's gates," he said to Nijiri as they stacked goods for the tax assessors. "You're no different from the rest, so relax."

But Nijiri could not relax. The sight of Gujaareh's familiar walls had stirred both homesickness and dread within him, and as they drew nearer, the dread grew. This was not dread for the inevitable duty he faced when the time came for Ehiru's Final Tithe; that particular misery was a steady, omnipresent thing. The new feeling was at once sharper and more alarming.

Troubled and restless, he went to Ehiru, who manned the second longoar so that they could steer more precisely now that other vessels had begun to appear with greater frequency around them. All the river's traffic had increased as they approached Gujaareh's gateway port; the crew joked that soon they would be able to cross the river by stepping from boat to boat.

"My heart flutters like a moth in my chest, Brother," he murmured, taking hold of the pole to assist Ehiru. "I've never had a true-seeing, but everything in me is frightened of returning to the city."

"We have no reason to fear," Ehiru said, keeping his voice just as low. "No one is looking for us, or at least not here. Gujaareh has grown wealthy by treating traders kindly; we have only to be calm and we should pass the gates with no incident."

"And once we pass the gates?"

"I would prefer to seek out our pathbrothers, but I don't know how we can reach them in the Hetawa without others—those I no longer trust, like the Superior—knowing of it." He looked briefly sour, then sighed. "For now, we have surprise on our side. That will count for something."

Nijiri frowned, then inhaled. "You mean for us to go to Yanya-iyan directly, then. And do what, Gather the Prince straightaway? Without—"

"Yes, Nijiri," Ehiru said, throwing him a hard look. "I mean to do just that."

*A Gatherer destroys corruption—and power, if he must,* Rabbaneh had said. And he'd been right to remind Nijiri to stop thinking like a servant-caste. True peace required the presence of justice, not just the absence of conflict.

So Nijiri bit his lip, stifled the part of himself that quailed at the idea of doing something so audacious, and set his mind to the task at hand. "We should seek Sister Meliatua," he said. "She and the Sisters have many allies around the city; they may be able to help us."

"Hmm." Ehiru seemed to consider this. "If she can get a message into the Hetawa…or hide a person…" He glanced at Nijiri, and abruptly Nijiri realized what he was thinking.

Nijiri scowled. "You will not enter Yanya-iyan without me."

Ehiru opened his mouth to argue, then apparently thought better of it. He shook his head, eyes creasing with amusement. "You have become a willful, rude apprentice, Nijiri."

"I've always been so, Brother." In spite of his mood Nijiri could not help grinning. But the moment was fleeting. Ehiru sobered and gazed out over the water. It wasn't difficult to guess the direction of his thoughts.

"Ehiru-brother." Nijiri hesitated, then blurted, "I've been thinking. Perhaps you could go before the Council of Paths. If you could face the pranje again, within the peace of the Hetawa—"

Ehiru took one hand off the oar and held it out. Even over the gentle bob of the barge, the tremor in his hand was pronounced. Nijiri caught his breath and Ehiru took hold of the oar once more, gripping it tightly to conceal the tremor.

"You see," Ehiru said. He turned his gaze to the river; his face was expressionless. "Within another fourday, I shall be as useless to you as I was in the desert. So I must act quickly."

It had been twelve days since he'd killed the soldier, but already Ehiru's reservoir was empty again—had probably been empty for days, if his hands were that bad. Shaken, Nijiri resumed turning the oar.

As they drew nearer the city, the river traffic grew thicker yet, forcing them to slow and even stop on occasion as boats gathered into knots and lines leading up to the looming arch of the Blood Gate. The crew murmured in annoyance. Pulling himself out of sorrow enough to pay attention, Nijiri watched as the captain called out to another boat nearby to ask why the traffic was so much worse than usual.

"Heard they're searching boats," the man replied with a shrug. "For contraband, maybe, or smuggled goods. Who knows?"

"Mnedza's Tongue," said one of the crewmen, frowning. "Why in the shadowlands would they tie up half the river with boat searches? Are they mad? It'll be Moonset before they go home tonight."

The captain glanced back at Ehiru and Nijiri, though he spoke aloud to the whole crew. "We've nothing to worry about," he said. "Our cargo is strictly legal—this time." This provoked uneasy laughter that Nijiri could not bring himself to share.

Their boat inched closer to the network of piers and bridges that made up the Gate. Soldiers wearing the gray loinskirts of the City Guard swarmed along the piers like ants, on both sides of the river. Nijiri's dread grew as he glimpsed a fisherman standing rigid with fury, watching a soldier poke a spear butt through his day's catch. As they finally reached a pier, a man wearing the indigo-trimmed headcloth of a tax assessor approached the boat, flanked by two soldiers. "Tie your boat for boarding," he said brusquely, and the barge's crew moved to comply. On the captain's orders, Nijiri and Ehiru pushed the barge's anchor stone over the side and then stood among the rest of the crew, watching.

The tax assessor stepped into the boat with the ease of long practice and began rummaging through the stacks of baskets and chests. The soldiers boarded less skillfully, but they moved with purpose as they came to where the crew stood. "State your name and business," said one. While the other soldier took notes on a wide scroll, the crew members began to speak in turn. When Ehiru's turn came he used the false name he'd given to Gehanu before the desert journey. Nijiri did the same.

"You don't look Kisuati, boy," the soldier said, narrowing his eyes.

"He was born in Gujaareh," the captain interjected smoothly. "My sister slept with a northerner and moved here when the family put her out. I've hired him on for the time being, since he isn't as lazy and shiftless as his father."

The soldier snorted at this and moved on down the line. Nijiri exhaled in private relief; the captain winked at him.

Finally the soldiers finished interviewing the crew. "All right, then," said the one taking notes. "Turn and raise your arms, and then we'll be done."

The captain started. "What is this? I have been riding the river between Kisua and Gujaareh for ten years and never—"

"New orders from Yanya-iyan," the other soldier said. He spoke wearily, clearly having said the words many times before. "There have been problems lately with spies and smugglers. You could have contraband hidden on you."

The captain's eyes widened in genuine affront. "Are you mad? I—"

The soldier drew his sword and put it at the captain's throat in a blur of motion; the captain fell silent immediately. "Orders from Yanya-iyan," the soldier said again, speaking slowly and coldly now. "The Prince's city obeys the Prince's law."

From the corner of his eye Nijiri saw Ehiru bristle at this perversion of Hetawa doctrine, but of course they could not take the man to task for it. The crew members tensed as well, angry on behalf of their captain, but there was little they could do without jeopardizing his life.

"This can be quick and simple," said the soldier with the sword, with a hint of exasperation this time. "If you've done nothing wrong, you have nothing to fear."

One by one, the crew members obeyed. Nijiri did the same, sighing at the indignity, but Ehiru turned only slowly. His eyes met Nijiri's as they turned, and Nijiri was startled to see that his mentor's jaw was tight with tension.

*But why is he afraid? We have no contraband and barely enough money to be worth stealing. Only—*

And then he remembered. Their black loindrapes, hidden under their Kisuati clothing. Their Gatherer ornaments.

His heart began to pound as the soldiers moved down the

line, patting each crew member and pulling out weapons, money-pouches, and the like. They were moving quickly, he noticed with the one part of his mind that could still function through rising fear. His ornaments were in a pouch tucked into the band of his Kisuati loinskirt. *Let them miss it in their haste,* he prayed silently. Perhaps they would feel them and dismiss them as dice or tehtet pieces or just a boy's rock collection—

The soldier's hands slapped roughly over his torso, and paused when they found the pouch. Through rising panic Nijiri felt the soldier tug the pouch out of his skirt; he heard the clatter of stones as the pouch was opened. When he heard the soldier's murmured oath, he knew they were lost.

He glanced at Ehiru; there was only one chance. He mouthed the word *fight?*

Ehiru's expression startled him, for the tension had been replaced by introspection. He shook his head minutely, then turned to face the soldiers. Swallowing, Nijiri turned as well, unsurprised to see a sword leveled at his own throat.

"Gatherer Ehiru," said the soldier; his voice shook. "Gatherer-Apprentice Nijiri. We were told to watch for you, but that you'd probably left the city."

"Obviously we have returned," Ehiru said.

"You will come with us now!" said the other soldier, nearly trembling in his excitement.

"Obviously we shall," replied Ehiru. He lowered his arms and gazed down at the sword pointed at him, unafraid. "To Yanya-iyan, I presume?"

That was when Nijiri understood. They had found a way into Yanya-iyan after all.

# 34

(⊙)

*A Gatherer may serve for as long as he passes Her test.*
*At the end of his service, he must offer up his soul's blood*
*for Her use. A Gatherer belongs wholly to Hananja, in life*
*and in death.*

(Law)

Deep beneath Yanya-iyan lay Yanyi-ija-inank, the Earthly Thrones of the Immortal Kings. Row upon row of shelves lined the silent, winding corridors, each shelf housing the funeral urns of Gujaareh's past Princes. Interspersed among the shelves were murals in embossed lacquer depicting each ruler's time upon the Throne of Dreams, accompanied by formal pictorals delineating his or her name and accomplishments in Hona-Karekh. In testament to the ambition of Gujaareh's founders, fewer than half of the shelves and walls had been filled in the thousand years of the city's existence—this even though many shelves bore the urns of favored spouses, acclaimed soldiers, and other noteworthy folk granted the honor of resting alongside their rulers. It would take thousands more years for the catacombs to fill completely.

But a temporary use for the empty space had been found, Ehiru saw. Three small, hastily constructed cages stood against one of the blank walls, marring the catacombs' graceful architecture with ugly iron latticework. The sight filled Ehiru with affront even as the soldiers pushed him into one of the cages and locked the door.

Nijiri yelped as a soldier prodded him ungently into the cage after Ehiru. Their hands had not been bound, but the soldiers seemed well aware of the dangers of physical contact with a Gatherer, using the butts of their spears to goad them along. Nijiri glared back at them and rubbed a fresh bruise on the back of one thigh as he crouched beside Ehiru. "What now, Brother?" He sounded tense but calm, and Ehiru suspected that his tension was as much eagerness as fear.

"Now we wait," Ehiru replied, examining their surroundings while the guards took up duty outside the cage. The cages were nothing more than flat grids of forged iron bars, tied with oiled lengths of twine to form a cube; the door was just a rough sheet of bronze, laid over an opening between the bars. The soldiers had to roll a carved wheel-stone in front of the thing to seal the door. The whole structure had been tied to iron rings set into a nearby wall of the catacombs, because clearly it would list wildly and perhaps fall apart otherwise. Flimsy in appearance, but nevertheless difficult to escape.

The cage nearest theirs was empty, but the furthest cage held one occupant. In the dim torchlight Ehiru could make out no details of the huddled form, which might have been only a pile of rags for all that it moved.

"Just wait?" Nijiri glanced toward the guards outside the cage, raising his eyebrows. They could not speak freely, but there was nothing to be said that their enemies did not already know.

"The Prince will be along soon enough," Ehiru said.

It did not take long for him to be proven right. After an hour's passing or so, the soldiers snapped to attention as the halls echoed suddenly with the rumble of chains and massive metal hinges. This was the mechanism which opened the heavy stone doors that sealed the catacombs during floodseason. A gust of fresh air and the jingle of sandals heralded the Prince's arrival, along with four of the Sunset Guard and the child who bore the Aureole. Two other child-servants trailed behind the guards, each carrying an armload of heavy iron chains.

The Prince, resplendent in armor of bronze scales and a blood-red linen skirt, drew to a halt before the cage.

"Ehiru," he said, smiling warmly. "I'm pleased to see you again."

"I am not pleased to see you, Eninket," Ehiru said. Eninket raised his eyebrows, smile fading.

"I see the Kisuati have filled your head with lies before sending you back to us." He sighed. "If only you had killed the woman. I could have spared you so much suffering."

"No more lies, Eninket," Ehiru snapped. "You have planned *war*, unprovoked and to suit your own greed, in violation of our every law. I name you corrupt—"

"You name me nothing." As quickly as the smile had vanished from Eninket's face, now a glare replaced it. "I should never have left you with the Hetawa, once I learned they had you. Better you had died with all the rest of our siblings than grow up to become another of their puppets." He stepped closer to the cage, though still not within arm's reach; Ehiru forced his tense muscles to relax. "Do you know what they did to our father, Ehiru? I saw him grovel once, abject as the most humble servant-caste, at the feet of a Hetawa priest. He begged, he wept, he promised to do whatever they asked, if only they would give him dreamblood. And they gave it to him, laughing at his humiliation."

Beside Ehiru, Nijiri made a strangled noise. Ehiru frowned, startled out of anger, disbelieving. "No," he said. "Dreamblood is used for healing."

Eninket threw back his head and laughed bitterly, the sound echoing throughout the tombs. *"Healing?"* He spun away, beginning to pace in his anger, fists tight at his sides. "Dreamblood is the greatest secret of power in this land, Ehiru! You and your pathbrothers collect hundreds of tithes every year; do you honestly believe all of them are used just to comfort grieving widows and ease injured farmers' surgeries?"

Ehiru stared back at him, aware in that instant of a terrible, instinctive dread building in the back of his mind. This was not at all what he had expected. *I do not want to know this,* he thought.

But Hananja's will could never be denied.

"Dreamblood is sweeter than any wine or aphrodisiac, more powerful than the purest timbalin," Eninket said. He had stopped pacing. His voice was edged as a sword—but soft, too. Like a Gatherer's. "A single draught can heighten the mind, soothe the heart, and make the body impervious to pain, weariness, even age, at least for a short time. But too much too often and even the strongest man begins to crave it. To *need* it. He will do anything to get more. You know this better than anyone."

He jerked his chin at Ehiru, and Ehiru flinched despite himself. Eninket smiled.

"Did you honestly believe the Hetawa would not take advantage of that, Ehiru? Where do you think they get the resources to run the House of Children, to build statues out of rare nightstone, to buy your food and clothing? The elite of the city pay half their fortunes every year for the Hetawa's favor—and for dreamblood." His lip curled. "A tithe for a tithe."

"You *lie!*" Ehiru sprang to his feet and ran to the cage's bars, his whole body trembling. If he had been free in that moment he would have killed Eninket with his bare hands, just to stop the terrible words. But Eninket only sighed at the sight of Ehiru's rage, his eyes filling with bleak pity. That, more than anything else, broke the back of Ehiru's anger. It meant that Eninket was telling the truth.

*No. It isn't true. No.*

"The forty and four years of our father's rule were a sham, my brother," Eninket said. He spoke heavily now, his anger gone; Ehiru's was too, numbed to nothingness. "He never made a decision without the Hetawa's approval, for fear they would cut him off and leave him to die in madness. The Princes are figureheads; Gujaareh is truly ruled by the Hetawa. When I learned this—and saw what it did to our father—I swore I would break the cycle. I accepted their poisoned honey when I took up the Aureole. It was either that or wake to find a Gatherer in my bedchamber some night. I lived as their slave for years. But in secret, I searched for the means to free myself."

He gestured at the two chain-carrying servants. They bowed acquiescence and then went past him to the third cage, which the guards unlocked for them. Ehiru heard whispers and the clack of metal, and a moment later they emerged, leading along the cage's occupant: a man who would have been twice their height if not for his hunched posture. He shuffled along between them, manacled at wrists and ankles. An open, hooded cloak had been draped over his head and torso, though he wore only a stained loincloth underneath. Once the man must have been hale, but some illness or famine had sapped the vitality from his flesh and left him emaciated, the skin of his legs ashen and mottled with sores.

Nijiri sucked in a breath and stumbled back, his eyes widening, terrified. Ehiru stared at the boy, then narrowed his eyes at the hunched figure as his mind filled with an ugly suspicion.

"You hate me now," Eninket said to Ehiru. His face was solemn. With one hand he plucked something from the waistband of his leather skirt. "I see that in your eyes even though *they* are the ones you should hate. But I've never hated you, Ehiru, no matter what you might think. I mean to use you, for they've made you into a weapon and dropped you at my feet. But know that I do it out of necessity, not malice."

He gestured again. One of the children reached up to remove the manacled man's ragged robe. And then it was Ehiru's turn to stagger away, so overcome with shock and revulsion that had there been anything in his stomach he would have vomited it up in helpless reaction.

"Una-une," he whispered.

Una-une did not respond. Once he had been Ehiru's mentor,

345

oldest and wisest of the Gatherers who had served Gujaareh for the past decade. Now he was a slack-jawed apparition who gazed unfocused into what was surely the most twisted of the nightmarelands. There was nothing of the Una-une Ehiru had known in the creature's eyes. There was nothing of *humanity* in those eyes—not any longer.

"He isn't at his best right now," Eninket said, still in that Gatherer-gentle voice. "His mind, what remains of it, comes and goes. I thought at first to use a Sharer; easier to control, and the deterioration wouldn't have been as severe. But the scrolls warned that only a Gatherer would have the power I needed. So I bribed a Sentinel to steal Una-une away as he meditated on the night before his Final Tithe."

Through shadows Ehiru heard Nijiri's voice. "The Superior said Una-une gave his tithe directly to the Sharers." The boy sounded more shaken than Ehiru had ever heard him, his voice quavering like an old man's. The Reaper's attack had left its mark on him. "I stood attendance on his funeral pyre with the other acolytes. *I watched him burn!*"

"You watched a body burn," Eninket snapped. "Some pauper buried by the Hetawa; I don't know. The Superior helped me hide the kidnapping when I threatened to tell the Gatherers about his corrupt use of dreamblood. Perhaps he thought to cut me off in retaliation, or perhaps it simply never occurred to him to wonder why I wanted a broken Gatherer; who knows? In any case, by the time he discovered my intent, it was too late. Una-une was mine."

Ehiru wept. He could not help it, witnessing the ruin of a man he had loved more than his father, more than all his brothers and sisters, more than even Hanaja Herself. He pressed him-

346

self against the hard, cold wall at the back of the cage, because that was the only way he could keep his feet. *My pathbrother, my mentor, I have failed you, we have all failed you, so badly—*

"Why?" It was a hoarse whisper, all he could manage. Beyond the cage Una-une twitched, reacting either to Ehiru's voice or to some conjuration of his broken mind.

"Una-une has no limit now," Eninket replied. "He takes and takes, far more than he ever could as a Gatherer. Much of the magic is consumed by his hunger, but more than enough remains for my needs." He turned to Una-une and lifted his hand, rapping the object in it with his fingernail; Ehiru jerked in reflexive response when he heard the faint whine of a jungissa stone. Una-une lifted his—no. *The Reaper* lifted *its* head slowly, blinking at Eninket as if trying to see him from a great distance.

"Come, Brother," Eninket said to the creature. Fixing the stone to his breastplate, he held out his hands in a posture that was sickeningly familiar. Like the Hetawa's statue of the Goddess, Ehiru realized with sinking horror—or a Sharer awaiting the transfer of a Gatherer's collected tithes. After a moment, the Reaper shuffled to Eninket's feet and knelt, taking his hands.

"No," Ehiru whispered. But there was no mistaking the Reaper's posture, a palsied mockery of the tithing ceremony. Nor could Ehiru deny the way Eninket suddenly caught his breath and stiffened, his face alighting in all-too-familiar ecstasy.

And even as Ehiru wept, a surge of pure, envious lust shot through him.

That was enough to send him to his knees, dry-retching over

the dusty stones. He felt Nijiri's hands on him, trying to pull him up or at least soothe him, but that was no help. By the time he finally lifted his head, blinking away tears and gasping for breath, the warped ceremony had ended. Eninket's shadow fell over him, right in front of the bars and within arm's reach at last—but so sickened was Ehiru that he could not muster the will to attack.

"I tell you this because you deserve the truth after so many lies, Ehiru," Eninket said. His speech was faintly slurred, his eyes still hazy with lingering pleasure. "Dreamblood has more power than you could ever imagine. You know what a single life can do. What you don't know—what the Hetawa has spent a thousand years hiding—is that the more lives one takes, and the more dreamblood one absorbs, the greater the transformations it triggers in body and soul." He put a hand on the iron lattice and leaned forward, speaking softly and emphatically. "Take enough lives all at once, and the result is immortality."

Ehiru frowned up at him, uncomprehending. Nijiri's hands tightened on Ehiru's back. "Impossible," Ehiru heard him say.

Eninket gave them a lazy smile. Above it, his eyes glittered like citrines in the torchlight. "It was so for our founder Inunru," he said. "Great Inunru, brilliant as a god, blessed by Hananja! Did you never wonder how one man could accomplish so much in a mortal lifetime? One hundred years after his first experiments he had not aged, did not die. More and more faithful flocked to the banner of Hananja as they saw him and realized the power of Her magic. The Kisuati Protectors finally banished his followers and outlawed narcomancy not because they feared the magic, but because they feared *him*. Inunru had made himself all but a god; they had to do something to destroy his influence."

"Lies," snapped Nijiri. "The Hetawa would have known of this. There would be records, the lore would have been chiseled into every wall—"

"The Hetawa had its own secrets to keep," Eninket said, smiling coldly. Ehiru fixed his gaze on Una-une, who sat slumped and quiescent at Eninket's feet. "Because another hundred years after his banishment from Kisua, right in the Hetawa's Hall of Blessings, Inunru finally died when his own priests killed him. They, too, had come to fear him, because his power had only grown in the time since—and with it, his greed. So they killed him. And they rewrote Hetawa ritual, rewrote history itself, to make the world forget such magic existed." Eninket leaned down, so that Ehiru had no choice but to look at him. "But I have found Inunru's scrolls, Brother, and now I know. A Reaper is the key."

He reached out and caressed Una-une's bowed head with a tenderness that had nothing to do with affection.

"When our armies and those of Kisua meet on the battlefield," Eninket continued, "their bloodlust and pain will draw the Reaper's hunger like a moth to flame. But this moth will devour the flame, and through him so shall I. Una-une will die at last, burned out by the power . . . but I shall become as eternal as a god." He paused, then gazed at Ehiru for a long solemn moment. "Then, however, I will need a new Reaper."

Ehiru's blood turned to stone.

With a soft sigh, Eninket turned away. "Rest well, Brother," he said. "I'll be back from Kite-iyan when the war is done. The guards will inform me when the necessary changes have taken place in you." He started to leave, then paused and glanced at Nijiri. "You may think this no kindness...but at least the boy will be a *willing* first victim."

With that, the Prince of Gujaareh walked away, gesturing for all the guards, even the ones who'd caged them, to follow. The children hooded the Reaper and coaxed it to its feet. It shuffled away between them, docile for the moment.

"Eninket," Ehiru whispered. He did not know if it was a curse or a plea. If Eninket heard, he gave no sign.

The great stone doors rumbled shut once more, sealing them within the tomb.

# FOURTH INTERLUDE

( ⊙ )

*Have you fathomed the secret yet? The thread of folly that eventually wove our doom?*

*There is a reason we Servants of Hananja vow celibacy. There is a reason the Princes were leashed. These were raindrops in a waterfall, a grain of sand flung at a storm, but we tried. True dreamers are both geniuses and madmen. Most lands can tolerate only a few, and those die young. We encouraged ours, nurtured them, kept them healthy and happy. We filled a city with them and praised our own greatness. Do you understand just how beautiful, and how dangerous, that was?*

*And yes, I knew. I've told you I was a talekeeper; I have always known the answers to these questions. We train our children to keep their own counsel. When I became a Gatherer, I watched, and would have spoken if the need had come. Fortunately there is no need. Is there?*

*Is there?*

*Ah, Superior, even without speaking, you are a poor liar.*

*Will you tell my brethren, at least, that I died? Ehiru. I should have told these tales to him, not you . . . but he has always been fragile, despite his strength. His faith sustains him—and faith is so easy to break.*

*So tell him I died. It will be true by the time you're done with me. And tell him that I love him. He'll need that in the time to come. And those words, I know, will be true until dreams end.*

# 35

(•⊙•)

*Speak all prayers in Sua, the tongue of the motherland,*
*that we may remember always who we were.*
*Speak of all dreams in our own tongue, that we*
*may embrace who we become.*

(Law)

Amid the thrones of the dead, the pranje begins.

\*     \*     \*

The first day.

"I'm not afraid, Brother. I can help you—"

"St-stay away from me."

\*     \*     \*

The first night: metal scrapes against oiled twine.

"What are you doing?"

"Forgive me for waking you. I thought perhaps I could cut some of the knots holding the ironwork together. If we can get out of this cage..."

Silence for a moment. "That was your hipstrap-clasp. The one your mother gave you."

"It was a child's thing." More scraping. "Are you thirsty, Brother? There's water, though no food."

"No."

"You haven't drunk since—"

"*No.*"

After a sigh, the scraping resumes.

\*     \*     \*

The second day: morning, or what passes for such among the thrones of the dead. Slow, even breathing overlaid by whispered prayer.

"Forgive me, forgive me, Hananja I beg You, I should have offered You my tithe after the Bromarte, I know it now, forgive my pride and selfishness, please please please do not let me kill him."

\*     \*     \*

The second day: afternoon. A brief draught of fresh air and the fading echoes of guards' boots.

"At least we won't starve. Here, Brother."

"I want nothing."

Silence.

A reluctant sigh.

"Now drink. Your mind will fight harder if your body's healthy."

"Have you forgotten your promise, Nijiri?"

"...No, Brother."

"Then why do you delay? You see what must be done."

"I see that you must eat and drink, and when our meal is done you must pray with me, and then while you meditate I'll resume work on those twine hinges. It may take several days, but I think—"

Unnatural fury splits the air. "Foolish, wicked *child*! Do you enjoy my suffering? Will you force me to perform another of those—perverted—"

"I want anything but your suffering, Brother. But if you take me it will be a true Gathering, because I offer myself willingly."

"Already my thoughts...the visions...I cannot..." A deep breath, a struggle for calm. "You gave your word, Nijiri."

"Have you considered what will happen if I take you, Brother?"

"What?"

"It might take longer with me—or it might go faster. I don't have your strength. But in the end, one Reaper will be as good as another to the Prince."

Long and terrible silence.

"Drink, Brother. When we've won our way free—and when there's no chance of either of us becoming the Prince's plaything—then I will send you to Her. That I vow, with everything that I am."

\*    \*    \*

The second night: silence in the halls of the dead, but for scraping.

\*    \*    \*

The third day: morning. Harsh and shaky breath.

"Brother?"

"The bars. They constrict. They, they will crush us."

"No, Brother. It was a vision—"

"*I saw them.*"

"Then come sit beside me. Death is nothing to fear, is it? Over here, the bars will take less time to reach us. Come."

Sandals shift on stone, slowly and reluctantly.

"Good. Feel my hand. I have calluses now, do you see? Camel reins, barge-rowing, twine-scraping…who knew the life of a Gatherer would be so hard? Gods, I should've stayed a servant-caste."

"You." The voice is gravel, groping for itself. "You are…too willful for that. You would've been…forced to find a new master every other day."

A rich chuckle. "Too true, Brother. I should be grateful at least that the Hetawa doesn't beat its children."

The harsh breathing stutters, then slows, calming.

After a long while—"Thank you."

No response, although a voice begins to hum a gentle, comforting hymn.

"It goes so fast this time, Nijiri."

"Shh." Another shift; now flesh strokes against flesh. "Here. You're here. In this world, this body. Stay with me, Brother. I need you."

"Yes…yes." An audible swallow. "I'd forgotten what true fear felt like. Nothing holds it back anymore."

"There's nothing to fear. All will be well. Rest. I'll be here when you wake."

\*　　\*　　\*

The third day: afternoon. The stir of fresh air. The stillness of the dead is broken by three new voices, peaceless and loud and disrespectful.

"Is he dead yet? I've got money on you, boy."

"Look at those eyes, Amtal! If hate could kill, you'd be dead already."

"No luck. The big one is breathing. He's just asleep."

"Sitting up?"

"Maybe that's how they do it. Maybe he's trying to kill you from afar."

"Maybe he's laying a curse on your family line."

"Maybe he's laying a curse on your family jewels!" Raucous laughter.

"Just feed them, you imbeciles, and let's go. I don't like this place."

Stone and chains; the return of silence. After a time, the scraping begins again.

*     *     *

The third night: early evening.

"You're shivering."

"N-not . . . cold."

"I know."

"Have I ever . . . harmed you, Nijiri?"

"Harmed me? No, why do you ask?"

"A v-vision. It was the pranje. I hurt you. Beat you. K-killed."

"Don't be foolish, Brother. I'm here, aren't I? I never sat pranje for you, though I wanted to, trained to. And I listened to the rumors about you, talked to others who attended you. Don't worry; you've never done such a thing."

A voice that trembles: "In the vision, I *wanted* to."

A voice that soothes: "I will never let that happen."

*     *     *

The third night, late, or the fourth morning, early: the small hours. The infinitesimal sounds of stealth. Death creeps on fingers and toes.

Slow, even breathing catches for a moment, then resumes.

"Welcome, Brother."

Silence.

"Do you want me?"

Silence, pent.

"Take what you need. Use it to free yourself. I'll wait for you in Ina-Karekh."

Silence. Stealth abandoned; now there is only breath, ragged with strain.

"N...nnh..."

Waiting.

"Nnnnh..." The voice breaks; it sounds barely human. "N-no. I will n-not. I will *not*."

"Brother— No, Brother, don't— Here. Yes. Yes, Brother."

The sobs that break the silence are without hope, but the soothing tones that overlay them are confident and loving.

"I wanted to...I would have...*Indethe a etun*—"

"Shhh. She has never turned Her sight from you, Brother. You're Her most beloved servant, and you have served Her long and well. She'll welcome you when the time comes. You will dwell in Her peace forever. I shall see to that myself."

"Now, Nijiri. It must be now. The next time—"

"The next time you'll do whatever you must. But try to hold on, Brother. I cut through the hinges a few hours ago. Now only a push will make the wall come loose. When the guards come again, we can break free."

"Can't...hold..."

"You can. I'll help you. Shhh. Close your eyes. Yes, like that. Shhh. I'll weave us a dream; would you like that? Not a Gathering, but perhaps enough to keep the madness at bay awhile longer. Now lie still."

"Nijiri."

"I've always loved you, my Brother. I no longer care what's right. *You* are my only Law. Rest now, safe in my dreams."

Silence.

\*     \*     \*

The fourth day.

"The Prince was right, Brother."

Massive chains rumble, sending forth echoes as stone doors shift. Fresh air wafts through the catacombs. Amid the thrones of the dead, life gathers itself for battle.

"You have indeed become a weapon, but not his. All things serve Hananja's will—even this. Remember that, no matter what you do."

The rumbling ceases; footsteps violate the peaceful sanctity of Yanyi-ija-inank as the guards approach.

"And no matter what happens, I shall never leave your side."

\*     \*     \*

The guards stop before the cage's door. "So, boy. Is he dead yet?" They laugh.

And Ehiru looks up, smiling a smile that chills their souls.

"Yes," the Reaper says.

# 36

(• ⊙ •)

*The Reaper is the abomination of all that Hananja holds*
*dear. Do not suffer such a creature to live.*

(Law)

The first guard fell when Ehiru kicked the loosened cage wall
off its hinges. The wall was heavy; it knocked one guard to the
ground while the other two, caught by surprise, stood there in
shock. By the time they reacted, Ehiru was out of the cage and
on them.

Nijiri ran out after him, ready to take down whichever one
Ehiru missed, but there was no need. Ehiru struck the first guard a
slashing blow across the throat, and in the same blurring movement twisted about and took hold of the second guard's face. Nijiri
saw the guard—screaming, blinded by Ehiru's fingers on his
eyes—fumble for his sword. Nijiri rushed forward to assist Ehiru,
but abruptly the guard made a strangled sound and sagged to his
knees. Ehiru released him. The man fell over on his side, dead.

All things were Hananja's will. Nijiri clung to that thought.
In Her name they would do whatever needed to be done.

The first guard gurgled and finally died, clutching his throat.

The third guard had managed to get halfway free of the entangling lattice of metal, but his leather breastplate had snagged on a spar. Ehiru, swaying in the aftermath of his Reaping, turned slowly, his attention attracted by the man's struggles.

Nijiri crossed the room in three strides, dropped to one knee beside the struggling soldier, and broke his neck in one swift jerk.

The glaze faded from Ehiru's eyes. He blinked at Nijiri, lucid again for however long the guard's dreamblood might last him. Sorrow flooded his face as he gazed down at Nijiri's handiwork.

"No more than is necessary, Brother," Nijiri said, standing. He wiped his hands on his foredrape. "Now come. We still need to make our way out of Yanya-iyan."

"Eninket." Ehiru's voice was deeper than usual, as rough and sluggish as if he'd just eaten timbalin paste. Even now, when he was newly flush with dreamblood, Nijiri could hear madness lurking near the surface of his lucidity.

*The dreamblood no longer holds it back. It keeps him alive, nothing more.*

Hananja's will. Setting his jaw, Nijiri replied, "He said he was going to Kite-iyan."

Ehiru nodded and turned on his heel, heading for the door. Startled, Nijiri hurried after him. The corridor beyond the catacombs' entrance was empty, for which Nijiri gave private thanks. The Prince must have limited the guards to three in order to minimize the chance that word of Ehiru's and Nijiri's capture would get out.

"Three's an unlucky number, anyway," Nijiri muttered to himself.

They went up the steps two at a time and then out into the brighter-lit corridors of Yanya-iyan's ground floor. Servants and courtiers stumbled in passing, staring at them. Doubtless they rarely saw hollow-eyed, unwashed men in Kisuati garb sweep through the palace like a flood, Nijiri thought cynically. If they raised any alarm it was slow, so Nijiri and Ehiru remained unmolested all the way to the courtyard. As they crossed the sandy expanse toward Yanya-iyan's bronze gates, for a fleeting moment Nijiri's mind was flung back to Hamyan Night, which now seemed ages ago and a thousand dreams away.

The guards on duty faced the courtyard gate, alert for unwanted intruders and unaware of the internal threat. They might have escaped relatively unscathed if someone up on one of the high tiers of the palace hadn't whistled an alarm. One of the men turned and spied Nijiri and Ehiru. Startled, he jostled his fellow, both of them turning; Nijiri broke into a run to close the distance, hearing Ehiru's steps speed up beside him. The first man grinned, seeing only an unarmed youth rushing toward him. Not bothering to draw his sword, he braced himself to grapple. Nijiri ducked his first grab, skidded to a crouch, and drove his fist at the side of the man's knee. The wet pop of cartilage echoed though the empty courtyard.

The man began to scream, dropping to the ground and holding his knee. Nijiri heard another scream behind him and turned to see Ehiru, his eyes glittering with unholy fierceness, letting a corpse fall from his hands. Before it fell onto its face, Nijiri saw an expression of starkest horror frozen on its features.

Arrows thudded into the sand not two feet away. Nijiri darted for the gate, grunting with effort as he raised the heavy bronze bar. Ehiru, disturbingly calm, turned to face the archers. Just as Nijiri managed to shove the bar aside and push open the gate, there was a blur of motion at the corner of his vision. When he looked around, Ehiru held an arrow in his hand. It was still quivering, two feet from the small of Nijiri's back.

*Impossible! Even for the best-trained Gatherer . . .*

"Go," Ehiru snarled, throwing the arrow aside. Too numb to think, Nijiri scrambled through the gate.

They emerged onto the busy avenue that circled Yanya-iyan as more whistles sounded from the palace's heights. Through the street traffic Nijiri saw men in the gray of the City Guard turning, craning their necks to see what had caused the alarm.

"This way," Ehiru said. He walked swiftly into the crowd and joined its flow, keeping to the center of the street where the human river moved most swiftly. Nijiri kept his eyes low, playing servant-caste again, though he darted a glance back. The guardsmen had just reached Yanya-iyan's gates. A palace guard ran out with sword unsheathed, looking about wildly; they saw him gesticulating at the city men. Nijiri quickly lowered his head again, noting that Ehiru had done the same. At the first juncture of streets they moved behind a lumbering wagon and turned south. Here was the market, where they could lose themselves easily in the sea of people.

Ehiru navigated his way through the milling folk so swiftly that Nijiri was hard-pressed to keep up. Around the stitch in his side—*too many days of inactivity; should have kept up my prayer dances at least*—he fumbled out a hand to catch Ehiru's arm. "Brother, the Hetawa is that way."

"No." Ehiru did not slow.

"Brother, we can't just walk to Kite-iyan! We need horses, disguises, supplies, replacements for our ornaments! And we must tell our pathbrothers all that has happened."

"Within an hour, the entire city will be on alert."

Nijiri's heart sank as he realized Ehiru was right. Even worse, the Sentinels at the Hetawa would be notified, as was customary in any city emergency—but the Sentinels, some of them at least, obeyed the Superior. Returning to the Hetawa meant recapture.

"Then we should take the south gate, Brother," he said. Ehiru slowed and glanced back at him. Nijiri offered a rueful smile. "It is not the closest gate to the Moonpath, I know, but the guard there is a friend of Sister Meliatua and Sunandi. Remember? He may even give us a horse."

Ehiru stopped, frowning as he considered this. A merchant brushed past him and he shivered, his eyes unfocusing slightly as they tracked the merchant into the crowd. His body shifted, the fingers of one hand forking at his side—

Nijiri seized that hand and squeezed it hard. Ehiru flinched as if waking from a daydream, then closed his eyes in momentary anguish.

"The south gate," he said. "Quickly. Get me out of this city, Nijiri."

Nijiri nodded. Keeping hold of Ehiru's hand, he pressed through the crowd in a new direction, praying that they reached Kite-iyan in time.

# 37

(• ⊙ •)

*The world is born*
*Echoes, dancing fires, laughter*
*We race through the realm of dreams, alongside gods*
*The world ends.*

(Wisdom)

The Prince of Gujaareh lay awake amid the cushions of his gauze-draped bed, contemplating the world he would one day own.

He had no particular desire for conquest. But he did desire peace—like any true son of Gujaareh—and he had long ago realized that peace was the natural outgrowth of order. This had been proven again and again throughout the grand dream that was Gujaareh. The rampant crime and violence that soiled other lands was alien here. No one starved, save in the most remote backwaters. Even the lowliest servant-caste had enough education and self-determination to control his own fate. Every child in the city knew his place from birth. Every elder in the city embraced his value in death. And on the strength of all who came between had Hananja's nation thrived, growing from a pathetic knot of tents perched precariously on the river mouth into a network of cities and mines and farmlands and trade-routes crowned by its capital, the glory of the civilized world. His beautiful City of Dreams.

But the rest of the world still struggled along in disorder, and what peace could Gujaareh have in the long term with such weak and petty neighbors? He had visited other lands in his youth, and been horrified by chaos and cruelty that made the shadowlands seem pleasant. Other rulers had tried to tame that chaos with might or money, sometimes succeeding, but it never lasted. How could it, when a human lifetime was only so long? Even the most noble warlord eventually grew old and died, passing on power to those who more often than not were ill equipped to maintain it.

Thus the solution: conquer the world, but for peace rather than power. And to hold the world once it was won, become a god.

The Prince sat up. Beside him his firstwife Hendet stirred. He looked down at her and stroked her cheek, greeting her sleepy smile with one of his own. After thirty years and more than two hundred other wives, he still felt honored to have her favor. In the way of southern women, she was still beautiful even with her youth long past; time had left few seams in her dark smooth skin. But she was old—past fifty, nearly as old as himself. He yearned for more children from her, and perhaps could have had them if he'd permitted her to accept dreamblood from the Hetawa. But tempting as the notion had been, he could not bear the thought of the Hetawa's setting its claws into yet another member of his family.

He kissed her forehead. "I would still rather you stay here. It will be dangerous."

She lifted a hand to trace his lips with one finger. "Don't be foolish."

He smiled and nodded, approving of her decision despite the flicker of grief that moved through him. He would lose her when the power made him immortal. Another decade or two, and then she would pass beyond his reach into Ina-Karekh, where he would never see her again.

More sorrow to lay at the Hetawa's feet, he decided. Then he rose, naked, to begin his war.

Servants draped a feather robe over him for the walk to the baths. There they sluiced his skin with purifying salt and lemon-water and dabbed him dry with oiled rose petals. When they finished dressing him in the armor of his ancestors and threading gold into his hair, he left the apartments to find Hendet and their son Wanahomen waiting for him. From his kneeling posture, Wana lifted a sword in a worked leather sheath. When the Prince took it, Wana raised his eyes to watch him belt it on, and not for the first time did the Prince marvel at the stark worship in his son's gaze.

So be it, he thought. Let Hananja and the Moons' children have the land of dreams. The waking world belonged to the sons of the Sun.

"Come," he said, and Wanahomen rose, immediately falling into place one pace behind and to the right as they walked. Ever proper, Hendet followed on his left, her head high in anticipation and pride. As they entered the public corridors, his

367

Aureole-servant leaped up to follow in his wake. The Prince considered waving the child away, but decided it would be more fitting to discard the Aureole afterward, when he had become a god in more than name. Charris fell in behind them, and thus they proceeded to the steps that led up Kite-iyan's highest tower.

Around them the marble corridors were empty. For their own protection the Prince had sent all his other wives and children away, and stationed the Sunset Guard on the lowest floor of the palace to protect against attack. Only these four—an auspicious and pleasing number—would witness his ascension.

They mounted the steps in silence, passing the landing where Niyes had faced his final moments, not stopping until they reached the topmost level of the spire. As Charris opened the door, a finger of light pierced the faraway horizon and spread as the sun's golden curve made its first appearance.

The Prince smiled. Far to the south, where the desert met the Kisuati border, the coming of dawn had signaled his armies' attack.

He stepped out onto the balcony, inhaling in pleasure as a brisk wind rose from the ground far below, lifting his hair like curling wings. To one side of the balcony a figure stirred, the rattle of chains breaking the morning's silence. The Prince glanced over at his Reaper, which crouched where the servants had chained it against the wall. The servants' corpses lay at its feet. The Prince was amused to see that some flicker of its old self must have stirred in the Reaper during the night; it had arranged the bodies in dignified positions.

The jungissa stone that the Prince raised was crude, ugly. It had chipped off a larger piece of Sun's seed, the peculiar stones that fell every now and then from the sky, and unlike the artfully carved jewels used by the Hetawa, this one was just a chunk of rock. Still, when the Prince struck it against a nearby railing, the Reaper shivered, lifting its head. "B-brother...?"

The Prince raised his eyebrows in surprise. The Reaper rarely spoke these days. The remnants of its personality had grown so weak that he barely needed the jungissa anymore; his will was enough to hold the creature's thoughts. Putting the stone away, he went over to it, crouching to peer into its confused eyes. "Here. Did you rest well, Una-une?"

The Reaper blinked against the sunlight, sighing and shaking its head. "No. Visions. There...there was pain. Ehiru. He suffered."

The Prince nodded to Charris, who unlocked the chain fastened to the collar 'round the Reaper's neck. "Yes, pathbrother," the Prince said, taking the end of the chain from Charris. He reached up to stroke the creature's slack cheek. "Unfortunately, he suffers. But now the time has come for your own suffering to end. One last task, one last glorious Gathering, and then you may rest."

Longing flooded the creature's eyes; tears welled in its eyes. "Yes. Yes. Oh please, Brother. I have served for so long."

"I know. Just a little longer, and then Her peace awaits you, I promise. Come."

He stood, tugging the Reaper's leash. It rose and flowed after him, predator-graceful even with its mind all but gone. He stopped at the railing, gesturing Hendet and the rest of them back.

But then, suddenly, the Reaper stiffened. It whipped about to face the balcony doorway, nearly pulling the chain from the Prince's hand. He caught his breath and gripped the leash, preparing to set his will against the thing's mad hunger—but then realized the creature's attention had not fixed on Hendet or Wanahomen. He followed the Reaper's gaze, and set his jaw.

"Enough, Eninket," snarled Ehiru.

# 38

⟨ ⊙ ⟩

*There is nothing to fear in nightmares, so long as you*
*control them.*
(Wisdom)

Like a vision, the Dreamer had raced across the nighttime sky
as their horses blurred along the Moonpath to Kite-iyan. Through
the rushing wind, the only constants Ehiru had grasped were
anger and Nijiri's voice, penetrating the blur now and again to
remind him of who he was. They entered Kite-iyan's welcome
hall and found it full of soldiers. With his mother's voice echoing in his mind, Ehiru hated them, and so fierce was his hatred
that some of it broke free and leaped forth. When he pulled it
back, their souls came with it, plump wriggling fish snared in
the net of his mind. He'd devoured them greedily, savoring their
pain and terror as a piquant spice, and guilt soured the moment
only a little.

Now he stood facing his Prince, his brother, his betrayer, and
the hatred returned—but this time he held it back. He would
cleanse this corruption from Gujaareh's soul in the proper manner, he had decided along the way, as a Gatherer and not a

monster. For justice and for Hananja, he would be himself one last time.

"Enough," he said again, stalking onto the balcony. Nijiri flowed behind him, a shadow ready to strike. To one side a woman, two men, and a servant-child stood in shock, their souls bright alluring flames that called out to him. He ignored them and the hunger that wanted them. "Yield. I still have enough control to give you peace. If you resist I can promise nothing."

Eninket gave him a cool smile, though Ehiru saw anger lurking underneath. "Don't be foolish, Ehiru. Death or godhood; which would you choose?" He put his hand on the Reaper's shoulder and the creature uttered a feral hiss at them.

"Control your beast, Eninket." Ehiru raised his voice. It was not the peaceful thing to do, but there was little peace left inside him, and he did not care besides. "The man it once was could have beaten me, but not this sorry thing. And if you unleash it, it may attack indiscriminately."

He glanced at their inadvertent audience. The man in the garb of a high-ranking soldier drew his sword; the youth did the same. The youth's features bore Eninket's stamp, Ehiru had already noted, and that of the shunha woman who stood with them. He saw too the fear that flashed across Eninket's face.

Keeping a hand on the Reaper's shoulder, Eninket spoke softly, but firmly. "Wanahomen, leave with your mother. Charris, protect them with your life."

The man looked ready to argue, though he threw an uneasy glance at the Reaper—which had fixed its gaze on Nijiri in blatant eagerness—and subsided. The youth had no such qualms. "Father, I will not!"

"*Do as I say.*" Eninket tore his eyes away from Ehiru long enough to glare the youth into submission. "Now. Go!"

After another moment, the youth slumped, and the woman pulled him toward the door by the arm. The soldier grabbed the arm of the child, who clutched a pole bearing the Aureole, and dragged him out as well. Once Ehiru heard their footsteps moving away down the stairs he stepped closer, keeping a wary eye on the Reaper.

"You've lost," Ehiru said to Eninket. "Face your death with dignity."

"Even now, after everything I've told you?" Eninket uttered a soft, bitter laugh. "A slave of the Hetawa to the end. No, Ehiru. *I'm* not the one who's lost here." He sighed. "So be it."

As he gazed down the Reaper, Eninket's face took on a peculiar look of concentration. The Reaper froze, expression going even more slack than usual—though it cocked its head, as if listening. Then Eninket took his hand away from its shoulder.

Even with that warning, the creature's speed caught Ehiru by surprise. He had only an instant to brace himself—but it flashed past him, and suddenly he realized that he was not its target. "Nijiri!"

But the boy caught the Reaper's hand before it could reach his face, twisting to turn aside its momentum. The creature stumbled, off balance, and Nijiri struck it in the middle of its sunken chest. It fell to the ground flailing and Nijiri closed in, his eyes more vicious than Ehiru had ever seen. Ehiru moved to assist, but abruptly a faint sound from behind impinged on his awareness. He whirled to face whatever trickery Eninket was attempting—

—And froze, staring at the humming jungissa stone in his

brother's hand. Eninket tensed, then paused, narrowing eyes at him.

"Come here, Ehiru," said Eninket. Ehiru took a step toward Eninket before it occurred to him to wonder why he did so. He stopped, frowning.

"So it works on you as well." Eninket stared at him with something akin to wonder. "The Superior said you had been deprived...and yet the boy is alive. Who, then, have you killed to preserve your own life, my brother?" As Ehiru set his jaw against shame, Eninket smiled, relaxing, a high gleam of victory in his eyes. "You're as corrupt as the rest of them, for all your pious talk."

The jungissa's song filled Ehiru's mind, throwing him back to a thousand nights and a thousand Gatherings, making him yearn for the time when things had been so simple in his life. When he had been pure, and there had been nothing but peace in his heart, and—

*What is this?* In confusion he shook his head, but the stone's whine pierced through his thoughts like a dagger.

"Another secret of the scrolls," said Eninket, drawing near. "A Reaper's mind grows in sensitivity as well as power, leaving you vulnerable to the simplest narcomancy."

Ehiru struggled to draw his eyes away from the jungissa as it grew in his vision, but he failed. The sound of the thing drowned out everything else—including the sounds of Nijiri's struggle against the Reaper behind him. He tried again to focus on Eninket, who was now unprotected and could be Gathered, but—

"Hananja's favorite, they call you. The most skilled Gatherer in recent memory; the dying dream of being taken by you. Yet look at the price you've paid for serving the Hetawa so well, Ehiru. You've become mine even faster than Una-une." The Prince sighed. "Perhaps this was always meant to be, my brother. Now *come*."

The word drove into Ehiru, backed by a will that parted his own like bedhangings and touched the most secret part of his consciousness where it lay. On some level he thought he made a sound, perhaps a strangled groan. He could not be sure. A hand touched his shoulder. He shivered beneath it, trying to let the hate loose again, but the mind that had woven its way into his gently pushed those thoughts aside. "Come, Brother," Eninket said again.

Ehiru turned and walked where the voice steered him, over to the balcony railing.

Behind him, from a distance, he heard someone cry his name. Nijiri. Fear for the boy nearly gave him the strength to turn back, but Eninket's will beat against his own.

"Shhh, Brother."

Now he was lost again, in the cage under Yanya-iyan, weeping against the hunger that had nearly driven him to murder Nijiri. The voice was different, but the words of comfort were the same, the hands on his shoulders almost as tender.

"It's all right," said the voice in his ear, twisting his memories further. Nijiri? No. There was no love in this voice. "I understand. So much corruption all around, so much suffering, and you helpless to stop it. But I can help you, Brother."

With a supreme effort Ehiru managed to close his eyes. But this was a mistake: the whine of the jungissa followed him into the darkness, and the voice spread its roots farther into his mind.

N. K. Jemisin

"Now. Reach out, Brother. Distance should be no barrier to you. Reach out, across the desert. Do you feel them?"

With his eyes shut, Ehiru had nothing to focus on but the voice. He fought it, but his mind stretched forth anyhow, falling away from him as though down a slanting pit. Visions formed around him: the desert, flying on skyrer's wings. There was the village of Ketuyae, there the oasis at Tesa. There were the foothills, and suddenly his descent changed. Something pulled him aside. He frowned, slowing, tasting blood and pain and nightmare-thick fear on the air.

And death.

Where there was death, there was dreamblood.

"Corruption, Brother. Do you feel it? Filth the likes of which our land has not seen in centuries."

Ehiru felt it. He whimpered as terror/cruelty/rage beat against his senses, driving thought even further beneath the surface of his mind. He could see them now, hundreds, thousands, men with swords and bloodlust, intent on hacking one another to pieces. The antithesis of peace. Then the vision changed and he saw only light where they had been—sparks that flared and then faded in death, others that burned steadily, together merging into a flickering whole. A Sun whose warmth promised to fill the cold and aching emptiness within him.

So many souls. So very many.

On another plane, Ehiru licked his lips.

"They will come here, Ehiru. Infect us with their savagery and chaos, destroy our peace—*Her* peace—forever." The voice moved closer to his ear, whispering its warning over distant screams of pain and rage and his own ravening lust. "Stop them,

376

little brother. Take them. Take them all now, and share them with me."

There was nothing left in him that could fight. The magic and the hunger had consumed it all.

Stretching out his hands and mind, Ehiru took hold of over twenty thousand lives, and began to Reap.

# 39

(•☉•)

*By the age of eight floods, a Gujaareen child should be able to read Law and recite the first four tenets of Wisdom, multiply and divide by fours and tens, and wield his soulname for protection in dreams.*

(Wisdom)

The sight of Waking Moon had been a comfort to Sunandi throughout her childhood. The hours of the Dreamer belonged to those who ruled Kisua's streets; that was the time of slavers and whoremasters, muggers and gangs. The strong who devoured the weak. But the setting of the Dreamer marked the end of their time, for by then the worst of the predators would have hunted, fed, and returned to their lairs to dream cold, bloody dreams. After that, only Waking Moon hung in the sky—the shy, plain sister of the heavenly queen, who had the heavens to herself for only an hour or so before the Sun returned. Less in the rainy season. But while Waking Moon's pallid light shone over the city streets, the weak had their time. The child called Nefe and her fellows at the bottom of the hierarchy could creep forth from their hiding places then, to nibble on the leavings of their betters. And if there was no food to eat and nothing of value to steal, at least there was safety, and with safety had come the few moments of happiness she recalled in that early life. Playing. Laughing. Feeling, for that one hour, like a child. She would never regret being adopted by Kinja—but neither had she ever forgotten those times, as dear to her as the mother she barely remembered.

Tonight the Waking Moon's light gave her no comfort, for beneath it she could see the armies of Gujaareh covering the plateau of Soijaro like a leper's sores.

*Too late, priest. We have failed, both my corrupt ways and your mad, rigid justice. And now both our lands will drown in blood.*

Sunandi's horse moved restlessly beneath her, perhaps reacting to the scent of fear in the air. She controlled the animal with a clumsy tug on the reins, and only then realized that Anzi Seh Ainunu had come up beside her, accompanied by Mweke Jeh Chi, chief Wisewoman of the Protectors. Anzi, the general of the Kisuati forces, was a tall hard sword of a man, brutally straightforward in speech and action. Mweke was a sharp contrast to him: a plump self-possessed elder, radiant with quiet power. The storytellers in the capital said she was a mystic whose dreams often came true. Rumor also had it she was not fully Kisuati, which would be a great scandal if true, though no one had managed to prove it yet. Sunandi wondered if she was part Gujaareen.

"The final attempt at parley has failed," Mweke said, reining in her horse beside Sunandi's. She spoke softly, though all the camp was awake and restless with the coming battle. "Our rider was given an arrow through the gut for his trouble."

Sunandi drew her robes closer about herself, chilled by more than the cool night air. "We knew a truce was unlikely, Esteemed."

"But you hoped." The old woman smiled at Sunandi's expression. "You have been waiting for your priest-friend to stop this somehow."

Sunandi opened her mouth to tell Mweke that Gatherer Ehiru was in no way her friend, but then closed it. It no longer mattered. If he had failed, then he was dead.

"I must go," Anzi said. His voice was deep, surprisingly gentle for that of a soldier, perversely reminding her of Ehiru. "The enemy waits only for dawn."

Mweke nodded to give him leave, but the general did not urge his horse away for a moment. "There's a wrongness in this," he said abruptly, looking out over the plateau. His forehead, Sunandi saw, was deeply lined in a frown. "The enemy's plan is flawed. They'll all die."

Sunandi frowned, trying to fathom how he had concluded this by looking at the army massing below. In the distance she could make out a line of masts along the coast; these were the mysterious ships whose existence Kinja and probably Niyes had died to reveal. Their deaths had not been in vain, for between those warnings and the Protectors' own suspicions, Kisua was ready to meet the Gujaareen attack, just. Anzi had managed to assemble twelve thousand soldiers, who surrounded the plateau and filled the valley beyond it—the only logical path the invaders could take to reach the Kisuati capital.

But although Sunandi was no expert in the strategies of war, she could see no reason for Anzi's confidence. Twelve thousand soldiers, many of them exhausted from being force-marched across half of Kisua to reach the plateau in time, were by no means a sure victory against ten thousand warriors who were fresh and chafing for battle.

"We have enough to hold them," Anzi said, as if reading Sunandi's mind. "And this is our land. We have ambushes set throughout the valley and the surrounding mountains. Our supply lines are reliable. We can keep them here days, even weeks if we must—long enough for our troops on the way from the south to arrive. It will be a war of attrition, which they will inevitably lose. Their commander is a fool if he doesn't see this."

Mweke watched him for a moment. "Perhaps they, too, have reinforcements on the way."

"Perhaps. Likely, in fact. But this is still *wrong*," Anzi said. Sunandi winced at his disrespect, but Mweke merely sighed. Perhaps the Protectors were used to him. "This was foolish from the outset. If they meant to win, they should have arrived with twice this number, if not more."

"What are you saying, General?" Sunandi said. "That they have no desire to win?" She could almost smell the Gujaareen troops' hatred. Many of them were northerners, the scouts had reported—barbarians who scorned all civilized folk as soft and decadent cowards. They were hungry for the chance to reap the riches of Kisua.

"I have no idea," he said. "You know these foreign madmen better than I. But if they've come to die on our shores, then I shall be happy to oblige them." He gave Sunandi and Mweke a curt nod, then wheeled his horse away. They saw him start down the trail that led from their encampment on the heights into the valley. From there he would lead the battle.

Which would be very soon now, Sunandi saw. The sky in the east had grown visibly paler in the past few moments.

"We should break camp, Esteemed," she said to Mweke. "Negotiation is no longer possible. We must return to the capital, where you and the other Protectors can be properly defended."

Mweke nodded, but did not move. "Anzi is correct," she said. "There must be something more to this. The Prince of Gujaareh is no fool. He has a maze of a mind."

Sunandi had never heard a more fitting metaphor, but they had more pressing matters at the moment. "We can do nothing but deal with the problem on our doorstep, Esteemed."

"No. We can make our own plans to foil the Prince, and have done. The relief troops from the south will not come here. The other Protectors and I have chosen to send them north."

Sunandi frowned in confusion. "I don't understand, Esteemed. There's nothing north but the Empty Thousand, and—" The realization came almost at once; she trailed off. Mweke read her face and nodded in cool approval.

"There can be no reason for the Prince to have built a garrison in the desert," the elder said, "other than to support an invasion by land. A *second* invasion. The Protectors believe this"—she gestured out at the Gujaareen army gathered on Soijaro—"to be merely a diversion. So we will deal with the true threat at its source."

Sunandi swallowed hard. "The general may have need of those troops, Esteemed. At the very least he should know to expect no relief."

"It is problematic to ask a soldier to risk his life for no good reason," Mweke said. "He doesn't fight as hard, thinking it hopeless; he welcomes death too quickly, thinking of the glory in sacrifice. We must have Anzi's full commitment, for this is *our* distraction as well. Kisua has defenses enough to deal with this rabble, should we lose the battle. But we shall win the war. When our relief troops are done with the desert garrison, they have orders to continue even further north, to Gujaareh's capital."

Struck dumb by pure horrified astonishment, Sunandi stared at her.

"So it must be," Mweke said. Her voice was soft, almost lost in the early-morning breeze, but implacable. "Gujaareh is a daughter gone wayward and spoiled, and now we must take her in hand. The correction will be painful for both our lands, but in the end all will be better." She glanced over at Sunandi, contemplative. "You've done very well through all this, Jeh Kalawe— better than expected, given your youth. Learn from these events. They may make you a formidable Protector, some day."

With that, Mweke turned her horse and rode away, back to where a party of soldiers and slaves were packing their encampment to leave.

Sunandi gazed after her, too numb to follow. Inadvertently she visualized a pitched battle at the gates of Gujaareh. The image of pale walls splashed red filled her with sudden nausea. She had always hated Gujaareh. And yet...

Behind Sunandi, dawn broke.

Below, on the plateau, the battle began.

Sunandi closed her eyes against the massed battle cry of twenty-two thousand men. Silently, for the first time in her life, she prayed to Hananja.

*Stop this. Only You can, at this point. Make the Prince see reason. Save Your city—and* both *our lands—from more point-less, useless death.*

For a long moment, as she had expected, there was no answer. Then the back of her neck prickled, reacting to a presence. Startled, she turned in her saddle.

Ehiru stood behind her horse, his shoulders slumped, his eyes on the ground. Sunandi caught her breath, more glad than she could ever have imagined to see him alive. But—

He lifted his head and Sunandi recoiled, shocked by what looked out at her through his eyes. *Insanity*, naked and glittering, so alien to his face that she barely recognized him. Insanity and something more: hunger.

Distantly, through the sudden pounding of her heart in her ears, Sunandi registered that the sounds of the battle below had faltered to a halt. *They all see him*, she realized, though she could not have said how she knew. Every soldier, official, and slave on the Soijaro plateau shared this vision.

Then Ehiru reached for her with arms grown impossibly long, his lips stretching in a ragged smile to reveal teeth sharp as rose thorns. "I bring you peace," he whispered, his fingers burrowing into her skin like roots.

In the world of flesh and blood, Sunandi went rigid on her horse and began to scream. Twenty-two thousand other throats screamed with her, but that world was meaningless. The dream-world was the Reaper's domain, the only world that mattered, and in that realm Ehiru dragged Sunandi to the ground, pinning her effortlessly. He crouched over her, still smiling his loving smile, and hunkered down to feed.

# 40

(•⊙•)

A Gatherer who refuses the Final Tithe shall be
deemed corrupt.

(Law)

*Die at last,* Nijiri thought fiercely, *and if you fall into the shadowlands I do not care.*

He kicked Una-une over onto his back and then straddled
him, taking hold of his chin and the back of his head.

But he had forgotten a Reaper's speed. Una-une's fist struck
him under the chin, the force of the blow nearly breaking his
neck. Stunned, Nijiri swayed back; Una-une heaved underneath
him and flung him to the balcony floor. An instant later Nijiri
found their positions reversed, Una-une's head blotting out the
dawn sky above him. Amber streaks of the rising Sun illuminated Una-une's gaunt face and one eye, which glittered with
malevolent glee.

"I remember you," the Reaper breathed, his thin body trembling with eagerness. His fingers scrabbled over Nijiri's arms,
trying to pin them. "Your soul was sweet."

Nijiri snarled in response and flung himself upward, driving his forehead into Una-une's mouth. Una-une uttered a muffled grunt of surprise as Nijiri set his feet against the floor and shoved with all his strength, throwing Una-une off to one side. Freed, Nijiri scrambled to his feet, stumbling back to try and recoup his wits.

Una-une was up as well. Quick as a dust snake he lunged, a skeleton's grin fixed on his face. Nijiri narrowly ducked a fist; the wind of its passing tickled his scalp. He snarled and shifted his weight for a kick, but before he could deliver it Una-une ducked under his guard and tackled him with a shoulder to the belly.

They were both lucky. Once Una-une had been a large man, shorter but heavier than Ehiru. Now he was skin and bone and shrunken sinew. His weight bore Nijiri back against the metal balcony railing hard enough to knock the breath from his lungs in an involuntary cry, but not hard enough to drive them both over to their deaths. Nijiri scrabbled at Una-une's shoulders for a moment, nearly panicking as wind soughed up his back and warned him of the danger. Desperately he clasped his hands and slammed them into the back of Una-une's neck with all his strength.

The blow should have driven Una-une to his knees. But the leather collar around his neck softened the blow, and in the same instant Una-une writhed aside and backed away. He swayed, arms and collar-chain swinging, grinning in blatant mockery.

*Playing with me*, Nijiri realized with a chill.

He pushed himself away from the railing, falling into a defensive crouch and trying to ignore the throbbing agony in his neck and ribs. His anger was gone now; it had been little more than a cover for his fear. Unbidden came the memory of the Reaper's cold touch on his flesh and in his soul, and despite the rising warmth of the day he shivered.

But without warning Una-une's mood shifted.

"Afraid," he whispered. A faint frown crossed his features; he cocked his head as if that would somehow shake loose his tangled thoughts. "Attendants... should not fear."

Nijiri frowned as he realized what path the mad creature's thoughts now traveled. Not the night in the alleyway. The pranje.

In spite of the drumbeat of his heart, Nijiri set his jaw. "You killed the boy who served you."

"It could have been you." There was a manic smile on Una-une's face; Nijiri suspected the creature meant to compliment him. "Lovely boy. For you, I would have fought the madness harder. You love Ehiru, don't you? As he loved me..." He trailed off, confusion flickering in his face for a moment, and then he lifted his eyes. Nijiri started at the sudden lucidity in them.

"Hananja's favorite," Una-une said. He looked away, radiating shame, as Nijiri stared in confusion. "Everything came to his hand like a tame bird. His skill in Gathering, Hananja's peace, and so many admirers. I loved him as a son... and hated him, too. Do you understand? That was when I knew. No peace left in my heart. Nothing but loneliness and anger. Time to go."

From the corner of his eye Nijiri saw movement. He dared a glance to the side and saw Ehiru turning away, stiff as an elder as the Prince guided him toward the railing. What were they doing? And why did Ehiru move like a man sleepwalking through some nightmare?

Visions of the Prince throwing Ehiru over the railing rang through his mind. "Ehiru-brother!"

For a moment it seemed as though Ehiru heard him. He stopped and began to turn back, but then the Prince murmured something and raised his other hand. A jungissa? Whatever it was, Ehiru seemed powerless to resist. He faced south again and continued to the railing.

"Even now," said Una-une. With a chill Nijiri realized he'd forgotten his adversary. But Una-une only watched him, hollow-eyed and radiating such deep despair that Nijiri's hatred faltered. And that reminded him of his one remaining weapon.

Swallowing, he lowered his hands to his sides, straightened, and took a step forward.

"There is still peace in you, Una-une-brother," he said. "A Gatherer belongs to Hananja, always, even now."

Una-une frowned at this, turning to gaze out at the horizon, but Nijiri saw that his words had been heard. Sorrow wavered in his ravaged face.

"I was ready," Una-une said. "I told them I wanted Ehiru to come and take my Final Tithe. But they took me away, and there's been no peace since." He sighed, then glanced at Nijiri. "Do you think I could've seen Her? Just once, in Ina-Karekh?"

Nijiri took another step closer. "Yes, Brother. You served Her well." He took a deep breath, trying to still the pounding of his heart, trying to feel the truth in his own words, trying not to think of Ehiru and whatever the Prince was doing to him. *A Gatherer's sole duty is to bring peace; for that a Gatherer must have peace within himself.* He tried to feel compassion for Una-une. To his own surprise, it was not difficult.

"Shall I send you to Her now, Una-une-brother?" he asked softly. "I know the way."

Una-une blinked at him. For one breathtaking, bittersweet moment his eyes filled with longing and Nijiri thought he would say yes.

Then Una-une's expression flickered. The confusion returned. And as it began to pass, Nijiri saw the Reaper's madness gleaming underneath. There would be no cat-and-mouse combat this time, he understood in that instant. The Reaper—for Nijiri could see Una-une fading away like morning mist—would pierce his mind and drain him dry.

Nijiri closed his eyes. "Forgive me, great Hananja. I can't do this properly and still be sure."

So he set his foot to brace himself, then made a blade of his hand and drove it into the Reaper's throat.

The Reaper staggered back. Reached up, scrabbling at the loose leather collar and the deep concavity where its larynx had been. Even as Nijiri watched the area turned bruise-dark. With that opening, Nijiri ran forward and slapped a hand against the Reaper's chest, driving dreambile through him as he'd done to Sentinel Harakha on the day of his apprenticeship trial. He was no Sharer; he had no idea what he'd managed to paralyze, just prayed it would be something important— And in the next instant, blood gouted from the Reaper's lips. Its mouth worked, fishlike, as it struggled to draw breath and failed. With a Gatherer's grace, it sagged to its knees. For just a breath its eyes focused on Nijiri, and there was peace in them.

Then Una-une fell and did not move again.

Taking a deep breath and clenching his fists, Nijiri pivoted to focus on Ehiru and the Prince. *Oh Goddess!*

Ehiru stood facing south. His hands quivered, each lifted before him with fingers forked. His body shook as well, harder than that of the afflicted child in Kisua; every muscle stood out like ropes beneath his skin. In profile Nijiri could see his mentor's face frozen in a hideous rictus of lust and ecstasy and desperate, terrified denial. His eyes were shut tight. Over the sound of the wind Nijiri could hear Ehiru's voice straining to utter a sound that might have been an animal's death-cry or the groan of an overstressed timber. It was the sound of nothing human.

"Uuuuuuh…"

And through it all the Prince stood behind him, hands on his shoulders, clinging to his back like a tick. His eyes had closed as well, but in pure bliss; in the dawn light he all but glowed as he drank in power.

"Nnnnnnnn…"

"Get away from him!" Nijiri lunged across the intervening space and grabbed the Prince.

It was like grabbing lightning. Power rammed up Nijiri's arms and seared into his brain before he could raise his defenses or pull his hands free. In that blistering instant he felt himself crumbling away, too weak to withstand such a flood of will and magic and dreamblood and life and—

"Nnn—No! NO, GODDESS DAMN YOU, NO!"

The torrent of power stopped. In the ringing silence and slowness that followed, Nijiri saw the Prince, torn loose by

Nijiri's effort, stagger back; his expression was wild and thwarted. And then Nijiri saw Ehiru's face contort in inhuman rage. Ehiru whipped about, still screaming—and put his fingers through the Prince's eyes.

Impact with the floor drove Nijiri back into himself. He gasped, disoriented. A breath later the Prince hit the floor beside him, screaming, his eyes bloody holes. An instant after that, Ehiru fell upon the Prince, roaring and tearing at his face with bare hands.

The sky wheeled above Nijiri's head. He closed his eyes, savoring flesh and blood and bone, more aware in that moment than ever before that his body was merely the temporary housing for his true self.

But it was good, strong housing, made by the gods themselves even if none would own up to the act, and he was grateful beyond words to have it.

\* \* \*

After a time Nijiri was able to think again. He turned his head to the side and sighed at the sight of the Prince's body. The face was unrecognizable, its limbs contorted in a bizarre sprawl. Dismissing it, Nijiri pushed himself up on one elbow and focused on Ehiru, who knelt facing the horizon.

"Brother."

Ehiru did not turn. "Nijiri. We've won." He chuckled, softly, without bitterness. "And lost. An army marches this way from Kisua."

Nijiri sat up, wincing as bruises he'd forgotten reminded him of their existence. He suspected a rib was broken, too. "You're certain?"

"I can taste them." The wind shifted again, carrying with it the muddy richness of the irrigation canals. Ehiru inhaled deeply as if savoring the scent.

Nijiri got to his feet, dusting himself off. The wind rippled the cloth of the filthy Kisuati shirt he'd worn since the catacombs. He pulled it off and tossed it away, reveling in the feel of light and air on his skin again.

"I suppose that's Hananja's will too," he said, and Ehiru nodded.

They remained that way for some while, watching the day brighten over the greenlands. Somewhere below, farmers tilled their fields and fishermen checked their nets and mothers kissed their children awake. War had come to Gujaareh and it did not matter, for whoever ruled in the palaces and fortresses would always need grain and fish and subjects to rule. For that, there would have to be peace. Hananja's will always won out in the end.

Nijiri turned to Ehiru and said: "Lie down, Nsha."

Ehiru glanced up at him and smiled. He lay back, his arms at his sides, and waited.

Nijiri knelt and cupped Ehiru's face between his hands, wiping away sweat and grime and flecks of the Prince's blood. When that was done he simply caressed Ehiru's face, memorizing its lines as if he hadn't done so a hundred times already. "I am Zhehur, in dreams," he whispered.

Ehiru nodded. "We'll meet again, Zhehur." He took a deep breath and let it out in a long, weary sigh.

The ritual words were in Nijiri's mind, but he did not say them. There was no need, and in any case no words were adequate. He drew his fingers over Ehiru's eyes to close them and then settled his hand in place. He had no jungissa—the Prince's defiled stone had probably fallen over the balcony railing—but it was an easy matter to push Ehiru into sleep. Even easier to pass through the thin layers that separated the realms, for Ehiru's soul was halfway to dreaming already.

The images that passed between them in the moments that followed were simple. Ehiru was more than skilled enough to construct his own paradise. Nijiri lingered only to make certain the proper connections were in place—Ehiru's mother and Kite-iyan, his hundred siblings, Una-une. He added small but unnecessary touches, like making certain the scent of the river hung in the air, and clearing the sky so that the Dreamer's light shone with that special strangeness he knew Ehiru loved. When the world was finished, he lingered more, reluctant to sever the final connection, but at last Ehiru gently pushed him out. Ina-Karekh was not a place for the living, except in short safe doses of dream.

So at last Nijiri withdrew from the dream and took hold of Ehiru's frail, fraying tether. He severed it neatly, collecting the tithe and setting the soul loose in its new home. Only when the last vestiges of Ehiru's umblikeh had faded to nothingness did he follow his own tether home, settling back into his flesh with a sigh.

"Farewell, Brother," said Gatherer Nijiri. "We shall indeed meet again." He kissed the smile on Ehiru's lips, then bent to lay another kiss on his breast. Those would do in place of his lotus signature.

Though no one would know they were there but him.

# Epilogue

(◦⊙◦)

Hananja's city burned beneath the Dreaming Moon.

Flanked by eight Kisuati soldiers, Sunandi walked through the debris-strewn streets with her face a mask and her heart full of grief. Here was the crafters' market, several stalls already destroyed by the fires that had flared in the city over the past several days. There was the hall where the famous chantress Ky-yefter performed, its facade destroyed by a stray catapult stone. Although the Unbelievers' District and parts of the southernmost wall now lay in smoldering ruins, the majority of the city remained relatively unscathed. The Gujaareen army had not fought hard before surrendering, for their Prince was dead. Since then, the Protectors had been adamant that there be no looting or rapine, and General Anzi had been ruthless in enforcing those instructions among the Kisuati troops who'd come north to see to the occupation. They would have a difficult enough time controlling Gujaareh as it was.

Yet it was clear that even with the Protectors' caution, something vital had been damaged in the city. Sunandi glimpsed some of the citizens forming water-brigades to combat the fires, but far more simply milled about in aimless confusion, their faces haunted and lost. Along the main avenues some of the citizens loitered with their fellows while watching the Kisuati soldiers move through their streets, but most sat or stood or rocked alone. In the pleasure quarter the Kisuati had found several raucous parties under way, with music and dancing in the streets. Gaudily painted timbalin-house women and youths beckoned to the soldiers, some lifting loindrapes to show nothing underneath and some wearing nothing to begin with, all of them smiling and friendly. But Sunandi had seen the haze of drugs or dreamseed in their eyes; she had heard the edge of fear in their sweet invitations. And among the whores she spied the yellow-clad figures of Hananja's Sisters, standing silent watch amid the revelry. Then she understood: Gujaareh's pleasure-givers offered themselves to the conquerors so that Gujaareh's weaker citizens might remain unmolested.

"They'll strike at any Kisuati-looking face," Anzi had warned Sunandi, when he heard of her plan to tour the city. "All our people will be targets for their vengeance—a pretty woman like you even more so." Clever of him to slip in that flattery, she reflected. Transparent, but clever. Well, he was handsome enough. Perhaps when the dust had settled and Gujaareh was firmly in hand... But not yet.

*See them, Anzi. Do you still fear vengeance? This city's spirit has been wounded, perhaps mortally. Gujaareh waits to see if death comes.*

They entered the Hetawa square.

Here alone something of Gujaareh's old peace lingered. The square was crowded with people of all castes and professions, some of them carrying bundles or pushing carts of belongings.

The street directly in front of the Hetawa had been turned into a makeshift infirmary, with pallets laid out on the cobblestones. Family members and Hetawa acolytes moved among the pallets, tending burn victims and wounded soldiers. Other folk lingered nearby, some scratching notices on the walls of nearby buildings, some huddled on the steps of the Hetawa itself. Yet despite the crowding of the square, Sunandi perceived a curious stillness in the atmosphere—an intangible sense of comfort that could be glimpsed on nearly every face. For a moment she puzzled over the feeling, and then abruptly understood: there was no fear. Gujaareh had been defeated, Gujaareh might die as an individual nation, but Gujaareh was not afraid. Not here, at its heart.

In spite of herself, Sunandi smiled.

She headed across the square. On the steps she stopped and turned to the soldiers. "Wait here."

The troop-captain, possibly acting on orders from Anzi, stared at her. "Impossible, Speaker. To let you go in there alone—"

"Do you imagine the Servants of Hananja would take her hostage? Or harm her in any way?" said a quiet voice nearby, speaking in heavily accented Sua. They turned to see a stocky red-haired man on the steps, watching them with a faint smile. Something about him stirred an immediate sense of recognition in Sunandi, though she could not recall seeing his face.

"Perhaps such things are done in barbarian lands," the man said, "but not here."

The captain bristled, but Sunandi threw him a stern glance and he subsided. "You must forgive us, sir," she said to the man. "It's a soldier's job to worry about even the most unlikely possibilities." She spoke in Gujaareen; his eyebrows rose in surprise and amusement.

"So it is. But I assure you, some things are *not* possible—not in the sight of Hananja. And if they were..." He glanced at the captain and although his smile never vanished, there was a momentary hardness in his eyes which, abruptly, Sunandi recognized. "There are only eight of you here. If we wanted Speaker Jeh Kalawe as a hostage, it would be simple enough to take her."

The captain looked ready to draw his sword, though the man's gentle warning had clearly had its impact. He glanced around at the square crowded with Hananja's faithful—most of whom were watching the tableau—then set his jaw and fixed his eyes straight ahead. Sunandi let out a held breath and turned to the man.

"It would seem my reputation in Gujaareh is greater than I thought," she replied. "Though of course it must be nothing to yours, Gatherer...?"

"Rabbaneh," said the man. He inclined his head to her, then turned to walk up the steps, gesturing for her to follow. "Nijiri notified us shortly after his return that you've been judged innocent of corruption. He suspected you might return to Gujaareh—though not so soon—and wanted to be certain you received no...unwanted blessings, shall we say?" He chuckled. "Very diligent, is our Nijiri."

She returned a sour smile, not entirely certain she liked this Gatherer's sense of humor. "For which I'm quite grateful."

"So are we all." He glanced over at her, examining her carefully. "I understand you and the others who were at Soijaro have mostly recovered."

Sunandi shivered at the memory. "A few died. Those already wounded or ill, several elders, a handful of others. But all the rest—yes, we have recovered, at least physically. I can't say how well any of us sleep at night." She sighed and made herself smile. "If nothing else, the tales of that monstrous event should keep Kisua safe for many years. The northern soldiers nearly fell over themselves getting back on their boats and fleeing home."

Rabbaneh's eyes were solemn, clearly seeing through her attempt at levity, but he smiled as well. "A peaceful result, then. Good."

The double doors of the Hetawa's main pylon had been thrown open. A line of people filed through it, spilling out onto the steps. Inside, the line ran down the length of a vast colon-naded hall whose ceiling was nearly out of sight above. But though the hall awed Sunandi, it was the sight of the titanic nightstone statue that made her stop and gape like a wonder-struck child.

While she stared, Rabbaneh stopped to wait, somehow radi-ating both nonchalance and possessive pride without uttering a word. After several long breaths, Sunandi swallowed and tore her eyes away from the Goddess with an effort. "I thought Yanya-iyan magnificent when I first saw it," she said. "I should have guessed that in Gujaareh, the Hetawa would be the great-est wonder."

"Yes," the Gatherer replied with a smile. "You should have guessed."

He headed into the shadows that ran behind the columns, walking sedately toward the back of the hall. Sunandi hurried to follow, trying not to stare at the columns and their carved tales, the sconces where moontear vines spilled down the walls in full bloom, the faceted glass of the massive windows. Between the columns she could glimpse other Hananjan priests in red-dyed loindrapes, guiding people into alcoves on the other side of the hall. Collecting tithes to heal the wounded, she realized. Of course.

The Gatherer stopped at a heavy curtain that led into what was clearly a different area of the Hetawa—the corridors, grounds, and buildings kept hidden from the public eye. Here Sunandi hesitated. But Rabbaneh smiled again, this time sincerely and with no hint of mockery. "Nijiri has told us many tales of his travels in the eightday since his return, Speaker," he said. "He'll be glad to see you again, I think."

She was not so certain of that. Nor was she certain she wanted to see him, now that she had come.

"We found Ehiru's body in Kite-iyan," she said. She noticed that one of her hands was fidgeting, unnecessarily smoothing a fold of her dress, and stopped herself. "The Prince was there, and the other...the Reaper too."

Rabbaneh nodded. "Our brother put his apprentice to a hard test. But Nijiri passed it, as we knew he would." He paused, then added more gently, "Come. It will be good for both of you."

What was it about Gatherers, Sunandi wondered, that could make her feel as though they cared about nothing in the world more than her? Was it the dreamblood that made them this way? Or did they deliberately seek out successors who possessed that fascinating, terrifying mixture of empathy and ruthlessness?

She pulled back her shoulders, nodded stiffly, and passed through the doorway.

The curtain opened into a vast courtyard at the center of the complex. Covered walkways edged the perimeter of this and crossed it here and there, each linking one building with another. Sunandi made an effort not to gawk, acutely aware that she had entered a world seen only by a privileged few. Still she could not help noticing some things. They passed vaulted storechambers whose shelves were stacked with a treasure trove of scrolls, stone tablets, and wooden placards. At the sandy far end of the courtyard, a stern-faced warrior in black stalked down a line of adolescent boys posed in some arcane combat-stance. Nearer by was a fountain surrounded by grasses and flowers, around which younger children chased one another and played in joyous, astonishing silence.

Within these walls, where peace was protected by the Goddess, the war might as well have never occurred.

Then the Gatherer led her into a new building, this one with walls of dark gray marble rather than sandstone. The halls here were completely silent, and utterly still but for her and Rabbaneh.

"Where are we going?" she asked. Instinctively, in such a still place, she kept her voice low.

"The Stone Garden," Rabbaneh replied. "He meditates there in his free hours."

They reached the building's atrium and passed from cool dim corridors into a space of sand and light. Two huge, irregular fingers of rock dominated the scene, one carved from nightstone and the other from white mica, each standing in a corner of the atrium. A handful of smaller boulders occupied the remaining space at random, some small enough to be used as seats. On the centermost of these, with his knees drawn up, sat Nijiri.

Rabbaneh stopped here, inclining his head to Sunandi. "I'll leave you in his hands." She nodded, and he disappeared into the corridors' shadows.

Silence fell, remarkably comforting. She felt herself relax, which seemed strange as she thought of the chaos and despair beyond the Hetawa's walls. Perhaps that, too, was Hananja's doing.

"I'm surprised to see you here, little killer," Sunandi said at last. "Have you been out there? Gujaareh's streets are anything but peaceful tonight."

It was difficult to tell from the angle and with only the Moon's illumination in the Garden, but she thought he smiled. "We'll go out soon, the three of us," he said. "The disruption in the city is terrible, true, but it can't be helped. Certain matters have kept us in the Hetawa these past few days."

"Such as?"

"Finding the Prince's co-conspirators. The Superior was dealt with by my brothers several fourdays ago, but there were others who abetted him." He sighed. "You were right, Speaker. The Hetawa had indeed become riddled with corruption. But we're working hard to make it clean again."

Knowing what that meant, Sunandi cleared her throat uncomfortably. "The Protectorate may want a few of the criminals for public trials. That's not the Gujaareen way, I know... but some things must change now."

"I understand. I will speak with my brothers. We'll keep a few alive for you."

She hesitated. "The Protectors will no doubt try to change you, too. You realize that?"

His smile returned. "Yes, I know."

He might have been speaking of the wash for all the concern in his voice. Shaking her head in consternation, Sunandi took a seat on a nearby boulder. Nijiri stirred from his meditative pose to face her.

For a moment Sunandi barely recognized him. He hadn't changed physically, but then it had been barely a month since she'd last seen him. There was nevertheless a new maturity in his features now. The weathering of experience, perhaps—or more likely a lessening of his youth. Gone was the frustrated restlessness that had been omnipresent in him before; gone too was the anger that had always churned beneath his calm facade. Now he was a Gatherer. Now there was only peace. But through the peace she could see sorrow, too.

"Tell me," she said.

He gazed at her for a long moment, then did.

By the time he finished the tale of Ehiru's death, she was weeping. He had spoken quietly, without embellishment or artifice—but there was no need for more. Even the simplest words conveyed the agony of Ehiru's final descent into madness, and the utter loss that the boy now felt. But to her surprise, Nijiri smiled when the tale was done.

"You grieve for him?" he asked.

For Ehiru. For Nijiri. For Gujaareh, which would never be the same. For herself. "Yes," Sunandi replied.

He got to his feet and crossed the sands to stand before her. "Then share this," he said, and cupped her cheek with his hand.

In that moment her body—her mind, her whole being—was suffused with a joy more powerful than anything words could capture. It warmed away the lingering scars of the Reaping and Lin's death, filled her with hope almost too keen to bear, blazed like a thousand suns in the core of her soul. Tears were not enough; laughter was not enough. Both at once were useless but she wept and laughed anyhow, for it would be criminal to leave such absolute joy unacknowledged, unexpressed.

When she once again became aware of herself, she found that she had pressed her face against the boy's chest, clinging to him because he too knew the bliss within her. That made them one. His arms around her shoulders felt like the most natural thing in the world.

"This is his peace," Nijiri said into her ear. "Now you understand."

She did. At last she understood so much.

He held her until the tremors stopped, stroking her hair and murmuring soothing nonsense words all the while. When she finally looked up, he stepped away, gracefully shunting aside the inevitable awkwardness that followed a moment of intimacy. When he offered his hand to her again it was as Nijiri, the rude fierce youth who had protected her in the desert, not Nijiri the Gatherer. The former was easier to deal with, so he had become that for her—even though the latter was his new reality.

She took his hand, and he helped her to her feet.

"Go to Yanya-iyan, Speaker," he said. "Tell the fools Kisua has sent to rule us how to do things. Hananja abhors clumsy transitions. Gujaareh will not resist if you treat us with respect."

She nodded, still too moved to speak. He led her out of the Garden then, and back to the hall where Hananja's statue stood watch over Her people.

Looking up at Her, Sunandi said, "Thank you."

"It's a Gatherer's duty to bring peace," Nijiri replied. When she focused on him again, Rabbaneh had joined him, and after a moment a third man with Gatherer's eyes stepped out of the shadows. Once upon a time she would have shuddered in their presence, but now she only smiled.

"Do your work well," she told them. "Your people need you."

Nijiri only nodded, though she saw warmth in his eyes. Then he turned to follow as the other two walked away. She watched them cross the Hall to the dais, where the Sharers immediately stopped their work and moved aside. Together the Gatherers knelt and bowed over their hands at Hananja's feet; a moment later they rose and left the Hall. They would exit the Hetawa by the Gatherers' Gate, she knew, and not return for many hours. They would leave corpses in their wake. But by their efforts, the soul of Gujaareh would once again find peace.

Nodding in satisfaction, Sunandi left the Hetawa and went forth to do her part.

# Glossary

**Abeyance:** A formal delay, pending further investigation, of any Hetawa-issued order. May be invoked by any Servant of Hananja sworn to a path, though the abeyance must be justified before the Council of Paths or the Superior.

**Acolytes:** Boys of between twelve and sixteen floods who have elected to pursue the Service of Hananja, but who have not yet sworn themselves to one of the four paths.

**Age of adulthood:** In Gujaareh and Kisua, four times four, or sixteen floods of age. The age at which young citizens are granted legal and all other rights of majority, and may be confirmed in their choice of vocation.

**Age of choice:** In Gujaareh and Kisua, three times four, or twelve floods of age. The age at which young citizens are counted old enough to pursue a chosen vocation, court a spouse, or undertake many other significant decisions.

**Age of eldership:** In Gujaareh, four times four times four, or sixty-four floods of age. The age at which citizens are counted old enough to hold positions of leadership or esteem. In Kisua, citizens are deemed elders at fifty-two years of age.

**Apprentices:** Youths who have passed the age of adulthood and begun higher training in an adult vocation.

**Assay of Truth:** The procedures required to determine whether and when a Gatherer's aid is required. Usually performed by the Council of Paths, although any Gatherer has discretion to perform an assessment in the field.

**Aureole of the Setting Sun:** Symbol of the authority and divinity of the Sunset Lineage. An emblem consisting of alternating plates of red and gold amber arranged in a sunburst pattern around a central gold semicircle, which sits atop a staff carved from white nhefti.

**Banbarra:** A desert tribe, enemies of Gujaareh.

**Body wrap:** A garment worn around the torso or waist by men and women in Kisua. A woman's wrap is usually ankle-length; a man's wrap may be knee-length or shorter and accented by a shoulder-drape.

**Bromarte clans:** A cluster of northern tribes whose territories lie just across the Sea of Glory from Gujaareh.

**Caste:** The social/vocational classes of Gujaareh and Kisua, ascribed at birth. An individual may transcend his or her assigned caste only by entering public service (such as in the Hetawa or the military).

**Charad-dinh:** A small nation to the southeast of Kisua, at the edge of the High Green Forest.

**City of Dreams:** Colloquial name for the capital of Gujaareh. Also known as Hananja's City. Officially, the city's name is simply "Gujaareh."

**Collar:** Decorative item worn in Gujaareh and occasionally in Kisua. Consists of a band around the neck and dangling ornaments that drape the chest and shoulders.

**Commission:** Official request for a Gatherer's service. Commissions are usually submitted by family members of the one to be Gathered.

**Council of Paths:** With the Superior, the governing body of the Hetawa. Includes senior members of the Sentinels, Teachers, and Sharers, as well as one (non-voting) liaison from the Sisters. Out of courtesy, Gatherers operate under the authority of this body, although they are officially autonomous.

**Dane-inge:** One of the divine children of Dreaming Moon and Sun. A goddess of the dance.

**Donation:** The monthly offering of dreams required of all citizens of Gujaareh.

**Dreambile:** One of the four dream-humors that form the basis of Gujaareen magic. Culled from nightmares, it is useful for discouraging harmful growth and destroying unnecessary tissue in the body.

**Dreamblood:** One of the four dream-humors that form the basis of Gujaareen magic. Culled from the final dream that occurs at the moment of death, it is useful for bringing peace.

**Dream-humors:** The magical energies culled from dreams.

**Dreamichor:** One of the four dream-humors that form the basis of Gujaareen magic. Culled from ordinary "nonsense" dreams, it is useful for repairing damage in the body.

**Dreaming Moon:** The mother of all gods and goddesses save Sun and Waking Moon, and mistress of the sky. Also called "the Dreamer."

**Dreamseed:** One of the four dream-humors that form the basis of Gujaareen magic. Culled from erotic dreams, it is useful for stimulating growth that ordinarily occurs only in the womb (e.g., new limbs).

**Easternese:** Collective term for people from lands far to the east of the Sea of Glory.

**Ehiru:** A Gatherer of Hananja; the black oasis rose. Once a son of the Sunset Lineage.

**Empty Thousand:** The desert that stretches from the southernmost edge of the Gujaareen Territories to the northernmost reaches of the Kisuati Protectorate.

**Endless, The:** The great ocean to the west of the Sea of Glory.

**False-seeing:** A dream that appears to be a vision of the future or past, but is too distorted for interpretation or is simply inaccurate.

**Final Tithe:** A Servant of Hananja's offering of all his remaining dreamblood to the Goddess, at the end of his service.

**Flood:** An annual event in which the Goddess's Blood river overflows its banks and fills the Blood river valley, renewing the fertility of the soil. Also: the marker by which valley-dwellers count perennial changes, such as age.

**Founding Sages:** The founders of Gujaareh, including Inunru.

**Four:** The number of bands on the face of Dreaming Moon. A holy number, as are its multiples.

**Four-of-four:** Four by four by four by four, or two hundred and fifty-six. A holy number.

**Gatherers:** Those in one of the four paths to the Service of Hananja, responsible for enforcing Hananja's Law.

**Goddess, The:** In Gujaareh, an alternative term for Hananja. In Kisua, may refer to any female deity.

**Goddess's Blood:** A river whose source is in the mountains of Kisua. Its mouth is along the Sea of Glory in northern Gujaareh.

**Gualoh:** Bromarte word for a demon.

**Gujaareh:** A city-state whose capital (also called Gujaareh, or the City of Dreams, or Hananja's City) lies at the mouth of the Goddess's Blood along the Sea of Glory.

**Hamyan Night:** The shortest night of the year, when dreams become so sparse that the Goddess Hananja starves. Treated as a celebration of the summer solstice in Gujaareh.

**Hananja:** One of the divine children of Dreaming Moon and Sun. The goddess of dreams, also associated with death and the afterlife.

**Hananja's City:** Alternate name for Gujaareh's capital.

**Hananja's Law:** The body of law that governs Gujaareh. Its principal tenet is peace.

**Hananja's Wisdom:** A collection of proverbs, prophecies, and other lore that faithful Hananjans must learn.

**Healing:** Any non-magical healing art, including herbalism and surgery.

**Hekeh:** A fibrous plant native to the Blood river valley, cultivated in Gujaareh and other river nations. Useful in making cloth, rope, and many other products.

**Hetawa:** The central temple of the Hananjan faith, and physical center of spiritual life in Gujaareh. The Hetawa oversees education, law, and public health.

**Hieratics:** A shorthand or "cursive" form of the Gujaareen written language.

**Highcaste:** The Gujaareen royal family, shunha, and zhinha; in Kisua, highcastes include the sonha and hunters.

**Hipstraps:** Straps used to hold loindrapes in place. Often decorated with clasps and used to carry wallets or tools.

**Hona-Karekh:** The realm of wakefulness.

**Ina-Karekh:** The land of dreams. The living may visit this land for short periods during sleep. The dead dwell here in perpetuity.

**Indethe:** Sua word for attention/honor/love.

**Inim-teh:** A plant grown in the Blood river valley. The seeds are harvested and ground to make a pungent spice useful in pickling and flavoring.

**Inunru:** A great and honored figure in the history of the Hananjan faith.

**Jellevy:** A small island nation in the Eastern Ocean near Kisua.

**Jungissa:** A rare stone that resonates in response to stimuli. Skilled narcomancers use it to induce and control sleep. All jungissa are fragments of the Sun's seed, fallen to earth from the stars.

**Ketuyae:** A small village in the southern Gujaareen Territories.

**King:** In Gujaareh, the most recently deceased Prince (may he dwell in Her peace forever).

**Kisua:** A city-state in the mideastern region of the continent, motherland of Gujaareh.

**Kite-iyan:** The Prince's alternate palace, home of his wives and children.

**Loindrapes:** A garment worn primarily by men in Gujaareh, consisting of two long panels of cloth (knee-length or ankle-length) linked about the hips by straps of leather or metal chain.

**Loinskirt:** A garment worn primarily by men in Gujaareh, consisting of a knee-length wrap of hekeh or a pleated drape of linen.

**Lowcaste:** A member of any of the castes at the bottom of the Gujaareen social hierarchy. Includes farmers and servants.

**Magic:** The power of healing and dreams.

**Manuflection:** A gesture of respect offered only to those who bear the gods' favor. The supplicant drops to one knee, crossing forearms (palms outward) before the face. A lesser version of this (arms held parallel before the chest, palms down, with an included bow depending on the depth of respect shown) is offered as a routine greeting or gesture of apology in Gujaareh.

**Merik:** One of the divine children of Dreaming Moon and Sun. Grinds down mountains and fills valleys.

**Midcaste:** A member of any of the castes in the middle of the Gujaareen social hierarchy. Includes merchants and artisans.

**Military:** Like the Servants of Hananja, a branch of public service in Gujaareh, and a caste into which one may be born or inducted.

**Mnedza:** One of the divine children of Dreaming Moon and Sun. Brings pleasure to women.

**Moontear:** A flower found along the Goddess's Blood that blooms only by the light of the Dreaming Moon. Sacred to the Hananjan faith.

**Narcomancy:** The Gujaareen skills of sleepcasting, dream control, and the use of dream-humors. Colloquially called *dream magic*.

**Nhefti:** A hardy, thick-trunked tree that grows near the mountains of the Blood river valley. Its wood is amber-white and has a naturally pearlescent patina when polished. Used only for holy objects.

**Nijiri:** An apprentice of the Gatherer path; the blue lotus. His mentor is Ehiru.

**Northerners:** Collective term for members of the various tribes north of the Sea of Glory. Polite term for barbarians.

**Numeratics:** Graphical/symbolic depictions used in mathematics, said to have their own magic.

**Physical humors:** Blood, bile, ichor (plasma), and seed.

**Pictorals:** The glyphic/symbolic written form of the Gujaareen language, based on written Sua. Used for formal requests, poetry, historical annotations, and religious writings.

**Pranje:** Ritual undertaken by narcomancers in order to test their self-control.

**Prince/Lord of the Sunset/Avatar of Hananja:** The ruler of Gujaareh in the waking realm. Upon death he is elevated to the throne of Ina-Karekh, where he rules at Hananja's side until a new King comes (may he dwell in Her peace forever).

**Protectors:** The council of elders that rules Kisua.

**Rabbaneh:** A Gatherer of Hananja; the red poppy.

**Reaper:** A myth. Abomination.

**Rogue:** A Gatherer or Sharer who has failed the pranje and refused the Final Tithe. Corruption.

**Sentinels:** Those in one of the four paths to the Service of Hananja. They guard the Hetawa and all works of the Goddess.

**Servant:** In Gujaareh, a member of the lowest caste. Servants are not permitted to accumulate wealth and may select their own masters.

**Servants of Hananja:** Priests sworn to the service of the Goddess.

**Shadoun:** A desert tribe, once enemies of Gujaareh, now tributaries. Allied to the Kisuati.

**Shadowlands:** The place in Ina-Karekh that is created by the nightmares of all dreamers. Those who die in distress are drawn here to dwell for eternity.

**Sharers:** Those in one of the four paths to the Service of Hananja, responsible for the health of the city. They use narcomancy and occasionally surgery and herbalism.

**Shunha:** One of the two branches of Gujaareen nobility, whose members claim to be descended from liaisons between mortals and Dreaming Moon's children. Shunha maintain the customs and traditions of the motherland (Kisua).

**Sisters of Hananja:** An order (independent of the Hetawa) consisting predominantly of women, who serve Hananja by collecting dreamseed in the city.

**Skyrer:** Nocturnal birds of prey who hunt the Empty Thousand. It is an ill omen to see skyrers by day, or away from the desert outside of the rainy season.

**Slave:** In Kisua, captive enemies, debtors, the indigent, undesirable foreigners, and criminals sentenced to involuntary servitude for a period of years. Slavery is illegal in Gujaareh.

**Sonha:** Kisuati nobility, who claim to be descended from liaisons between mortals and Dreaming Moon's children.

**Sonta-i:** A Gatherer of Hananja; the indigo nightshade.

**Soulname:** Names given to Gujaareen children for protection in Ina-Karekh.

**Southlands:** Collective name for the various tribes beyond the source of the Goddess' Blood river, many of which are vassal-states of Kisua.

**Stone Garden:** A meditation-space in the inner Hetawa.

**Sunandi Jeh Kalawe:** A maiden of the Kisuati sonha, assigned to Gujaareh as Voice of the Protectorate.

**Sunset Lineage:** The royal family of Gujaareh, said to be descendants of the Sun.

**Superior:** The administrative head of the Hetawa, whose decisions are made in conjunction with the Council of Paths and the Gatherers.

**Taffur:** A small canid found in the Blood valley and Empty Thousand, sometimes kept as a pet in Gujaareh and Kisua.

**Teachers:** Those in one of the four paths to the Service of Hananja, responsible for education and the pursuit of knowledge.

**Territories, The:** Collective name for the towns and tribes that have pledged allegiance to Gujaareh. Often referred to as simply "Gujaareh."

**Tesa:** An oasis in the Empty Thousand, around which a thriving trade-center has developed.

**Timbalin:** A popular narcotic in Gujaareh. Allows uncontrolled dreaming.

**Tithe:** A Gujaareen citizen's due offering to Hananja.

**Tithebearer:** One designated by the Hetawa to receive Hananja's blessing, in return for a tithe of dream-humors.

**True-seeing:** A dream-vision of the future or past.

**Umblikeh:** The tether that binds soul to flesh and permits travel out of the body into other realms. When severed, death follows instantaneously.

**Una-une:** A Gatherer of Hananja, recently deceased. Ehiru's mentor.

**Voice of Kisua:** An ambassador of Kisua, who speaks for the Protectors. The proper title for a Voice is "Speaker."

**Waking Moon:** Younger sister of the Dreaming Moon. Visible only shortly before sunrise.

**Water Garden:** A meditation-space in the inner Hetawa.

**Wind Garden:** A meditation-space in the inner Hetawa.

**Wood Garden:** A meditation-space in the inner Hetawa.

**Yanya-iyan:** The Prince's main palace in the capital city, seat of Gujaareh's government.

**Zhinha:** One of the two branches of nobility in Gujaareh, whose members claim to be descended from liaisons between mortals and Dreaming Moon's children. Zhinha believe Gujaareh's strength lies in its ability to adapt and change.

# Acknowledgments

My thanks here are mostly for resources rather than people, but only because the list of people to thank would be another book in itself.

The list of helpful resources would be, too, but I'll single out a few for particular note. First is *Mythology: An Illustrated Encyclopedia* by Richard Cavendish, a coffee-table book that attempted the impossible—a survey of all the world's myth systems. It had some notable problems of cultural bias and the usual problems of any broad survey, but it was helpful in one way: when I first read it, I began to see the common structure underlying most human cosmogonies. I used this common structure, as I did in the Inheritance Trilogy, to create the gods of Kisua and Gujaareh.

Also, *On Dreams* by Sigmund Freud, and *The Red Book*, by Carl Gustav Jung. The latter I was able to see "in person" at last thanks to a lovely exhibit at the Rubin Museum in New York. Early psychoanalysts got a lot of things wrong in their studies of human nature, but in their partly spiritual, partly intellectual quest to understand their fellow human beings, I got a sense of how a faith can be born. To some degree, Gujaareh's founder Inunru—er, sans mass murder and megalomania—is inspired by them.

Also, the Brooklyn Museum's Egyptian and Nubian collection. The British Museum's collection is much bigger and more impressive, but I don't live in London, and that museum was too crowded and anxiously guarded to allow the hours of close study I needed. No quick visit can give you a real sense of the day-to-day life of ancient city-dwellers: how they combed their hair, how they cleaned their teeth, how they traveled from home to work, how they gossiped about that guy down the street who looked at them crosswise and didja hear he worships *that* god? In Brooklyn nobody cares if you sit in one place and stare at something for hours, as long as you don't then get up and shoot somebody.

Oh, and I'll allow myself one bit of people-thanks: to my first writing group, the BRAWLers, who were the Boston Area Writers' Group until we decided we needed better branding. You guys tore this book apart and put it back together better, and you loved it and cheered for it before anyone else. (No, Jennifer, they did not have sex.) Thank you.

# extras

orbit

# meet the author

N. K. Jemisin

N. K. JEMISIN is a career counselor, political blogger, and would-be gourmand living in New York City. She's been writing since the age of ten, although her early works will never see the light of day. Find out more about the author at www.nkjemisin.com.

# interview

So my editor has asked me to interview myself, for the benefit of my readers. Gotta admit, that's a new one. I kind of like the idea, in principle: now I have the opportunity to ask myself questions I find interesting, while avoiding all those incredibly annoying questions interviewers always seem to ask, like "Where do you get your ideas?" And I can even be rude to myself! Hey, this is kinda cool. So here goes.

*Where did you get your—*
*SLAP.* See, this is fun already!

*Ow. So, the land of Gujaareh. Why'd you pattern it after ancient Egypt?*
I've always been fascinated by ancient empires in general, but particularly those that have remained mysterious to—or been ignored by—"Western" historians and scientists. Egypt's not really the worst of these, but that was part of the reason I chose it: because there is so much scholarship already, and there are so many archaeological and artistic finds to be explored. That made research easier.

But beyond that, I was fascinated by Egyptian magic,

which seems to have been a seamless blend of the religious and medical disciplines for them. I was surprised to learn a few years back that the "four humors" philosophy of medicine was employed there, because I'd always been taught that this was something that came from the Greeks. (But then, ancient Egypt, ancient Greece, and ancient Rome all did a lot of cross-pollination.) That made me wonder what other surprises there might be in the study of ancient Egyptian lore, so I started exploring further. And around that time, I discovered a new branch of modern science that seemed to dovetail nicely with the Egyptian stuff: psychodynamic theory.

*Oh, so* **that's** *what possessed you to create a magic system based on Freudian dream theory and Egyptian medicine. Because that stuff's crazy.*

Well, no. (And Freud would say there is no "crazy.") Modern medicine recognizes the power of the subconscious mind. You've heard of the placebo effect—I know you have because you're me—in which people who are given a sugar pill (or something else that has no medicinal content) often respond to treatment just as well as people receiving actual medicine. Sometimes their recovery is nothing short of miraculous, and they get better because they *believe* they should be better. The power of the mind to affect the body is something that's been understood, and exploited, since ancient times. It's not a far stretch from there to the idea that directed, lucid dreaming might somehow be used to harness the placebo effect. This is something Jung openly contemplated and explored through a religious context, in particular the Hindu mandala...but I digress.

*So that's the religious connection. Okay, admit it; you're secretly trying to proselytize for Hinduism!*

No, that's stupid. I know diddlysquat about Hinduism, beyond what I've read in a few books. And anyway, I'm not Hindu.

*No?*

Nope.

*But you mentioned a Hindu influence with the Inheritance Trilogy.*

Yeah, and Zoroastrianism, and Greco-Roman and Norse mythology, and American Indian trickster tales, and the loa of vodoun, and the Christian Holy Trinity. I always find it interesting how people pick one thing out of a list of influences to fixate on. I gave a list because they *all* matter.

*Dammit.*

That's not a question.

*Okay, then are you proselytizing for* something? *Because you keep exploring religion in your writing, and that has to mean something.*

Well, I consider myself an agnostic—not in the sense of doubting the existence of God, but in the sense of doubting the capability of any human religion to encompass the divine. More specifically I think religion alone is *not enough* to encompass the divine. Religion is a handy guide to living, assuming you're still living in the society that existed at the time of the religion's founding. It's useful for unifying and motivating a population. But to understand ourselves and the universe, we need to explore other schools of thought—the complexity of the human consciousness, the limits of science, and more. I believe we will eventually need to interact with other intelligent entities, and exchange ideas. And we need to be wary of the ways in which letting others do this thinking and learning *for* us can come back to bite us on the ass. So if there's any one religious theme in my work, it's that.

*Lolwut?*
Look, just write it down.

*Okay, but…Ina-Karekh—the Gujaareen "land of dreams." Is that meant to represent the Christian Heaven? With the shadowlands as Hell?*
Nope. Ina-Karekh is based on Jung's collective unconscious. And the method used to enter it is rooted in Egyptian belief—the separation of the ka, the life-energy of the soul, from the ba, the physical embodiment of the soul, wherein the ka is contained in various organs and on its own might have trouble traveling into other planes of existence—

*Yeah, whatever, let's move on to something juicier. The Gatherers are all gay, right? They're totally gay.*
There is no "gay" in Gujaareh. In Gujaareen society, people love whom they love. But if we used modern American labels on any of them, Nijiri would be gay.

*And the rest?*
They're harder to categorize. Most Gujaareen are opportunistic: they'll happily schtupp anyone they're attracted to, so we'd call them all bi. But that label doesn't really fit, because being bisexual is about more than whom you sleep with. Anyway, Ehiru was heterosexual before he became a

426

Gatherer—that changes them in more ways than just the spiritual. As it is, all Gatherers are closer to asexual.

**Is everybody in these books African?**
No. It's not Earth. There's no Africa.

**You know what I mean. Are they all black?**
Some are. Some are sort of reddish- or yellowy-brown, and some are tan with freckles, and some are white enough that they don't go outside at noon. I know what you're getting at, though. Gujaareh is modeled on ancient Egypt. (And Kisua is modeled on ancient Nubia.) Egypt, despite what my middle school geography textbook tried to tell me, is in Africa; ergo, its people are African. But "African" has no one set look, any more than "Asian" or "European" does. Also, Egypt was the crossroads of trade for that side of the planet in its day. Traders from what would become China, the Persian Empire, Greece, the Roman Empire, the Malian Empire, the Vikings, the Nubians—they all passed through Egypt's ports. Everything we know of ancient Egypt, from modern genetic studies of mummies to their own art, suggests it was a multicultural, multilingual, multiracial society. So that's what I've tried to depict here.

**You could've done this story in a medieval European setting.**
That's not a question, and no, I couldn't have. For one thing, the magic system is rooted in ancient Egyptian science and medicine, and medicine in medieval Europe was a completely different animal—

**WHY DO YOU HATE MEDIEVAL EUROPE?!?!?!!?!**
Uh, could you calm down? We need to keep our blood pressure in the healthy range.

*Hater.*

::sigh:: Look, I don't have a problem with medieval Europe. I have a problem with modern fantasy's *fetishization* of medieval Europe; that's different. So many fantasy writers and fans simplify the social structure of the period, monotonize the cultural interactions, treat conflicts as binaries instead of the complicated dynamic tapestry they actually were. They're not doing medieval Europe, they're doing Simplistic British Isles Fantasy Full of Lots of Guys with Swords And Not Much Else. Not all medieval European fantasy does this, of course—but enough does that frankly, they've turned me off the setting. I might tackle unsimplified medieval Europe myself someday... but honestly, I doubt it. I loved the challenge of writing the Dreamblood books, but I've learned that I prefer creating my own worlds to emulating reality. World-building from scratch is easier.

*If you liked writing the Dreamblood books so much, why are there only two of them?*

There might be more. I have many tales of the Dreaming Moon in my head. But I have more ideas than I have time to write them in, alas.

*That's because you're lazy and disorganized and have no discipline—*

*SLAP.*

*U R so meen.*

Are you done yet?

*Okay, last question. Is that a gas giant in your pocket, or are you just happy to see me?*

. . .

*Don't hit me again!*

… Yes, the Dreaming Moon is a gas giant. The world of the Dreaming Moon is one of its moons; Waking Moon is another. The Gujaareen are aware of this, as their astronomy is about as developed as that of ancient Egypt, but the habit of referring to the Dreamer as a moon is something that long predates these discoveries, so it stuck. I did actually try to work out the astrophysics, for which I thank the instructors and my fellow attendees at NASA's Launch Pad astronomy workshop for science fiction/fantasy authors and other creative types, which I was privileged to go to back in 2009. Not much of that made it into the duology—maybe one day it will, if I write a story about the Teachers—but it was fun to play with. Any errors are mine.

*I didn't ask you all that. You just like hearing yourself talk, don't you?*

Oh, for—That's it. I'm done.

*You suck as an interview subject, you know that, don't you? Hey, that's a question!*

*Wait, you really did go? Ah, c'mon. You're no fun. Come baaaaaack…*

In retrospect, I don't think I liked being the one doing the interviewing. Ah, well. In peace, y'all.

# introducing

If you enjoyed
THE KILLING MOON,
look out for

## THE SHADOWED SUN

Book Two of the Dreamblood series

*by N. K. Jemisin*

There were two hundred and fifty-six places where a man could hide within his own flesh. The soldier dying beneath Hanani's hands had fled to someplace deep. She had searched his heart and brain and gut, though the soul visited those organs less often than layfolk thought. She had examined his mouth and eyes, the latter with especial care. At last, behind a lobe of his liver, she found his soul's trail and followed it into a dream of shadowed ruins.

431

Piles of rubble loomed out of the twilit mists—crumbling structures so titanic that each single brick would dwarf a man, so foreign in design that she could not fathom their purpose. A palace? A temple? Camouflage, regardless. Beneath her feet the dust gleamed, something more than mica: each step displaced a million stars. She took care to put them all back in her wake.

To find the soldier, Hanani would have to first deal with the setting. It was simple enough to will the ruins into order, which she did by crouching to touch the ground. Threads of dreamichor, yellow-bright and gleaming, laced from her fingertips and etched the ground for a moment before vanishing into it. A breath later, the dust skittered up to seal cracked stone; the harbinger of change. Then the earth split and the ground shook as great bricks righted themselves and flew through the air, clattering together to form columns and walls. All around her, had she chosen to watch, the outlines of a monstrous city took shape against the gradient sky. But when the city was whole, she rose and moved on without looking. There was far more important work to be done.

["This takes longer than it should."

"The injury is healing."

"That does no good if he dies."

"He won't. She has him. Watch."]

After first passing a stone archway, Hanani paused and turned back to examine it. The arch was man-height, the only thing of normal proportions in the dreamscape. Beyond the arch lay the same shadows that shrouded all—no. The shadows were thicker here.

Prowling carefully closer, Hanani attempted to step through the archway.

The shadows pressed back.

She imagined illumination.

The shadows grew thicker.

After a moment's consideration, she summoned pain and fear and rage instead, and wrapped these around herself. The shadows' resistance melted; the soldier's soul recognized kindred. Passing through the arch, Hanani found herself in an atrium garden, the kind that should have helped to cool the heart of any home—but this one was dead. She looked around, ducking splintered palms and wilted moontear vines, frowning at a suppurating mess of a flowerbed. Then she spied something beyond it: there at the garden's heart, curled in a nest of his own sorrow, lay the soldier.

Pausing here, Hanani shifted a fraction of her attention back to the waking realm.

["Dayu? I'll need more dreambile soon."

"Yes, Hanani— Um, I mean, Sharer-Apprentice."]

That done, Hanani returned to the dream of the hidden garden. The soldier lay with knees drawn up and arms wrapped about himself as if for comfort. In the curve of his body, a gaping wound spilled his intestines into a hole at the nest's heart. She could see nothing beyond the hole, only that perverse umbilical connecting him to it.

*Death*, said the air around him.

"Not here, petitioner," she replied. "These are the shadowlands. There are better places to die."

He did not move, hungering again for death. Again she demurred. *Memory*, she offered, to entice him.

Anguish flared up in cold, purple-white wisps, wreathing the area around the nest as a new form coalesced. Another man: older, bearded in the way of those who bore northern blood, also garbed as a soldier but clearly of some higher rank than Hanani's soldier. A relative? Mentor? Lover? Beloved, whoever he was.

433

"Gone," Hanani's soldier whispered. "Gone without me."

"May he dwell in Her peace forever," she said. Extending her hands to either side, she trailed her fingers through the ring of mist. Where she touched, delicate deep red threads blended and pulsed into the white.

["She uses *more* dreamblood? She'll run out at that rate."

"Then we'll give her more. The desert scum have nearly cut him in two, man, what do you expect?"]

Hanani's soldier moaned and curled into a tighter ball as red threads stretched forth from the walls, soaking into his skin. Abruptly the mists flickered, the bearded soldier's image growing insubstantial as shadows. New scenes formed instead, appearing and overlapping and fading with each breath. A lonely perch atop a wall. Sword practice. A barracks bed. A river barge.

Hanani coaxed the memories to continue, inserting gentle suggestions to guide them in a new direction. *Loved ones. Life.* The scenes changed to incorporate the bearded soldier and others—doubtless the petitioner's comrades or caste-kin. They laughed and talked and worked at daily tasks. As the images flowed, Hanani reached carefully around the man and into the hole that was devouring him. The first contact sent pain slamming up her arm like a blow—but cold, so terribly cold! She gasped and fought the urge to cry out as her fingers stiffened and froze and cracked apart—

No. She formed her soulname's syllables within her mind and clarity washed through her, a reminder that this was a dream and she was its master. *This pain is not my own.* When she drew her hand back, it was whole.

But the man was not; the pain was devouring him. She focused on the images again, noting one of a tavern. The petitioner was not there, although his dead beloved and other comrades were, laughing and singing a lusty song. There was danger in this, she realized abruptly. The petitioner had been injured in a raid, his beloved killed. She had no idea whether the rest of his companions had been cut down as well. If so, then what she meant to attempt might only increase his death-hunger.

There was no choice but to try.

["—As though you *want* her to fail, Yehamwy."

"Of course not. The Council simply wants to be certain of her competence."

"And if *the Council* knew the first thing about healing, that would be—"

"What is that noise?"

"I'm not certain. It came from the tithing alcoves. Dayu? Everything all right, boy?"]

Distractions could be dangerous, even deadly, in narcomancy. Focusing her mind on the task at hand, Hanani reshaped the tavern scene around her soldier. His comrades stopped singing and turned to him, offering greetings and reminiscences and sloshing cups. The beer shone a warm deep red in the dreamlight. Behind them, Hanani quietly faded the bearded soldier away.

"Look here," she said to the petitioner. "Your fellows are waiting. Will you not join them?"

The man groaned, uncurling from his nest and straining up toward his comrades. A great wind soughed through the dreamscape, blowing away the city and the shadows. Hanani exerted her will in concert with the man's and the garden swirled away, its shadows suddenly replaced by bright lanterns and tavern walls. The nest lingered, though, for the man was bound fast to his pain. So instead Hanani touched the edge of the nest and caused it to compress, shrinking rapidly into a tiny dark marble small enough to sit in his palm. He gazed mournfully at Hanani and clutched the marble tightly to his breast, but did not protest when Hanani caused the rope of intestine to fall free, severing his linkage. She pressed the dangling end against his belly and it vanished, as did the wound itself. Lastly she summoned clothing, which blurred for a moment before his mind shaped it into the gray-agate collar and loinskirt of a Gujaareen city guard.

The soldier nodded to her once, then turned to join his companions. They surrounded him, embraced him, and all at once he began to weep. But he was safe from danger now—and *she* had made him so, made him whole again, body and soul alike. *I'm a Sharer now!*

But no, that was presumption. Whether she'd passed the trial to become a full member of the Sharer path was a matter for her pathbrothers to decide, and the Council to confirm, no matter how well she'd done. And it was utter folly to let her emotions slip control while she remained in dreaming; she would not ruin herself by making a child's mistake. So with a deep sigh to focus her thoughts, Hanani released the soldier's dream and followed the faint red tendril that would lead her soul back to its own housing of flesh—

—But something jolted her awareness.

She paused, frowning. The dreamworld of Ina-Karekh lay behind her, inasmuch as such things had any direction at all. Hona-Karekh, the waking realm, was ahead. She opened the eyes of her dreamform to find that she stood in a gray-shadowed version of the waking realm, where the tension and busy movement that had filled the Hall of Blessings a few moments before were suddenly still. She stood on the dais at the feet of the great, looming nightstone statue of Hananja, but her petitioner was gone. Mni-inh and Teacher Yehamwy, who had come to oversee her trial, were gone. The Hall was silent and empty, but for her.

The realm between waking and dreams. Hanani frowned. She had not intended to stop here. Concentrating, she sought her soul's umblikeh again to complete the journey back to waking—and then stopped, hearing something. There. Over near the tithing alcoves, where Sharer-Apprentices and acolytes drew dreams from the minds of sleeping faithful. A slow, deep sound, like nothing she'd ever heard before. Grinding stone?

Or the breathing of some huge, heavy beast.

["Hanani."]

Nothing in the between realm was real. The space between dreams was emptiness, where the soul might drift with nothing to latch onto—no imagery, no sensation, no conceptualization. An easy place in which to go mad. With her soulname and training, Hanani was safer, for she had long ago learned to build a protective construct around herself—the shadow-Hall in this case—whenever she traveled here. Still, she avoided the space between if she could help it, for only Gatherers could navigate it with ease. It was troubling to say the least that she had manifested here unwittingly.

Squinting toward the alcoves, she wondered: had she forgotten some step in healing the soldier, done something wrong in the transit from Ina-Karekh? A man's life was involved; it was her duty to be thorough.

["Hanani. The healing is complete. Come forth."]

Something moved in the stillness near an alcove's opening. Emerged from it, behind one of the Hall's flower-draped columns, which occluded a clear view. She perceived intent and power, a slow gathering of malice that first unnerved, then actively frightened her—

*["Hanani."]*

The shadow-Hall shivered all over, then turned bright and busy with people and breezes and murmurs. Hanani caught

437

her breath, blinking as her soul settled back into her own flesh. The waking realm. Her mentor stood beside her, a troubled look on his face.

"Mni-inh-brother. There was something…" She shook her head, confused. "I wasn't done."

"You've done enough, Apprentice," said a cold voice. Yehamwy, a heavyset, balding Teacher in his early elder years, stood glowering beside the healing area. Before her, on one of the wooden couches set up for Sharer audiences, Hanani's soldier lay in the deep sleep of the recently healed. Automatically Hanani pushed aside the bandages to check his belly. The flesh was whole and scarless, though still smeared with the blood and gore that had been spilled prior to healing.

"My petitioner is fine," she said, looking up at Yehamwy in confusion.

"Not him, Hanani." Mni-inh crouched beside the couch and laid two fingers on the soldier's eyelids to check Hanani's work. He closed his eyes for a moment; they flickered rapidly beneath their lids. Then he exhaled and returned. "Fine indeed. I'll have someone summon his caste-kin to carry him home."

Less disoriented now, Hanani looked around the Hall of Blessings and frowned. When she'd begun work on the soldier, the Hall had been full, humming with the voices of those come to offer their monthly tithes, or petition for the Hetawa's aid, or just sit on pallets amid the moontear blossoms and pray. The sun still slanted through the long prism windows, but now the Hall was empty of all save those on the dais with Hanani, and a cluster of Sharers and Sentinels near one of the tithing alcoves.

The same place she'd seen something, in the realm between. That was strange. And it was far too early for the Hall's public hours to have ended.

"Hanani had nothing to do with this," Mni-inh said. Hanani looked up in surprise at the sharp tone of her mentor's voice. He was glaring at Teacher Yehamwy.

"The boy was fetching tithes for her," Yehamwy said. "Clearly she is involved."

"How? She was too deep in dreaming even to notice."

"The boy was only thirteen. She had him ferrying humors like a full apprentice."

"And? You know as well as I that we allow the acolytes to ferry humors whenever they show an aptitude!"

The councilor shook his head. "And sometimes they aren't ready. This incident is the direct result of your apprentice's excessive use of humors—"

Mni-inh stiffened. "I do not recall *you* passing the Sharer-trial at any point, Yehamwy."

"And the boy's desire to please her? One need not be a Sharer to understand that. He followed her about like a tame hound, willing to do anything to serve his infatuation. Willing even to attempt a narcomantic procedure beyond his skill."

Hanani's knees had gone stiff during the healing, despite the cushion beneath them. She struggled clumsily to her feet. "Please—" Both men fell silent, looking at her; Mni-inh's expression was tinged with sudden pity. That frightened her, because there was only one boy they could be talking about. "Please, Mni-inh-brother, tell me what has happened to Dayu."

Mni-inh sighed and ran a hand over his hair. "There's been an incident in the tithing alcoves, Hanani. I don't know— There isn't—"

With an impatient gesture, Yehamwy cut him off. "She should know the harm she's caused. If you truly believe she's worthy of becoming a Sharer, don't coddle her." And his expression as he turned to her was both bitter and satisfied. "A tithebearer is dead, Sharer-Apprentice. So is the acolyte Dayuhotem, who assisted you."

Hanani caught her breath and looked at Mni-inh, who nodded in sober confirmation. "But..." She groped for words. Her ears rang, as if the words had been too loud, though no one would shout in Hananja's own hall, at the feet of Her statue. Hananja treasured peace. "H-how? It was a simple procedure. Dayu had done it before, many times; he knew what he was doing even if he was just a child..." A Moon-wild, joyful jester of a child, as exasperating as he was charming. She could not imagine him dead. As well imagine the Sun failing to shine.

"We don't know how it happened," Mni-inh said. He threw a quelling look at the councilor, who had started to speak. "We *don't*. We heard him cry out, and when we went into the alcove we found him and the tithebearer both. Something must have gone wrong during the donation."

"But Dayu—" Her throat closed after the name. Dead. Her vision blurred; she pressed her hand to her mouth as if that would push the horror from her mind. *Dead.*

"The bodies will be examined," Mni-inh said heavily. "There are narcomancies that can be performed even after the umblikeh is severed, which may provide some answers. Until then—"

"Until then," Yehamwy said, "on my authority as a member of the Council of Paths, Sharer-Apprentice Hanani is prohibited from further practice of any healing art or narcomancy, pending the results of the examination."

VISIT THE ORBIT BLOG AT

# www.orbitbooks.net

FEATURING

**BREAKING NEWS**

**FORTHCOMING RELEASES**

**LINKS TO AUTHOR SITES**

**EXCLUSIVE INTERVIEWS**

**EARLY EXTRACTS**

AND COMMENTARY FROM OUR EDITORS

WITH REGULAR UPDATES FROM OUR TEAM,
ORBITBOOKS.NET IS YOUR SOURCE
FOR ALL THINGS ORBITAL.

WHILE YOU'RE THERE, JOIN OUR E-MAIL LIST
TO RECEIVE INFORMATION ON SPECIAL OFFERS,
GIVEAWAYS, AND MORE.

## imagine. explore. engage.